MOKAD IS COMING . . .

Just as Sugar went to grab the handle, the door opened. A huge bearded man stood there. His clothes were dark. His eyes were orangish-brown, but it wasn't their color that filled her with dread. It was the shape of the irises—horizontally slit like those of a goat.

Sugar stumbled back.

"Ho there, Darling," he said.

Someone else entered the front of the house.

Sugar tried to dart around the big man, but he was quick and blocked her path. Were these two of the Famished? Had they drained the life out of this village and now come for her?

He raised his voice and grinned. "I think we've found what we've been looking for."

John D. Brown
CURSE
The Dark God Book two

BLACK
SWORD
BOOKS

Illustration copyright © 2014 Victor Minguez

Map copyright © 2008 Isaac Stewart

Cover design by Mythic Studios

ISBN 13: 978-1-940427-08-9

ISBN 10: 1940427088

First edition: August, 2014

For Nellie

Contents

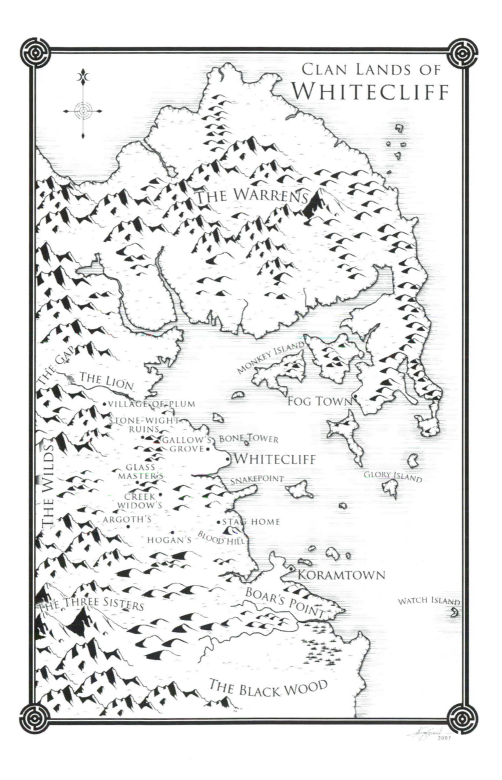

1

Skull and Weave

TALEN HAD ALREADY died once this season, and it was not something he wanted to do again. Not anytime soon. And yet here he was, well past midnight, sneaking into the heart of enemy Fir-Noy territory.

Sugar, River, and five of Shim's soldiers were with him, all of them crouching in the moon shadow cast by a tree next to a pile of stones some-one had hauled out of the adjacent field. All of them but River wore weaves of might, increasing their strength and speed, which was one of the reasons why all of them had sizeable Fir-Noy bounties on their heads. And not only in Fir-Noy lands. Five of the nine Mokaddian clans had sided with the Fir-Noy against Shim and the Shoka.

Talen and a number of the others held bows, arrows ready. They had risked coming to the village of Plum to retrieve a cache of weaves and other unknown items of lore from the ruins of Sugar's house. Her mother, upon her deathbed a little over three months ago, bid Sugar to retrieve them. Sugar had wanted to go immediately, but Uncle Argoth prevented that, tell-ing her she needed to wait until the right opportunity arose. It appeared tonight was that opportunity, for all over the New Lands, Mokaddians and Koramites had been distracted with the Apple Dance, one of the biggest festivals of the year. So while Talen and the others were sneaking through the woods, most everyone else was dancing and feasting and becoming groggy with large quantities of hard cider. And thus far the strategy had worked, but it was one thing to sneak through the darkness of the woods and quite another to enter a village washed with moonlight.

Talen preferred his dark spot under the tree. It was much better than the moonlit fields that spread about the village. Out there anyone with an eye in his head could spot them coming from a hundred yards away. And it was better than the moonlit road running in front of them that led to the village where those that had shot Sugar's mother with arrows and murdered her father all lay, he hoped, dreaming in their abominable beds.

Except this wasn't right. Talen and the others were supposed to have come out across from the ash ruins of Sugar's old house. The one these fine folk had burned to the ground. "I think you've brought us to the wrong end," Talen whispered to Sugar.

"No, I'm just coming to get something important first." Sugar pointed up the road to the entrance of the village.

Talen followed her finger. The Fir-Noy here had begun to build a wall around their village, presumably to keep sleth like him out. It was a wooden palisade atop a mound of dirt. But she wasn't pointing at the half-finished wall with its timber supports still showing like bones. She was pointing at a tall pole that had been erected at the gate of the village. Something had been fastened to the top of that pole. Talen peered closer and saw a human skull shining pale in the moonlight.

It took him a moment, and then he knew whose it was. "That's your father's."

"You're going to help me," she said. "He deserves better than that."

Talen nodded. He deserved much better than that.

The night shadows of the clouds played over the fields and road that ran its crooked way through the village. Talen started to rise, bow in hand, but Sugar suddenly put a hand on his shoulder to keep him down.

A small longing ran through him at her touch, and it surprised him.

She motioned to the right. He turned. Something moved in the shadows a bit farther down the half-finished wall.

A patrol? The wall wasn't finished, but it was still large enough in many places to hide a number of men. Two of Shim's soldiers prepared to draw their bows. A minute passed, and then a solitary dog showed itself on this side of the wall, snuffling the ground.

The dog wasn't on a leash, but that didn't mean its owner wasn't following behind. A slight breeze blew in Talen's face, and that was a good thing because it meant he was downwind of that dog. But Talen wasn't thinking so much of the dog as the spot on his shoulder where Sugar's hand rested. That small longing had grown.

The last few weeks he'd started to feel odd things, vague sensings of another's Fire and soul. But those stirrings had never felt like this. He pulled away from her, the electric feeling of her touch lingering, and felt a hunger jangle along his bones.

River had warned him that the awakening to the lore was as big a change as that of going from boy to man. The ways of the lore were odd, and sometimes the body reacted in strange ways, but nobody had ever said anything about this.

Maybe this had nothing to do with the lore. Maybe this was simple attraction. Sugar wasn't one of those voluptuous soft ladies, but lately he'd caught himself staring at her, her dark shining hair and honeyed skin, her eyes. A spark often lit those green eyes, and Talen knew there were all manner of thoughts running like wild horses behind them. She had nice lips as well—

The man next to Talen froze. And Talen realized he'd lost his focus. He shook his head and cursed himself. Now was not the time to lose his concentration to some idiot Fire-induced twitterpation.

He looked at the scene in front of him and realized everyone was still watching the dog. It had raised its head as if it sensed the fist of soldiers under the tree. It sniffed the wind for a moment, turned their way and sniffed more, then dropped its head and padded off down the length of the wall away from Talen and the others.

When the dog was out of sight, River blew out a sigh of relief. "Dogs are the last thing we need."

Talen whispered, "You'd think that if they're worried enough to build a wall, they'd be worried enough to have a guard to go with it. You'd think they'd have a night patrol."

"You're assuming 'thinking' and 'Fir-Noy' are two words that go together," whispered Sugar. She rose. "Come on. We don't have time to waste."

She ran onto the dirt road and up to the half-built gate where the tall pole with her father's skull stood. Talen glanced about, saw the area was clear, and followed her out, running over the hard-packed dirt in his bare feet. He ran with the quickened pace that a weave of might imparted, bow in hand. River and three of the soldiers followed Talen and Sugar, taking up flanking positions to keep watch.

In this fist of soldiers, River was the only one who could multiply her might fully. She had mastered that lore years ago. The rest of them wore the weaves of candidate dreadmen, those that were in training. A candidate weave increased the wearer's abilities maybe by a fourth or half, preparing them for the large multiplication that came when you wore the weave of a full dreadman.

But candidate or full, no weave made a man invulnerable, as Talen could testify. He had plenty of bruises and cuts from training. There was a stitched gash on his arm from a practice with spears. And the pointer finger on his left hand was still wrapped tightly to its neighbor to give it support after it was broken a few weeks ago.

He followed Sugar to the half-finished village gate and the pole that stood next to it.

Sugar looked up at her father's skull. "Dirty whoresons," she spat.

The pole looked to be about eleven feet tall. The villagers had fastened a wide board below the skull and written something on it in dark script. It was hard to make it out, but there was just enough light to catch the letters. It said "Sparrow's End."

It appeared these villagers were trying to claim some honor for having killed Sugar's father. They probably hoped to change the name of their village. The irony was that Sparrow hadn't known a thing about the lore. The Fir-Noy mob had murdered an honest man, not some vile sleth.

Talen whispered, "The Fir-Noy are greasy goat lovers. When Shim ascends, they'll rue their cabbage brains."

"Just get me up," she whispered back.

Talen set down his bow and took a knee next to the pole. He said, "So, I heard you agreed to the *Sower's Jack* with that Koramtown weaver, him with the fancy blue tunic and shiny boots."

"I thought the boots were striking."

"Too bad you had to miss them. Shall I tell him that instead of dancing with him and his fancy boots, you decided to cavort around a village pole with me in the wee hours of the night?"

"Not if you value your life," she said.

"You like him that much?"

"He's got all of his teeth."

"I always thought his nose was a little too dainty for someone like you."

"What's that supposed to mean?"

He held out his hand to help her climb up onto his shoulders. "Just pointing out the facts."

Sugar took his hand. "Well, the fact right now is that you need to not drop me." She steadied herself with one hand on the pole, took one step up on his leg and another onto his shoulders. Talen grabbed both of her legs just above her ankles to stabilize her, and stood.

And as he did, the intoxicating scent of her Fire and soul flowed down over him like a river. He staggered back a step.

"What are you doing?" she hissed.

"Sorry," he said and moved her back to the pole.

She unsheathed her knife and sawed at something. And he struggled not to lose his wits as the delicious smell rolled down.

A moment later she said, "I've got him. Let me go."

Talen barely heard her.

"Talen!" she hissed.

"Right," he said and let her go.

The next thing he knew she was on the ground with the skull in her hand.

"What's wrong with you?"

He shook his head to clear it. "What kind of magic is the Creek Widow teaching you?" he asked.

"Same as you. What kind of a question is that?"

The Creek Widow, that old plotter, had probably been teaching the women some secret glamour. And Sugar had set it all in motion for that weaver and his boots, only to be sent off behind enemy lines.

"You could have told me," Talen said.

"Told you what?"

"Nothing," he said. It *was* a glamour. He was sure of it.

Sugar shrugged. "Whatever," she said and held the skull out to him. "Take this."

Talen took the skull, careful not to touch her again, and was surprised to find the skull as light as an apple. All the flesh had been burned off and the soft matter burned out when the Fir-Noy had cast the bodies of Sparrow and every other living thing he owned into the great inferno they'd made of his house and workshop. But someone had fetched the skull out, cleaned it, and painted the mark of sleth upon its forehead. The mark was made with a line running horizontally through a V to make a triangular face with two sets of horns. The face represented a man; the four points represented the twisted horns of a beast possessed by Regret himself.

The dark eye sockets and grinning mouth of the skull looked up at him. Someone had used thin leather strips to keep the bottom jaw firmly attached. They obviously took great pride in this kill. And they obviously thought themselves very brave indeed, for the bones of sleth were usually ground and scattered in the sea.

Sugar slipped off the leather sack she carried at a diagonal across her shoulders. She loosened the flap tie, retrieved a square cloth, then held out her hand. Talen passed her the skull, which she gently wrapped in the cloth and slipped into the sack. Then she tied the flap tight again. "We'll go back into the woods and circle around to get the other items. We don't want to be trying to sneak past Solem and his dogs."

And so they moved silently back to the woods and began to skirt around the fields. As they made their way, Talen stayed away from Sugar and her womanly conniving, but the odd haze of desire continued to afflict him. And that annoyed him. It was risky enough having to sneak behind enemy lines—he didn't need his fistmates increasing that risk by dulling his mind. He sighed in frustration and forced himself to think of something else, and his mind ran to his own father. The images of what had happened down in the stone-wight cave still tormented him. On a regular basis he would dream of the monster grasping his father's throat, drawing out his soul and Fire. Dream of that soul and Fire being transferred into the rough earthen body of that other creature with its vicious muzzle. And in all those dreams the monster would gape its mouth wide, then turn its awful head to look at him.

He hated the Divines. Hated what they'd done. Hated what they did to the humans they ruled, drawing out their souls and feeding them to their masters. He hoped these things Purity had hidden were indeed powerful weapons.

The fist of soldiers followed Sugar along a dark trail under the moonlit trees. Talen's throat felt dry. He'd been multiplied for a number of hours already, and he could feel the strain in his body. He twisted his water skin around, un-corked the top, and drank to slake his thirst.

As he slowed, one of the other soldiers, a big brute named Black Knee, put a hand on Talen's shoulder, then brushed past.

And as he did, Talen smelled sausages and sweat, and then a desire similar to the one he'd felt with Sugar washed over him.

Talen stumbled to a halt. A tingle lingered where Black Knee's finger had brushed his skin.

By Regret's rotted heart, was he now wanting big hairy men?

River came up behind him. "What are you doing?"

"Losing my wits," Talen said, still feeling the scent of Black Knee's Fire and soul. At least he hoped that's what it was. He shoved the cork back into his water skin.

"You don't need to be worried," she said. "We're prepared for this raid. You're going to do fine."

"Right," he said and began to think all those warning against the lore might have some merit.

Up ahead Sugar dropped down in a dry streambed and signaled for them to follow.

The streambed ran like a black snake out of the woods, through a field, and to the village. It was maybe twelve feet across, three or four feet deep. It appeared this was their way in, and so the fist followed Sugar, crouching and picking their way over the rocks and dry silt beds, keeping their heads below the grass that grew along the bank.

Partway through the field, they came around a bend and ran into a group of cattle standing in the bed. Sugar stopped, trying not to spook them. But the cattle startled anyway, lowed, then clambered up and out of the streambed.

Sugar motioned for the fist to keep down. A cloud passed over the moon and away again. The cattle moved away. And the fields fell silent as death. Sugar motioned the group forward, and they continued on, crouching low and following the streambed all the way to the village.

The fist slipped below the shuttered windows of a home standing next to the streambed. They slinked forward to a stone bridge, and then Sugar motioned them up.

They climbed out of the streambed, keeping themselves low and in the shadow of the bridge. The village was made up of about twenty homes strung along a road. They were surrounded by garden spaces and barns and sheds and other outbuildings. The streambed bisected the village almost in half. The ash ruins of Sugar's old house lay two houses down the road from this bridge.

Sugar silently ran to the shadows of the first house. Talen followed, arrow nocked in his bow. They paused long enough to look about and hear a man snoring loudly on the other side of the wall. Then they scampered to the shadows of the next house. Inside, a dog gave a weak woof.

Talen and Sugar froze, but the dog fell still.

Behind them the others ran one by one from the shadows of the bridge to the shadows of the houses.

Then Sugar left the side of the house and stole across the open space that used to be her yard. Talen followed. Behind him River gave hand signals, and she and the others followed, spreading out and watching the village around them.

The villagers had burned the home, barn, and smithy completely to the ground. It was nothing now but ash and charred timber. Only the stone hearth and a part of the chimney rose into the night sky.

Talen followed Sugar into the ash, which slid soft as silk between the toes of his bare feet, and picked his way through a number of charred timbers until he stood next to Sugar by the hearth. She leaned in close. "It's under one of these bricks," she whispered. "Start there and work my direction."

Again, the delicious scent of her washed about him, and he gritted his teeth and moved to where she'd pointed. She moved a bit in the other direction, knelt, wiped off a swath of thick ash covering the hearth with her arm, and pried at a brick with her knife.

Talen knelt at his spot, set his bow to the side, and wiped away a section of ash. He picked at the bricks there with his knife, found nothing, wiped another spot, and began again. Every move they made sent up puffs of dry ash that rose to waft about in the breeze, filling his nostrils and making him squint. He wiped another section with his arm, powdering himself, and tried another brick. He moved to another brick and wondered if the Fir-Noy had already found the cache.

A few houses down a dog barked. He froze. Another dog joined in, but then both fell silent. And Talen moved to the next section and wiped away more ash. They were out in the open here with plenty of moonlight. All it would require was some old grandfather who couldn't sleep to come outside to take a leak and look their direction.

Then Sugar popped two bricks that were neighbors and removed them to reveal a hole. "Ha," she whispered and reached her arm in.

Talen looked about the village, but all was quiet in the moonlight. He had expected this to be harder. They weren't in the clear yet, but so far this raid had been a pie bake. Surely there was a military proverb in this. Something like "hard cider makes a poor defense" or "festival night is time to fight."

Sugar retrieved what looked like a small box from the hole and reached back in for more.

It was then that a bow thwumped. The next moment Rooster cried out with an arrow buried in his arm. Another arrow snicked down, a dark flit in the corner of Talen's eye, and took Rooster in the chest. Another arrow struck Black Knee in the leg.

"The roofs!" River cried. Two men with bows rose up on the shadowed slope of the rooftop closest to Talen. Another man rose from the roof across the way.

Talen went for his bow, but an arrow struck a timber in front of him. And then another. And another, and he dodged back to take cover behind the hearth.

River shot her bow at a man on a roof trying to get a better angle at Talen. The arrow took him in the chest. Shroud, one of the Shimsmen that had come with them, moved for cover and shot his bow.

Sugar crouched by the hearth, still fishing for something in the hole.

Talen needed his bow. He prepared to make another run to grab it, when yet another man rose from a house opposite him and shot. Talen ducked and the arrow whizzed past his head.

There was no way those men had just climbed up there. And even if they had seen him and Sugar retrieving the skull, there was no way they would know Talen and the others would circle around the village through the woods and come back to this very spot. These men had been waiting.

It was ambush. "We've been betrayed," Talen said.

Another arrow whizzed past through the darkness, and Talen ducked down to where Sugar was. "Time to move," he said to Sugar.

"Almost finished," she said.

Across the way the double doors to the barn banged open. A number of men roared and rushed out, their helmets glinting in the moonlight. They carried swords, spears, and bows.

Fear shot through Talen. "There's no time!"

The men spread out in a line on either side of the barn doors. Those with bows already had their arrows nocked. They drew their strings back. There were at least forty men, far more than a village militia, and all of them had been waiting.

A large man walked out of the pitch darkness of the barn into the moonlight. The upper half of his face was painted black, the lower half white. About his neck hung a leather cord festooned with a cluster of boar tusks, signifying the Fir-Noy clan. He did not wear a helm, but did wear a cuirass of brass scales that glinted in the moonlight. Over the cuirass was a leather harness that held the discs signifying his honors. In the middle of that harness, directly over his breast was the eye of Mokad. The paint, the cuirass, and eye—they were all the distinctive garb of a Mokaddian dreadman.

"The boy's mine," he shouted. "Slaughter all the rest. And keep the ears. There's no reward without an ear."

2

Dogs

SUGAR CROUCHED OVER the cache at the hearth. She'd already retrieved a small box and something else that felt like a codex. Both were in her bag. But Zu Argoth had told her to leave nothing behind.

"Come on!" Talen said.

Sugar reached back into the cavity. Her hand fell on one last item—something that felt like a necklace wrapped in soft cloth. She grabbed it.

"Now!" one of the Fir-Noy shouted.

"Lords!" Talen exclaimed and dove at her. Bows hummed. And Talen's tackle carried them both behind a jumble of charred boards. He landed upon her, the impact sending ash billowing up, filling her lungs and eyes. A moment later arrows thudded into the wood about them.

Talen pushed himself off her, wheezed. "To River!" he said. "Now!"

Sugar sprang up, but her sack with her father's skull and mother's items yanked her back. It had been skewered by an arrow to one of the charred logs.

Across the way, the archers pulled their bows back, took aim again.

She tugged with all her multiplied might, and the arrow broke, allowing the sack to slide free. Talen shoved her forward over the charred heap of logs that used to be the outer wall, then dived after her.

She waited for the arrows to thud about her, but they didn't, and she realized her mistake. The archers were waiting for them to rise again, and there was nothing but open ground for a good number of yards all around Sugar's and Talen's position. They were going to be easy targets, and when she and Talen popped up to run, the Fir-Noy would send their arrows flying.

An arrow buzzed from one of the house roofs toward them. It clacked off a log close to her head. The archer on the roof would be making an adjustment. If he was any good, the next arrow wouldn't miss.

"So much for our dance about that pole," Talen said.

"Go!" she said.

And they shot forward.

"We're up!" Talen hissed. They took a few steps.

"They see us," she continued. Another two strides.

"We're down," both of them said at the same time and dove to the dirt. Bows twanged.

"Roll!" Talen said, and both of them rolled away from the spot where they'd just landed. She went right; Talen went left.

A host of arrows whistled around and past them like a swarm of angry insects.

They sprang to their feet again. They'd practiced this advancing movement in the face of arrows during their training these last few months. It only took a few seconds for a good bowman to mark you. Another second or three for the arrow to strike. And so you timed it as if you were the bowman yourself, shouting out what he saw. "I'm up," a few strides, "they see me," a few more strides, then down behind some cover. But there was no cover here, so they dove to the dirt again and added a roll.

Sugar lunged to her feet again. "We're up," she said under her breath again and ran for the gap between a barn and a house where River and two of the soldiers had retreated.

"They see us," Talen said. Then, "Lords! They see us!"

He was looking up. On the steep roof of a house in front of them, a man rose up out of the shadow, his bow was drawn and pointing right at them.

Talen shoved Sugar away from himself, out of the path of the arrow.

The bow thumped. Talen cried out.

Sugar glanced back. Talen was running another direction, but she couldn't tell if he'd been hit. An arrow at this range could easily slide clean through a man. She turned back. "They see me," she said and threw herself to the ground and rolled. Arrows sank into the ground next to her, and she lunged up again, but with all the distraction, she'd missed her angle on the lane River had disappeared into. So she dashed toward a privy that stood on the other side of a short fence up ahead.

Off to her left Talen shouted, "I hear the Fir-Noy had a good crop of goats this year! A fine bevy of Fir-Noy wives!"

"They see me," Sugar said to herself. The neighbor's fence was only a few strides away. Multiplied, she covered the distance in a flash. "I'm down," she said. But she hopped the fence instead and only then dove behind the privy.

"You'd think your women would complain!" Talen shouted again. "But maybe they've been lying with the billies."

His insult rang across the village. What was he doing? He could never keep his mouth shut.

"Get that Koramite rot!" someone yelled.

Sugar thought they meant her, but a number of the Fir-Noy chased after Talen. Was he drawing their attention with insults, distracting them, giving her and the others time to escape?

A new appreciation for Talen welled up in her. If she made it out of this, she was going to kiss him. Over these last few months he had become a true friend. He wasn't the massive bull his brother Ke was, but she decided at that moment maybe such things didn't matter.

"Go back to your goaty beds!" Talen yelled and sped off behind a house.

Sugar peered around the privy corner to see if she was being followed. Back by the barn the Fir-Noy dreadman unsheathed his knife. "That one's mine," he roared and shot out after Talen. His strides were powerful, huge, and in a moment he disappeared behind the house where Talen had run.

A handful of Fir-Noy ran out to finish Rooster. Another group chased after Shroud who was running for the bridge. Someone a few lanes away shouted, "Here's one, by Springman's barn!" All about the village dogs barked.

In front of Sugar stood a fence, then the open fields and the woods beyond. She prepared to make her escape, but just as she chose her course, men rose in groups from the field where they'd been hiding.

She had to move. A few seconds more and dozens of those men would see her. She looked back toward the houses in the village. A lane ran between the Waterman's house on the left and old Glib's house on the right.

Black Knee was in that lane, axe held high, the arrow still sticking out of his leg. A Fir-Noy blocked his way. The soldier lunged with his sword, but Black Knee knocked aside the thrust and struck the man in the head with the axe, sending him sprawling. Black Knee hobbled off behind Glib's house. The Fir-Noy stayed on the ground. It appeared Black Knee had also benefited from Talen's insults.

She waited for arrows, but none came, which meant nobody had a clear view of her position. Nor did they seem to be focused on Black Knee, so she darted out from behind the privy and raced down the lane between the two homes after the big man. Back by the ash ruins of her house, some Fir-Noy were arguing over the body of Rooster and who got his ear. Beyond them, shouts of triumph rose from the streambed.

Her stomach curdled. Poor Shroud. Poor Rooster.

She darted for the corner Black Knee had disappeared behind, but before she reached it, shouts rose from the men coming in from the field.

"That's her!" one shouted. "The sleth daughter. Get the dogs. The dogs!"

She rounded the corner and saw Black Knee at the other end of the house grasping his leg. He heard her and whirled around with his axe, then recognized her.

She ran to him. "Where's River?" she asked.

"Running with half these whoresons on her tail." A large blotch of blood darkened his trousers in the moonlight. He'd taken another wound to the head that was bleeding something awful as well.

Black Knee suddenly pulled her back into the shadows of the house.

Two houses down a Fir-Noy bowman clambered up the roof of a barn. He looked about, searching for targets, then turned his back to them and moved down the roof watching the lanes below him.

Very soon there would be men on every other roof and more in the lanes. She and Black Knee needed to get out, now. She looked about. Farmer Stout's house and outbuildings lay just across the lane. Her heart leapt—Stout kept a fine riding horse in his barn. "Come on," she said.

"You go ahead," Black Knee urged. He wiped the blood from his brow. "I'll watch your back and follow."

He wouldn't follow. He was going to make some fool-headed heroic stand. The memories of the terrible morning three months ago came back to her: Da hammering away in the smithy, the smell of the hay. When the mob came, she'd fled the fight instead of trying to help. Fled, and then watched as the murderers shot her mother with arrows and hacked her father's head from his shoulders.

If she'd stayed, they would have probably killed her. But they might not have. She might have provided the little bit of distraction necessary to turn the tide, to allow her mother with her wicked speed to send that mob of sleth hunters into a panic.

Sugar took Black Knee's arm. "You're coming with me."

Back on the lane by the privy, a man shouted, "Skirt around that way." And Sugar knew he was sending men to cut off their escape.

"Go," Black Knee said and turned to face the mob that would at any time come around the corner. "I've been waiting a long time to get my hands on a few Fir-Noy scum."

"You won't get your hands on anyone," she said. Black Knee was a large man; she only came up to his chest, but she was one of Shim's fell-maidens. Fire burned in her arms. She remembered Mother manhandling Da that awful morning, throwing him like a child across the room. Sugar bent down, looped her right arm behind one of his knees. With her left she grabbed his arm above. Before he could move, she hefted him up and across her shoulders.

He let out an exclamation of surprise. "What are you doing!" he demanded.

"Goh!" she said and adjusted his weight. "You're as fat as an ox."

"Put me down!" he demanded.

But Sugar just ran out from behind the house, him on her shoulders, and made for Stout's barn. Black Knee was a boulder, but she carried him along well enough to dash across the space without being shot by an arrow. And then she was into the deep shadows of Stout's fence.

Someone shouted somewhere off to her left, but she kept running, Black Knee bouncing on her shoulders. Just before she made it around the corner of Stout's barn, the Fir-Noy that had been chasing her exited the lane where she and Black Knee had been standing.

"There! By Stout's," one of them cried.

She darted out of their line of vision, around to the front of Stout's barn, and set Black Knee down in front of the doors. A horse neighed nervously inside. If she and Black Knee both hid in there, the Fir-Noy would know it, and the chase would end in Stout's barn.

"In," she said. "Close the door behind you. Stout keeps his bridles and saddles on the left. You wait until this rabble runs by. That will be your chance. And don't be getting any ideas about making some pea-brained attack. If you don't come back to the fort, I swear I'll have the Creek Widow work up a sleth curse that will hound you into the world of souls."

"No need to involve her," Black Knee said.

"Then get," she said.

Black Knee hesitated.

"Get!" And even though Sugar had no idea if the Creek Widow had any sleth curses, it seemed it was enough to cow the big man, and he slipped through the doors into the dark barn. She stepped back into the lane where the Fir-Noy could see her.

"There!" one of them shouted.

She ran away from the men. Just before disappearing behind another house, she glanced back. Black Knee was standing in the barn. He put his fist to his heart in salute to her, then closed the barn door. The Fir-Noy mob hurried up the side of the barn, unaware the big man was just a few paces away on the other side of the wall.

She turned away and darted into another lane and dashed along the house. In front of her the moonlight shone on the main road that ran through the village. At the edge of the village a large group of Fir-Noy hollered. She suspected that was where Talen and River were.

She hoped they made it. Ancestors, she prayed, let them make it!

She realized she should have said something to Talen about the dance. She'd actually wanted a dance with him, but the idiot had seemed impervious to all her hints and had waited so long others had stepped in. The fool.

Sugar burst from the lane onto the main road. River had planned escape routes and a rendezvous just in case something happened. If she could run down the road to the gate of the village, she might be able to make it to the woods and hopefully hook up with the rest of the fist at the rendezvous.

She turned and ran for the town gate, the dirt hard under her bare feet. All over the village men yelled and dogs barked. And she thought about the men who'd been hiding in the field. There could be more such men up ahead. She felt the candidate's weave of might about her upper right arm. It was a thin copper braid that gave her strength but also limited her.

There were two ways to multiply your powers. The first was to wear a weave of might, a device that reached into you and controlled your powers for you. This is what the dreadmen controlled by the Divines wore. The Divines would start their dreadmen on less powerful weaves and as the dreadman's body matured, they would move them to more powerful weaves until, after a year or two, the dreadmen were truly fearsome. The dreadmen marked their levels. Full dreadmen were usually of the second or third levels which meant they had doubled their natural strength and speed.

The most elite and mighty were of the fourth or fifth, tripling themselves. But few could multiply their powers to that degree.

Using weaves, the dreadmen didn't have to know any lore. And they didn't have to worry about losing themselves to the firelust. Or using up their own Fire. But wearing a weave meant you were limited to the weave's strength and the Fire within it. Once you depleted the store of Fire in the weave, your magic was gone until a Divine quickened the weave again.

The second way to multiply was to control your powers yourself, to wield the lore as Divines did. Using this method, you didn't need an external source of Fire—you simply consumed your own Fire at a more rapid rate. Yes, you depleted your own stores and hastened the time of your death, but you could use it with more precision, multiplying and diminishing yourself to fit the need. And because a body had a much greater store of Fire and used it much more efficiently than a weave, you needed less Fire and did not need to worry about running out in the moment of crisis.

However, Fire was tricky. Fire sometimes flared. Until you had the skill to control it, you risked being carried along into what was called the firelust where you'd burn up days, weeks, months of your life all in a moment. The body couldn't handle such a surge and would break. At that point the Fire would recede, but such people never recovered. They usually died within a few days, if not hours.For this reason, all of those in Shim's army who were new to the lore wore candidate weaves.

A door began to open in front of her. She was tempted to remove her weave, but drew her knife instead. She couldn't afford someone calling out her position. A quick slash to the throat, and they wouldn't know what had happened.But a little boy stepped out. Soby, the son of Lavender and Brash, who she'd tended a number of times just this last year.

He turned and saw her.

She brought a finger to her lips. "Shush," she said and flew past.

She took a few more strides, thinking maybe he'd actually listen to her, but he soon found his tongue. "Mam!" he cried out. "She's here!"

Thanks, Soby. She flew down the crooked road, past the last two houses, and then through the half-built gate. She lengthened her stride, her bare feet hardly touching the hard road, and passed the pole where her father's skull had hung. She scanned the fields that stretched out on both sides of her and saw nothing but a dark cluster of sheep in the distance.

Shouts and barking rose behind her. She glanced back.

A group of men were hurrying down the lane. Leading them was a man holding the leashes to six or seven straining dogs. The moon shone of the man's bald head and revealed his long beard and massive single eyebrow. It was Solem, the hound breeder. There were dogs that hunted their prey mostly by scent and others that hunted them mostly by sight. Solem's were sight hounds, which meant they were fast. And these were especially so.

Fear shot through her.

The dogs were barking, straining to be set free. Solem stopped and, with his two sons, removed the leashes. Then he pointed at her.

"Stu, boys!" he shouted. "Take her!"

And the dogs surged forth.

3

Dreadman

TALEN RAN DOWN the lane between two houses, his bare feet flying over the hard ground. Those greasy bowmen had certainly seen him, but now wasn't the time to dive for cover—they'd catch him for sure. Now was the time run like a hare and put as much distance and as many buildings as he could between him and those whoreson, clay-brained, shriveled manhood, goat loving—

Someone moved on the roof of the house on Talen's left. A Fir-Noy, gray in the moonlight, released an arrow. His bow hummed.

Talen darted left under the eaves of the house.

A moment later the arrow smacked into the dirt just behind him.

If he'd been unmultiplied, that arrow surely would have been his funeral! Talen ran past the junk the owner of this house had stacked against the wall. He leapt over a broken chair and smacked face first into a wind chime. The chime broke free, bits of metal and stone tangling about his head. Talen ripped the thing off and flung it to the ground.

"The boy's here!" the man on the roof yelled.

"Go shag your nanny!" Talen yelled back and ran for the corner of the house, realizing that if he cut out into the lane beyond, the bowman would have another clear shot. So he stopped at the corner and pressed himself to the wall.

But that wasn't going to do him any good, for another group of Fir-Noy turned into the lane a few houses down. And then the Fir-Noy dreadman entered the lane behind Talen, his half black, half white face looking like a horror.

Lords, Talen thought and darted out into the lane beyond, making himself a splendid target for the man above. He jagged right, ran a few paces, jagged left. An arrow whispered past. Then he raced into an alley between a house and a barn. Someone had cobbled it, and his bare feet tapped as he ran over the smooth, cool stones.

He had only taken half a dozen strides when the dreadman entered the alley behind him. Holy Six, but that man was fast. Panic rose in Talen's breast.

The alley opened up onto a lane. Talen didn't look to his left or right. He ran straight for the other side and the chest-high stone wall that stood there.

Behind him the dreadman ran over the cobbles in the alley.

Talen rushed the wall. He was multiplied. His whole body was tense with power. He sprang to the top of the wall with one foot and leapt, soaring out over the enclosure below. To his right was a house or barn. Below him a herd of huge piebald pigs huddled together, sleeping on their sides in the moonlight.

He was going to land on them. *Lovely.* He cursed and tried to aim for a clear spot. It didn't work—there were too many pigs, too close together. He landed squarely on the flank of one of the large animals. Ribs bent, then broke underneath him. The pig squealed with blood-curdling pain. Talen's momentum carried him forward, and he stumbled and slammed into two of the huge brutes.

The pigs squealed. He scrambled up, got his feet underneath him, and trod upon the sides of two other pigs as he tried to get out. All about him pigs were struggling up in alarm, grunting, squealing. Behind Talen, the dreadman leapt to the top fence, surveyed the scene, and sprang for an open spot. Farther back, Fir-Noy soldiers raced along the cobblestone alley.

Ahead, the wall on the far side of the yard beckoned, but Talen knew he wouldn't make it. That dreadman was too close. But Talen could slow him down if he could get into the house next to this pig yard and bar the door from the inside. Talen spotted a semi-open path through the pigs to the door. He hurdled one pig, then another, and raced for the building. When he got closer, he saw the door was already barred—from the *outside*.

His heart sank. This wasn't a home, but a barn or shed of some type, which meant he wasn't going to be able to slow anyone down. But the dreadman was too close for Talen to change direction.

He flung the locking bar up, yanked open one of the two double doors, and charged into the darkness, looking for an exit. The strong smell of blood and hanging meat slammed into him. He ran into a body hanging from the rafters, recoiled, knocked over a pail full of sticky liquid, and bumped into another hanging body.

Short stubby arms and hooves poked him in the face. Pigs, slaughtered and drained out. This was a large butchering shed. And the sticky liquid that was all over his foot was blood. Talen kicked the blood bucket away and weaved through the two rows of pigs to the back.

The dreadmen entered the doorway. The moonlight silhouetted his large frame and glinted off the edges of his brass cuirass.

Talen backed up, bumped into another hanging pig.

"Not a smart place to run," the dreadman said. "I'd hoped for some intelligent sport. But I guess you are part Koramite, aren't you? Shouldn't have gotten my hopes up. Still, we won't have to fetch a meat hook to string you up, will we?"

There weren't more than a few dozen dreadmen in all of the New Lands. Talen had watched this one compete in the games at Whitecliff. His name was Tenter. He was large, powerful, and murder with a blade.

"You're the one that grew up in the swamp," Talen said, trying to stall. "A bit of pond scum given a weave of might. I think I saw your woman lying out there in the yard. That one with a big snout."

Tenter chuckled with satisfied menace and took another step forward, the white half of his face pale in the darkness.

Talen backed up. Drew his knife. The dreadman's brass wasn't the strongest metal, but it would still protect the big man from slashes. And even if Talen could break through with his knife, a direct thrust wasn't going to be easy. Tenter would be wearing a padded tunic underneath which would help stop the blade. But attacking Tenter was madness anyway.

Maybe he could maneuver Tenter around the pigs so that the way back to the door opened up. But just then another one of the Fir-Noy caught up and entered the shed, ruining that idea. A third arrived and opened the double doors wide to let in more moonlight.

Talen took another step back. Tenter advanced past a swinging carcass.

Talen bumped into a table set against the back wall of the shed. His hand brushed the handle of something, and he grabbed it only to realize he'd picked up a large frying pan.

"You could join us, Tenter," Talen said.

"Then I really would be mating with pigs."

Talen hurled the pan at Tenter, but Tenter dodged, and the pan struck the side of a hog carcass and thudded to the floor.

Tenter yelled back to his men. "Wait by the doors. He comes your way, just stick him. This one's nothing but a mouth."

Talen was going to lose this fight. He was fast, multiplied, and had learned much in these last three months, but Tenter had been a dreadman since Talen was a boy. He was mature in his power. And he'd done nothing but study how to fight and kill.

Talen readied himself with his knife. Swallowed. He tried to remember his training. He glanced around one last time to fix the lay of his surroundings in his mind—the last thing he wanted to do was dodge himself onto a meat hook—and then he saw something behind him and to his right. The moonlight spilling into the shed was just enough to outline the frame of a small window. It was closed with a simple hook latch.

On the table lay a skinning knife, a coil of rope, and a few pots. Talen grasped the knife and hurled it. Tenter flinched to the side, and the knife flew past. Talen flung the rope. Tenter batted it away, but when he did, Talen reached up with the point of his knife and flicked the window's latch off.

Tenter saw Talen's intent. He lunged. Talen grabbed the edge of the table and swung it up, right into Tenter's face. The dreadman tried to dodge, but he'd not expected the move, and the sound of Tenter's head colliding with the wood made a satisfying thwack. Tenter staggered to the side.

Talen ripped open the small window and half leapt, half heaved his head and shoulders through the window. He pushed and wriggled forward, frantically trying to bring the other half of his body out.

"Rotted sleth!" Tenter said and grabbed one of Talen's bare feet, crushing his foot bones in his iron grip.

Talen struggled, kicked with his free foot and connected with Tenter's face. Three of his toes slipped into the man's mouth and felt the hard teeth, the wet tongue. Talen kicked again with all his might. Connected. And suddenly, his foot was free, and Talen slid the rest of his body free. He tumbled to a garden below and landed between two rows of kale. Behind him was the pig yard; in front of him was freedom. He scrambled to his feet and shot down the rows of cold weather vegetables.

Behind him Tenter roared. The window was too small for that big man. But the wall was made of thin plank, not sturdy rock or wattle and daub.

Tenter kicked a hole in the planking. He kicked again and another board made a sickening crack.

Talen leapt over the garden fence and out onto the wide lane. Across the way stood a barn and a hedge row. Beyond it lay the open fields and woods. It was the perfect escape, and therefore, exactly where Talen shouldn't go. Tenter was fast, and if he broke free, Talen suspected he'd fail to outrun him in a straight race.

Back in the slaughter shed, Tenter cracked more boards with another kick and widened the hole. Other men shouted from the pig yard.

Off to the left stood a number of houses and outbuildings. All was silent there, and so Talen raced for them.

Behind Talen, Tenter broke another board and began to push through, but Talen rounded the corner of a house before Tenter got free. He ran to a barn, turned its corner, and saw River and Oaks sneaking along a fence line up ahead.

He hissed and raced toward them. They looked up in alarm.

"We've got to get across the field now," he said.

"Where are the others?" River asked.

"No idea."

"But you were with Sugar."

"We split. I was hoping she'd joined up with you."

"Last I saw, she was running," River said. "We were forced a different way."

Talen's heart sank. Just then a pack of hounds began to bay over in the direction of the village gate.

"Shouldn't we do something?" he asked. "We can't just leave the others."

"Sugar knows this land better than any of us—if anyone's going to escape, it's going to be her. As for the rest, Rooster was killed at the house. I'm fairly sure they got Shroud down by the bridge. And Black Knee—how far can you run with a shaft in your leg?"

"What about Felts?" asked Talen.

"He wasn't even around the house when the arrows started," Oaks said. "He'd gone to take a more forward security position."

Talen sighed in frustration, sick with the thought of those that had fallen. To leave their bodies felt like a betrayal: the Fir-Noy would surely mutilate them.

"We'll meet Sugar where we planned to rendezvous," said River. "Now let's move before it's too late."

Oaks hopped the fence to the field and ran out into a patch of scythed grass. River gestured for Talen to follow while she brought up the rear. The three of them were about halfway across the field when someone called out to them from behind. They turned to see Felts leaping over the fence. Felts was like an uncle.

Talen's hopes rose. Maybe Sugar would make it as well.

But then Tenter entered the next field. A number of soldiers followed him as well as two men with dogs.

Oaks groaned. "Tenter. Of all the Fir-Noy, we had to pull that straw?"

"Just get to the woods," River said. "We'll lose them there."

They ran, but before they slipped into the dark trees, Tenter spotted them. He yelled to his men and sprinted toward them, the men with the dogs following behind.

A few paces later, Talen and the others entered the first of the trees with Felts not far behind. Because these woods were close to the village, they'd been cleaned by those that gathered wood. There were also a number of trails leading deeper into the trees that shone in the wan moonlight that reached the forest floor.

They found a path and followed it as it snaked its way in for about a hundred yards, dodging branches, straining to see their way with the little moonlight that made it to the forest floor. Behind them the dogs barked.

They leapt a gully, and River stopped. She was breathing heavily, but not too hard. Talen himself felt good, strong, ready to run a few more miles. In the fight with Tenter, he'd lost the tie binding the finger he'd broken to its neighbor. He flexed his digits. His finger had felt strong for a number of days now; it was probably time to lose the binding anyway.

River said, "I swear we should have already come to the horse breeder's place Sugar told us about."

Talen thought back to the maps Sugar had drawn in the dirt as they had prepared for this sneak behind enemy lines. They'd discussed their escape routes and what to do if things went awry. Off to their left was what appeared to be a thin line of light, a clearing shining in the moonlight. "Is that it?"

The dogs were baying now, getting closer.

"If it's not," Oaks said, "I think we'll feed you to Tenter first."

"You're far more juicy," Talen said.

Felts had joined them by this point. He was an older man who kept his long graying beard in two braids. Despite his age, he was a strong, loyal, and formidable fighter. He caught his breath and said, "That whoreson has already eaten enough of our crew. How about we feed him nothing."

"Come on," said River, and they struck out for the clearing, speeding through a clump of bushes. Oaks followed her. Talen went next. And the thin branches that Oaks ran through sprang back and whipped Talen in the face.

Moments later they broke out of the woods and into the clearing with a fence. At the end of the field stood a house and a large barn.

This was surely the farm Sugar had described to them.

Back in the woods, the dogs barked, and men called to each other.

River hopped the fence which circled the field. The others followed, sprinting across the grass, passing by obstacles that had been set up for horse jumping, and came to three interconnected pens on the far side. Half a dozen horses stood in one of them. But River ignored those mounts because Sugar had said the horse breeder kept his best mounts in the stalls.

The group rushed to the barn's double doors. River and Oaks pulled them wide and went in. Talen followed them. Felts stood guard, fearing those in the house across from the barn had heard them. The strong smell of horses and hay filled Talen's nostrils. There were eight stalls. Five with horses. A post ran along the right side of the barn. A number of saddles and blankets sat on it. Hanging on pegs above the saddles were accompanying bridles.

Talen grabbed a saddle, bridle, and blanket that looked to be the right size for him and rushed to a stall. The chestnut gelding there jerked its head back when it saw Talen, an obvious stranger. "Are you ready for a little ride?" Talen asked the horse calmly, trying to sooth it. "Just a little moonlight." He opened the stall door. The horse snorted a warning. "Apples and oats, I promise," Talen said and took the horse around the neck.

Immediately, he felt the animal's soul and Fire, and his desires flared.

By Regret's eyes, they flared!

He cursed. He couldn't stick to Sugar. No, now it had to be stinking men and sleth-rotted horses!

He grunted in anger and frustration, and pushed forward, trying to ignore the ridiculous feelings, and began to fit the bridle over the gelding's head, vowing to give the Creek Widow a piece of his mind.

In the woods at the far end of the field the dogs with Tenter bayed. Surely that would wake the horse breeder in his house.

This was going to be close.

Then Felts turned at the entrance to the barn. He grabbed one of the two doors and closed it.

Oaks was already leading his horse out. He looked up.

"Sorry," Felts said, then ran over to the other door and began to shut it.

The plan wasn't to hide here. What was he doing?

"No!" Oaks shouted. He dropped the reins to his horse and rushed the closing door. "You filth!"

Talen was confused, then realized what Felts was doing. There were only a handful of people who had known about this mission. Talen had assumed the person who had betrayed them was back at the fortress, someone who had been spying and overheard. But who said the traitor had to stay behind? Rooster, Shroud, and Black Knee were dead. That left Oaks and Felts. And Felts had, curiously enough, missed all the excitement.

It was impossible, but there was no other conclusion—Felts was the one that had betrayed them.

Oaks crashed into the door just before Felts slammed it home and dropped the locking bar. But even though Felts was older, he was anything but weak. And he probably had the door braced with his foot, for the door didn't budge.

Oaks must have realized this, for he suddenly rolled to the other door and shoved, throwing that door open. Oaks drew his knife, but Felts knocked his blow aside and struck Oaks in the face, an open-handed, multiplied blow with clawed fingers to his eyes. Oaks stumbled back.

Felts struck again, knocking Oaks to the ground. He turned and rushed back to shut River and Talen in. But River left her horse and raced forward. She had been using the lore for many years and had the power of a mature dreadman.

Felts saw her, drew his own knife, and slashed at her face, but she snatched his knife hand and with her other hand struck his windpipe.

Felts reeled back, dropped to a knee, and clutched at his throat. He wheezed terribly, trying to get breath.

River looked down upon him and cursed in frustration and dismay. "Why?" she demanded. "Why? What could they promise you!"

But Felts only fell to his side writhing, struggling for breath, his face full of fear and pain.

Talen was sick. Felts had been joking with him over a mug of watered ale not two days ago. How was this possible?

Oaks's horse side-stepped away from its stall. Its eyes were wide with fear at the strangers and commotion. It made a dash for the door. Talen yelled a warning and grabbed for bridle, but it was too late, and the animal charged past River into the night, its reins trailing on the ground.

River turned and helped Oaks up.

Talen quickly buckled the bridle on the chestnut gelding. He tied the reins to a post to keep him still and fetched the blanket and saddle. By the time he finished adjusting the stirrups to fit the length of his legs, River was back at her mount, cinching up the belly strap.

River said. "Get the horses in the pen. Get them running."

Talen ran out of the barn and caught movement at the house. Someone had been at one of the windows. "The house is awake," he shouted and ran to the pen that held the other horses. He opened the gate. Beyond the pens, at the far end of the field, Tenter, a number of Fir-Noy, and the dog master burst out of the trees.

"They've found us!" Talen yelled back. "There's no time to saddle a third." The horses in the pen began to move. He ran around the edge of the pen, clapping and hollering. The horses startled. One found the open gate and darted out. The rest followed, and then the horses River had chased out of the barn joined them out in the yard.

The door to the house burst open. An older man and what appeared to be his son stepped out with clubs. "What's going on here?" one demanded, but Talen yelled and clapped, and the rest of what the man said was drowned out by more than a dozen horses galloping past him.

Oaks rode out of the barn on the black mare River had saddled. River vaulted to the saddle of the chestnut gelding.

"See here!" the older man shouted.

Talen ran to River, took her outstretched arm, and swung up behind her on the saddle. Then she put her heels into the horse. The horse surged forward, and he clung to it with his thighs.

He felt the horse through the legs of his trousers. Felt its flanks with his bare feet. The animal's rotted soul and Fire were all about him, and the desired flared up his rotted legs.

Ahead of them Oaks put his heels into the stallion's flanks, and the animal shot after the mob of horses they'd scared out of the pen and barn. Talen glanced back. Tenter was running full out, taking impossibly long strides, approaching the house, the dogs trailing behind him.

"Go!" Talen shouted. "Go!"

River kicked the flanks of the gelding again, and they shot away from the barn, but he could see they weren't going to outrun Tenter. The dreadman was already rushing past the pen, his half black, half white face looking like something out of a nightmare.

River was wearing her strung bow across her chest and back. "Give me your bow!" Talen said and grabbed it, sliding it up and over her head. He snatched an arrow from her quiver, nocked it.

They galloped past the house. The strapping son rushed forward and tried to strike River with his club, but she leaned away from the blow and kicked him hard in the arm. The club went flying. And River and Talen flashed past.

Tenter was already in the yard, rushing past the barn, his face all business and murder.

Talen continued to hold the horse tight with his thighs, the Fire and soul of the beast calling him, and brought the bow around, but the bow was too long, and he had to cant it sideways to avoid the horse's rump. Talen drew the string. His muscles bunched as they had thousands of times. His father had been the captain of a hammer of Koramite bowmen. He'd made sure his children had learned the art. Talen brought the string back as far as he could at this angle.

Tenter saw it and, incredibly, put on some speed.

That's right—come closer. At this range that brass cuirass wasn't going to provide much protection.

Tenter took two more strides. One more and he'd have the horse's tail.

"Go back to your pig lovers!" Talen shouted, then released his arrow.

Tenter dove off to the side. The arrow flew past him, its white, goose feather fletchings flashing in the moonlight, and almost took one of the men of the house. Talen turned and grabbed another two white fletched arrows.

Tenter rolled to his feet, but Talen already had the string to his cheek. He released again.

Tenter twisted to the side, then came again.

The horse was at a full gallop now, thundering down the moonlit road, leaving the house and barn behind. The animal's gallop was strong and smooth and would have been a pleasure to sit if Talen hadn't felt his rotted thirst for the animal growing.

Talen shot the third arrow. It flew true and struck Tenter, but the angle of the shot and the metal of the cuirass were just enough to deflect it, and the arrow skittered off into the shadows by the barn.

Talen grunted. He should have had that shot.

Tenter came again, but he must have taken a wrong step, for he tumbled, rose, and tried to run again, but only managed to limp a few paces. He took a few more injured strides, then stood in the middle of the road, yelled, and gestured an insult.

The dogs flew past Tenter, continuing the chase. Three others from the horse breeder's house ran after them. But Talen nocked another arrow and shot one of them in the chest. The dog went down in a yelp. The other dogs slowed, and then the owners called the rest back.

River urged the horse to the right, and they raced past a number of low-hanging branches that forced Talen to duck. When he came up again, he saw their pursuers had indeed given up the chase.

He blew out a breath in relief, but knew it wasn't over. Tenter would return to the village. Anyone who had been captured, and was still alive, was going to face a horror. And Sugar was still out there. He turned around and leaned in close to River.

"We've got to go back," he said.

"It's too dangerous," River said.

He said, "We've got to go back for her."

4

Water

SUGAR PUT A good two dozen yards between her and the village gate, minding the road, for a number of wagons and horses must have come through after a rain, leaving ruts and tracks that had dried hard with deep edges that could break a toe or twist an ankle. But she couldn't slow because she'd seen Solem's dogs in competitions. Seen them run down deer, their teeth ripping into hamstrings and throats.

Holy ancestors, she prayed, *give me speed* and immediately realized she could answer her own prayer. A candidate's weave multiplied, but it also limited the Fire. It was given to those new to the lore to keep them from killing themselves. Her weave was a copper arm ring. If she took it off, she could multiply herself beyond the power the weave gave her.

She grabbed the copper ring, knowing if she lost control, if she gave into the firelust, it would be the end of her. But she was going to die if she couldn't run faster than those dogs. So she slipped the copper weave of might off her arm and shoved it into her sack.

Immediately, her Fire began to diminish. The strength in her legs slackened. But this was to be expected. When the weave was on, it controlled the flow. Now that it was off, she was forced to manage it herself. She began to build her Fire in the way River had taught her: carefully, in increments, so that it didn't flare and run away with her.

A surge of life and vigor rushed back into her limbs. But it wasn't enough at her current speed.

The dogs galloped behind her, quickly closing the distance. She was dead if she kept this pace.

She increased her Fire. Felt it in her heart. Felt it in the quickening of her lungs. She measured her strides as she had practiced. She'd been warned that if she multiplied herself too much, she would overpower her breath. And then she'd fall to the ground panting or pass out completely. Breath was the key.

But she'd never multiplied herself to that point. She didn't know her limit. And she wondered, not for the first time, how she would know when she was approaching it. How could you tell when you were on the edge when you felt the surge of joy she did now? River had never been able to give a satisfactory answer.

She pumped her legs faster. Her Fire grew, and she flew down the road. Her strides lengthened to nine or ten feet. Eleven. She sped down one swell and up another. The dogs barked behind, full of vicious bloodlust, but she felt so good she wanted to laugh.

A small gust of wind blew across the fields, carrying bits of detritus with it. Straw from the fields, insects, dirt—she didn't know. One speck went up her nose; others flew into her eyes and cut like sand. Sugar lost her vision for a moment. She blinked furiously, rubbed, almost stumbled. And then the flecks moved. Her eyes cleared, even though the grit still hurt.

She was lucky she hadn't taken a wrong step and twisted her ankle. *Lords, to be undone by a speck in the wind.*

She glanced back. The dark forms of the dogs sped along the sunken lane. They approached the bottom of a swell behind her, sprinting in the moonlight, gaining on her, terrible and smooth, like shadowy pike shooting through dark waters toward their prey.

She pushed herself faster. The edges of the fields flew by, but she dared not look back. She needed all her concentration on the road and the ruts that could undo her with one bad step.

The thudding of a galloping horse sounded across the field on her right, and she realized she was not going to be able to return the way she'd come. They would be fanning out, hoping to flank her. Sugar built her Fire further. Her limbs surged with joy, and she shot forth.

She felt the same giddiness rising in her chest as she did when jumping off the top of the Swan Creek waterfall to the pool below, and this time she couldn't help herself and gave voice to the joyful thrill with a shout.

She was panting, her lungs burning, and yet, lords of the sky, she didn't care. Riding this surge of life was like riding a wild and ferocious horse without saddle or stirrup. Perhaps if she just let it go. If she just flowed with it . . .

This was probably what they had warned her about: the crazed mind-lessness of the firelust.

Her strides were huge, light as a feather, and quick. She was flying. Flying. The sounds of her pursuit receded behind her.

Could she go even faster?

An alarm sounded in her mind. With a great effort she tried to reign in her flow, but it would not respond. She tried again. Focused. Bent all her might.

And she realized why the firelust was so dangerous—she didn't want to rein it in. She wanted to soar. A tiny fear shot through her. She was at the edge. She was right at the precipice.

She fought harder although she did not want to. This time her Fire diminished ever so slightly. The road flew beneath her. She shook herself and tried again, fought to rein in her Fire, and the Fire shrank back.

Lords, she had almost lost herself. And she was still in danger of doing so, for the joy still surged through her. The wild delight still ran along her skin like the electric caress of a lover.

Slower, she thought. *Slower*. And she fought to reduce the flow yet again.

She risked one glance back. The dogs were still behind her, flying over the road. Three riders galloped behind them.

You could run your body, just as you could a horse, to death. Or to damage. Long-lasting damage. She didn't know how long she could run like this. She didn't feel pain, but they'd warned her about that as well—the firejoy buried the pain.

It didn't matter. She had to maintain this speed.

The fields raced past. The wind made her eyes water. More shouts rose from behind, but she focused on her breathing, focused on her lungs working like bellows, focused on the ruts and patches of good ground along the road which bent in a great dogleg to the next village.

She realized that someone racing a horse straight across the fields would get there before she did. He would rouse the inhabitants. He'd make sure they got their bows. When that happened, those that wanted her dead would then be both in front and behind her. And even though she was fast, she wasn't running fast enough to outrun a storm of arrows.

Ahead and to her left stood the beginning of the plum tree tangles the village was named for. Those thickets would stop a mounted rider, but they wouldn't stop the dogs. In fact, the dogs would probably gain the advantage there. She needed terrain that would eliminate the advantages of both the horse and the dogs. She needed to get to moving water.

The Lion River was close, just over a mile away. If she immediately cut through the woods at the edge of the fields on her left, she could slow the horses. Her path would take her to the trail that led to the shacks of the river folk. She knew the river, and there wasn't a ford for a few miles in either direction. Which was perfect.

With her next step, Sugar slowed, then took one leap, flying up over the lip of the sunken lane and into the field on her left. The field had been mown, and the stubble was hard. Sugar rarely wore shoes, so the calluses on her bare feet were thick. But she was running faster and harder than she was used to, and before she'd taken a dozen strides, the hard stubble stabbed her on the inside of her toe where the callus was thin.

Behind her, the dogs leapt up out of the road and onto the field.

The field was a few hundred yards wide, and Sugar raced across, the hard stubble stabbing and cutting her feet. Just before she exited the field into the wood, she trod upon a sharp rock that surely broke something in her foot. She cursed, favored her foot for a stride, then continued on despite the pain. Obviously, her calluses weren't sufficient for these speeds. But she couldn't stop. She crashed through the woods toward the main trail leading to the river folk. And then had to slow, for while this wasn't a thick wood—the villagers felled trees for firewood here, as they did in all the woods around the village—there were still stray branches that could poke out her eyes, thicker ones that could skewer. There were rocks and uneven parts.

The dogs entered the woods behind her. They were not barking now, just running with deadly intent. She knew if the dogs were going to catch her, this is where it would happen. Fear rose along her back, but she couldn't increase her speed.

Sugar kept to the clearest parts where the moon could give some illumination, but the dogs with their galloping strides and awful breathing were coming closer. She risked another glance back. They saw her fear and increased their speed.

A branch whipped her, and she snapped her attention back to her path ahead. Through the trees she thought she saw a break, a lighter ribbon of moonlight cutting through the woods. As she ran, the ribbon of light grew larger. It was the main road to the river folk snaking its way through the trees. Just a little farther, she told herself. Just a little more. She sprinted for the road, but the dogs closed the distance behind her. One growled deep and low, anticipating the first bite. Then Sugar broke from the wood onto the trail.

Now, she thought. *Now!* And she put on a burst of speed. Despite the risk, she flared her Fire.

The ground was hard, the way clear. A dog snapped at her heels. She thought she'd flared too late, but then a surge of power coursed through her limbs, and she lengthened her strides. The dogs were right behind her, snarling at her heels, wanting to rip and tear.

She pushed herself harder. A wet muzzle brushed her ankle, but in the next stride she pulled ahead of the dogs and their teeth. Two more strides and she gained another few yards.

If I have to die tonight, she thought, *I will do it with joy*. Better that than being dragged down, a dog on her leg and another ripping her throat out. Her Fire blossomed, and she flew down the trail, the sounds of the dogs slowly receding behind her.

She knew Solem's dogs were fast, but they couldn't sprint at top speeds forever. And sure enough, they slowed to a lope. She kept her pace just a little longer, and then pulled her Fire back from the brink. As she did so, she felt a twinge in her knee.

Dreadmen and fell-maidens ate like they were starving and slept whenever they could. They had to in order to replenish the stores used in their times of action. She'd been eating and training and sleeping, but her body wasn't ready for this. She knew the twinge was only the first sign of damage. However, the river was not far away.

She ran another quarter of a mile until the houses of the river folk rose ahead of her. They were dark. Nothing was stirring. She sped through the habitations, setting a few dogs barking, and raced down the steep river bank.

Along this stretch, the Lion was a wide river, great swaths of it shining in the moonlight, other parts sliding by, as black as coal, in the shadows of the hills. She ran past a number of shacks where the fisher folk kept their nets and other implements of their trade and down to the spot where she knew two families hid their skiffs, hoping they still kept them there.

The waves of the river lapped upon the shore. Crickets filled the darkness with their singing. She spotted one of the skiffs in the moonlight and shadow. She ran to it, untied it, dragged it out into the cold water, and jumped in. The smell of the river enveloped her.

Behind her, Solem's dogs appeared at the top of the river bank. Farther back the riders entered the fisher folk village and shouted, raising the hue and cry.

Sugar picked up a paddle from the bottom of the skiff, dipped it in the water, and stroked deep and strong, keeping as low as she could. The skiff shot away from shore. She paddled again, and the river's current grabbed her.

The barking dogs ran to where she'd taken the skiff.

Sugar froze, letting the current carry her silently along the shadows.

A couple of the dogs splashed into the water, sniffed about in confusion, but they didn't pursue her along the bank.

The skiff moved along like a log. Up at the top of the bank, the river folk roused. Lights descended the river bank. But by that time she was moving into a bend in the river. The current carried her around the point and out of view. Only then did she paddle into the moonlight to get across the river and into the faster waters on the other side.

A mile or so later, she looked back. She could see no boats following, which meant she'd given them the slip. She couldn't quite believe it, and knew this reprieve was only temporary because she still had to make it out of Fir-Noy territory and back to Lord Shim's stronghold. Her murderous former-neighbors would be sure to wake the whole countryside to prevent that. But for now she was safe.

She sighed in relief, and thought of Talen and River. Of Black Knee. She hoped the others made it out. The image of Rooster and Shroud taking arrows rose in her mind. They were surely dead. She shook her head in dismay. They had been good men. Good, honest loremen.

The thought of the lore brought her back to her own Fire, and she retrieved the copper arm ring from her sack and slid it back on. Moments later it took control of her Fire, and the surge of energy began to recede from her limbs. The crazy joy faded. In moments her breathing slowed, and a huge weariness settled upon her.

She sank onto her back in the bottom of the skiff and looked up at the stars and the scattered clouds shining in the moonlight, clutching the sack to her chest, feeling her father's skull and her mother's secrets through the fabric.

She was hungry and thirsty, but she didn't eat the food she'd brought with her or dip her hand to drink from the river. The memories of that awful morning rose in her again: the inferno, the black sword coming down on her father's neck. She thought about Mother. It all combined with the deaths of Rooster and Shroud, and the sorrow of so much loss filled her.

Ancestors, she prayed, her eyes stinging. *Let them avoid the terrors in the world of souls. Let them all be gathered into safety.*

* * *

Miles away, Talen, River, and Oaks rode hard into the night. When they were confident they hadn't been pursued, they circled back to the village of Plum and found the village and surrounding fields crawling with groups of men. There was no way to get past all those men, but Talen did find a tree just back from the edge of the woods with a good view. He climbed it and looked over the field at the village. A fire burned in the main square of the village. Strung up next to it were the stripped bodies of Rooster and Shroud. Talen looked carefully over the village and fields, but didn't see any commotion. If they'd captured Sugar, she would have been strung up with the others, which meant they hadn't caught her yet. He climbed back down and reported what he'd seen.

"Black Knee and Sugar both knew our contingency plan," River said. "They'll make it back, or they won't, but there's nothing more for us to do here. Although I hate to leave Rooster's and Shroud's bodies behind."

"Vengeance is what their spirits will want," said Oaks. "We can get their bodies later."

"Come on then," River said to Talen. She held her hand out to help him up behind her on the horse.

Talen waved her off. He didn't want to be anywhere near that horse. And he didn't want to ride off and leave Sugar.

"Killing yourself won't help her," River said. "Come on."

"I'm going to run," Talen said, telling himself it was logical to leave Sugar and Black Knee to their own skills, but knowing it was betrayal.

"Talen," River warned.

"Just go. I'll keep up."

And keep up he did, walking when the horses walked and running when they trotted. An hour or so later when they came to open country, River insisted he conserve his strength, so he climbed up behind her and rode, hating his coward's heart and cursing his rotted desires.

It was early morning and still dark when they sneaked their way across the border between Shoka and Fir-Noy lands. Two hours later, in the early pre-dawn light, Talen jogged along the road that led to the fields surrounding Rogum's Defense, the fortress where Uncle Argoth and Lord Shim had been training up their army of dreadmen. Trees rose on both sides. A few yellow autumn leaves littered the road. They were cool and moist with dew under Talen's bare feet. Maybe Sugar *had* found her way back. Maybe she was here.

5

Visitors

ARGOTH, FIRST CAPTAIN of the Shoka clan, sat upon his horse in the middle of the main road running through the village of Rogum and watched the naked man up ahead in the morning light. Well, he wasn't all naked; about his neck he wore a bright blue scarf. But the rest of him was bare and revealed a strong body that had been shaved all over. It was quite the sight. And not only was the man naked, but he was muttering, holding a herring out to a number of gulls, trying to coax them closer. The gulls, however, seemed more interested in pecking the remnants of last night's Apple Dance festivities that still lay about the village square.

Shim, warlord of the Shoka, sat upon his own stallion next to Argoth. He said, "That's a lovely picture. Do you think I could impress the ladies with a scarf like that?"

"They'll be astounded, I'm sure," said Argoth.

"I would place it a bit more strategically," said Shim. "A woman wants mystery, Captain. A bit of the old hide and peek."

"Indeed," said Argoth. "I shall inscribe that into the annals of wisdom."

"You doubt me?"

"Never, Lord."

One of the black-headed gulls walked away from the rest of the noisy flock to eye the naked man and his herring. The bird walked with a bit of a limp and looked like it was missing one toe.

Two of Shim's body guards rode with him today. Shim turned to the new guard behind him. "Armsman, you're a middling to handsome man. Perhaps a bit more handsome than our Captain Argoth. So we're going to run a small test. On our next feast night I want to see you in that." He pointed at the naked man. "I'll have Captain Argoth show up in more strategic wear."

Shim was as hard a man as Argoth had ever met. He looked like he was made from boiled leather and revealed just as much in his expressions. And so when he said such things, people who didn't know him had a difficult time determining whether he was serious or joking. This guard was new and looked at Shim with shock.

"What?" demanded Shim. "You don't fancy ladies?"

"I," the armsman stammered. "It will be done, Zu."

"Indeed it will," said Shim. Then he turned back around. He glanced out of the corner of his eye at Argoth, the smallest hint of a grin betraying his intent.

All of Shim's guards went through some hazing. Argoth had no doubt this new one had been prepared by the others to know that Shim was a hard and eccentric man who tested his men's loyalty with odd demands, which meant this armsman would surely show up at the next feast night wearing nothing but a blue scarf about his neck.

Argoth smiled. Then up ahead the leader of the hammer of men guarding the village along with two other soldiers and a couple of men from the village marched up to the naked man. A number of the gulls startled, then, in a rush of flapping wings, the whole flock took flight, including the one brave bird the naked man had been courting.

The naked man watched in dismay as the birds wheeled around the square, then cursed. But he did not curse in Mokaddian. Argoth couldn't see the man's wrist tattoos clearly from this distance, but knew they were not those of any Mokaddian or Koramite. This was a foreigner.

Then the man turned, and Argoth saw the tattoos on his face and the brownish orange color of his eyes.

"What's a Mungonite doing here?" Shim asked.

The hammerman approaching the man said, "See here. All foreigners need to have a token to travel these parts."

The man ignored him.

"Mungo, I'm talking to you."

The naked Mungonite watched the birds, and when they settled upon the gables of the inn, he struck out after them. The hammerman tried to block his way, but the naked Mungonite was quick, and he dodged past the soldiers and village men and ran for the inn.

"Stop him," the lead guard called out.

Two other guards standing on the porch of the inn strode out toward the man.

But the Mugonite ran away to the side of the inn. He put the tail of the herring between his teeth, leapt to the seat of a wagon, up to the porch roof, then climbed up the face of the inn to the gables.

"He's a squirrel," Shim said.

"He's something," Argoth replied. And it wasn't a squirrel. The man was a bit too fast. Too strong. "That's not a drunken reveler who extended last night's festivities. I think we've got ourselves another *visitor*."

That was the code word that allowed them to mark a man as sleth without proclaiming it for all to hear.

When Shim had indicated he wanted to raise a kingdom of loremen on these shores, Argoth sent a call to all the Groves of Hismayas, asking them to join with them. He also sent word to groups that were not part of the Order of Hismayas. The problem was that not all loremen were as strict in their practice of the lore as others. Some crossed the line into abomination.

Argoth had known it would be a problem. And the issue had indeed raised its head as soon as the "visitors" had begun to trickle in. Not a week ago they'd had to hang one when he'd been caught stealing Fire from children. And so it was important that all visitors be identified and brought to Argoth and Matiga to be questioned before they caused a stir. Argoth had positioned men to catch them as they came off the docks. Obviously, this one had slipped through. But that wasn't the only problem here. This was a Mungonite sleth, and Argoth had sent no message to any group in Mungo.

The soldiers stood back and watched the man, trying to figure out if someone should go up after him. Then one of them spotted two boys, one with a sling.

"Are you any good with that?" the hammerman asked the boy.

"Good enough for pins at thirty paces."

"What about your friend?"

"Better than him," the second boy said.

"Why don't you give our friend on the roof a bit of motivation? No head shots. Maybe a sting in that hairless butt of his."

The two boys looked at each other. Then they looked past the soldier at Shim.

"Go ahead," Shim called.

The boys looked at each other again, then grinned. The first loosened a sling he'd tied around his waist as a belt. It was woven of dark hair. He slid the loop at one end over his middle finger, then held the knot on the other end in a pinch. He fetched a brown oval stone the size of a small egg out of a pouch tied at his waist and slipped the stone in the cradle. Then he stepped back a number of paces to get a decent angle.

Up on the roof the naked Mungonite muttered and approached the gulls with his fish.

The boy whirled the sling three times over his head and cast the stone. Not with all his might, but with enough to hurt. The stone flew up and over the roof a little to the left of the Mungonite, who paid it no mind at all. A moment later the stone smacked into a wooden roof beyond the inn and clattered to the ground.

"Ha," the second boy said. "Stand back." He whirled his sling a bit faster, this time the stone flew straight and struck the Mungonite in the side of his thigh.

The Mungonite turned and glared at the boys.

"Good slinging," said Argoth to the boy. Then he yelled up at the Mungo. "Friend! Can you understand me? Come down."

The Mungonite didn't move.

By now a crowd of people were gathered to watch.

"Give him some more motivation," Shim urged the boys.

The first boy whirled another stone. It was a straight shot, but the Mungonite snatched it right out of the air.

The second boy cast another stone. It was a bit faster than Argoth would have liked, but the Mungonite ducked, then threw the stone he'd caught at the boy.

The boy turned, tried to dodge, but the stone nailed him in the back with a solid thud.

He cried out.

Then the gulls scattered again, a number flying to the peak of the roof next to the inn.

The first boy slipped another stone into the cradle of his sling, but the Mungonite raced down the slope of the roof and leapt across the lane between the inn and its neighbor.

The distance between the two roofs was a good twelve feet, and a number of people in the crowd exclaimed their surprise with a chorus of ooh's.

Then the Mungonite scrambled up the other roof.

This would not do. The man was clearly multiplied and not in his right mind.

"Bring him down," Argoth said to the captain of the guard.

"Aye," the man said and motioned to his men, sending some to circle around behind the roof where the Mungonite was.

"Come down," the hammerman called. "Or we'll start hitting you with blunts."

The Mungonite ignored the captain and started in with his herring and muttering again, trying to coax the one bird with the missing toe closer.

The hammerman motioned to his men. Two of them strung their bows, then began a series of small pulls on the strings to waken the wood. A third soldier went into the inn and came back out with quiver of practice arrows.

The Mungonite crouched and held his herring out.

A few birds squawked and flapped back, but the one brave bird eyed the fish.

"Come down," called the hammerman.

But the Mungonite ignored him.

The hammerman nodded to his men, and they withdrew a number of blunt tip practice arrows from the quiver.

The hammerman called to his men that had gone around back. "He's going to come your way. Be ready."

The soldiers nocked the arrows and drew their strings back. They were all using warbows with heavy pulls. The first loosed his arrow, and it shot forth with a velocity that was going to hurt.

But the Mungonite saw it at the last moment, twisted, and snatched the arrow.

The second solider loosed his shaft. It flashed up toward the man.

The Mungonite batted it away.

"Ho," said Shim in appreciation.

A big man with long blond moustaches and plaid pants pushed himself off the wall of the inn where he'd been lounging. "Zu," the man said, using the honorific. "You'll not catch him that way."

"Oh?" Shim asked.

The man wore a sword, gloves, and tall brown riding boots. He walked toward Shim and Argoth.

One of Shim's bodyguards moved to block his way.

Argoth looked at the man's wrists. His hands were covered with tattoos. Those who wore their tattoos from the wrists up were said to wear their honors on their arms. This man wore his honors on his hands, as was the custom of many of the coastal clans in Mokad.

"No," the big blond said. "Blunts won't do it. I know. I sailed with the blighter, and he was murder to fetch out of the rigging."

His accent marked him as a mainlander.

"And who might you be?" asked Shim.

"Flax from Lem," he said.

"Lem," said Shim thinking. "That's old country."

"Yes," he said. "My cousin Silver wrote me about the wonders of this place. I've come to join him. Maybe see if one of the clans will let me open up new land."

Argoth perked up his ears. That statement was part of the code he'd written in his call to the Groves. In order to make more land arable, the clans would sometimes make an offer to any who would do the work. If they cleared the land, they could get the tenure on it as well as the first year's rent. And so making such a claim wouldn't seem unusual. The part that marked him as someone from a Grove or order was the cousin named Silver.

Shim knew the code as well. He said, "There are a lot of Silvers here. Which one were you referring to?"

"A hayward with the Vargon clan," he said. His left hand hung non-chalantly down by his side, but it was held with the index and small finger pointing straight out, the other fingers and thumb in. It was the first sign and identified a man as a user of the forbidden lore. Of course, knowing the sign didn't mean he was a fellow loreman. The Divines had their spies and infiltrators as well. This Flax could very easily be one of them. Only when he'd passed the other tests would they know.

Then the blond made the sign that identified him as part of the Hand of Mayhan. The men of the Hand were killers. Sleth of the darkest stripe that hunted down dreadmen and priests. In their long years as an order, they had even killed a handful of lesser Divines.

Argoth had sent no message to any in the Hand. All those in the Hand that he'd known personally had died or disappeared long ago. But that didn't mean his message might not have been passed on.

Argoth eyed him warily. "I don't know you, Zu," he said.

"No, but there's one of yours who can vouch for me, even though he might not like to do so."

Argoth was going to ask who, but one of the soldiers shouted out, "Got him!"

Up on the roof the naked Mungonite glared, then turned back to the bird. The second soldier loosed his shaft. It too struck the man in the back and glanced off.

The man flinched, but crabbed a bit closer to the bird.

"That's going to make a smart bruise," Shim said.

The soldiers nocked more arrows. The Mungonite crabbed a bit closer to the bird, which eyed the fish. Then the Mungonite sprang forward and caught the bird in a great flapping of wings and loud squawks.

The solders raised their bows.

The Mungonite looked down at them, gritted his teeth, then ran down the far side of the roof.

The bowmen moved to get a clear shot, but the Mungonite jumped to the next roof, scrambled up to the top, ran to the back, and leapt to the roof of a barn.

The hammerman yelled to his soldiers to give chase.

The Mungonite ran to the end of the barn roof, jumped, flying out over a girl in a pea green frock who was leading a cow out to its pasture. It was an amazing leap. An inhuman leap.

He broke his fall with a roll, then was up in the blink of an eye, running for the woods.

The big blond said, "Even if your men catch up to that Mungonite priest, they're going to have a time roping him. Our naked friend has *skills*." He emphasized that last word. "It would be easiest if someone with equal *skill* went after him. Let me fetch him for you. We'll call it a gift of good intent."

A Mungo priest? If that were true, it would mean he wasn't sleth. But if Mungo were going to send a spy, it would not have been a lunatic wearing nothing but a blue scarf about his neck.

Shim regarded the big blond for a moment. "Flax, is it?"

"Yes, lord."

"You bring him to me at the fortress, and we'll talk."

The naked man raced across the pasture, bird in hand, heedless of the effect his speed was having on the people in the square, who were all moving down the road to watch him.

Flax smiled. "I'll have him before the morning's done." Then he walked over to a hitching post, untied a fine saddle horse, and mounted it. Then he rode off after the crowds.

Shim watched the big man for a moment, then turned back to Argoth. "That Mungo has no sense of fashion, but, Regret's arse, he can move. Did you see that?"

"It was hard to miss," said Argoth.

"Scampering around like a squirrel, batting away arrows—I want him in our army."

Argoth looked around. Almost everyone was trailing down the road after the spectacle, including a pack of village dogs.

Argoth pitched his voice low. "No. A man like that can't be counted on." There were indeed many that might bear the title of sleth that would be useful, but it was clear that the Mungonite was damaged. Argoth knew his call would bring all sorts, and he wondered now if he'd made a mistake.

"I didn't say put him up front," said Shim. "I said we could use him."

"You know what your opposition claims." There were those in the Clans who feared Shim was controlled by dark masters. "Someone like that would only confirm their bad assessment."

"Captain," Shim said, "you fight lies with the truth. Our friend has skills. If we can learn them, we will. If he turns out to be unstable, then we'll use him to remove some of the fears the people feel. We don't want to hide him or make him mysterious. That simply starts rumors and turns him into something to be feared. If we were Divines, that's exactly what we'd want. But we're not. I'm going to let the people get up close. I want them to see that he's nothing more than a man. I want to make him common."

Shim had no caution. And yet, hadn't Hogan said the same of Argoth? He found it ironic that he had taken the role of the conservative now that Hogan was gone.

"He's from no group I know," said Argoth. "We have no idea where he's from, no idea of his purpose. We need to be careful."

"Careful is my name," said Shim.

This from the man who was bringing the Order out into the sun. "In your world," said Argoth, "careful is nothing but a soggy flatulence."

6

Meat

BEROSUS, WHO HAD GIVEN the false name of Flax to Lord Shim and the sleth with him, rode away to follow the naked Mungonite. Berosus was blessed. There was no other explanation. During Berosus's recent voyage across the sea, the Mungonite had learned what Berosus was. Being a priest, the Mungonite knew what to look for. But Berosus had prevented him from revealing the secret. However, the Mungonite had still escaped him out at sea.

All thought he'd jumped overboard and drowned, but here he was, like an offering from the Creators. A gift that would help Berosus begin to earn the trust of Lord Shim and his sleth, Argoth.

The naked Mungonite ran into the woods. Berosus followed. A few of the villagers wanted to tag along, but Berosus motioned them back. He followed the priest for a mile, and when he was sure he was beyond the eyes of any of the villagers, he called his dreadmen to join him.

Some priests were nothing more than menial servants, cleaning the living quarters, keeping records. But some were taught the lore and wielded the vitalities, helping with the sacrifices, working in the forges of the Kains, hunting sleth. No spy or messenger would make a spectacle of himself as this man had. So Mungo hadn't sent him. Something else was afoot. But he'd find out. He'd find everything out.

When he succeeded here, the Sublime's approbation would shine down upon him. She would bless him. She might even put him above the Glory himself. He could almost feel the bliss rising through his bones as he and his men chased the priest down a road and into an abandoned barn that lay in the woods near the beach.

The distant sound of the surf mixed with a flock of gulls that wheeled and shrieked high above. This barn and house had probably belonged to a fisherman, but that had been some time ago. The roof of both the barn and the small house that went with it sagged with holes. There were no shutters on the house. No door. Someone had hauled them off long ago. Weeds grew up all around the base of the structures and in the yard.

And yet Berosus smelled the remnants of wood fire. As if someone was hiding out here.

Movement in the small farmhouse drew his attention. Berosus motioned for one of his men to deal with whoever was there. He assigned two others to search the perimeter for anyone else, and then he turned to the barn. Its old doors were closed.

"Friend," he called. "You escaped on the ship, but there are no prying eyes to hold us back here. Come out, and we'll talk."

Something knocked inside the barn.

"Come," said Berosus. "Do not try my patience."

Berosus had multiplied himself. He'd been multiplied for some time now. There were levels of dreadmen and Divines. Most breeds of men could not progress past the second or third level. There were a few individuals who could multiply themselves to the fifth. But Berosus went beyond even that. He was as different in his breed from those who were meat as a staghound was from a lapdog mutt. As different as a lion was from a gummy-eyed barn cat. There were things that happened when you could multiply at this level. Things beyond strength. For example, he knew exactly where the priest stood, for he could hear his breathing.

Berosus signaled his men to stay back. Then he walked up to the barn doors and opened both of them wide. The priest stood exactly where Berosus knew he would be, a two-tined pitchfork in his hands. He lunged forward and stabbed Berosus in the gut with it. Berosus let him. If you did not know the bitter, you could never taste the sweet. Pain blossomed inside him, and he savored the sensation.

The pain would soon pass. His blood would soon clot. The wounds to his bowels would mend. When multiplied at this level, the healing process became miraculous. Yet another sign of the Creators' favor and his superior breeding.

"That won't do," said Berosus. "It really won't."

The priest pulled the pitchfork out and lunged again. He was fast, but

Berosus caught the fork. He wrenched it out of the man's hands and cast it aside.

The priest picked up a fishing knife that lay on a table and slashed. But Berosus grabbed the priest's knife hand, twisted, and broke the man's wrist.

The man winced with pain, wrenched his arm free, and stepped back.

"Who is your master?" Berosus asked and stepped forward. "Who sent you?"

With his good hand, the priest picked up an old wooden mallet and hurled it at Berosus's head. He was a strong man, multiplied. The mallet would have smashed a normal man in the face, for none of the lesser breeds would have been quick enough to avoid it. It would have struck a dreadman of the third. But to Berosus it was as if a child were tossing him a ball. He batted the old mallet away and took another step forward.

The priest backed up against the wall of an animal stall, eyes darting. He was going to try to bolt past Berosus, but before the priest could move, Berosus reached out and grabbed the man by the throat, hauled him off his feet, and slammed him into the wall. Not to kill him, only to daze him a bit.

The priest tried to swing at Berosus, but Berosus slammed him into the wall again, bouncing the Mungonite's head smartly against the wall, then dragged the man out of the barn and into the light.

The priest might have been of a lesser breed, but he was strong. And he did not quail. Berosus had to give him credit. There was nothing but murder in his orange eyes. And they were wonderful eyes—wild with darker flecks.

"Hold him," Berosus said.

Two of his dreadmen converged on the man, grabbing his arms and twisting them behind his back. When they'd secured him, Berosus pulled down the blue scarf. He expected to see a thrall, but there was only a scar where a thrall had been.

The priest looked up with angry satisfaction in his orange eyes. "You can't hold me," he said with a thick Mungonite accent. "There's no thrall that can catch me."

"We shall see," said Berosus. Thralls grew into a person. In some instances, depending on the type of thrall, the weave itself became unnecessary. He felt the man's neck, expecting to encounter the binding of master to servant, but none was there.

Now, that was interesting.

Once someone was accepted into the service of the priests, they never left. It was forbidden. They were thralls for life. But the fact that nothing was there meant this priest had escaped his thrall.

Berosus pulled a weave from his pocket. It looked like a thickly segmented necklace.

When the priest saw it, he bucked, but the dreadmen held him, and Berosus placed the weave about his neck and clasped it shut.

It was a king's collar, a weave that prevented its wearer from using many forms of the lore. It would cut the priest off from his ability to multiply his Fire. Berosus waited a few minutes for the weave to fully take hold.

He said, "I have always appreciated the Mungonite form. It's a good breed, and your eyes—the amber in the sun is quite amazing."

Above them the gulls cried.

"You're sleth," said Berosus. "Did you also receive a call from Argoth?"

The priest shifted.

"You are going to tell me everything. There's no sense in fighting. The only question is whether you'll be of any use to me. If so, I'll let you live."

Berosus wore his honors on his hands. It was common enough, and wouldn't raise any questions. Many clans wore their honors there. However, he also wore the eye of Mokad in the palm of his left hand. It was a weave, grown into his skin, that allowed him to reach into the souls of those who'd been marked. It was not made with metal, but with a part of the Sublime's own flesh. Anyone looking at his palm would see nothing more than common tattoos. But to those upon whom he laid his hand it would burn like flame.

Berosus placed his hand upon the priest's head and pushed through the bindings of flesh and soul. Oddly, he did not feel the normal initial wall of resistance. He pushed farther, and suddenly there was nothing. It felt like he'd entered a broken and windswept room.

Usually he would find an intelligence waiting for him. He would ride it, bring it to heel. There would be a struggle. But there was none of that here.

The priest began to laugh.

Berosus searched for the man's soul, but found gossamer tatters. Thoughts passed by him, but they were as elusive and insubstantial as cobwebs.

"Fish," the priest said, laughing. "The skin that shines, the belly that's soft and white. You won't have me, Seeker. You'll never have me. I will never again be someone's dog."

Berosus stepped back and thought. The gulls cried above them. One lone black-headed gull stood upon the peak of the house roof. It stutter-stepped to one side, revealing that it was missing one toe. This was the bird the priest had been courting back at the village. Berosus looked at the priest.

His mind flashed back to the ship. When he'd gone for the priest, the man had escaped up the rigging. Just before Berosus had reached him, a gull had cried and flown away from the crow's nest where the man had secured himself.

That too had been a black-headed gull.

Suddenly it all became clear. "Friend," Berosus said. "That's a dangerous and tricky lore. Easy for things to go wrong, eh?" It explained the priest's behavior at the village. The lore had indeed gone wrong, and the Mungonite was trying to get his pieces back. Of course, the bird must have been at turns confused and terrified, fighting the soul that tried to inhabit its body. It would only get worse as time wore on. A poor saddling could never be a long-term arrangement.

"I could use a man like you," said Berosus. "Come back to the fold, live a good life in the service of your betters."

"Never," said the priest, murder still in his eyes.

"Never's a long time," said Berosus. He turned to one of his dreadmen. "Get that bird. I need it alive."

When the dreadmen moved to capture the bird, the priest bared his teeth in a snarl. He kicked back, yanked one arm free. He spun and wrenched his other arm free, then snatched the knife from the sheath of one of the dreadmen and hurled it at the dreadman going for the bird.

The hilt of the knife hit the man in the head and bounced off.

The dreadman turned.

In that moment the gull screamed and launched itself from the roof.

"I am free," the priest said with manic glee. "I am free." Then he turned to run.

Berosus caught him.

The priest struggled.

The man was astonishingly strong. Too strong. Then Berosus realized the king's collar, having no soul to constrain, wouldn't have worked on this man. The priest was still multiplied, anger burning in his marvelous eyes.

The priest chopped at Berosus's grip, but Berosus kicked the man's feet out from under him and dropped him face first to the ground. Two more dreadmen fell upon him. The Mungonite heaved and bucked, but the dreadmen held him there.

The dreadman who'd been charged to get the bird picked up a stone and hurled it at the black-headed gull, but the bird veered, beating its wings wildly, then shot behind the house, then swooped up between two trees. Up to the sky beyond.

Without the soul that lived in the bird, Berosus couldn't compel the priest. The bird wheeled higher and higher into the sky. There would be no catching it. Which meant there was nothing more Berosus would get from this man.

No matter. Lord Shim hadn't stipulated he bring him back alive. Berosus pulled out his knife.

The priest gritted his teeth, struggling against his captors, but satisfaction shone in his wild orange eyes. "I am free," he gasped.

"You are meat," said Berosus, "and will be collected with all the rest." Then he slit the man's throat. Blood pumped out of his neck, and then the priest's eyes rolled up in his head, and he slumped in the men's grasp.

Berosus stood and looked up at the sky. The black-headed gull climb to join a flock high above, riding the wind blowing in from the sea. The birds were small and pale against the blue sky. He soon lost track of the one gull amongst its fellows, but it didn't matter. The priest was up there, trapped, having nowhere to which he might return. The bird he rode would soon go mad. It would die, and the priest would find out that you are never free.

Berosus looked down at the body. "Get him up on my horse," he ordered.

Shouting arose in the old small house. Moments later a young man in a gray hood dashed out the door and off the porch, but one of the dreadmen who had gone to search the house shot out the door after him, caught him, and bore him to the ground. There was a tussle, but the dreadman soon had the boy by the hair and an arm twisted up behind his back. He hauled him to his feet. The second dreadman came out holding a small cask.

The first dreadman marched the boy forward, and Berosus saw it wasn't a boy at all. It was a young woman who'd cropped her dark black hair to shoulder length. She had caramel skin. And as she came closer, he recognized her beautiful jade eyes. He'd seen those eyes on the ship.

She saw the priest's body lying on the ground, saw the blood, and her face fell.

The second dreadman popped the lid off the cask he carried and said,

"Bright One, you'll be interested in this." He brought the cask over and tipped it so Berosus could see inside.

In it lay a number of items wrapped in fine linen worked with an alternating black and white border design that belonged to Lumen, the former Divine of this land. Berosus unwrapped a number of the items and found half a dozen dreadman weaves, some Fire stomachs, two codices, and other implements of the lore. From the right buyer any one of these items could fetch enough to live on for a year. Some far more.

Berosus turned to the young woman. "You're the one that cut loose the ship's boat, aren't you? You cut it loose for your master. That's how he survived after he jumped overboard. He rowed to shore while we were resupplying and getting another ship's boat. And then both of you left on another ship that sailed from Karsh before we did."

She said nothing.

"Very clever," Berosus said. He grabbed her wrist and examined the tattoo there. "Cath. That's a long way from Mungo."

But it made sense. If the priest had somehow escaped his master, he'd want to get as far away from the Mungonite Seekers as possible.

"Do you know any lore?" Berosus asked. "Was he teaching you?"

"She's a bit too strong," the dreadman holding her said.

The young woman twisted, trying to get free.

Berosus nodded. He held up one of the Fire stomachs from the cask and examined it in the light. "It's not your everyday thief that can break into a temple and steal the holy implements. You have to know where to look for the secret chambers. But he would have known, wouldn't he? There are lords and chieftains and sleth that would pay a great price for such a thing."

She took a long look at her master, then glared at Berosus in anger.

"This isn't your first robbery, is it?"

They'd probably been stealing and selling weaves for quite some time. And this team of thieves wouldn't be the only ones attracted to this land and its temple that lacked its Divine.

The young woman said with a heavy accent, "I can show you more. Make him let me go."

"You don't know what I am, do you?" Berosus asked. "But you will know soon enough." He fingered her lovely hair. "Soon enough, my pretty girl."

7

Eresh

TALEN TROTTED OUT of the cool woods with River and Oaks following behind on the horses they'd stolen from the Fir-Noy barn. Across the fields rose the fortress of Rogum's Defense, which had been built at the edge of a plain that dropped down to the Sourwood River on the north and the sea on the east.

When the original Koramite settlers had first come to these lands, their primary threats came from the woodikin and other creatures already here. So the settlers had built a string of forts ten to twenty miles apart, depending on the terrain. Some guarded ports, others fords or settlements, and still others entrances to valleys.

Rogum's Defense was one of those early fortifications, build of stone in the shape of a smaller square inside a larger one with towers at intervals along both walls. The lower, outer wall stood fifteen feet high and eight across; it ran roughly 400 feet on a side, and enclosed about three and a half acres. There was 70 feet of space between that outer wall and the inner one; this open space is where Talen and the others trained.

The higher, inner wall was double the height of the first and ran 250 feet on a side. Inside that inner wall lay another bailey of little less than an acre, ringed with the barracks, smithy, hall, and the other structures.

Rogum's Defense was not as tall or as large as the massive fortress in Whitecliff, but it was formidable enough. Besides, Rogum's Defense was out of the way, which allowed for the secrecy Lord Shim and Uncle Argoth required. Upon the walls, Shim had erected banners showing his new device—a field that was half white, half blue, with a blazing yellow sun in the middle. The banners waved in the lazy breeze above the outer gate.

Talen trotted with the horses across the open field surrounding the fortress to the bridge that crossed the shallow stream that wound its way through the wide field in front of the fortress. At this time of year the stream was at most a few inches deep. At a bend in the stream, a handful of geese bravely rested in the water next to a clump of reeds. If the geese stayed much longer, Talen suspected they would become this evening's dinner, for those that trained in Shim's new army had, as all who used the lore did, an enormous appetite. Just the thought of roasted fowl made him salivate.

He crossed the bridge, the wood smooth and hard under his bare feet. Behind him came River and Oaks, the horse hooves clopping loudly. The water below was clear in the early light, allowing him to see the stones at the bottom and water plants growing in between, their dark emerald lengths undulating in the current. Watching that flow had always given him peace, but not today, for his mind was too full of worry for Sugar and Black Knee.

He jogged with the horses to the gate of the outer wall, and then River and Oaks slowed their mounts to a walk. The gutted and rotting body of a man hung from the felon's pole that stood outside the gate. His white beard was stained. His brown teeth made an awful grin. A crow sat on his shoulder and pecked at the dried flesh of his neck.

Argoth had sent his call out to the secret groves and orders of sleth weeks ago, but it took a few weeks to sail across the sea, weeks for the message to spread, weeks for those to make the journey down to the ports and across the sea to the New Lands. Only a few had responded at this point. The man hanging from the felon's pole called himself Pinter. He was one of the first sleth to answer Argoth's call.

He'd demonstrated wondrous skill with his axe and bow. He had a knife he called The Judge with a fabulous hilt. He'd wowed Lord Shim with his ability to scamper and climb the buildings of the fortress, but the Creek Widow had caught him stealing Fire from a captured Fir-Noy, a mere boy with flowers in his pocket. It didn't matter that the Fir-Noy had been a spy. All those that knew the lore in Shim's army had been forbidden to steal Fire—"We will *not*," the Creek Widow had said, "practice the abominations of the Divines and their masters that devour us!" Pinter had disagreed.

The crow pecked another bit of flesh.

"Ho!" River shouted to the guard above. "Any news of Black Knee or Sugar?"

The man above was eating a meat pie, probably left over from the previous night's festivities. "Nobody's come through this gate in the last four hours. They're probably out sleeping off the dance like we all should be. And where have you been?"

The guards didn't know about the mission Talen and the others had been sent on to the village of Plum. Shim was a strict commander and didn't share knowledge unless he had to. Butter jaws had cost more than one life, as had been so clearly demonstrated this last night.

"We were in Mount's village, sleeping with a bunch of goats," River lied.

"You went to Whitecliff against orders," the guard said.

"Oh, I wish," Oaks said.

And so did Talen. River and the guards bantered back and forth a bit more as those below opened the gate. When the trio passed through, the guard up on the gate said to Oaks, "You know, if you didn't have the brother in tow, I'd suspect you of some bravery. Not everyone can handle a tumble with the Koramite bowmaster's daughter."

"There are things a man can only dream of," Oaks said. "But wooing her is like wooing a bear."

River rolled her eyes.

"You're a bit of a weakling," the guard said. "And look at your hair. Maybe I should have a go."

Oaks shrugged. "It's your own death."

The guard grinned. He made an exaggerated bow to River, meat pie in hand. "I propose a wrestle in the outer bailey, one-on-one, you and me. We'll see who the bear is."

"I really don't enjoy beating up on children," River said.

The other guards hooted. River normally would have teased the man further. Or taken him up on his offer. Not only because that's the way she was, but also because he was Shoka, one of the Mokaddian clans. As Koramite half-breeds, Uncle Argoth had told them they needed to make a concerted effort to help the Koramites and Mokaddians get along in Shim's camp.

River waved good-bye as she passed the man.

"Better luck next time, boys," Oaks said.

The trio crossed the outer bailey, passing three fists of dreadman candidates practicing close combat with wooden swords. As they approached the inner fortress, the smell of frying fish and cook fires wafted out at them on the breeze. Hunger gnawed Talen's belly, but it would have to wait because Legs stood by the gate of the inner wall, a blanket wrapped around his shoulders.

A big-boned man, all sinews and weathered muscle, stood next to him. He had a long moustache and plaid pants. Next to him stood a horse with a dead and naked man lying across its back.

"Sugar?" Legs asked.

"She's not with us," River said.

Worry filled his face. "She's still down by the gate?"

"No . . ." River trailed off.

The newcomer spoke. He had a booming voice. "The little man says he's been here all night. I asked him why all the fretting, but he's tight as a drum."

"As he should be," said River.

"Aye," said the man. "Aye. Your Lord Shim runs a tidy operation. It's to be commended, as is that gentleman hanging on the pole outside the gate with his crow friend. If you're going to have rules, you had better be willing to enforce them."

Talen said, "I don't think we've met. I'm Talen, Hogan's son."

"Ah, the famous one," the blond said. "I'm Flax of Lem. You two look to be brother and sister."

"Yes," River said.

"So you must be River."

She said, "You know quite a bit for having just arrived."

"A prudent man gets a lay of the land before charging in. I've been here for a few days."

"Lem," said Talen thinking. "That's old country."

"Indeed it is," said Flax. "Old and satisfying. But as fine as the fields of Lem are, they're too quiet. I thought my skills might be useful elsewhere."

River nodded. "And who is that?" she asked, pointing at the dead man.

"Someone Lord Shim wanted me to catch," said Flax. "But our Lord is otherwise occupied at the moment. I'm waiting to deliver him."

"You said skills," Talen said. "Are you looking for Silver the Vargon?"

"Perhaps," said Flax. "But I don't think now is the time to talk about that." He patted Legs on the shoulder. "I sense this one wants to hear about his sister."

River took Legs's hand. "Let's you and I walk to Argoth's quarters."

"Please tell me what happened," said Legs.

"I will," she said. She turned to Flax. "Welcome, Flax of Lem."

"I truly hope Shim shares your generosity," said Flax.

As Talen moved to follow River, Flax pointed at the tattoos on Talen's wrists. "Those are honors I haven't seen before. Although Legs had something similar. Is that a Koramite clan?"

At one time it had been. But since the events down in the cave, Talen's tattoo had been changing, which was another odd thing—tattoos didn't change. He thought it might have to do with the fact that he'd died and been stuffed back in his body by a monster. In fact, he was wondering if that's where those rotted lusts were coming from. "It's Koramite," Talen said. "I'm a half-breed."

Flax nodded. "Myself, I've never held with those that say Koramite blood has rot in it. In fact, a number of years ago I employed a Koramite in one of my fists. He was a fine man. Died well."

Talen nodded. "Death is overrated."

Flax's eyes crinkled in confusion, then curiosity. "It sounds like there's a tale there. I heard you were in the caves. I'm putting in a formal request to hear about it." He clapped Talen on the shoulder.

Talen suddenly felt a faint gnawing. He'd felt it before, down in the caves with the Mother, something probing the edges of his soul. He stiffened and closed himself tight against it.

Flax gave him a knowing look. "Very good," he said. "Very good. Talen half-breed." Then he let Talen's shoulder go.

What had that been about?

They parted, Talen and Oaks hurrying through the thick gate and wall of the inner fortress to catch up to River and Legs.

"He seems a likeable fellow," said Oaks, "even if he is a foreigner."

"Yes," said Talen, still uncomfortable with the probing. Who would probe like that? It was like running your hands up the leg of someone you'd just met. But perhaps that was just the way of sleth. Talen had a lot yet to learn. And unlearn.

They exited the tunnel made by the gate and thick wall. Off to their left were a number of cook fires with fish spitted and roasting above them. Talen kept moving. They passed a number of carpenters hammering iron nails into an extension of the barracks and caught up to Legs and River as they walked through the door that led to the ante-chamber of Lord Shim's quarters.

The door, like the others in the fortress, had been painted with Shim's blue and white device with the brass sun.

One of Lord Shim's clerks sat at a desk with a pile of tally sticks at one end, scratching something down on a piece of vellum. A fat fly buzzed in a circle about him. He looked up as they walked in, then pointed to a bench set against the wall.

"We need to speak to Argoth," Talen said.

"Lord Shim and Argoth will be out soon."

"This can't wait."

The clerk leveled his gaze at Talen. "They asked not to be disturbed."

Talen said, "I think—"

Then the door behind them flew open, and a Kish stomped in from the bailey. The Kish were lighter-skinned than Mokaddians or Koramites. Their lands were north of those of Mokad, Koram, and Urz across the sea in the old country. This Kish looked like an old bear. He was muscled, but much had gone to fat. His face was grizzled and jowled. His nose had a bump as if it had been broken a few too many times. One of his eyes was milked over, but the other flamed with intelligence.

"Where's that sluggard Argoth?" the Kish demanded.

"Zu," the clerk said. "He's in conference with Lord Shim."

"Get him out here."

The clerk hesitated. "They have asked—"

"They've asked for my report," the Kish said. "Go, man. Be quick. Or I'll have you replaced."

The clerk rose, slowly laid down his quill.

"Go!" the Kish commanded.

The clerk jumped, then exited through a door and shut it behind him. The Kish put his hands on his hips, then turned and spotted Talen, River, Legs, and Oaks. He grunted and motioned at them with his chin. "So you're the monster slayers, eh?"

"Not I," said Oaks. "I'm merely escort the notables about. But these three were down in the caves."

Eresh openly looked each of them from head to toe. When he finished with River, he said, "You're a well-turned thing, but can you fight? Can you fight as well as your brother?"

"Which one?"

"Well not that one," said the Kish and motioned at Talen. "I'm talking about the bull."

"Ke's a pie bake," she said.

"Is that so?" he said and folded his arms. "I don't know that it's wise to have women in the army. I think they distract the men and waste precious Fire. We want to multiply killers, not posies, however pretty they look in a box."

River said, "I guess you've not heard of deadly nightshade. I think you underestimate the uses of flowers."

"I rarely underestimate."

At that moment Argoth emerged from the hallway.

"Uncle," Talen said.

Eresh cut in. "You told me you had an army. That's a joke. Your operations are flabby. Undisciplined. Full of maggots and worms, and worse—I understand you made an invitation to that blond goat turd from Lem. We're going to talk about him."

Talen expected Argoth to bridle at the Kish's offence, but he laughed instead. "Maggots? Coming from you I'd say that's a compliment."

"The one bright spot is your armory. You tell that leather bag Shim he can keep his smithing crew."

"I'm sure the warlord will be happy to know you've given your permission."

"Look, you haven't got time for coddling. If Mokad is already under sail, you're dead. Dead. I would recommend a few Fire sacrifices." He pointed at River. "And I would wait on the fist of fell-maidens."

"No, old friend," said Argoth. "There will be no sacrifices."

Eresh licked his bottom lip, playing with a flake of skin there. "You're too fastidious," he said. "I can promise you Mokad is not sparing its Fire."

River cut in. "Master Kish, I'm sorry, but we need to report. Uncle, our situation has changed." Then she looked at the Kish in a way that suggested they move to a different location.

"It's all right," Argoth said. He put a hand on the Kish's shoulder. "This is Eresh the Horlomite—dreadman, terrorman, and all around bane. He's as bloody as they come. And he's going to get this army ready to battle Divines. He's an old friend who has left his tidy den of aged iniquity at my request."

"And a fine den it was," Eresh said.

"But not finer than being able to strike such a blow that the enemy may never recover. Eh?"

"I told you I wouldn't commit until I'd seen what I needed to see. You're no match for Mokaddian terrors. Not yet. But that can change. Especially if we can grow the ranks as that Shim thinks he can."

"So you accept?"

"You will provide me a cook and a woman. The cook will be mine and mine alone. The woman will need a little bit of brain about her, but not too much."

"We can provide the cook," said Argoth. "As for the woman, you'll have to convince a willing victim on your own."

"Mokaddians," Eresh said with disgust. "I'll do it without the woman then. But I tell you this: the cook had better rotting well be able to serve up the stars and moon every morning, midday, and night."

"You'll have lark tongues for breakfast," said Argoth.

"I don't like lark," said Eresh.

"Then you'll be served worms. Isn't that what you Kish eat?"

"Only when it's time for love making."

"That's right. I forgot the Kish needed help."

"Do you know why Mokaddian don't eat worms?" Eresh asked.

Argoth waited.

"Because they have nothing to enhance, which explains why your women are so unsatisfied."

Argoth groaned. "Ah, yes, I had forgotten the dizzying intellect. May the Six save us."

"I can assure you," Eresh said, "the Six will have nothing to do with it."

"Zu," Oaks said and inclined his head at Eresh. "I have heard many things about the Kish. Were you in the Eastern wars under the Red Lord?"

The Red Lord had been savage. He'd expanded the holdings of the Kish, but only with extreme blood and terror. It was said he beheaded two-thousand men, women, and children in one day with his own hand. His troops had shown no mercy. Nor were they shown mercy by their commanders.

Eresh spat. "The Red Lord was nothing more than a great wobble of pudding. We murdered the Eastern hordes despite him."

Talen spoke up; they were wasting time. "Uncle, we were betrayed. Sugar is missing. As far as we know, Black Knee is still out there as well."

Argoth's eyes narrowed.

"I want to go after her," said Talen.

"Come into the main chambers," said Argoth. "We'll discuss it there with Matiga and Shim."

Argoth turned back the way he'd come, and they all followed him, filing past the clerk to clomp up a stairway that led to a chamber above. In that room, three tall windows opened onto the inner bailey, letting in the smell of the cooking fish, the sounds of the carpenters banging away, and the early morning light. Shim and the Creek Widow stood at a large table in the middle of the room where two oil lamps glowed, illuminating a map. Across from the windows, the plastered walls were painted with a scene of a woodikin battle.

When everyone had filed in, River and Talen proceeded to report what had happened at the village of Plum. When they finished, Shim said, "Felts is one of the last I would suspect." He shook his head.

"Was Felts wearing any odd necklaces or collars?" Argoth asked. "Any rings? Anything that might be a thrall?"

"I saw nothing," said River.

"Nor I," said Talen.

"Send someone to talk to his family," said Lord Shim. "Felts wouldn't sell out for money. Somebody got a lever on him."

Eresh said, "I'll tell you somebody who would sell you out for money. That maggot of the Hand."

"The Hand?" asked Argoth.

"That blond pustule outside with a dead man on his horse."

"Flax?" Talen asked.

Eresh's face filled with disgust. "The Hand is not to be relied on."

"We will see," said Shim.

Eresh grimaced but held his tongue.

"Send Urban to find Sugar," said the Creek Widow.

Urban was another one of the few sleth that had heeded Argoth's call. He had a crew of men that did not mingle with the rest of Shim's soldiers. In fact, they quartered themselves elsewhere, but none had seen where. Talen said, "I want to go with him."

"I think not," said Argoth.

"It's important to me."

"No," said Argoth. "Work it through. Tenter's weave was empty. All the weaves of the Fir-Noy dreadmen were empty. So who filled it?"

Only Divines and sleth knew the lore.

"There are no Groves or orders among the Fir-Noy," said Argoth. "That means it was filled by a Divine. But I do not think Mokad would send a solitary Divine to these shores. Not after losing two Divines already. They'd come in force, which means—"

"Which means you don't have until next spring," Eresh said. "If the Divines are already here gathering Fire for the weaves of their dreadmen, then you don't have any time at all." He spat. "We're all swimming in the cesspit."

Shim sighed heavily.

His and Argoth's plan had been to build up an army of a two thousand dreadmen by spring. But these would have been more than simple dreadmen—they would have wielded the lore. It would have been more like an army of Divines. With such a force, the clans would have had to rethink their opposition. They would see brothers and cousins and fathers wielding the lore. They would hear the stories of those abominations that held the reins of the Divines. They would see with their own eyes the lies they'd been told. The ranks of Shim's army would have then swelled, and they would have been joined by the ranks of sleth—loremen and lorewomen of great power—from lands all across the Western Glorydoms. It would have been an army unlike any other in the world.

Then another thought struck Talen. If a Mokaddian Divine was here, he would have brought all his ranks of protection, which meant it wouldn't be some idiot Fir-Noy lord they'd be rescuing Sugar from. It would be a Divine and his acolytes, who also knew the lore, all guarded by a whole force of mature dreadmen.

"We need to find Sugar now," Talen said. "Before it's too late."

"That dreadman singled you out," the Creek Widow said.

"I don't know that he singled me out."

Oaks cleared his throat. "He said, 'The boy's mine'."

"Anyone else in the party mentioned?" asked the Creek Widow.

Talen gave River a pleading look.

"Sorry son," Oaks said. He turned to the Creek Widow. "It was just Talen."

"I'd say that was singling out," said the Creek Widow. "And why would he do that?" she asked rhetorically.

Talen wasn't going to answer that. They both knew why. But how would that dreadman know that Talen was the one the Mother had claimed as her own down in her cave? The only person who knew the full details of that awful fight besides those that had taken part was Shim. For everyone else, Talen's role had been played down. In the public version, it was all Argoth and Ke and the others who'd played the parts of heroes.

"You're going to stay here for a bit," said the Creek Widow, "until we sort out what's going on."

At that moment there was a commotion on the stairs. Shim's clerk knocked, then opened the door to the room. "Black Knee has returned. And he's going to need some doctoring."

* * *

Talen and the others found Black Knee on the far side of the bailey looking pale. He lay on the ground, a number of women crowding around, cutting off one blood-soaked leg of his trousers.

A blood-soaked strip of cloth was wrapped tightly about his leg. One of the women took a knife and cut through it. The wound underneath was a wide puncture that went right through the side of his thigh.

The Creek Widow pushed past Talen and knelt by the big man. She felt his forehead, checked his wrist for his pulse. "Are there any other injuries?" she asked.

He looked at her wearily, the sunlight blinding him. "Just my pride," he slurred looking away. "Tell Lord Shim it was a trap. They got Rooster."

"We know," said the Creek Widow. "River, Oaks, and Talen made it back as well."

"What about the girl?"

"Don't you worry about her." She looked up and pointed at a group of women. "You two, clear the cabbages off that table." The she turned to Talen and River. "Help me get him up."

Two women moved away the cabbages. Talen and River each slid their hands under an armpit while Oaks and Argoth took his knees. Then they hefted him onto the table that was still strewn with cabbage leaves.

The Creek Widow turned to River. "Fetch me my bag. I'll want some wine and oil, and warm water and soap. And bring me the opium with goat's milk."

"This leg is going to want some maggots," Black Knee said.

"Not yet," she said. "First we'll clean it and make sure it's stitched up right. Then we'll see." She bent his leg up and examined the exit wound. "Did you get the whole shaft out?"

"Aye," said Black Knee. "Pushed it through. That was a delight I won't be wanting to try again anytime soon."

She smoothed back his hair. "You're going to be fine. A weave and a couple of days of rest, that will see you out of the woods."

The Creek Widow looked at Argoth. "We really could use Harnock's skills here."

"You might as well try to move a mountain."

Harnock was a member of the Grove, hiding in the Wilds. He'd refused Argoth's call. Talen had heard only bits and pieces about him. Foremost was the fact that he was not all man, but the result of Lumen's attempts to create a new type of warrior. He was unstable and, from what Talen could gather, would probably end up like Pinter, eaten by crows.

Talen grabbed Black Knee's hand. His relief at seeing his fist mate was immense.

The big man looked over at him. "Where's the girl?" he asked.

"I'm going with Urban to find her," he said.

"Not on your life," the Creek Widow said.

8

The Queller

BEROSUS WATCHED THEM work on Black Knee's leg for a moment. He watched Talen. The boy was a fledgling Glory not attached to any Sublime Mother. That is what he'd felt when he probed the boy. It was impossible, but there he stood.

If the Sublime of this Glory had been killed and consumed by one of her sisters, that sister would now hold the reins. So that meant the Sublime who had started Talen had not been consumed by a sister. Something else had killed her. And that posed another puzzle because if the Sublime of this fledgling Glory had died, it was impossible the one enthralled would survive it. Lesser thralls had been known to survive the breaking of their bonds. But those bound directly to a Sublime Mother did not. So what was going on here?

Before he'd been killed, Rubaloth the Skir Master had communicated through the bond he held to the Glory of Mokad. He'd communicated across a sea. Over such distances the link was always tenuous and difficult, but the Glory of Mokad had insisted he'd felt another Sublime Mother when Rubaloth had died. A Mother that had the power to raise a son of Lammash, although Berosus doubted that report.

Rubaloth had been a powerful Divine—one of Mokad's mightiest Skir Masters. And he'd died in this place.

Berosus had been here two weeks now. Two weeks to study the sleth. They were using weaves of might, but none were in the pattern of any of the houses of Kains he knew. There were no Guardian Divines, no tethered skir, no Fire sacrifices. There simply were no signs that would indicate an enemy Mother was here, controlling this human herd.

It would appear the sleth claims were true. But who here was so mighty as to overthrow a Mother?

He was going to have to be careful. He was going to have to watch his back. True danger walked these shores.

But that wasn't necessarily bad. In fact, the thought of it brought a rising joy. There was no bitter without sweet. No light without darkness. No peace without fear. And it had been some time since he had felt fear. It made him feel alive.

He felt for the Glory of Mokad across the sea. *There is no Sublime Mother here*, he reported.

He waited, listening intently, trying to shut out the banging of the carpenters in the fortress and the soldiers practicing their forms. The faint distant reply came: *Queller, you will destroy everything that has been infected.*

It was the Mother of Mokad that replied, not the Glory. He felt the wonderful thrill her attention always brought.

Save what you can of that herd. The rest we shall lay up in store against our need.

It shall be done, he replied.

He waited for more, but the tenuous link faded.

The Queller—that was her nickname for him because he, better than any of the other Divines, could quell a rebellion. Better than any other, he was the one that could restore order to a herd and make it productive. She had sent him to clean this mess up. And that's what he would do.

His first business was to secure Talen. You didn't want a fledgling Glory running about as a loose end. That could come to no good. Once Talen was secure, he would identify who it was that defeated the Mother. And then he would begin the harvest.

It was going to be a big job—tens of thousands of souls. A small sleth nest could be useful at times in managing a herd or in attacking another Mother's holdings. He himself had infiltrated one branch of the Hand and directed them as the Mother saw fit. But this army Shim was raising was a pestilence.

Ideas and knowledge spread like disease. In these situations, you couldn't just kill the leaders because the infection didn't end there. No, in these situations, it was best to simply destroy them all.

He took in a great breath of air and surveyed the fortress around him—the candidates, the cooks over by the fires, the soldiers upon the walls. Harvest wreaths hung above doors and on posts, remnants from last night's celebration. Such wreaths hung above doors in villages all throughout the New Lands. He thought it ironic: they had indeed celebrated a harvest, but not the one they supposed.

After Black Knee was doctored, Shim and Argoth called to him. He led the priest over on his horse.

"He's dead," Shim said.

"He fought me, Zu. He was quite out of his mind. I've got a tidy hole in my gut to prove it. But if I recall, you didn't specify that I bring him to you alive."

"What would I want with a dead body?"

"If I could have taken him alive, I would. But you saw him. People are talking. Someone like this was going make them uneasy."

Shim considered him.

"I don't mean to offend," said Berosus. "But I came here because of a call. I'm sorry that he's dead. But I know these types. They can't be relied on."

Argoth looked over at Shim.

"You're wasting your time with that one," Eresh said, his one good eye burning. "The Hand offers nothing but a knife in the back."

"Fools will often blame others for their own misfortunes," said Berosus. "I've found that to be especially true among the Kish."

Eresh bristled. "It wasn't foolishness that slaughtered a company of men at Amon ford. It was an ally that sat and watched other men burn."

"You've muddled the facts," said Berosus. "But that does happen with age."

Eresh narrowed his eyes and moved his hand to his sword, but Shim held his hand up. "Hold, commander. We don't need any blood today."

"I told you one of your own would vouch for me," said Berosus.

* * *

Argoth watched Eresh release his sword, then draw an apple from his coat pocket. He expected the Kish to give it a furious bite, but, quick as a snake, Eresh hurled the apple at Flax's face instead.

Flax flinched but wasn't fast enough. The apple smacked into his forehead and sailed into the wall of the fortress. Eresh followed the apple. There was a flash of steel and before anyone could move, Eresh held the point of his sword at Flax's throat. "It appears I am not too old to take you, maggot."

Flax grasped the hilt of his knife, the only weapon a stranger would have been allowed to carry inside the fortress. Eresh did not have the best position on the blond even though he held a sword. If Flax turned just so, he could stick his knife into Eresh's belly.

But Eresh wasn't someone to make such a mistake. It was sloppy, and Argoth realized Eresh was tempting Flax to pull his knife, to give him a reason.

"No!" Argoth said and stepped forward, pushing them apart.

Shim turned on Eresh, his face cold with anger. "We have within our grasp the opportunity, not of a lifetime, but of an age. It is not the time for squabbles."

"The Hand needs to pay its debt of blood."

Flax had not yet released the hilt of his knife.

Argoth said, "Listen, you two, if we are to fight our true enemy, we must put aside such issues—the blood between Eresh and the Hand is nothing compared to that between you and those that devour our souls. Would you stop to chase a horsefly when a ravening lion was at your heels?"

Eresh licked his chapped lips, then stepped away and sheathed his sword. "The next time I draw my sword on this walking goat turd, I will kill him."

Flax shook his head ruefully and released his hold upon his knife. He put his hand up to placate Eresh. "Argoth speaks wisdom. Let us deal with our common enemy first. After that, you and I can settle our differences."

"That might be far too late," said Eresh.

"Commander," Shim warned, his face iron. Then he turned to Flax. "You will come and state your purpose. And if you're too beetle-brained to keep your smug arrogance to yourself, then I will loose Eresh. And may the Six have mercy upon you."

Flax inclined his head, and Shim turned to walk to his chambers. As he did, Flax gave Eresh a level stare, and Eresh gave it right back, his milked eye looking like a horror.

Argoth had learned long ago never to trust someone you didn't know. And even though Eresh had now confirmed that this Flax was actually a man of the Hand of Mayhan, Argoth was still wary of him. He would wait and see. Action, more than anything else, proved a man. And just because he was a man of the Hand, didn't mean his goals aligned with Shim's.

The group followed Shim to his upper chamber. They lit candles, then shuttered and curtained the window that looked out on the court so the conversation could not be overheard. Shim sat behind his mahogany table that shone with a dull luster from the candlelight. The tanned hide of a bear he had speared as a youth was draped over the back of the chair. Behind him on the wall hung the new device of his army. It was in the shape of a shield. The field was half blue, half white, and in the center, was a large sun made of brass. The blue for courage and loyalty. The white for purity. And the sun to represent knowledge and power.

Shim's fathers had preserved it and kept it hidden. From generation to generation they'd passed it down. One of Shim's ancestors had been a lore-man who had been hunted down by the Divines. But a scion had survived the extermination of that line and kept both the tale and the device.

As they filed into Shim's chamber, Matiga stood with Argoth. Eresh stood off to the other side, disgust on his face, never taking his one good eye off the blond man. Flax came in last and stood before them.

Argoth said, "I never sent a message to the Hand."

"But you did send one to Bream of Darkbridge," Flax said. "The grove I'm in is affiliated with his. Bream himself could not come, but I have his token and a letter." Flax retrieved a piece of parchment from his pocket along with a plain scarf.

Argoth took both, then walked to the window and pulled the curtain back and unshuttered the window. He examined the seal of the letter in the strong light. It looked like it hadn't been tampered with. Furthermore, it was Bream's special seal featuring three horse heads with a line across the bottom. He motioned Matiga over who examined it as well.

"That's Bream's," she said.

Argoth broke the seal and read the note. It simply said, "The bearer returns your token at my behest. We are interested in your proposed venture, but feel reluctance. Convince him."

Argoth held the scarf up and found the corner. In it was stitched the simple figure of a bear. Matiga pulled out her knife and cut the stitching on the back to reveal the smaller image of a stork.

"This is the token that was sent out," she said. Then she and Argoth stepped back from the window, shuttered it, and replaced the thick curtain. Argoth handed the letter to Shim and nodded. It all could be faked, but someone would have to be deep in Bream's counsel to get it all right.

Shim read the note and said, "Reluctance?"

Flax said, "Bream is being watched. He dared not risk come out of hiding. I volunteered to come here and see if this was a trap or an opportunity."

"And what have you found?"

"I don't know yet," said Flax. "With all respect to your efforts, what I see is, well, not an army of dreadmen. Your candidates wear weaves that are poorly made. What's worse, they're almost all running dry. And how many lore masters do you have here that can replenish them when they do fail? Half a dozen at the most. There's no way so few can sustain an army even half the size of this one."

"You have no idea how many lore masters we have," said Eresh.

Flax continued, "And even if someone were able and willing to bleed his life away to fill these weeds you call weaves, you don't have the right ratio of full, seasoned dreadmen to candidates for proper training. Five-to-one is ideal. You have, what, twenty-five or forty to one? So I don't know. Joining such a"—he searched for the word—"hasty operation might lead to our doom. On the other hand, having a whole hammer of loremen who are intimately versed in blood and Fire might tip the balance in your favor."

Argoth had to give Flax credit. He'd opened his negotiation strongly. Shim's army *was* in desperate need of more loremen.

"I don't see a hammer," said Eresh. "I see a single man."

"If I send word, they will come."

Matiga folded her arms. "This Kish is bad enough. I do not think we want men of the Hand."

But if Shim were to succeed, they needed more loremen. Only a handful had come so far. Perhaps they were too wary, or perhaps they were on their way. But weeks mattered. Numbers mattered. And they couldn't be choosy.

She continued. "The Hand, for all its will to fight the Divines, has never created the opportunity you see here. But even if it had, we wouldn't allow you to join us."

"The Order of Hismayas disapproves of some of our methods," said Flax. "Tell me something new."

"You have no conception of who your real enemies are," said Matiga.

"My life has been dedicated to throwing off the yoke of the Divines. I've lost brothers, parents, friends. I know whom I fight better than anyone here."

"No," said Matiga. "You don't."

Flax's mouth set in annoyance, but he didn't give voice to it. Or was this the ruse of an expert in these games? All men wore masks, but there were some who never took off the mask. Argoth could not tell which kind of man Flax was.

Matiga said, "You may kill every Divine, but you will still lose the war because the Divines are merely tools, thralls, of far more powerful masters. Kill the Divines, and the masters will simply raise up others in their stead."

"What are you talking about?"

"Humans are ranched like cattle, Handsman. Their souls harvested to feed the creatures that rule over us."

Flax narrowed his eyes. "Harvested?"

"Shocking, isn't it?"

"I would need proof."

"Why would we lie?"

"Because lying's useful," said Flax.

"We are eye-witnesses. We have fought one of the Devourers and pre-vailed. But you don't have to trust our testimony alone. We have tangible proofs. And I will tell you this—killing a Divine is an easy thing compared to fighting one of their masters."

"If these masters do exist, then why don't we know of them? Why do we never see them?"

"If our cattle knew they were being bred for slaughter, do you think they would feed at our very doorsteps, docile and trusting? The Devourers are not stupid. They raise human overseers to rule over us as Divines, breed-ing them to be able to wield great powers. And so well have the Divines spun their lies that humans go willingly to their various harvests."

Flax said, "I would need to see these evidences. If it's true, it simply widens the number of our targets."

Matiga said, "The point that you have lost is that our enemy preys upon us. We will not join them in that evil. And so if any member of the Hand wants to ally themselves with us, they must take an oath to cease to prey upon others for their Fire, and the soul that comes with it. We will not be-come the very thing we fight against."

"There is no crime in stealing from an enemy."

Matiga looked at Shim. She was clearly not impressed with Flax.

"He's of the Hand," said Eresh and tapped his forehead. "You've got to speak slowly."

"Commander," Shim warned.

Argoth stepped in. "Let me paint the vision. We are not here to overthrow the Divines and take their place. We are here to free every willing brother and sister of the human race. And the only way to do that is to teach them to master their own vitalities. Give them power. There is enough power in the people of this land, if freed from the darkness of ignorance, to overthrow those who rule over the Glories forever. We are going to raise a nation of loremen."

Flax looked around the room. "A nation of the old gods, eh? You're going to bring everyone out of darkness and put the lore into the hands of thieves and murderers."

This was an old argument among those who used the lore. Was it best to monopolize the power like the Divines did, or did every man have the right to use or misuse the powers? "It's already in the hands of thieves and murderers," said Argoth. "Better our own poison than that of another."

Flax considered for a moment. "Let's say that we agree to join your cause. Your army is still too weak to fight Mokad. You will need us. You will need our Fire. That does not come for free."

Shim waited.

"We'd want land, and paid passage. We'd want our members to fight together. There will be no splitting of our ranks unless we agree to it. And we want a portion of Lumen's hoard."

"The weaves in our possession do not belong to any one of us," said Shim. "Their use is assigned based on need and ability. To be given one is to be given a stewardship, not ownership."

"Do not split hairs," said Flax. "Whoever determines need and ability controls the weaves. That's the same as owning them."

"No one person controls them," said Argoth.

Flax shook his head. "You're making it difficult for me to convince the others in my order to join your cause. They would need to see a clear value."

"The hope of what we're doing should be value enough," said Shim.

"We will share whatever powers we have with those who join us," said Argoth. "But if you are to join us, you must do so in very deed. There's more that's required."

"More?"

"A gift of Fire," said Argoth. "To show your intentions."

"A payment in earnest," said Eresh. "If you prove yourself, you'll be re-paid. If not, we'll keep it."

"I would think such a sacrifice would by itself prove my intentions."

"Two weeks ago," said Matiga, "a man showed up at the gates of the fortress, having, like you, answered our call. He was known to us. Powerful, a master, and he was wild. He'd eaten the souls of crocodiles. You couldn't see the sign upon his body, but there lurked in him a darkness. He came promising to fight with us. He would have been a formidable addition to our ranks. But in not too many days it became apparent he also came think-ing he could feed where he pleased."

"The one hanging from a pole outside the gates of this fortress?"

"No," Matiga said. "This one we elected not to publicize."

Flax shrugged. "If it's Fire you want, Fire we have aplenty."

"We do not want that which you've stolen from others," said Matiga. "We want *your* Fire. An Opulence at the very least. This is a personal sacrifice."

Flax raised his eyebrows. "Are you joking? That's three years of my life. I'm sorry, but this is foolish. Besides, if I give you of my Fire, I'll simply re-plenish it from the stores we already have. Let us not play games."

"We are not playing games," said Argoth. "But we do not want to per-petuate the very abominations we seek to fight. What's been stolen from others is tainted. Your oath, if you join us, requires you give up your stolen Fire to the winds."

As Argoth spoke these words, his mind ran to Nettle, his son. Stealing Fire *was* an abomination. And his grief at having practiced that abomination upon his son, even though he'd been a willing victim, curdled his heart. He had stolen Fire from his son to battle the Skir Master. He'd lost the battle and been enthralled. In the process, he'd lost his son. Nettle still lived, but parts of his mind were missing.

Flax shook his head in disbelief.

Argoth had known these requirements would cause many to balk at joining them. They asked applicants to make too large a change. Two potential allies had already refused or said they needed more time to think which amounted to the same thing. He wondered again if these standards were too high. They so desperately needed the Fire this man could bring to the Order. But he thought of Nettle again. He thought of their enemy.

The price wasn't too high. They had to draw a line. And if it meant their doom, then at least they would die with a clear conscience.

"Goh," Flax said and shook his head. "You people are mad."

Argoth knew they'd lost him then. Lost his Fire. Lost the experience of those in his hammer he could have persuaded.

Flax continued, "Only lunatics would dare challenge the powers as you have. I've studied you since I arrived on these shores. And I now have heard and seen enough to know that this is not an opportunity, but a trap. A trap set with bait so incredible I'm finding it hard to resist. So, while I cannot make promises for any others of the Hand, I will pledge myself. I will take your ridiculous oath. I will pour out my Days, but only half an Opulence. And then I'll send back word. And if others join me, then you will provide them passage and lands. And you will assign them 'stewardships'."

Argoth couldn't quite believe what he'd just heard. Perhaps Shim's vision was enough for this Flax. Or perhaps Flax had always been willing to join and had just started high in his bargaining. Or maybe it was a bit of both.

"I can accept that," said Shim. He looked at Argoth and waited for his opinion.

What was there to dispute? Argoth nodded in agreement.

Eresh grunted. "A full Opulence. No less. Because he will turn his back on you."

Flax said, "Once I set my hand to a tiller, I do not look back."

"A full Opulence," Matiga agreed.

Flax gritted his teeth. "A full Opulence with a guaranteed return plus interest."

Shim looked at Argoth who nodded. "Accepted," he said. "You've made a good choice."

"That remains to be seen," said Flax. "I tend to think that the intelligence of any one choice depends on all the choices that follow."

"So it is," said Shim. He rose. "Welcome, brother."

Flax nodded at Eresh. "He's not really part of this family, is he?"

"Och," said Eresh, his one good eye hard and cold and disapproving, "I've just become your loving uncle."

Argoth smiled. "You can still back out."

"And let the Kish have all the glory? I think not. In fact, I want to deliver my part now. Let's be done with it."

"This way then," said Matiga and motioned to where Flax could make his offering.

Sometime later when they were finished, Matiga led a sweating and drawn Flax out of Shim's chamber.

"May I quarter here in the fortress?" Flax asked.

"Yes," Shim said. "Matiga will make arrangements."

He nodded. "I'll go gather my things from where I was staying and will return in a few hours."

Argoth led him out of Shim's chambers. When they stepped into the sunlit bailey, Flax said, "What I need now is a tankard of strong ale and some oysters."

"To celebrate?" asked Argoth.

"Gods, no," said Flax. "I think I've just sealed my own doom. I need something to help me forget."

Argoth smiled. Despite his wariness, Argoth suspected he might end up liking Flax after all. He led him back to his horse and then the outer gate. When Flax was well on his way, he went back to Shim and the others.

When Argoth walked back into Shim's chambers, Eresh looked at him in disgust and shook his head.

"We know of your reservations," Argoth said to Eresh. "But he gifted Fire. He passed our tests."

"And so you just take him into your bosom?"

"No," said Argoth patiently. "Now we watch him, just as we're watching all our old friends, including you."

"Save yourself the trouble," said Eresh. "Let me rid you of that stinking pus today. We'll come out an Opulence the richer."

Shim held his hand up for Eresh to stop. "No more. You have free rein to watch him. If he proves out, you will swallow your anger and welcome him."

"If he proves out, I'll be all hugs and kisses," Eresh said.

9

Redthorn

SUGAR WAS BEYOND exhaustion. She'd run all night and through the morning. She was nearing some kind of breaking. She thought she'd given the Fir-Noy the slip, but they'd raised the hue and cry throughout all the surrounding villages. They'd sent riders downstream. She'd tried to keep to the cover of the trees, but then she'd accidentally run upon a group of woodsmen taking a morning breather, and it had all started up again.

She paused in a wood thick with pines and shadows. The scent of the trees was rich and deep. Above her a breeze swept through the tops of the trees, but the thick carpet of needles upon the ground under her bare feet muffled the sound. Here and there, shafts of light filtered down, dust motes shining, to illuminate the forest floor. A moth flew into a fat shaft of light and then out again.

She listened for her pursuers, but heard nothing. Her weariness settled upon her, and she sat on the trunk of a fallen tree to regain her strength.

Her lips were dry. Her mouth was dry. So dry that she found it difficult to swallow. She felt twinges in her knees and other joints. She felt light-headed. Three times she'd almost lost herself to the firelust. The last time she had almost failed to put her weave of might back on. Lords, but the Fire was sweet. All she'd wanted to do was burn and burn.

She knew she'd just consumed a large quantity of her Days. Most living things were made up of three vitalities—body, soul, and a store of Fire, or Days, as some of the masters called it. Fire was consumed or "burned" like wood or grass. When a person used up all their Fire, the binding of the three vitalities broke. The body died. Every time you burned Fire, you hastened your own death.

This danger was compounded because when you built your Fire to multiply your might and speed, you couldn't do so in a linear fashion. If a man wanted to increase his strength by half, he might have to use double or triple the normal amount of Fire. If he wanted to double his strength, he might have to burn five to eight times the normal rate. Sugar couldn't gauge exactly how much Fire she'd burned. But she was sure she'd shortened her life by a number of days. And such a multiplying took a toll on the body, especially one that wasn't used to it. She needed to get back to Rogum's Defense. Needed to talk to River and make sure she hadn't done permanent damage.

She slid her pack around and opened it yet again to look at the items she'd retrieved from her mother's secret cache.

Of the items she'd taken from the cache by the hearth, Sugar could only remember seeing one of them before. And that had been when she was very young. The first was a codex of parchment sheets as square as a roof shingle. Five bands of soft leather ran along the spine of the sheets. Groups of sheets had been sewn together and put in a stack. The sheets had then been sewn to the bands of leather along the spine. The bands also secured two thin wooden boards—one covered the front of the codex, the other the back. The boards were lacquered red. Two brass clasps attached to the front held the codex shut. She'd unclasped the codex earlier and looked at a few pages of the writing. Mother had taught her how to read, but the blue script on these pages would take some deciphering.

The second item was a necklace. The chain was made of silver, segmented every few inches with carved figurines. Some of the figures were made of wood, some stone, two appeared to be woven of wire. There was a horse, birds, a man, a woman, a bear and other animals. The necklace had been wrapped in a cloth with a sprig of godsweed.

The third item was a lacquered box that contained another sprig of godsweed as well as a metal otter as long as the flat of her hand. It was black and heavy and felt like it was made of gold wire. The other item was an armband much like the candidate's weave she had been given by Argoth and the Creek Widow. She wondered if that was the weave that had awakened her mother to the lore. Was it one she had planned on using to awaken Sugar herself? The thought of Mother teaching her filled her mind and brought with it a sharp pang of loss.

Sugar sat there a few moments, contemplating her mother's things, and caught a whiff of wood smoke. More than anything else, she needed water.

She needed it now, before her body became enfeebled and found herself unable to go on.

She knew the village of Redthorn lay somewhere up ahead. It was Fir-Noy, but she didn't have a choice. She needed food and water.

Sugar brought her dark scout scarf up around her face. Despite the brief rest, she still felt a bit light-headed, but she hooked her thumb through the strap of her sack across her chest and, with a sigh, heaved herself to her feet.

She traveled some distance through the pines, then came to the edge of an apple orchard. Sugar squatted to get a good look through the rows of trees. Nobody was in the orchard.

She listened, expecting to hear the sounds of the villagers up and about their daily tasks, and heard nothing but the breeze. Maybe Redthorn was one of those places that celebrated the Apple Dance a bit too heartily. Maybe the inhabitants were all still asleep.

She entered the orchard, her feet sinking into the smooth cool grass, and immediately saw an apple lying under a few long blades. She picked it up. It was partially rotted, gone to soft brown goo and fungus on one side. But the other side was whole and blushed with red. She bit into that part. The apple flesh burst like honey and sunlight on her tongue. But even better was the juice that ran down her throat. She found another apple lying in the long grass, a small thing with a couple of brown dots indicating worm holes. She devoured it in three bites. She made her way down the row toward the village, but only found one other apple. It was clear the Redthorn folks were diligent with their fruit.

Something moved a few rows down.

Sugar's heart leapt to her throat, and she froze.

A moment later a handful of spotted deer moved into view. They had come, like her, to eat what fallen fruit the tidy villagers had left. She sighed in relief, and then one of them saw her, stopped, and bounded away in a fright. The rest followed.

Sugar shook her head. She should have seen them. Her thirst and weariness were making her stupid and slow. They were going to get her caught.

The villagers had begun to prune this part of the orchard. The cut branches were gathered in piles between the rows. Sugar crouched down behind a pile and peered through the tree trunks at the village beyond.

Nothing moved.

She thanked the Creators for Fir-Noy reveling, hoping they weren't anywhere close to sleeping off their cider binge.

She proceeded to the end of the orchard and crouched behind a low stone wall to scan the road running past the orchard and the village on the other side. Her throat still ached for water.

A number of homes lined a main road. About them stood outbuildings, gardens, fields, and three large orchards. The upland villages grew apples and cherries far sweeter than anything that could be grown in the lowlands. Heaps of pruned branches stood in the other two orchards. There probably should have been crews of adults and children finishing the pruning in this orchard, but all was silent. The only thing that moved was a thin ribbon of smoke rising from the chimney of a house down the road. Behind that house stood a community well with a number of paths leading to it.

She looked down the main road, looked the other way, and saw nothing but three brown chickens a few houses down the lane, pecking at something in the dirt. So she hopped the stone wall, hurried across the hard dirt road, and slipped into the shadows alongside one of the houses, silent as a cat, and moved to the back.

She turned the corner and almost trod upon a brindled bulldog lying on its side. Her heart pounded, and she jumped back, expecting the animal to rise up. But the bulldog didn't move. It just lay there. A fly buzzed about, landed on the tongue hanging out of the dog's mouth, then flitted to the dog's nose.

The dog's ribs weren't moving. It was positioned oddly. Sugar looked closer. The dog was dead.

She blew out a soft sigh and paused a moment to relish her luck. She looked about. The early morning sun lay softly on the yard fences, the privies, and gardens being prepared for winter. It illuminated the well's small wooden roof and very clearly revealed that nobody was out. A large set of wooden windpipes had been fastened onto a pole at the edge of the garden. These were uplanders, after all, and believed in giving the wind a voice. The morning breeze whistled through these pipes and a number of others throughout the village, making an eerie, lonely sound. This village's Apple Dance must have been quite the reveling.

She darted across the garden. The rows of beets and carrots were covered with a thick layer of leaves against the coming cold and held down with a thin layer of dirt. She hopped the fence on the far side to a path leading to the well and almost landed on a pale ox lying on a swath of yellow birch leaves. Its large dark eyes had dried. Its mouth hung open.

Sugar paused. Beyond the ox lay a man. He was sprawled along the fence, wearing red festival trousers embroidered with blue loops around the cuffs and a festival shirt embroidered about the shoulders with leaves and fruits.

Alarm ran up Sugar's neck. She carefully approached the ox and man, circling around until she could see the man's face.

The man's face was painted with festival swirls. There was no wound she could see. No blood on the leaves or ground or clothing. Farther down, a boy lay slumped alongside another house. The body of a woman sprawled in the grass by the orchard fence across the road.

Her arms goose pimpled. Her senses went on full alert.

This wasn't cider, unless the cider had been poisoned, but then who would be giving an ox cider? It could be the effects of too much of the herb sinnis. But again, who would be giving that to dogs and livestock?

She used the shaft of a garden fork to roll the man at her feet over. He was heavy and stiff and moved more like a big log than a man. She used the end of the stick to raise his tunic, examining his belly and chest. She lifted the tunic higher to check his armpits. Nothing. There was no sign of any pestilence.

Woodikin lived in the Wilds beyond the borders of the land. Half the size of a man, they made their homes mostly in groves of huge trees called tanglewoods. When the first Koramites had settled in the New Lands, the woodikin had fought them. They were wily, using ambush and poison and insects, but in the end, they had lost, and their tanglewoods here had been destroyed. The woodikin themselves had retreated into the Wilds. It was rare to see them within the borders of the land, but in the last few weeks there had been a number of sightings.

She looked for the markings of woodikin darts. But there were no wounds, no insect bites, nothing at all. The man was just dead.

She felt someone watching her and spun around. A small flock of sparrows swooped over a garden and perched on the peak of a roof.

She needed to get out of here.

But she needed water more. She was still dizzy with thirst, a small ringing in her ears. The well stood just a few paces away. The gate at the end of this path stood open. Despite her fear, Sugar left the man and quietly walked to the well. The smell of cold sweet water rose up from the depths. She carefully dropped the bucket down, the whole time keeping an eye out.

The house closest to the well was a simple structure: board and plaster, thatched roof, with a main room for living and cooking and another to the side. This was the home she'd seen before with the thin stream of smoke coming from its chimney. Painted on its back door were two stalks of barley which announced this as the residence of an ale-wife. The door stood ajar, revealing a hallway to the main room, the end of a table there, a chair, and three baskets sitting on the floor. A covered ceramic pot sat in one of the baskets. The contents of the other two baskets were covered neatly with cloths.

Food, it had to be. Leftovers from last night's festivities.

The well bucket hit the water below. Sugar let it sink. When it felt good and heavy, she gently cranked it back up. The water was cold and clear, but part of her said it could be poisoned. Maybe that's what killed these folks. She held the bucket up, sniffed it, tasted it. It was sweet and pure. She took a large gulp, and felt the lovely relief washing down her mouth and throat. She lifted the bucket higher and drank, the delicious cold water spilling down her chin and into her tunic. She drank until she knew she couldn't hold more, then filled her waterskin.

She needed food. She didn't know how long she might be on the run. She might be in Rogum's Defense by the end of the day. But it also might take her another day to make it back. It had been drilled into her that you took your opportunities when they presented themselves. You ate and slept when you could, because you might not be able to eat and sleep later.

She didn't know what had killed these people, but she didn't think it was the food. No one would have brought enough for everyone to eat. They would have all brought a dish or two, which meant the food wasn't poisoned, if poison is what killed these people.

There were tales of the Famished, the souls of sleth that refused to move on. They would enter the bodies of the living and, in perfect disguise, drain all those about them for their Fire. After a number of days or weeks, when the neighbors and loved ones were all consumed, the famished soul would travel to a new out-of-the-way place, jump to a new victim's body, and begin all over again.

But those were tales told by Divines, and who knew if they were true?

Like all the rest of their lies, it was probably part of their propaganda. Nevertheless, she drew her knife, then sidled up to the house and listened.

She heard only the breeze whistling through the windpipes in the gardens. She looked through the door. The house was still.

She pushed the door open with her foot. It glided silently on its iron hinges, uttering one creak. The main room had one window that stood unshuttered, allowing the light of the day to dimly illuminate what was inside.

Sugar stepped inside, her knife ready. The door swung gently behind her. The floor in this main room appeared to have been replaced in the last month, for the boards were unpainted and so newly cut she could still smell the wood.

She crept quietly to the baskets and bent down. The lidded crock contained a dish of beans cooked in hog fat. The fat was white and congealed at the top. She dipped a finger in and scooped some out. It was savory and delicious. The other baskets contained bread, roasted mushrooms, and a half-eaten cherry tart. She took a bite of that tart. The flavor burst in her mouth, and she couldn't help but take another, then another.

She was amazed at how good this food tasted and wanted to eat more, but told herself she could do that when she was well away from this village. She wrapped the other items up and put the crock of beans in her sack, then heard horses clopping down the road. Moments later the voice of men carried through the window at the front of the house. "Check here," one said.

Regret's eyes! She'd lingered too long. She backed up, then hurried to the door she'd come through. Just as she went to grab the handle, the door opened. A huge bearded man stood there. His clothes were dark. His eyes were orangish-brown, but it wasn't their color that filled her with dread. It was the shape of the irises—horizontally like those of a goat.

Sugar stumbled back.

"Ho there, Darling," he said.

Someone else entered the front of the house.

Sugar tried to dart around the big man, but he was quick and blocked her path. Were these two of the Famished? Had they drained the life out of this village and now come for her?

He raised his voice and grinned. "I think we've found what we've been looking for."

Sugar drew her knife to strike, but the man who had entered the front of the house rushed up behind her and caught her arm. Sugar twisted, threw her elbow back, and slammed it into his face.

He grunted, but he did not let go. She struggled, but he grabbed her hand. A sharp pain shot through it, and she dropped the knife. She tried to yank her arm free, but his grip was iron. He twisted her hand and wrenched her arm around into her back. Pain shot up her arm. She lashed out with her free arm. Kicked back.

"Great lords," the big man said, "we've got ourselves a tiger." He grabbed her free arm, and the two of them pushed her face-first against the wall.

"She's Koramite," the big one said. "It has to be her."

"Sugar," the one that had disarmed her said, "we've been sent by Shim. We're friends."

She stamped down hard on his foot.

"Oh!" he grunted and loosened his grip just enough for her to yank herself free and whirl around to face them.

Then she recognized the one that had come up from behind. It was Urban, one of the foreign sleth, the one that had all the women talking. That meant the big one was not one of the Famished, but part of Urban's crew that kept themselves out of sight.

The big one backed up and held his hands wide to show her he meant no harm.

Urban felt his eye. "Goh," he said. "Remind me next time I rescue someone to suit up in full armor."

"That's going to be a pretty one," the big one said. "Swell up real nice."

Sugar's heart was still beating wildly from the fight, her breath still coming fast.

"You can drop that fighting stance," Urban said and stepped back.

"I'm sorry," she said, but didn't dare relax.

In the scuffle, she'd dropped her sack. She'd not tied the top shut, and the necklace she'd found in her mother's cache had spilled out along with the cherry tart and lay on the floor.

Urban went to pick up her sack for her and saw the necklace. "Now that's a pretty piece," he said and picked it up. He fingered the segments, then held it up to get a good look at it. When he fingered the horse, he immediately winced as if it had bitten him and dropped the necklace.

He looked at her with a bit of puzzlement on his face, then squatted down and used the point of Sugar's knife to pick up the necklace again. "Is this what you went in for?"

He was a handsome man. His clothes were not sumptuous, but they were well tailored and the green of his shirt set off his dark hair and eyes, making him a striking figure. But she didn't know what to tell him or how much to trust him. "Just put it in the sack," she said.

He held it out to her instead. "Grasp the golden figure of the horse."

Sugar took the necklace, felt the weight of it. The memory and loss of her mother welled up in her, but she refused to let it show on her face. She curled her fingers around the horse.

"What do you feel?"

"Nothing," she said.

"No pricking, no fear?"

"No," she said a bit confused.

Urban nodded. "Do you know what it is?"

She said nothing.

He shook his head in disapproval. "Sometimes I wonder about the Grove here."

"They've been good to me," said Sugar.

"I do not doubt their intentions," said Urban. "But their methods, well, that's something we can discuss later. Right now we need to get you back. You've got a lot of people worried."

Behind them in the main room another soldier shouted. "Gods!" he said. "Urban!"

Urban turned and hurried back down the short hallway. Another one of his crew held the door of the main bedroom open with the tip of his sword. "They're like leeches."

Sugar picked up her sack and followed to get a view. A man with dirty feet lay on the floor in the room. He was naked except for his small clothes. All about him, lined up like suckling pigs, were a dozen grotesque creatures. Some were the size of rats, others as long as his arm. All of them looked starved. They were knobby and twisted, the color of pale driftwood. Their many fingers, as thin and spidery as the roots of a tree, grasped their prey. They were attached to his thighs, his stomach. One at his neck. The mass of them moved and undulated in the dim light, sucking the Fire from him.

"Frights," Sugar said.

One of the things turned and looked up at her with one cancerous eye. Then the man on the floor opened his mouth and gasped.

"Godsweed," Urban said. "Fetch the godsweed!"

The soldier ran out and came back moments later with a braid of godsweed, then took it to the hearth. He lit the braid in the embers of the dying fire, then brought it to Urban who took the smoking knot from him and walked into the room.

Frights were creatures not wholly of the world of flesh. They fed on Fire, and so it was common to find them lurking about the sick and dying. They haunted battlefields. For reasons unknown to Sugar, when feeding they sometimes became visible to the naked eye. It was said they could kill a man, but there was one thing they didn't like.

Urban waved the smoking braid, spreading the sweet godsweed smoke about, poking the braids at the creatures. The frights began to become agitated. One struck at Urban. The soldier brought another smoking braid and waved it about. Urban waved his braid closer to the frights. Then one of the smaller frights detached from the man and fled out the window.

Urban and his man continued to wave the smoking braids about. As the smoke in the room thickened, a number of the other frights detached. Then they all fled out of the room, some disappearing through the window. One of the bigger ones charged between Sugar's legs and out into the common area.

Sugar yelped and danced aside.

"Creator's love," the big one cursed. "The filthy beasts."

Urban walked over to look down at the dying man. He was glassy-eyed and drooling. Urban bent down and took the man by the face. "Zu, what's going on here?" he asked the man. "What happened?" But the man didn't respond. It was clear he wasn't long for this world.

Another one of Urban's crew entered the house. "Urban," he said. "We've found the bulk of the villagers."

Urban gave orders to keep the room smoked and wait to see if the man revived. Then he followed the other crew member out. Sugar, not wanting to stay another moment in the house, joined them.

They found the villagers lying at the edge of a cherry orchard by the remains of a bonfire. There were sixty-three in all, men, women, and children.

The bodies were crawling with frights.

Like the others, these villagers showed no marks that would indicate how they'd died. There were a lot of footprints, but nothing special.

Another one of Urban's men called out. He was crossing the road, carrying a girl and a boy in his arms. He was followed by another man carrying a second boy. All three were alive. None of the children looked older than seven or eight years. Their eyes shone with weary shock.

"We opened the hay door to let some light in a barn, and there they were, three little owls lined up in a cubby."

Urban addressed the oldest boy. "What's your name, son?"

The boy did not speak, just looked at the dead bodies arrayed before him, dismay filling his face.

"It's all right. We'll protect you."

Sugar stroked the girl's hair. "Where's your mother, Sweet?"

The little girl's face broke into tears. Then she leaned forward, holding her arms out.

She was Fir-Noy, but it didn't matter. "Come here, Precious," Sugar said and took her. She clung to Sugar, heavy and solid as a little stone.

"It's okay," Sugar said and stroked her hair.

The girl buried her face in Sugar's chest and panted like she would cry at any moment, but she didn't cry. She just kept panting.

"Boys," Urban said to her brothers. "We need to know what happened here."

The older boy closed his eyes, his face scrunching up in pain.

"The woods filled up with darkness," the smaller boy said. "Da came running, and a man yelled, and the whole wood was breathing. And mother ran with us to the barn and told us to hide. But when we got to the cubby mother was gone." His lip began to quiver and he stopped, the horror of that moment filling his eyes.

The older boy finished the thought. "They took her to the horned evil in the smoke."

10

Grass

ON A HILL a few miles from the Fir-Noy fortress of Blue Towers, Berosus squatted next to the body of the young woman that had been with the Mungonite priest. She was a thing of beauty: dark hair, stunning jade eyes, and clear skin the color of caramel. But her body was merely a husk now because Berosus had removed the vast majority of her soul in preparation for the harvest.

The remnant soul which lingered within might live on for a few days, maybe even a few weeks, but there was no point in allowing that to occur. The body would seek the familiar; it would walk back to some place it mistook for its home, go about its old habits. Maybe it would sit in a favorite chair, eat a piece of bread or go through the motions of drawing water. It wouldn't respond to the conversations of those about her, or their later pleadings. Nor would it be able to resist the frights and other creatures from the world of the dead. Eventually it would succumb to them.

But Berosus did not want to think of her that way. Such an untidy end would spoil this moment. So he killed the young woman's body with a sharp twist to the neck and laid it down upon the dried autumn grass at his feet.

The captain of Berosus's guard had brought a small meal, and Berosus picked up a salted herring from the cloth spread upon the grass and took a bite. "Life is meant to be lived consciously," Berosus said, "deliberately."

"Yes, Bright One," the dreadmen said.

Berosus ran a handful of the female's luxurious dark hair through his fingers. He traced her brow and the ridge of her cheek bone, the delicate curve of her lips. She was so beautiful in her repose. As graceful and sensuous as the rich petals of an iris.

"Every day a banquet is spread, Captain. And if you're not careful, you'll miss it." Berosus disdained the Divines who sent others to do their work. Life was full of gifts, full of opportunities such as these. And every day they missed it. In their excess they thought they lived more, but in reality their excess constrained them like blinders upon a horse.

He took another bite of herring.

The captain said, "This fledgling Glory, do you want him alive or dead?"

Berosus ignored him. The breeze blew gentle waves through the dry meadow grass about the girl. The heads of the grass nodded to and fro, as if reaching out to touch her.

He contemplated her a moment more and picked up the rough, black gloryhorn where the essential parts of the girl's soul still lived on and put it in its sack.

The gloryhorn was the weave he would use to call the souls, including those that had escaped during the time this land lacked a Divine. He could have used anyone's soul to quicken it, but it pleased him to think of the girl in there, for every time he saw the horn, he would also think of her, this hill, and the grass rippling in the breeze. Sooner or later the soul in the horn would degrade, and he'd have to find another. Until then, he would relive this moment of beauty, this reminder of the fierce, short fire of life.

Humans were grass—designed by the Creators to feed greater beings. It made no sense for grass to spend its days complaining about its lot. It made no sense to think about the dark when the sun was shining. Better to spend your days reveling in the feel of the wind and the sun and your roots growing deep.

And yet, there were some who were spared, by the grace of the Mothers, to live on. For whom death wasn't the end. He might become one of those. Then again, he might not. Other Divines soured the moments of their lives, jockeying for position and approbation. But he'd learned long ago that was fruitless. The Sublime Mothers graced who they would with a long life in the world of souls for their own reasons. And even those souls did not live forever.

He finished the herring and sucked his two fingers clean. The dreadman captain stood silently waiting for his answer. He was a good man. One of the best. But he too one day would be grass. And another would grow up in his stead.

In the distance, the blue towers of the Fir-Noy fortress rose above the trees. Berosus looked out at the towers and said, "The fledgling Glory is a holy thing, Captain. And useful. We would not want to lose the part of the Mother that quickened him. Take him alive. We'll find out who fashioned him soon enough. And the Sublime Mother of Mokad will be pleased. If nothing else, she'll feed upon him. And Her Exquisiteness shall add to herself the power placed in him. She will smile upon us. You have felt her approbation?"

"One glorious time," said the Captain.

"Do well, and you shall feel it again."

"It shall be done, Bright One."

Berosus looked down upon the body of the girl. She had solid bone structure, wide hips for bearing children, a full set of teeth. She was good stock. She would have grown up to bear many fine children and increase the herd. She would have provided many souls as meat for the Mothers.

"I need to get back to the traitors," he said. "Be ready."

"Yes, Bright One."

Another of his dreadmen came up the hill. "We have a report, Bright One."

The wind gusted about the hill. Above them two red-tailed hawks circled. Berosus waited for the dreadman to continue.

"There is an upland village called Redthorn. One of the sleth fled through that village earlier this morning. All of the inhabitants there are dead, including many animals and livestock."

Berosus shrugged. This was not news. One or two dreadmen, of sleth or Divine making, could easily kill any number of unorganized villagers.

"I sent men," the captain continued. "They say the frights are feeding, thick as fleas. There was no sign of struggle, but there was a living blackness, a wisp of mist. It lay upon the floor of a barn. When they opened the door, it attacked one of the men."

Berosus looked over at the captain. "A mist?"

"That is their report, Holy One."

He narrowed his eyes. These sleth were turning out to be more formidable than he thought. How delightful. After all these years, had he found a true sleth challenge? "I want to see the bodies," he said. "I want to see the ground."

* * *

A few hours later Berosus stood before a pile of bodies that lay in front of an orchard of the village of Redthorn. A hammer of dreadmen had spread out in a perimeter around him. The rest of the hundred he'd brought with him were stationed back at the Fir-Noy fortress of Blue Towers. More were coming on the ships that should arrive in just a few days along with thousands of troops from Mokad and three other Glorydoms. His Skir Masters, who were going to be necessary both for the fighting and the harvests, would arrive with that armada as well.

He bent down to the body of a dead woman. She was older, short, her hair beginning to streak with gray. There were no wounds upon her. No blackening of the skin around her neck or wrists that would indicate a Fire harvest. He cut open her tunic with his knife. The skin was clear, but there was a bruising that spread over her chest.

He leaned in. Sniffed. There was something here. He'd smelled it when he'd first gotten close to the village. He leaned in closer and sniffed again.

Magic. Old magic. Something about it tugged on his mind, but the memories were so old they had fallen to dust.

Berosus stood and surveyed the stiffened bodies about him.

"What is this?" the captain of his dreadmen asked.

"I don't know," he replied. But it was powerful. He could feel it in his bones.

"It's a Fir-Noy village. Do you think Shim's sleth drained them to fill their weaves?"

"I think we'll find out many things when we take the boy."

11

Lust

TALEN WALKED THE PARAPETS of Rogum's Defense with Legs, watching for Sugar, until the captain of the guard told him if he was going to just walk around, he might as well be useful and help move some builder's lime up for repairs. Workers sat on platforms that hung down the length of three towers, sealing gaps in the mortar and limewashing the wall.

Talen helped work a crane atop one tower to haul two barrels of lime up. When he finished, there was still no sign of Sugar. The mistress over the washerwomen saw him at the well rinsing the lime powder off his arms and told him some nannies needed milking.

The Mistress was not someone you said no to, and he needed to divert his thoughts, so after washing, he went to the pens. Legs decided to stay by the inner gate and wait.

The goat pens were located on the north side of the outer bailey. In the early morning, those tasked with herding the goats would take them out to the pastures surrounding the fortress and bring them back in the afternoon. Only about a dozen goats were in the pens now, and it was easy to see which nannies needed to be milked. He opened the gate and walked through the wattle fence. The brown and white goats milled about him, and the smell of their Fire and souls called to him.

He groaned inside.

The Mistress carried in a bucket of feed for the chickens and saw him standing there. "You actually get down and squeeze it out," she said and made the motions with her hands. "It's called milking."

"Maybe you should demonstrate?" Talen asked.

The Mistress rolled her eyes. "Take it into the kitchens when you're done."

Talen faced the goats again. He wasn't going to let this craving get the best of him, so he rolled up his sleeves and selected a nanny whose bag was so full it was almost half as big as she was and led her over to the stand. The milking stand looked like a rectangular table that stood about a foot off the ground. It was a little longer and wider than a goat. At one end was the head gate that consisted of two vertical boards with a narrow hole in the middle big enough to comfortably fit a goat's neck. He moved one board of the head gate to the left, tempted the nanny with a bit of grain to stick her head between the two boards, and then he move the board back and locked her in. He gave her the grain, then took the leather hobble strap hanging on the board, brought the strap around her back legs just above the hocks, and cinched it up nice and tight so it squeezed the ligaments. When he was satisfied she was secure and wouldn't kick, he fetched a bucket of water and a cloth.

In a neighboring pen, the kid goats gamboled about a tree stump. In this one, another nanny came up and gave him the eye. Her Fire smelled delicious, but he waved her off. "Be gone," he said.

The goat regarded him.

"Shoo."

The goat tilted its head and watched him like an old wife watches someone new to the task.

"Fine," Talen said and turned to the nanny on the stand. He mustered his courage, sat on the stool, and began to wash the nanny's somewhat hairy udder with a cloth. As soon as he touched her, the smell of Fire and soul doubled. And by the blasted Creators, he wanted it.

The first three squirts of milk from each teat went into a cup. He looked for abnormalities such as clots or blood. When he didn't find any, he brought the wooden bucket around and went at it, the warm milk squirting into the bottom. She bleated. He cursed. And every second his hunger grew.

Then next nanny hopped right up onto the table. He secured her and went through the whole process again. By the time he finished the third goat, he was beyond frustration. His hunger consumed him, and he had to concentrate like a mad tallystick man to simply get the job done.

He put the lids on the two buckets and hauled a good six quarts of milk back to the inner bailey, passing Legs who was still standing at the gate, which meant Sugar still hadn't returned. He was now truly worried for her. He went to the kitchens, set the buckets down where the cook directed him to, and walked back out into the bailey.

Regret's eyes, but this wasn't right. Sugar missing, and him with these blasted desires for men, horses, and goats—it angered him!

Why had Tenter singled him out? Probably for the same reason the Mother had singled him out down in the caves. He was different, maturing differently than others who had been awakened to their powers. Bred to be that way. Isn't that what the Devourer had said?

I will not become a villain, he told himself. *I will not!*

But he'd felt the power of the Devourer—whatever sort of creature she was—down in the stone-wight warren. She'd been stunning, an object he'd wanted to worship. He didn't want to become a villain, but what if he couldn't help himself? What if that's just what he was?

He saw Scruff, River's new horse, tied up outside the smithy, waiting to be shod. Ke had been taking him out on patrol, working with him, which meant Talen had been so flustered with the goats, he'd not even noticed Ke had ridden in.

Despite his name-sake appearance, Scruff was a stellar animal, one of the few horses being made into a firesteed. Talen walked over to the smithy. Scruff nickered at him for a scratch, but Talen wasn't going anywhere close to another living thing. He skirted around and looked in the doors. Two far-riers stood at the fire forming horseshoes. He asked where Ke was, and they directed him to the great hall.

Like all of the buildings in the inner fortress, the great hall was built snug against the inside wall. It was a large building with a high ceiling and four hearths big enough for men to stand in them. When Talen entered the hall, he found two of the long tables laden with leftover food from last night's festivities. Twenty or thirty people milled about, eating. Ke was among them, standing next to one of the tables.

Talen made his way over. Ke looked up, chewing some morsel with delight. "You're a little black thunder cloud."

"We've got to talk," Talen said.

Ke, the big bull, shooed a few flies away and picked up a pie, a small thing no bigger than a plum. He held it out to Talen. "Try this. It will make you feel better."

Talen didn't want to eat, but he accepted it and took a bite and immediately regretted it. It was a nasty little wad of leek with a few miserly grains of unidentifiable meat hiding in the corners. "Who brought these?"

"The rat catchers from Lind," Ke said. He picked up another and plopped the whole thing in his mouth. He chewed, let out a sigh of satisfaction, then picked up another.

Talen shook his head—there was no accounting for taste.

Ke's hair was cropped short. He wore a rust cloak. The gash on his face from the battle down in the bowels of the ancient stone-wight warren had healed. The stitching made from sheep guts had been removed weeks ago, but a scar from the gash and suture holes remained. Scars remained on everyone that had been there, and not all of them were visible like Ke's. Or as lauded. He looked like he had some brutish pin cushion for a head, yet that seemed to attract quite a number of the women.

A small black and white dog sat very politely by the table. He looked up at Talen and wagged his tail.

Talen tossed him the remainder of his leek wad and turned back to Ke. "Something's wrong."

Ke folded his muscular arms.

Talen motioned for Ke to step to the side, away from the others in the hall. Then he related the events as he knew them, including Felts's betrayal. Ke shook his head when he heard about Rooster and Shroud. He rubbed his face. "Felts won't be the last to turn traitor."

Talen said, "The next one might be me."

"What are you talking about?"

"Lust," Talen said.

Ke looked down at him. "What?"

"It's overrated. I can tell you that. Maybe the Divines are speaking a little bit of truth about becoming sleth. My passions are running amok. Goats and horses. Black Knee."

Ke looked at Talen as if he'd sprouted another head.

"It's not natural," said Talen. "And don't look at me that way."

"Brother, you're a strange little man. If I were going to go that way, it wouldn't be with Black Knee. He's as ugly as they come."

"No," said Talen. "It's the Fire. I can feel it in every touch. It isn't normal lust. It can't be." There was no blood-thumping glamour in it. He knew what it was to desire someone physically, and this was different. "Here," he said and grasped Ke's big hand. His hunger surged. "There, do you feel that?"

"I feel nothing."

"Exactly. *You* feel nothing. But I feel an appetite. I can smell your soul like I can that ham roasting over the fire. It doesn't matter who or, apparently, what it is. I just finished milking goats, and the whole time it was there, looping about me like the smell of freshly baked bread. I'm not right."

"Well, that's not news," Ke said. "You've never been right."

"Ke," he said, exasperated.

River entered the hall. She spotted them and walked over. "What are you two stewing?" she asked.

Ke shrugged. "Our brother here fancies Black Knee."

Talen groaned. This wasn't funny. "Something's off inside of me," he said, keeping his voice low. "I can feel the Fire in those I touch. And I want it. It calls to me. I'm telling you: I don't think the monster put all my pieces back correctly."

River considered him. "It's not uncommon to go through a period of confusion, although that usually occurs when you go from candidate to full dreadman. I told you the awakening triggers a second change in the body, not unlike the change from boy to man. Your body becomes different. You feel different things. We all go through it. That's probably all this is. You'll just have to ride it out."

"You say that, but did you feel this when you awakened?" he asked. "Do you know anyone who has?"

"I remember when I was first awakened," said Ke. "For me it was euphoria followed by moods as black as the underside of night. One day Da found me in a corner of the barn loft. I had just learned to diminish, to slow the rate of my Fire until I was barely breathing. It's a very hard thing to do, but can sometimes save your life. Imagine being trapped under water. You can diminish yourself to the point where you almost don't need breath anymore. So I should have been celebrating my accomplishment, but there was no joy in me. I wanted only to be smudged out, forever. Once in a while the darkness still comes, but I've grown past it."

"You're telling me it doesn't go away?"

Ke said, "I'm telling you that when the wild patterns fall into place, brother, you'll never want to go back. It's like trying to learn how to swim and you're forever struggling and choking. And then one day you finally relax, and you're suddenly diving down to the emerald weeds in the pool below the falls like an otter."

"For all we know," River said, "this is right as rain."

"And what was your trial?" Talen asked River.

"Trial?" Ke said in disgust. "I think she suffered a burp and a bit of indigestion. It always comes easy for her."

"Oh, it does not. Look, the storm will come, and then it will pass."

"We hope," Ke said.

"And if not?" Talen asked. He'd been changed, guided by the Devourer herself from conception to fit her terrible plans. His own mother had tried to fix the changes, but had died trying. Nobody had any idea of what he was or what he would become.

"We roll with it," said Ke. He put his strong hand on Talen's shoulder. Talen flinched at the delicious smell of his soul, but Ke's eyes bore into him. "I know you're a little disoriented. That comes with the territory." He motioned at River with his chin. "Trust us. Nothing's going to happen to you. And if it does, we'll be there."

"Right," Talen said.

"And if you turn into something abominable, well, we'll get it over quick. Cut your head off just to be sure the job's done right."

River gave him a look.

"He knows I'm joking," Ke grinned, "mostly."

Mostly was right. River herself had tried to kill him down in the caves. He had no doubt, if it came to it, that both of them were prepared to try it again.

Ke elbowed him. "Come on, smile. Life's meant to be lived. Even when the seas get high." He pointed at some boiled crawfish a good five inches long. "There's some living right there." He picked one up and cracked it open with his thumb and forefinger, exposing the red-tinged flesh inside. He sucked a bit of meat out. "Lovely," he said and chewed. "Have one."

Talen sighed.

"Fill your belly," Ke said. "And I'll tell you what I found today. Because dreadmen and goaty lust aren't the only odd things to show up in the last twenty-four hours."

"It wasn't goat lust," Talen said.

Ke waved the comment off. He pointed at a small pie filled with cheese, onion, and mushroom. "Eat that."

Talen picked one of the pies up. He took a bite. It didn't help.

Ke said, "We had a report this morning of something in the Sourwood River. It came sniffing about the hot pool. We went to investigate."

The Sourwood was the river that ran next to Rogum's Defense. A hot spring ran down the bank at a bend in the river, and a pool had been at the confluence. It was a favorite spot for Shim's dreadmen to relax. "And?" Talen prompted him.

"Two miles up we saw it. A massive shadow under the water. It was huge, thirty or forty feet long at least. And it was a good thing the men in the pool had gotten out. It certainly had the other fish spooked. The carp sprang in bunches into the air, trying to get out of its path."

"A whale?"

"None that we see around here. And when have you ever heard of a whale coming up the Sourwood or even the Lion and scaring the fish?"

"Never," said River.

"We followed it for a mile or so," Ke continued, "and then it was gone."

"Back to the bay?" asked River.

"Or down so deep in the river we couldn't see it."

"So much for the pools," Talen said. He'd actually been thinking about going to take a dip.

"Wurms have been sighted at the borders of the land as well," said River.

"So we have our hands full of things to worry about," Ke said. He turned to Talen. "Hold your course. It will pass. And now I need to report to Uncle."

Ke picked up a sweet apple tart from Bain, and then he and River left.

"Talen," Black Knee called and motioned for him to come over. The man was sitting over by the barracks on a chair with his wounded and bandaged leg propped up on a barrel. The wives of Rooster and Shroud sat with him.

Talen walked over to them. Black Knee had sawn off his beard and hair to mourn the loss of those two good men. Big clumps of hair still lay on the ground about him. Both women's eyes were red. Talen loosened the purse at his waist. It contained dice and a small bit of money. He removed the money and, as was customary for a fist mate, shared it between them. "It's not much," he said. "But it's what I have." They accepted the money. Black Knee asked Talen to relate his tale from that night, and Talen did. When he finished, they talked about Rooster and Shroud and their children. Talen knew what it was to lose a parent. Eventually the conversation wound down, and the two women left.

When they were gone, Black Knee said, "I have no doubt the ancestors came to collect those two. They were good men from good lines."

"And Felts?" Talen asked.

Black Knee shook his head. "That one I can't explain. Half of me hopes some fright or howler shreds his soul. The other half hopes he makes it. I don't know what turned him."

"Does it matter?"

Black Knee shrugged.

"Sugar isn't back yet," said Talen.

"She carried me out of danger. You know that, don't you?"

Talen nodded.

"She's not your everyday girl, that one."

"No," Talen agreed.

"From here on out, I'm going to be looking out for her. And I won't be standing for any louts." He gave Talen a look meant to include him.

"I don't think Sugar is susceptible to louts. Of course, if any suitable men find out you're involved, it just might turn them off."

"I'll show you turned off," Black Knee threatened.

"Except you'd have to catch me first. A highly improbable proposition."

Black Knee lunged forward in his seat, but Talen danced back.

"Get back here, you runty thing," Black Knee said. "Let's try that again."

"I think I like my current position."

"Oh," Black Knee said. "The young lad shows signs of intelligence. I'll tally one in your favor."

"Splendid," Talen said, but a fat lot of good it would do if she didn't come back.

"Don't be fretting about her. She outran the Fir-Noy once. She'll do it again."

"I earnestly hope so."

"She will," Black Knee said. "Mark my words."

* * *

About fifteen minutes later Talen was out with the other eight members of his fist unloading a cartful of firewood in the outer bailey, when Sugar came riding through the gate with that foreign sleth Urban, him with his fine clothes and glittering eyes. Two of his crew rode behind with three children up on their horses with them.

Talen dropped his wood on the pile and ran to meet them. Legs beat him to her. Despite his blindness, the boy could move quickly when he knew an area.

Sugar lighted off her horse to embrace her brother. Legs clung to her tightly.

"Took you long enough," Talen said, coming up from behind.

Sugar turned. "Well, if you hadn't shoved me, I could have gone with you and River."

He gripped her shoulder. He wanted to embrace her, but the maddening smell of her soul called out to him, and he quickly turned and took the reins of her horse. Urban dismounted. His one eye was puffed up and dark with bruising.

"You ran into trouble then?" Talen asked.

"I ran into her elbow," Urban said. "Or rather, it ran into me."

Talen looked at her questioningly.

Sugar said, "I thought he was one of the Famished."

"The Famished?"

"He grabbed my knife hand. I was half out of my mind with thirst and hunger."

"Lucky for me she wasn't full strength," Urban said with a smile.

"She's a bruiser for sure," said Talen. "Always pummeling the candidates with her fists."

"You think she'd look worse for the wear," Urban said.

"Not when I fight slow boys like you."

Talen laughed.

"Thanks for finding her," Legs said.

"Oh, it was our pleasure," said Urban. "In fact, you might say it's our specialty, finding lost and abandoned things."

They began to walk toward the inner bailey. As they did, Sugar reached out and squeezed Talen's hand. It startled him.

"Thanks for what you did back in Plum," she said.

The scent of her Fire and soul, her attractive eyes, they all disoriented him a bit. "What are you talking about?"

"Drawing their attention."

"Drawing their attention?"

"The insults and loud shouting."

"Ah," Talen said, and realized he had done that. He took on a feigned noble air. "I was rather heroic, wasn't I? I don't suppose your dainty-nosed weaver would have thought of that."

Sugar groaned, rolled her eyes, and tossed his hand.

Despite his hunger, he wanted to grab it back again. "Who knew my mouth could prove to be so useful."

"The weapon of kings," Legs said.

The oldest child with Urban rubbed his eye. His tattoo proclaimed him a Fir-Noy. "Who are these?" Talen asked.

"We found the children and Sugar in Redthorn," Urban said.

"Redthorn? That's not the most direct route out of Fir-Noy lands."

"I wasn't thinking of direct," Sugar said. "I was thinking of not dying."

"But why bring them?" Talen asked.

"It was awful," she said. "The village was slaughtered. Talen, some great evil is abroad. We need to find Argoth and Shim."

They hurried into the inner bailey and gave their horses to grooms to take to the stables. Then Talen hurried with Sugar and Urban to Shim's quarters. On the way, Black Knee saw her and rose up on a crutch. He tried to hobble over, but Sugar ran to him instead and gave him a hug. "You didn't play the fool after all," she said. "I'm so happy you avoided yourself a curse."

"Aye," said Black Knee. "I didn't dare disobey." He grimaced from the pain in his leg and sat back down. "I'm going to be wanting to hear your tale," he said.

"You'll have the long version," Sugar promised.

Then Sugar went into Shim's clerk and had him call the lord. A little while later, Talen, Ke, River, Argoth, Shim, and the Creek Widow all assembled in Shim's chamber.

12

Plan of War

ARGOTH LISTENED to Sugar and Urban make their reports. When they finished, Argoth knelt down in front of the children and took the girl's hand. "I have a daughter about your age. What are you? Five years old?"

The girl nodded.

"She's four," the oldest boy corrected.

Argoth looked at them. "I need you to tell me everything. We need to stop whoever did this. Maybe you saw something that can help us."

"You're Shoka," the oldest boy said.

"You're right. The Fir-Noy and Shoka are angry with each other. But we're all still Mokaddians, aren't we?"

"We want to go to our Uncle's," he said.

"We'll take you back, I promise. But I need you to tell me what happened. I need you to start from the beginning and not leave out any details. Will you do that?"

The boy nodded.

Then he told the story. The whole village as well as some neighbors had turned out for the Apple Dance festivities. It had been a celebration like all the others that had been held with dance and food and laughter. But just at dusk that all changed. The heart of the cherry orchard had turned black. Nobody had noticed until the pained cry of a hound drew their attention. They thought the darkness was a trick of the evening shadows, so a man went into the orchard, calling for his dog. He disappeared into the blackness and never came out.

They were about to send more men in when long ragged arms of black vapor began to stretch out between the trees and down the rows. The arms of vapor reached out to the grassy spot where the villagers were celebrating. Snakes of it curled up and around people's limbs. At first nothing happened, and then one of the old farmers cried out and fell. The whole village turned to run, but it was too late. The mists attacked them.

The children's mother hid them in the upper reaches of their barn. But she wasn't able to close the barn doors and the mists caught her. One slithered into her mouth and she fell to her knees. The second boy had wanted to go to her aid, but other mists flowed into the barn. And then a pair of men came along, hauled their mother to her feet, and dragged her away. The mists in the barn did not bother the men, but the children didn't trust it for it lay along the dirt at the bottom of the barn, moving even though there was no wind.

The children peered through a knot hole to see where the men were taking their mother. They saw something come out of the orchard, something tall with horns. Odd lavender flames flashed around the thing, but they never could get a good look at it. The children soon turned from the peephole, pressing deep into the hay and plugging their ears. But it didn't block out the cries of pain that rose throughout the village. Sometime later the cries ceased.

"And the men who took your mother," Argoth asked, "what did they look like?"

Tears began to spill from the little girl's eyes.

"Their faces were painted red and yellow," said the boy.

"Did you see their tattoos?"

"Like Bone Faces," he said.

Argoth asked them a few more questions, but it was clear the children had told all.

"I bet you're hungry," Argoth said.

They nodded.

He called Shim's clerk in to take them. But the children wouldn't go with him and clung to Sugar and Urban.

Matiga said to Sugar, "Leave the things you retrieved here. Find them food and a place to sleep and where their uncle lives." She pointed at Urban. "You go with her. And you, Talen, tell your brother I want a chat."

Sugar led the childred out with Urban, followed by Talen. When the door closed, Shim said, "We've fought the Bone Faces for years. This isn't Bone Faces."

"Maybe the Bone Faces and Mokad are in league," said Matiga. "We pose a common threat to both."

"It's clear our plans need to be speeded up," Shim said.

"Argoth's original time table was already too short to build an army of dreadmen by next spring," said Eresh. "You can accelerate some learning, but the body can only be stretched so far. Developing someone into a dread-man takes time. Rush it, and you'll just end up with a lot of broken men."

"What other options do we have?"

"You can't fight them here, bottled up in a fortress," said Eresh. "You have no Skir Masters. If you try to stand against them toe to toe, they'll pin you down with a barrage of wind. You'll shoot your rain of arrows only to have their skir winds throw them off course. Then the winds will pound you with sand. You can wear goggles to keep it from blinding you, but mixed in with the sand will be shards of shale that will cut like knives. And then they'll bring up the larger skir. They'll slam hundred-pound stones into your gates and knock them to splinters, blow your men off the parapets. You cannot beat them by playing their game."

"That was never our intent," said Shim. "We always meant to fight them with ambush and raid, with sabotage and subterfuge. We meant to assas-sinate the Divines first. And when the snake's head was cut off, we would then chop up the body. Without the Divines, the weaves of their dreadmen would soon run dry. Our army, on the other hand, would never run dry because we would teach each man and woman the lore. Because we wouldn't be relying on weaves, Mokad would grow weaker as we grew stronger."

"Killing a Divine is not as easy as it sounds," said Eresh.

Argoth said, "We could flee. As distasteful as that is, it must be on the table."

Shim shook his head. "You can't disappear a whole people. We'd have to leave the bulk of our clans behind. Leave our fair wives and children to become like Redthorn. I can't do that. I won't do that."

"It might be your only option," said Eresh.

"No," said Shim.

"You cannot send candidates to contend with the terrors of Mokad," said Eresh.

"Then let us force them to the next level," said Argoth.

"I just told you," said Eresh. "You'll end up with broken men."

Argoth said, "That's not entirely true. It can be done in a way that minimizes the loss."

Ke and Matiga raised their eyebrows in surprise.

"I've done it before," Argoth said.

"How big is this loss?" asked Shim.

"Ten percent. Maybe a bit less."

"Or maybe a bit more," said Eresh. "Maybe a lot more."

Forcing a man was like stuffing a burlap sack with something that was much too big for it. Some sacks stretched. Other sacks broke instead, ripping along a seam or some weak part of the weave. Likewise, some men could bear, up to a point, a sudden multiplication of their powers. In time their bodies and the bindings of the three vitalities matured and strengthened, and they could be forced again. Others could not bear the added stress. Their bodies and bindings tore. And through the gaps their Fire poured forth in a rush. If it was not stopped, those who broke would die, sooner or later, in a muggy haze of firejoy. Of those that didn't die, some of them could heal over a few months or years and try to wield their Fire again. Others became brittle and had to wear a governor the rest of their lives.

Shim sighed heavily. "I don't want to lose one of our candidates."

"That's not your only problem," said Eresh. "Three hundred weaves eat a prodigious amount of Fire. I've looked at your weaves. They are starting to run dry. I don't think you have two week's worth of Fire."

"Then I will make another sacrifice," said Shim.

Shim had already given huge amounts of Fire. Argoth didn't know how much more the man had.

Shim saw Argoth's look. "These soldiers follow me. They risked everything trusting my word. If I have to sacrifice all my Days in their service, I will do it."

"I didn't speak against it," said Argoth.

"I will," said Eresh. "You pour too much of yourself out, and you'll be dead. Then who will lead them?"

"If this fails," said Shim, "we're all dead anyway."

Up until this point, River had stood in the corner keeping her silence. She spoke now. "We'll all make another sacrifice. And we'll pray the ancestors bless us. But there's more. Harnock has Fire," said River. "He has the Book of Hismayas. There might be lore there that could help. We should send someone one more time to fetch him."

"He will not leave the Wilds," said Matiga. "Especially not with Divines here."

"The book of Hismayas?" asked Eresh.

Argoth sighed. The book was supposed to contain great treasures of lore, the crown great treasures of power. Many had fought and killed for it. The Divines had stolen it; the Order had stolen it back. But the Book was beyond any of the Order.

"Lords, man," said Eresh, "where is it?"

"It cannot be opened," said Argoth. "It has killed all who have tried."

"It hasn't seen the likes of me," said Eresh.

"And it won't," said Matiga. "It's in Harnock's hands. If you try to go there, he will slay you. I'm telling you: it is not an option."

River shook her head. "He didn't act that way toward me when I went with my father."

"Harnock and your father had a bond," Argoth said. "If we had time, we could work it out with him, and I would send you. But even if you got in, the book is sealed. What we need are Fire and dreadmen. We need you here helping us raise the candidates, not chasing a dicer's dream."

River sighed.

"Let us do as we planned at the beginning," said Argoth, "although our chances are now stretched even thinner."

"You cannot take retreat off the table," said Eresh. "I suggest a time limit. We fight not just for the people in these lands. If we lose, there will be no mercy. They will exterminate every living thing associated with us. And the truth about the Divines will be lost."

Matiga said, "The truth will only sound like lies until we can prove it over and over. What mankind needs is proof. We can shout the truth from the rooftops, but until we can prove it in their eyes, the truth will be labeled as just one more vile sleth heresy and turned against us."

Eresh learned over to Argoth. "That one has some brains. A nice form. I think she'll do nicely."

"Careful," said Argoth.

"Indeed I shall be," said Eresh, delight shining in his one eye.

Matiga raised one eyebrow and gave him a look that pegged him somewhere slightly above a toad.

Shim said, "We'll prepare to carry the truth into the wilderness. But now is not the time to retreat. Now is the time to kill the snake that is before us."

"We'll need reconnaissance," said Ke. "And tactics. They're going to bring a Skir Master or three in. The chief Skir Master is the one we need to target first. He'll have rings of security about him. And you can be sure he'll bring kitemen. It's going to be very tricky approaching him with them watching everything from the skies."

"And," said Argoth, "if I know Mokad, they will have a few dogmen on the ground."

"Toth," Eresh spat. "I never liked that country."

"It's going to be very difficult to find a weakness," said Argoth. "Especially if we only have a matter of days to do it."

"What about the Victor's crown?" Shim asked. "Have you repaired it?"

Argoth sighed and shook his head. They had thought it impervious, but later found that the Devourer had damaged it in the battle in the cave. The lore was ancient, and none that now lived fully understood it. "We have tried everything we know; it still eludes us."

"What about that Flax of the Hand?" River asked. "Why don't we bring him into this council?"

"No," Eresh bristled. "The Hand thinks only of itself. You will rely on them to your sorrow."

"Surely they have dealt with this before," said River. "More than any of us, they know how to hunt Divines."

"What they know is how to turn their backs on their allies. That is all they know."

"They have killed Divines," said Shim.

"They have killed loremen as well."

"Master Kish," said Matiga. "You're going to have to get along."

Eresh licked his bottom lip. "Oh, I'll get along, your most formidable loveliness, right up until the time he and his betray you. And then I'll be there with my knife to carve out his throat."

"I'll take that as an oath," said Shim. "And seeing how much you protest those who break their oaths, I expect it will be worth something."

"Aye," said Eresh, "worth my weight in Hand blood."

"We still don't have a decision," Matiga said.

Shim said, "We will prepare to move out and break into smaller units that can hide more easily. Two days from now there will be nothing but a small number left here to make the enemy think this is still our base. For the rest of us, our mission is to locate the Divines sent against us."

"The Skir Master must fall in the first stroke," said Eresh. "He must be the prime target. We'll be lucky if we get one chance, and we don't want to be wasting it on lesser targets."

"Agreed," said Shim. Then he turned to the pack Sugar left on the table. "Now let us see if Purity left us anything that might be helpful."

13

Chicken Bone

SUGAR AND URBAN took the children to the kitchens, Legs in tow. The odors of the thick dreadman's stew the candidates called swamp rose from the cooking pots and wafted across the fortress. The stew was made of many things: barley, fish, beef, cabbage, and probably twelve other ingredients. All candidates ate it every afternoon and evening. The weaves multiplied the powers of the body, but they also multiplied hunger and thirst. And this stew slaked both. To her surprise, Sugar actually had grown to enjoy it. She and Urban took three wooden dishes and filled them with swamp for the children, telling them that they would be taken back to the border later, for it appeared they had an uncle that lived in a village not far from Redthorn.

An old cook filled Sugar's bowl with swamp, then fetched a basket from a shelf behind her and pulled away the cloth cover to reveal half a dozen mushroom and cheese pies left over from the Apple Dance. She asked Sugar how many she wanted, and Sugar asked how many she could get. The cook simply gave the basket to her, telling her she was a brave lass. Sugar offered Urban a pie, but he waved it away. "I need to talk to Argoth about your special skills."

Sugar took a bite of pie. The cheese was soft and pungent. The mushrooms were spiced and mixed with sweet onion. And the pastry shell flaked with every bite. She thought she might pass out for the joy of it. She took another bite. "What skills?" she asked around the mouthful of pie.

But Urban only smiled and walked back across the bailey.

Sugar thanked the cook profusely for the pies, then made her way to some tables with Legs and the children.

When they sat, Legs said, "I hate the fact that I couldn't be there to help you."

"It all turned out."

"One of these days, I'm going to pluck the eyes out of a goat to see if they won't grow in my own head. Then the next time you go to Plum, you won't have to go alone."

"Yes, and both of us would have then fallen into the trap."

Legs shook his head. "Tenter's famous for his love of garlic. If I'd been there, it's likely I would have smelled him out."

"But would you have smelled Redthorn?"

"I'm telling you, one of these days," said Legs, "I'll have my goat eyes and be able to fight. Then you won't have to shoulder everything alone."

"You and your goat eyes," said Sugar. "If you're pining after eyes, why not long for something that will bestow superior sight, like a hawk's?"

"A hawk?" asked Legs. "Too small. Can you imagine? Those little things, rolling around in my sockets."

"Why are we even talking about this?" asked Sugar. "You can't grow an eye."

"If the Green Ones can bring back the dead, they can bring back an eye."

"So say the Divines, but I don't know that we should believe everything that falls from Divine lips. It's probably just more propaganda."

"It's propaganda I want to believe," said Legs.

"And that's the problem with propaganda," she said.

Sugar ate with Legs and the children until she thought she might burst, and then she found a fist of men who were on patrol later and could take the children back. Shortly after that, the leadership filed out of Shim's chambers along with Urban. Argoth gave the command for the candidates to form ranks. Shim's army was a little over six thousand strong. A number of hammers were out of the fortress on various duties, and there were terrors and cohorts of men stationed at various places around the clanlands, but almost two thousand soldiers were in the fortress, and they lined up. Of these, 327, including her and Talen, were dreadman candidates. The rest were waiting expectantly to be awakened to the lore.

The army stood at attention in sharp lines, grouped by their units. The smallest units in Shim's army were fists of ten or so soldiers. Two to four fists combined to make a hammer. Four or five hammers made up a terror. Shim's army had enough men for three dreadman terrors, although almost all were still only candidates, their bodies still in the beginnings of change brought about by their awakening. With time, they would increase their capacity and move to more powerful weaves, then no weaves at all, wielding the lore as Ke and River and Argoth did.

Sugar took her place and watched as Argoth and Commander Eresh reviewed the soldiers. Next to Sugar stood River and the other eight females of her fist. They were the only women who had been given weaves. The plan was to teach the lore to all men and women, but priority had to go to the strongest and fastest of those already skilled as warriors. The Creek Widow, however, had insisted on a fist of women for spies, if nothing else, and had put River in charge. Legs stood behind Sugar, outside the official ranks. The big blond foreigner came in after everyone was formed up and stood next to him.

Commander Eresh walked down the line of candidates. He took one man by the ear and pulled his head back and forth as if appraising how well it was connected to his shoulders. He sniffed another man. Another was told to open his mouth and show his teeth and gums. Sugar herself was told to look up so he could see the whites of her eyes.

Eresh said, "There are better uses for pretty things than putting them in front of a great mass of brutes."

"Zu," said Sugar, "with all respect for your fearsome power, the pretty things here can beat half the fists in this army."

Eresh looked at Argoth.

"They're good," Argoth said.

Eresh grunted and moved down the line. When he finished, both he and Zu Argoth returned to the front to address the group.

"Candidates," said Zu Argoth. "Before you stands Eresh the Bloody. He was one of those that stopped the black hordes and sent them back to their mountains. He once led two terrors of Dreadmen. He has joined our cause and is now the master of candidates and will oversee your training."

But Commander Eresh had wandered over to the cooking pots. He took the ladle from one of the cooks and took a sip of the hot and steaming broth. He rolled it around in his mouth and smacked his lips.

Sugar wondered if all Kish were so rude and distracted. Or was this simply the first sign of incompetence? She stole a questioning glance at River who shrugged. Sugar could tell the other candidates were having the same questions.

Commander Eresh dipped the ladle again and fished out a chicken leg from the pot. He put the leg into his mouth and with one bite dragged the meat off the bone. Then he handed the ladle back to the cook.

All watched in silence.

As he chewed, he nodded. "Not quite," he said. "But good, very good." He bit the cartilage end off the chicken leg and munched it.

"Commander," said Argoth. "They're yours."

Eresh walked back to the soldiers. "Never underestimate the importance of a cook," he said, the meat and cartilage still in his mouth. "Dreadmen are nothing without their cooks. But, of course, that's not what you want to hear. You want to hear of battles and tactics and awe-inspiring feats. The power feels good. As fine as a silky woman's skin." He worried a stubborn pieced of flesh off the bone with his teeth. "The power is like a lover. You've all felt it." He pointed at a man. "What do you say?"

"I'd say that she's a succulent thing."

"Succulent, indeed," said Eresh. "She caresses you. Flatters you. You're quick, she tells you. You're strong. Invincible. But if you listen to her, that will be your doom."

He turned to Argoth. "I need a formidable volunteer."

"Bags," said Zu Argoth. "Step forward."

A soldier of many years broke from the lines. The tattoos on his forearms proclaimed him an armsman, fully trained, with many kills to his name. He was in the top group of candidates and often helped with the skills training.

Commander Eresh cleaned a morsel from between two teeth with his tongue. He eyed Bags. "Very good," he said. "Zu Bags, do you wear your lover?"

Bags pulled up the sleeve of his tunic and showed his candidate weave.

Eresh pulled up his sleeves and tunic. Then he dropped his trousers and stepped out of them to show he wore no weave. He looked ridiculous.

"I'm an old man," he said. "Fat, half-blind. And I'm going to strike you. Avoid it if you can."

Bags nodded. "And do I get to strike back, Zu?"

A number of the candidates chuckled.

"If you think you can land a blow, do it. In fact, I will make you a promise. If you land a blow, I will be your servant for a day. I'll wash your feet. Pick your toenails. Bring you cake. Agreed?"

"Throw in some good wine," said Bags.

Eresh grinned. "Breakfast, lunch, and dinner."

Bags stretched his arms wide, loosening himself. He was a big man, a seasoned warrior. He was not someone to toy with. As he approached, Eresh bit the chicken's leg bone in two. He sucked loudly on half of the bone, extracting the marrow and juices. Then he began to munch it.

Bags stopped two paces away from Eresh.

Eresh pointed at him with the other half of the leg bone. "Have you prepared yourself, Candidate?"

"Aye," said Bags.

Commander Eresh struck. One moment he was standing casually, the pointed half of the chicken bone in his hand. The next moment Bags was reeling backwards, clutching at his forehead.

Eresh stood back and spat a bit of bone shard off his tongue.

Bags got his feet underneath himself. A part of the chicken bone stuck out of his forehead. The other part was shoved up under his skin. Blood began to pour out of the wound. Bags steadied himself, yanked the bone out, and looked at it in dismay, and then the blood began to run down his brow and into his eyes.

"And in such a manner," said Commander Eresh, "is one of the mighty slain by a chicken." He looked at the other candidates. "Is that the best you have to offer?"

Nobody moved.

"Come," said Eresh. "If any one of you lands a blow, I will grant him a boon. Or is it true that Mokaddian clansmen are nothing but old women?"

Another man stepped forward. A tall Burundian with a massive beard. He went straight at the commander. His blow should have landed, but Eresh dodged, took him by the throat, and before the man could react, Eresh had him bent backwards over an empty vegetable wagon. He slammed the man's head into the side board and stunned him.

"Mokad comes," Eresh said. "They know you're something now. Seafire. Slain Divines. The mighty Grove of the New Lands. They come with all their powers to kill every last one of you." He slammed the man's head into the side board again. "And you present this?"

Another man stepped forward.

* * *

Talen watched the old Kish in amazement. These men were some of the fiercest fighters in Shim's army.

Flax had been standing behind Talen. He leaned forward and whispered, "Are you going to let a Kish talk to you that way? Show your comrades what a Koramite is worth."

"Are you mad?"

"I'll go at him from the front. You get behind him, on his blind side. Hit him with anything you can find."

"That's not fair."

"You think the Commander is playing fair?"

Eresh tripped another man and sent him to the ground.

"Don't let me down," Flax said, and then he began to circle around in front of the Commander.

Talen hesitated. Flax wanted him to strike a superior officer in the back?

Flax looked back, motioned for Talen to get moving.

The Hand were Divine killers. Maybe Flax knew things Talen did not. What did he have to lose? If this was how you fought in the mad world of dreadmen, then so be it. Talen moved. He wasn't going to close with Eresh. He'd seen the results of that. Instead, he looked for a rock.

A fourth man came forward, but he did not close immediately with Eresh. Instead, he paced back and forth like a wildcat in a cage. He was a fighter known for his murderous kicks. He feinted. Commander Eresh, his naked legs looking ridiculous, rolled his eyes.

Talen circled around behind. There weren't any rocks, but there was a crookneck squash at the base of the vegetable wagon.

The fourth man kicked at Eresh's blind side, but Eresh caught his ankle and lifted his leg up high. He grabbed the man by his crotch. "Good-bye walnuts," he said and squeezed. "You're Mokaddian. You don't need them anyway."

The man groaned in pain and fell back.

"And so your lover betrays you," said Eresh.

"May I play?" Flax asked.

Eresh turned. "Ah," he said, "the fearsome Hand."

"I don't want to take advantage of your age."

The other candidates laughed.

Eresh looked over at Shim for permission. "I won't hurt him too much. I promise."

Shim didn't looked convinced, but he nodded his assent with a warning look.

Eresh turned back to Flax and rubbed his hands together. "Let us see what a man with such fine pants is good for."

Talen picked up the gourd. He couldn't believe he was doing this.

Flax began to close the distance. He moved to the side. And Talen saw it was to make sure Eresh turned so Talen would be behind his blind spot. Flax stepped to the side again. Eresh turned, putting Talen in his blind spot.

This was Talen's moment. He took two steps and hurled the gourd at the back of the commander's head. The gourd flew straight and true. And at the last moment commander Eresh must have seen the faces of the candidates who noticed it, for he turned like lightning and caught it.

Flax flew into motion. He kicked. Eresh spun back. The blow landed on Eresh's back, but not squarely. Eresh caught Flax's leg and twisted. Flax went down to the ground, Eresh on top of him. There was a flash and Eresh held Flax's own knife at the man's throat. Hate and disgust twisted Eresh's face.

"And so your lover lies to you," Eresh said and moved the knife closer.

"Commander," said Argoth evenly.

A beat passed. Then Eresh pushed himself up off of Flax and stood back.

Flax grinned. "I believe that counts as a blow."

"Indeed it was," said Shim. "Which means he'll receive the promised boon, won't he commander." It wasn't a question.

Eresh threw the knife into the ground at Flax's feet. "Of course he will. I keep my oaths, unlike others."

Flax motioned at the candidates. "I give my portion of wine to you. And I'll throw in a barrel more. I think you'll remember the lesson better that way."

Eresh pitched his voice so low that it was a strain for Talen to hear. "I see through your game, Handsman; you may have scored points with them. Not with me."

Flax smiled and shrugged.

Eresh turned to the candidates. "If you're going to beat Mokad, you need to think differently. You underestimated me. You came to me on my own terms. Even our blond wonder only thought to pair with one of you. The whole lot of you should have turned on me. Do you see now? Mokad will come, and if you try to stand against them man-to-man, you will die. And then, bish-bash, there goes your pretty field of blue and your brass sun. There goes your wife. Your pretty children. There goes your soul.

"You cannot beat them at their game. You cannot beat them as individuals. You will only beat them by breaking off a part and attacking it with the odds in your favor. And even then, you won't be enough. So you will fight with cunning. You will ambush and harry. You will trap. You will flee." He pointed at Talen. "You will take your enemy unawares with any weapon at hand. You will sing your enemy to sleep. You will not fight his war. You will fight your own. And you will remember that the fist is everything. There will be no single heroes in this army. You will stand together, or Mokad will scatter you like chaff before the wind."

Commander Eresh paused and surveyed the candidates. "Mokad's troops have already begun to arrive. So tonight you will prepare yourselves for the first quickening. We do not have time for luxuries. Those who pass will become dreadmen of the first level. Some of you will break. But even if we had time to wait for every last one of you to mature, some of you would still break. More will break when you go through the second quickening a few months from now. Still more will break when you move to the third. But you'll never make it to the second or third if we don't field a stronger force today."

14

Gifts

ALL AROUND TALEN the candidates talked excitedly, some with surprise and eagerness, others with grim concern. As far as Talen was concered, the quicker he moved through the changes that the lore were awakening in him, the better. He could smell the army about him. Smell the sweat of their bodies and clothes that hadn't been washed in a week. Somebody's bad breath kept assaulting him. Mixed in were the smells of the horses in the stables and the cooking swamp. And underneath it all were lovely whiffs of Fire and soul.

Lords, but he couldn't wait until that craziness was gone.

Sugar came over to him, leading Legs along by the hand. "Well done. Very brave going against that wild man."

Legs spoke up. "Indeed. Such valor deserves a poem. Luckily, I have sounded one out." A few of the men in the immediate area overheard him and turned. Legs cleared his throat.

The Kish was insulting our men,
Dealing death with his boiled chicken.

A few of the men chuckled.

Mighty weapon in hand,
Talen said, "this won't stand!"
And with his gourd he did the foe in.

Talen rolled his eyes. "That's it?"

"A saga for the ages," Legs said.

"I think your rhythm is off in that last line."

Legs said, "I believe I shall call it 'Talen, mighty wielder of lettuces and sundry vegetable products'. Or maybe 'The Gourd Warrior'."

The men about Talen hooted with laugher. A few clapped him on the shoulder. He smiled, going along with the joke, but would they have laughed as hard if they knew at every touch he wondered what it would be like to taste their souls?

Flax walked up then. He put his arm around Talen and held a jug of wine high. Talen tried to shrink away from his embrace, but the big man was strong.

"For Talen and the spoils of war!"

"Ho!" a number of men cheered.

"That's not much spoils," a skinny man said and pointed at the jug. "Divide that up, and each of us won't get more than a lick."

"Which is why," Eresh said, cutting in, "I've ordered a barrel up from the buttery."

The men turned to look at him.

Eresh continued, "Bring your cups with you when you come for your swamp this evening. We shall celebrate your quickening."

Someone shouted, "Bloody Eresh!" The crowd responded with another "Ho!"

"Bloody Eresh!" the man shouted out again. This time more of the army picked up the refrain. The man shouted once more, and this time the "Ho" rose from the whole host, ringing about the walls of the inner bailey in a deafening chorus.

Eresh pinned Flax with his one good eye and gave him a look of contempt. Flax just smiled.

"He doesn't like you very much," said Talen.

"I can't imagine why," said Flax. "Do you think it's my pants?"

This time Talen laughed.

* * *

Talen and Legs stood in line in front of the large cooking pots and got their bowl of swamp and a section of hard bread. Sugar said she'd already eaten, but made sure to get a generous serving for Black Knee.

They went and sat by a group of men asking Flax about his background and exploits as he ate. Someone asked him about the Hand and if he'd ever himself killed a Divine.

"Divines do not die easily," he said, gesticulating with his spoon. "And killing a Divine isn't always the objective." Then he told a story about how he once was smuggled into the palace of an Urzarian Divine by a eunuch to steal weaves and scrolls of lore. He told another story about rescuing five of his fellow sleth from a hanging in Cath. He showed them a puckered scar on his back that he'd gotten from that exploit when a guard had skewered him with a knife. He showed them another scar from a tumble he'd taken out of a tree while avoiding a giant of Trolumbay.

The men listened raptly. Some added anecdotes of their own. Eventually the conversation wound around to whether there were more of the Hand coming. "Perhaps," said Flax. "A few of the leaders have died. The others sent me to observe and report. I hope they join us." He stood. "And now I need to run an errand." He took his wooden bowl and spoon to the washing cauldron, rinsed it out, and put it in the stack to dry. Then he waved to them as he walked out of the bailey. The men turned back to the last bits of their meal.

"He appears to be a quality fellow," said Black Knee.

"Aye," said Talen, "that he does. What do you think, Legs?"

Legs had removed his father's skull from Sugar's pack and was soberly running his fingers over every crack and bump. Legs had told Talen many stories about his da; it was clear he loved the man. Talen hoped that skull brought him some solace.

Legs said, "Earlier, when I was waiting, Flax said he had things he might be able to teach me."

Talen felt a little pang of jealousy. "Like what?"

"Things," Legs shrugged.

"Maybe these are things I might benefit from too."

"I don't know if you'll have the chance," Black Knee said. "I'm hearing that Shim has decided the army needs to be out more, not squatting here at the fortress where it's easy to find us. This won't be a war of fortresses. And the speech our commander of chicken bones gave confirms it. So I think we'll be splitting up."

"What do you mean?" Talen asked.

"The army is going to be going out more. Patrols, raids, spying. I think Shim wants us to practice communication and maneuver, breaking up and disappearing as smaller groups, and then suddenly joining up in great numbers to surprise the enemy. I'm thinking we'll camp in terrors. And they'll send hammers and fists off on specific missions." He looked at Sugar. "I don't know what they'll do with the women."

"Commander Eresh seems to have other plans for them," said Talen.

Sugar said, "Let him tell the Creek Widow to keep us out. I'd like to see that."

"That's indeed a fight I'd pay to watch," said Talen. "But I doubt you'll be coming with us. I bet the Creek Widow has plans for her fell-maidens."

"How can I get myself in that fell-maiden fist?" Black Knee asked. "That's what I want to know." Then he looked down at Legs who was still running his fingers over the skull and said, "What are you going to do with that?"

"I don't know just yet," Sugar said. "Mother's ancestors are buried back in old Koram across the sea. Da's are in Koramtown. But part of me wants to keep him about."

"Nothing wrong with that," said Black Knee. "In fact, it's a good idea to have some bones close by. It helps the ancestors find you. Myself, I keep a bone about my neck to help my grandfather remember me." He pulled up a necklace with a small bone threaded through it.

"His finger bone?" asked Talen.

"No. This is from one of his dogs; they were his pride and joy. I imagine they're in that place with him. They'll snuff me right out."

Sugar nodded.

"What about the other items you retrieved?" Talen asked Sugar. "What were they?"

"I don't know," said Sugar. "The Creek Widow is examining them."

Over by the great hall, Argoth called out for the first fist of men to report for the quickening. All the eyes in the bailey watched the fist of men walk over and disappear through the door.

"Creators bless them," said Black Knee.

As the men went into the hall, Ke exited. He spotted Talen and began to make his way over. A number of the women by the hall said something to him. Ke grinned, and they laughed. Sugar watched Ke, and then she looked at Talen. He looked over at her and her green eyes. She smiled, her teeth white against her honey skin, and something thunked inside of him, disorienting him a bit.

She got this look on her face.

"What?" he asked.

"Nothing," she said and looked away. "I'd better go see if I can do anything to help the Creek Widow with these forcings."

"Aye," said Talen.

She gave him another look, hugged Black Knee, then left the three of them there. Talen watched her go.

When he'd died the first time, he'd been laid out on the dusty floor of the Mother's cave like a doll with all its straw scattering to the wind. He'd been floating above himself until the monster stuffed him back into his bones and made a request. A request which Talen had fulfilled. And now, having met death once, Talen did not want to go into that peril again loaded down with regrets, if-onlies, should-haves, and small cowardices.

A man could die not having ever really lived. Life was like the setting sun—the spectacle lasted but a few moments, and if you were too stupid or afraid to seize the moment, it would be gone. He'd begun to think that Sugar was just such a moment. And if he delayed, that sunset would be gone forever, snapped up by one of the men here with the guts and sense to act.

"What are you looking at?" Black Knee asked.

"Nothing, grandfather," he said. "Just contemplating the task of hauling you up the stairs."

"Legs," said Black Knee. "Let's save Talen some effort. Why don't you take me to your quarters instead?"

Legs bunked with Sugar and the fist of women training to become fell-maidens. "You're a bit large to sneak in," said Legs.

"I'll pretend I've been blinded like you."

"Oh, that will fool them for sure."

Ke threaded past a group of soldiers and hailed them. "Still milking that leg wound I see," Ke said.

"Indeed," Black Knee said. "I was just telling Legs that it appears I'll have to bed with him and his crew of women."

"Maybe I need a leg wound," Ke said.

"You've got plenty of admirers," Black Knee said. "Leave the leg wounds to us less favored folk. Besides, I thought you were helping Argoth with this forcing, which means you won't be using a bed anyway tonight."

"No, I've got other duties."

"Oh, other duties he says. Would these be duties with that milk maid from Grib?"

Ke groaned. "No. A bit of eyes and ears work."

"Ah," said Black Knee. "Well, watch out for Fir-Noy dreadman. That's all I can tell you."

"We shall," Ke said. "But I'm not going to be gone long. I'll be back in an hour or so. You keep a bed warm for me." He turned to Talen and fished about in his pocket. "I've been meaning to give you something. I thought I'd better do it before all of the chaos tomorrow will bring." He removed a length of ivory from a pocket.

The ivory was carved all over with intricate designs and banded in silver. Parts of it had yellowed. "Da's sending," Talen said and took the ivory.

It was like a whistle, as long as a finger, but a little thicker. There was a hole carved in one end that would allow it to be strung on a necklace. It was heavier than it appeared. A sending was supposed to be able to allow someone in the world of the flesh to communicate with the dead. Talen said, "I thought Da said these didn't work."

Ke shrugged. "I don't know the lore. But I'm not giving it to you to call the dead. I thought you'd like to have it to remember him by."

Da had secrets. Even Ke and River didn't know them all. He had been the head root of the Grove of the Order of Hismayas here in the New Lands. He was obviously a man of great power. Who knew? Maybe he had actually called the dead with this.

"Thank you," Talen said. The relationship between him and Ke had changed since the battle in the stone-wight's warren. They'd become closer. Talen had always wanted to be like his older brother, always wanted Ke to be proud of him. A great sense of gratitude welled up in him at this gift.

"There are many stories of sendings working," said Legs. "I think the legends are true."

Ke looked down at Legs with his wild hair. "Oh?"

"My ancestor, he saw one of the shining ones."

The shining ones were those from the world of the dead who had made the perilous journey to the great brightness and clothed themselves in flame. A soul all by itself was a weak thing, but clothed in everlasting burnings it became formidable. Of course, there were more than the souls of men who journeyed to the great brightness.

"You sure it wasn't an herb-induced hallucination?" asked Black Knee. "Some old reprobate in your line?"

"He was indeed a reprobate, but I don't think it was something he smoked."

"So what happened?" asked Talen.

"Old Ethem was on a great cliff running from a bear. He knew he was going to die one way or the other. So he figured it would be better to die quick at the bottom of the cliff instead of in bits and pieces to the bear. He blew his sending and yelled for his grandfather, but just as Ethem was about to jump, that bear stopped. It walked back and forth a number of times as if something stood between it and its prey. Then it spooked. Ran off as if Ethem himself was the predator."

"Sometimes bears bluff a charge," said Ke.

"True," said Legs. "But Ethem swore he saw the ancestor. Saw him like a flame. And then he was gone. Didn't even linger to bind Ethem to a task."

"All those old stories," Talen said. "Why don't you hear about the ancestors visiting someone now?"

"You do," Legs said.

"Not like that."

Black Knee nodded. "The dead seem to only communicate with the dead these days."

"There are many things that are yet mysteries," said Ke. "I don't doubt the tale. Maybe this Ethem was spared for great things."

"No," said Legs. "He was tried and executed not much later for stealing his own lord's mare."

Black Knee laughed. "Which goes to show there's no sense saving a man who lacks brains."

Ke looked at Talen. "Do we just give up on you now then?" he asked.

"Har," Talen said.

Ke grinned and clapped Talen on the shoulder. "Hold your course. Make Da proud."

"I will," Talen said and put the sending in his pocket.

Ke bid them a goodnight, then made his way to the stables.

"That's a fine thing for your brother to give you."

"Aye," said Talen. It was a very fine thing.

By this time the sun had sunk low in the west. The shadows of the fortress walls stretched almost all the way across the bailey. The cooks and their helpers began cleaning up, the smoke of their extinguished fires filtering away. A number of hammers put on their gear went out to patrol or change places with those on the walls. Others were moving to their barracks. A few of the washerwomen who slept with Sugar's fist in the grain cellar were retiring as well.

"Looks like it's time to haul my carcass up," said Black Knee. He motioned at Talen. "Give me a hand, will you? This leg is going to be murder."

Ringing the inner wall of the fortress were two stories of buildings. Barracks ran along two sides. Each fist had its own quarters. Talen's and Black Knee's was on the second level.

Talen looked at the big man. "Murder on me you mean."

"You're young and strapping," Black Knee said. "I'll be like a feather." He used a staff to get to his feet and groaned.

Legs had stopped running his fingers over his da's skull.

"Do you need help finding your way?" Talen asked.

"No," Legs said. "This bailey is easy."

So they bid Legs good evening and, despite his odd craving, Talen helped the big man up the stairs to their quarters on the second level. There were two rooms to each fist's quarters. The backroom held twelve bunks, three to each wall. The front room, where the men stowed their weapons and gear, was smaller.

Black Knee moved to the back room. Talen lingered in the front room. He used a striker to light one of the lamps, then pulled out Da's sending and examined it in the light.

A moment later Black Knee shouted. There was some banging, then the dark body of a weem came flying out the door and landed on the floor by Talen's feet. A weem was a large relative to the centipede. It was big enough to eat mice and had a poisoned bite.

Talen scrambled back, but the weem was dead.

"I'm going to kill Crane," Black Knee said.

Talen put the sending down, then walked into the back room with the lamp and found Black Knee standing next to his bed. A small cord hung down from the upper bunk.

"He had it hanging right here," Black Knee said. "Its legs were on my face!"

Talen smiled. Crane was such the jokester. "You sure he put it there?"

"Who else?" Black Knee said.

Talen helped Black Knee search for other surprises. When they'd cleared the room, he went back to sit at the table and examine the sending. Some of the whorls and loops on its exterior had symbols carved into them, but Talen didn't know what any of them meant. Nor did he have any guess how a person was supposed to use this to enhance his words so that his dead ancestors might hear them.

He remembered one old story of an ancient king who lived in a desert and used a sending to speak with his ancestors to help him find a new well during a drought. In another story, shining ones had crowded into the room of a greedy and arrogant man who was contemplating the murder of his brother. With the eyes of so many ancestors upon him, he gave up his plans. But only for a while. He eventually murdered his brother and turned to wicked magics, trying to avoid death. He lived far longer than he should have, but death caught him anyway. He went weeping into the world of souls because there were none that would guide him to brightness. Some tales said he wandered there still, a ravening and mad soul.

But those tales and others he'd heard were of people dead many ages ago. He turned the sending in his hand. Wouldn't it be marvelous to talk to Da again? And to visit with Mother?

He blew on the sending. "Da," he said quietly. "I hope you are safe." The image of Da, his booming laugh, his great strength rose in his mind. Talen mused on the many hours he'd spent teaching Talen how to draw and aim his bow.

It was just a little over three months now since Da had been killed by the Devourer, his soul and Fire ripped from his human body and stuffed into one of her monsters of earth. But Da had not become her servant. Talen had released him from that body with the Skir Master's raveler.

Talen did not weep at the memories any longer, but there was a huge hollow inside where Da had been. He wondered if that emptiness in his heart would ever leave.

"Hoy," a voice sounded from the doorway.

Talen looked up to see Flax standing there.

"So this is where my accomplice lives." Flax held up the jug of wine he'd won from Eresh. "You didn't get your fair portion. I saved you some. I suggest you drink it before your fist mates come back and gulp it all down." He held it out to Talen.

Talen took the jug. "Thanks," he said.

"Go on, have a sip. You earned it."

Talen uncorked it and sniffed. It smelled delicious. "You know, the Creek Widow says none of us should drink spirits. Says it weakens the defenses of your soul."

"That Creek Widow," said Flax and shook his head. "A little drink can't hurt a flea. Moderation is the key. Even Eresh gave the troops drink."

Talen brought the jug to his lips and took a drink. It was sweet and smooth.

Flax fished a crock out of his pocket. "I also brought something for the big man's leg."

"Who is that?" Black Knee called out from the back.

"Someone come to make sure your leg doesn't rot off," Flax said.

A moment later Black Knee came hobbling out of the back room.

Flax held out the crock. "This is old country. Put on a clean smear every morning and night. Being multiplied will do most of the work for you, but this will cut the healing time down by half."

Black Knee took the crock, removed the lid, and sniffed it. "It doesn't smell very potent."

"Stink doesn't heal," said Flax. "Trust me. It's plenty strong."

"What I need," said Black Knee, "is some more of the Creek Widow's goat's milk, laced with a little of the poppy."

"Ah," said Flax. "I thought you looked a little too much at ease. Now, that is a drink you do need to be careful of. We don't want to be too much at ease, not with what I heard happened in Redthorn. Or with that thing in the river."

"Aye," said Black Knee.

"You think Mokad's turning the fish against us?" Talen asked.

"I don't believe much in coincidence," said Flax. "Not where Divines are concerned."

At that moment the horn sounded giving the troops a half hour warning to get to their quarters before curfew.

Flax said, "Well, looks like I'd better get back to my quarters before some nanny catches me out past my bedtime. You two sleep well."

"Oh, I'm already primed for a wicked dream," said Black Knee.

Flax turned to Talen. "Reward yourself, boy."

"I will," said Talen, putting his hand on the jug.

A look of satisfaction flashed across Flax's face. "See you on the morrow lads." Then he exited.

Black Knee set the salve on the table. "I think I'm liking these foreign sleth more each day."

"Yes," Talen said. He looked down at the jug of wine. "Do you think Sugar got any?"

Black Knee unwrapped his awful wound and placed the bandage on the table. "If you want to woo her, you need to use some brains to out-think your competition."

"Who said I was wooing?"

"You did with all those looks and sighs."

"I wasn't sighing."

"You were melting like butter in the summer sun."

"Sugar's a friend."

"And that's what she'll stay unless you use your brains."

Talen waited.

"If you're going to give a woman a gift," Black Knee said, "you want to make it a true gift."

"How is wine not a true gift?"

"You want to give her a thing that is exactly what she wants or needs, but is precisely not what she is expecting. Give her a surprise like that, and she'll be filled with delight. It shows you've been thinking about *her* wants, not just yours. So the wine is good. It's a nice gesture, but any fool can take wine. You want to take what she is wanting, maybe without even knowing it."

"That sounds good, but what does she want or need?"

"Use your brains, man. What were she and the boy carrying around like it was made of gold?"

"Their da's skull."

"And what does that skull need?"

Talen imagined it in her bag, jostling around, getting banged about. Insight blossomed. "It needs a place where it can be protected. A small box."

Black Knee touched his nose, then pointed at him. "Now you're thinking."

"Make it pretty," said Talen. "Fill it with straw."

"That's the way to a woman's heart. Add some flattery, and a strict rule to never discuss her bunions. And a manly chest, like I myself possess, and you might be in the running. But, of course, you're just friends."

"Right," said Talen.

Black Knee examined the wound on his thigh, then dipped his finger into the crock Flax had left and gingerly smeared a bit around the stitching.

"A box will take time," Talen said. "So I can take the wine tonight. A box tomorrow." He picked up the jug.

"So says the young man who wasn't sighing. But you're still forgetting something."

"What?"

"I don't know about Sugar, but most women don't fancy the smell of horse sweat."

15

Ferret

SUGAR FOUND the Creek Widow in the great hall. She spent about a half an hour helping the other women heat water and make a special tea before the Creek Widow spotted her and marched over. "What do you think you're doing?" she demanded.

"Getting the tea ready for the candidates and warming blankets."

"Nonsense. The biggest thing you can do to help is take care of that body of yours. The last thing we need is a sick fist member."

"I feel fine."

"Did you not hear me? You go get some rest. Now be gone," the Creek Widow said and shooed her out of the hall.

So Sugar left the women. Outside, the sun had sunk below the horizon, and the deep shadows of evening were gathering in the bailey. She turned back to her quarters and saw Talen on the other side of the bailey by the kitchens with his shirt off and a pot of water at his feet, soaping his chest and armpits.

These last few months of work with the weaves and lore had changed him. She could see it in his walk and the thickening of the muscles in his limbs and chest. If they were horses, Ke would be a big destrier. Talen, on the other hand, was turning out to be more of a courser, built for a different purpose. His slick shoulders and chest looked quite nice from this angle. Surprisingly nice.

She and Talen had started out at the same place in their slethery, competing against each other, but he had outdistanced her. Ke and River now took him out for special lessons sometimes, but it was clear he was bred for great things.Or terrible things. The Devourer had, after all, claimed him as hers down in the stone-wight warren.

Talen began to wipe his arm with a cloth and saw her watching him. She waved a small hello. He grinned, then soap ran from his hair into his eyes and he fumbled for the rinse pot.

Sugar crossed to the cellar where she and the other fell-maidens slept. Soft candlelight spilled out the open door onto the paving stones of the bailey. The cellar was full of barrels of grain and other food, beds, and a cage with three ferrets. Ferrets, in addition to being muzzled and sent into a hole to scare up rabbits into the teeth of hunting dogs or the cudgels of the hare beaters, were also used to hunt mice and smaller rats. A cat was good. But in a room like this, stacked with barrels, there were too many places a cat could not go. And so the ferret master had tasked Sugar and the others with releasing the ferrets each night to hunt any vermin who thought it clever to steal the lord's food.

Two candles illuminated the bunks and the stacked barrels of barley, wheat, and peas. The Mistress, a handsome, large-boned woman with big hands, two of the other washerwomen who slept there, and Legs were talking with Urban.

They all looked up when she entered.

"There's our beautiful Koramite warrior now," said the Mistress. "Although why you'd want a young inexperienced thing I cannot tell."

The bruise about Urban's eye was deep purple. He said, "I'm surely not worthy of one such as yourself."

"I'll be the judge of that," said the Mistress. "Besides, you've already seen the bruising that one gives her suitors."

"Lucky for me," Urban said, "I'm actually here on other business. Sugar's being reassigned to another hammer."

She wondered if she'd offended Commander Eresh with her comments earlier. She said, "I think I like my fist, thank you very much." Besides, she couldn't imagine the Creek Widow allowing her fist of fell-maidens to be broken up.

Urban looked over at the three ferrets. Two were normal black and brown with bandit mask coloring. The third was white. He reached through with a finger and scratched one of the bandits behind the ear. It enjoyed the scratch for a moment, then bounded away. "Ferrets are interesting fellows," he said. "A bit too much musk for my taste, but they sneak into places cats and terriers cannot. Quiet useful, wouldn't you agree?"

She folded her arms. "Sure," she agreed.

He reached into the sack he carried and retrieved the yellow cloth that held her mother's necklace. He unwrapped it and held up the necklace. "Every army needs a ferret or three to chase things out into the light that others cannot."

"What has that got to do with my mother's necklace?"

He smiled. "Come outside with me, and we'll chat."

"I've got a better idea," said the Mistress. "How about *she* goes outside and you chat with *me*?"

"And risk the safety of my brilliant parts?" Urban asked.

"You haven't seen anything yet, honey pot." She patted the bed beside her. "Stay a while."

"Duty calls," said Urban with mock regret.

"Duty keeps a cold bed."

"Alas," Urban said. "I shall rehearse the memory of your face to keep me warm."

The Mistress sighed. "Talker." She turned to Sugar. "You be careful, girl. Foreigners are slippery things."

"I shall remember that," Sugar said. And, indeed, she would. Despite what he'd done for her, she didn't quite trust this Urban. Still, she followed him out of the cellar and back into the bailey. An apple tree grew over by a plot of ground next to the great hall that was used as a garden. The garden had been used for normal vegetables when Shim's army had come here, and a few rows of kale still grew, but most of it was godsweed now. Urban led her to a bench in the dark evening shadows under the apple tree.

Across the way, a now-clothed Talen emerged from the base of the stairway leading up to his barracks on the second story. He was carrying a jug and walked quickly across the bailey to her cellar and disappeared inside. A few moments later he walked out again without the jug. He paused at the doorway and looked about the bailey, then spotted her and Urban. For a moment she thought he'd come their way, but he turned and walked back to the stair.

Urban patted the bench next to him. She sat down. He smelled nice: a little of man mixed with some spiced oil he had in his hair that had mint in it. Above them the first stars of evening shone in the dark blue sky.

"Your mother left you an incredible gift," he said and held out the cloth and necklace to her.

She took them. "This is a weave of some sorts, isn't it?"

"Did you mother talk much about the dead?"

"No more than anyone else," she said. Then she stopped. That wasn't entirely true.

"What?" he asked.

"Well, she told me once she'd met her great, great grandmother. But I could never figure out how."

Urban nodded.

"I know she saw things later with the Devourer. When she died, she said she was going to help my da. Said something was wrong in the world of souls. But that didn't have anything to do with this necklace."

Urban said, "I'm sorry she's not here. Your mother was quite the lore mistress. That isn't just a common weave. With it you can see things, go places that others cannot."

What was he talking about?

"We're fairly sure it will let you send a portion of your soul forth into the yellow world."

The yellow world was the world of souls and skir. Sugar was taken aback. Such things were only done in tales told at the ale-house.

"Argoth and Matiga both agree that you need to be trained."

Sugar looked down at the necklace.

"Once you can soul walk, you can go behind enemy lines without being seen, gather intelligence. You can direct a hammer of men so we can hit the enemy the hardest or avoid being seen."

Sugar marveled that her mother would have such a thing. And for not the first time she wondered how much her mother really knew. "I would leave my body? Isn't separating soul from body dangerous?"

"Very much so," he said. "But becoming a fell-maiden is dangerous. Taking a swim in your river, it appears, can be dangerous. People have killed themselves digging in the garden."

It seemed odd, them trusting her with such a thing. "Why me? Why not use it yourself?" Despite his pleasant nature, there was something secretive about Urban.

"Because I cannot."

"You mean you won't. You don't want to risk it yourself."

"No," he said. "I would if I could. But I cannot. The weave itself prevents me, which was made very clear when I picked it up in Redthorn."

Sugar knew of two kinds of weaves. There were wildweaves that could be handled by anyone. Dreadmen used such. Their weaves of might would magnify any who put them on. But there were other weaves that only someone with lore could use. "You don't know its operation, but you expect I will? My mother never spoke a word about the lore to me."

"Someone of great skill can weave a part of themselves into a weave. A very small part of themselves, but enough to recognize friend from foe. They act as gatekeepers."

She narrowed her eyes and looked at the weave. "A piece of my mother is in there?"

"Maybe. Or maybe not. It looks old. It could be from an ancestor or someone else entirely. Every natural weave requires a soul. Some just a little. Some substantially more. Your body is a weave, and the soul and Fire quickens it. This type of weave requires more soul than a dreadman's weave of might. And that soul protects it. Not like you protect your body, but the principle is the same. And that's to be expected with weaves of such power. You can't have just anyone using them. There must be a way to recognize authorized use. Whoever is there recognizes you as friend. That is why you did not feel the pricking of daggers that I did."

"Someone is in here?" she asked again, not quite willing to believe.

"In a manner of speaking," he said.

Mother, Sugar thought. But then she tamped down that idea. It was possible the weave had been handed down to her from some relative or friend. But if Mother had indeed put herself in it . . .

"Can you speak to the soul inside?" Sugar asked.

"It doesn't work that way."

"Why not? Have you tried?"

"I have not," he said. "But others have. It's not . . . reliable. It's not a complete soul, only a portion."

Sugar didn't understand why that would matter. But even so, the possibility that a living part of her mother was there, in her hand—her heart lurched.

After a few moments, Urban said, "You're very quiet."

"I don't know what to say."

"We want you to become part of my crew. I proposed the idea to Argoth earlier. He agreed to it. But I'm not the type to force. The Order of Hismayas has its fine points, but I also disagree with it over a number of things. You've already met Soddam and know the kinds of people you'll be dealing with."

She'd be dealing with true sleth—a possible problem, but not the biggest. "I don't know enough lore."

"You can learn the lore. You're quick, and you won't be doing it alone. You'll be working with someone familiar with that place."

"Someone in your crew?"

"Our cook," he said, "who makes honeyed buns that would tempt the Creators themselves. What do you say?"

"And Argoth knows and agrees with your intentions?"

"I wouldn't have the weave otherwise. Mokad is here, and Shim needs eyes. This is an opportunity, Sugar. It might well be that the information you provide will give mankind the power to stand."

"That's a lot to expect," she said.

"Well, you're Purity's daughter," he said as if that explained everything.

She considered him. This was Mother's, and she'd sent her to find it. She obviously wanted it to be used. And if Zu Argoth had agreed, who was she to gainsay him? "Tell me what I have to do," she said.

"Later we can talk about what you owe me for this black eye, but what I need now is your hand."

She felt a small apprehension, but pushed it aside. She turned her hand palm up and offered it to him.

He took her hand in his. His skin was rough and warm. "You said you didn't know the lore well enough. Tell me what you know of the three vitalities and how they operate."

The three vitalities, the powers in all living beings, were flesh, soul, and Fire. Everyone learned that as a child. Those who were blessed by the Creators could use the vitalities to work wonders. Sugar repeated this, then told him what River had taught her these last months and what she'd learned about the Devourers and their fight to subdue humans.

When she finished, he said, "Very good. Now I'm going to teach you something new. Just as there is an intimacy of flesh, there is also an intimacy of soul. And just as you protect your flesh, you want to be able to protect your other vitalities. I want to see your defense."

Suddenly she felt something change inside her. A moment later it felt as if someone was taking all her air. She couldn't breathe. She struggled to pull her hand free from Urban's grasp, but he would not let go.

Then as suddenly as it had come, the menacing presence departed, and she took in a great breath.

He shook his head in disapproval. "A weave opens up a door to the soul," he said. "That's how they operate. And if you're not careful, anyone with the skill will walk right through it. Do you understand?"

She yanked her hand away.

"Do you understand?"

She was breathing hard. "I wasn't ready."

"The Grove here." He shook his head in disapproval. "They haven't taught you how to close the doors of your soul?"

"They have," she said. "I'm just not as quick with it as some."

"You're going to need to be. This is what you will practice tonight and tomorrow and the next day and the next until it's second nature." He held his hand out for her to take it again.

"If you misuse me," she said in warning.

"If I misuse you at any time, you are free to go," he said. "I told you I do not compel those who follow me."

Sugar gave him her hand. "What about curfew?"

"An exception has been made," he said.

They spent what must have been the better part of an hour there under the apple tree by the garden, the sky fading to black, the stars coming out to shine in the darkness above, Urban holding her hand, prompting her and probing her soul. At first, all she could think of was his terrifying presence. But after the dozenth try, she suddenly figured out how to close her doors against him. Her relief was immense. But he didn't stop. He forced her to continue to open and close, and as she gained more control, she noticed how gently he held her hand.

Eventually, he told her it was time to take a rest and broke contact. She could still feel where he had held her, and she could still feel the workings of her soul. It was like suddenly finding you had a new limb.

"You will practice that until it's as natural to you as breathing," he said. "That one skill alone will save your life many times over."

"Why don't they teach that earlier?"

"Because the Grove follows the techniques used by the Divines, and the Divines don't want their dreadmen learning much lore. But we're not tools of the Divines, are we?"

"I think you'd be hard put to accuse the Creek Widow of being a tool."

"True enough," he said.

She looked at him. "So if you're not of Hismayas, then what are you?"

"We can talk about that another time. You just remember that the closing defense not only protects you with weaves in general, but it's required to use your mother's weave safely. When you walk, you open your doors, and you must be able to shut them again. Now, I think you need to begin to learn one more thing. I want you to put the weave on. Have you learned how to give and take Fire?"

"We were just beginning that."

"There are a number of ways to quicken weaves. Some require one method, some another. This weave, if I'm not mistaken, just needs you to feed it Fire."

Sugar put the necklace on.

"Can you feel the weave's pattern?"

"River's tried to help me with this, but the patterns make no sense."

"Just be calm. Open your doors."

"There's nothing."

"Feel."

Sugar concentrated on the weave. "It's a tangle."

"Focus on the tangle," he said. "See if you can't follow one thread."

Sugar focused. She found a thread, lost it, found another. She tried to follow this one, but it kept slipping from her just as it had every time River tried to help her in these last few weeks. She sighed heavily. "I can't do this."

"If you say you can't, you never will. Why do you think you should be able to do this hard thing on the very first try?"

Above them the moon had come out. A wind had also picked up, and she felt a chill. "It's not my first attempt."

"Why should you expect to succeed on the tenth, fourteenth, or even twentieth try? Where is that written? Keep at it. If you can find a thread, you can learn to feel the pattern. Once you do that, you will find the weave's mouth. And then it's just a matter of sharing your Fire."

Sugar concentrated one last time, but the threads slipped away. "I'll try," she said.

"Good," he said and stood, his eyes glittering in the moonlight. "Very good. I will tell Argoth it appears Shim's army will soon have itself a ferret."

* * *

Sugar walked with Urban back to her cellar. At the doors, he bid her good-night. Then she hurried inside to get out of the chill and shut the door behind her. The cellar was pitch dark. She listened for a moment and heard the slight snore of the Mistress. She also heard the patter of small feet somewhere off to the left behind the barrels, which meant Legs must have opened the cage to let the ferrets out to do their work.

She tiptoed over to her bunk and sat down on it, holding the weave in her hand. She couldn't quite believe she was going to walk in the world of souls. She thought of her mother and father—would she be able to find them there? She sat up straight. Was that possible?

Something stirred in her bed. "Talen was by," Legs whispered.

"I saw," she whispered back.

"Left you some wine."

That was thoughtful of him. There were a number of other girls who talked about him. He'd certainly been enjoying himself with that sailor's daughter a few days ago.

"I think the Mistress drank half of it," Legs said.

"Figures," she said.

"So?" Legs whispered.

"You should be sleeping," she whispered.

"What did your foreigner want?"

She took a breath. "He wants me in his crew."

"The crew nobody sees?"

"I saw them."

"I don't know if you should trust this Urban. I overheard River and Ke talking about him. They themselves don't know what to think."

"Argoth agreed to his idea. So even if he is a bit dangerous, I'm not going to protest. Besides, there's more to it than that." She found Legs's hand and pressed the necklace into it. For some reason he picked up on patterns faster than anyone. "Feel this," she said.

Legs ran his fingers over the segments of the necklace. "It's a weave."

She envied his quick ability. "It's Mother's."

Legs was feeling each of the figurines, running each of the segments through his fingers. "This pattern is strange."

"Oh, is that what the great Kain Legs says?"

"Well, it doesn't feel like one of the weaves of might."

"That's because it does something very different. And it's made differently. This one has a guardian of sorts in it."

"I've heard of that," whispered Legs.

Sugar sighed in exasperation. Did everyone know more than she? "Were they taking you out for special lessons as well?"

"I can't help it if I hear things," said Legs. "River was talking."

"The point is, well, who do you think it might be?"

"How should I know?"

"Think," she said and waited.

Legs kept fingering the weave and then suddenly stopped. He grabbed her hand. "Mother?"

"It could be," she said. "But even if it's not, this weave lets you walk in the world of souls."

"You could talk to Mother and Da," he said, his voice full of excitement and wonder.

"Maybe. Of course, that's not what my job will be." She told him about Urban's offer to spy behind enemy lines.

"Do you think Mokad will bring soul walkers here?"

She hadn't thought of that frightening prospect. "I suppose so."

"They could be here now, watching us this very moment."

"Now you're scaring me."

"I could be a Walker," said Legs. "I could fight as a Walker."

"I don't know—"

"You'd bar me from the one thing that would make me useful?"

"We only have one weave."

"We can make another."

She sighed. "We can ask, although you'd think Argoth and the others would have done so if they knew the lore. But we'll see. In the meantime, they're expecting me to learn."

"But you'll ask," he said.

"I promise."

He felt along the segments a bit longer. Then she told him to scoot over, and she climbed in bed next to him. When she was in the bed, Legs snuggled up. His feet were warm. She put her arm around him, and soon his breathing changed to match the breathing of the women sleeping about them.

She took the necklace from him and again tried to follow a thread, listening to the ferrets scamper and patter in the darkness over and between the stacked barrels.

16

Yellow Dream

TALEN LAY ON his bunk thinking of the events of the day, listening to the members of his fist in their beds and the wind whistling along the door and window of the front room. He'd been able to gather some wood for Sugar's box, but now wondered if the idea was silly. She'd seemed very content holding Urban's hand under that apple tree. Blasted foreigners—what was it about them that fascinated all the ladies?

Out on the balcony, a fist of men moved past the front window. They were going to the great hall to be quickened. Talen still remembered the day Da had put the weave of godsweed about his arm. Not knowing what it was or what Da was doing, he'd worn it. Da had wanted to begin Talen's awakening to the power. And it had awakened him. It had multiplied him like a dreadman and almost killed him.

Every person had different capabilities. Some were of a breed that could multiply themselves more than others. Some, with even the most powerful of weaves upon them, might feel no effect at all. Talen multiplied with only the slightest touch of power. That's why his Da's weave had almost killed him. He hoped these candidates fared better than he did that first time. And may the Six preserve them from his maddening lust. He could feel the desire gnawing at him even now, but put it out of his mind and thought about how he was going to join the edges of Sugar's skull box.

Outside, the wind gusted and blew along the walls. The grogginess of sleep descended upon him more quickly than usual, and suddenly he was dreaming of the Apple Dance, of succulent meat pies, and dancing with Sugar and the girl who sold vegetables in Stag Horn. Then his mind turned to the Sourwood River that ran past the fortress. He dreamt he was with Ke, fighting a tentacled creature. One of its arms shot out of the water and wrapped around Talen's leg. He felt the tug, the sharp pricks of its barbs. Ke fought the creature, tried to save Talen, but the creature yanked him under the water.

And then Talen was back in his fist's bunkroom. He could see the faces and exposed arms of the members of his fist as they slept. There was a yellow cast to the room. In it the skin of his fistmates shone as if there was a light within. He hungered for that light.

He moved like smoke from his bunk to the one below, flowing over Black Knee. He flowed to the others in turn. He dreamed he was the creature in the river, sending out a long smoky tentacle to taste the candidates in the room.

The oldest member of their fist was of the Vargon clan. He wore a withy weave about his wrist. A small tendril of Fire, thinner than a spider's thread, rose from the weave and dissipated into the air.

Talen-as-smoke swallowed the Fire up. But when the small thread was gone, he was not satisfied, and so he sent his shadowy self out of the room and onto the balcony, slipping through the cracks of the shutters of the adjacent quarters, tasting the men in their sleep and finding nothing. One man lay on his back awake, fingering a knife.

Talen had dreamed this dream before. It the last few weeks it had come with increasing frequency. He'd leave his chamber, like a smoke, and travel about the fortress. Tonight he wanted to see the river, and so he slipped his long and twisting self up to the battlements. The world of his dream was cast in yellow twilight. About him the towers rose into the night, repair platforms still hanging down their lengths. He moved unnoticed among the soldiers keeping watch and rose above the battlements. Just a little ways away, the Sourwood River flowed like a shining black ribbon out to the bay.

He thought about dipping into that river to see what lay beneath the surface but something caught his eye on the outside of the fortress wall. Something dark. It was a man scaling the sheer stone face with a rope, moving as quick as a dreadman. Talen flowed down the side of the fortress to get a better look at him.

The man was clad in dark cloth, but did not wear the clothes of Shim's army. His wrists and honors were exposed, showing he was not of any clan in the New Lands. An intruder then. On his neck clung a small thing, all gray and twisted. Talen looked closer and saw it was a fright the size of a large grasshopper.

Talen pulled back in disgust, but the man seemed not to notice and continued to climb. Was he a spy or an assassin? Or one of Argoth's visitors? Either way, a warning needed to be sounded. Talen raced back up the wall to the guards and tried to alert them, but they couldn't hear. One man put a finger to his nose and blew a snotty discharge out and over the wall into the night.

Talen raced back down the battlement to where the rope had been thrown over the wall and peered over only to find the man right there—an inch from Talen's face!

In his bunk, Talen started awake, his breath catching in his throat. He saw double, the man on the wall in the yellow dream world and the darkness of the bunk room. It was disorienting, frightening. Then his dream flowed back from the wall, down and back into his room, and he was left lying on his back, looking at the dark ceiling with the longing for Fire still coursing through him.

He blew out a breath and became annoyed. This awakening to the power was like a burr in his small clothes. He tried to fall back to sleep, but the image of his dream was still too vivid in his mind. Besides, Black Knee and another one of his fist mates were snoring. So Talen silently got out of bed and dropped to the floor. He slipped to the front room, thought about dressing, but decided not to. He opened the front door and stepped out onto the balcony in nothing but his underwear. He shouldn't technically be here with the curfew, but it was only for a moment to clear his mind. The cold wind stole along his belly. The stones beneath his bare feet were chill, but he welcomed the cold. He crossed to the stone railing and leaned on it to look out over the bailey below.

The wind gusted strongly. A flash of lightning briefly lit the inner walls of the fortress, but the sound took a few seconds to arrive. He looked up at the night sky and realized the storm must still be some distance away because the sky here was still clear enough to see the stars.

He listened to the wind and watched the empty bailey and movement of sentries upon the far walls. And a man cried out. At least, that's what it sounded like over the wind.

Talen cocked his head. The wind had masked it, but he was sure he'd heard something.

He poked his head out of one of the wide arched openings along the balcony and looked down, but nobody was there in the windy shadows of the night. When he pulled himself back in, a dark figure swung through one of the arched openings farther down the balcony on a rope and dropped to the floor.

Talen froze.

It was the man from his dream. The one with the fright clinging to his neck.

17

Slayer

THIS WAS IMPOSSIBLE. Was he still in a dream?

"Who goes there?" Talen asked. His voice rang loud and clear along the balcony. He was most assuredly *not* in a dream.

The man said nothing. Instead, he sprang from his crouch toward Talen. He was fast. Too fast. And Talen knew he didn't have time to fetch a weapon from his quarters.

"Breach!" Talen shouted, hoping the wind didn't drown out his cries. "On the balcony!" Then he turned and sped toward the stairs, pulling the governor weave from his arm.

The man sprinted after him with terrifying speed. Talen flared his Fire, but knew it would take a moment to build. Knew it wasn't going to come quickly enough for him to outrun the man. He looked at the bailey below. He could lead the man out into the open there. Talen leapt up to the lip of the balcony's stone railing. With the next step he soared out over the bailey.

He yelled as he jumped, trying to maintain the right body position for landing. Surely somebody would hear him! He sailed over a cart, hoping his training would pay off and he wouldn't twist his ankle. When he landed, he collapsed into a roll that flung him back to his feet, and ran toward the gates where someone would be on watch.

But the dark form of the attacker flew over Talen's head and beyond. The man landed and rolled, and was on his feet in front of Talen, blocking his escape.

"Guards!" Talen shouted. "Intruder!" He turned and sprinted back toward the barracks and the stair that led up to the battlements. He needed a weapon.

Upon the walls, a number of soldiers called out.

"Behind me!" Talen shouted. "Somebody shoot!"

The man was silent and quick, and if the guards above didn't move, Talen would soon be bleeding his life out into the cobblestones of the bailey.

Barrack doors opened. Three candidates rushed into the bailey wearing nothing but their small clothes. Two more exited from a room father down, but at least they had weapons.

"Here!" Talen shouted.

The candidates charged. Talen flew past them trying to get his own weapon.

One of the candidates behind him grunted. Another cried out in pain. Talen glanced back and saw the candidates fall to the ground.

Talen fled to the stairs. His Fire had finally built, and the vigor coursed through him, multiplying his strength and speed. He took the stairs five at a time.

Behind him the dreadman reached the stairs and began to follow him up. Talen sped higher, but the dreadman was quicker. He caught Talen just as he reached the second story.

Talen turned to fight, expected to feel a sword run him through. Instead the man bore him to the ground. Talen tried to strike out, but the dreadman punched him twice. Once in the gut, stealing all breath from him. Then in the forehead with the palm of his hand, bouncing the back of Talen's head off the stone floor, dazing him. While Talen tried to regain his senses, the dreadman hefted Talen over his shoulder like a sack of turnips and stood.

And that's when Talen knew the dreadman wasn't an assassin or spy.

Shouts and calls of alarm rose around the bailey. Out on the balcony, candidates began to pour out of their rooms. The dreadman paid them no mind. He raced up the stairs.

Flax's words rang in Talen's mind—there were no coincidences with Divines.

Fear shot up Talen's back. He was not going to be taken! Not back to some Divine. Not back to one of the Devourers.

He tried to twist from the man's grasp. He kicked, but the man held him fast. Then he saw how he could strike. He arched up as far as he could, then curled himself down, slamming his elbow into the man's kidneys.

The man grunted, but did not loosen his grip. Talen rose up to do it again, but the man slammed Talen to his feet. He punched Talen in the gut so hard it knocked the breath out of him. Then the dreadman pulled out a cord and began to tie Talen's wrists.

Talen regained his breath and tried to headbutt the man in the face, but the dark dreadman turned to the side, and Talen headbutted the man's shoulder instead.

At that moment guards from the battlements above came rushing down the dark stairs with axes and swords.

"Here!" Talen shouted.

The dreadman moved down two steps and drew his sword. More candidates entered the stairway below, blocking the dreadman's retreat.

Talen saw his chance and shot up the stairway. "He's a full dreadman," he shouted.

The men charging down the stair recognized him, and they let Talen push through. He needed a weapon. An axe or sword would be best in these close quarters. Even a staff would be good. He ran to the top of the stair and out onto the battlement, but there was nothing here except bundles of stones and arrows. But there were weapons in the tower. He sprinted down the wall walk to find one.

Shouts rose from behind, and the dreadman emerged from the stairway.

Regrets eyes! Talen didn't need a weapon, he needed an army!

The wind gusted. Lightning flickered, illuminating a large storm blowing in. All about the fortress men yelled shouts of alarm. Bows twanged and Talen hoped they weren't shooting at his attacker from directly behind.

The dreadman sprinted after Talen, and Talen knew he wasn't going to make the tower door. He looked down the wall at the dark shadow of the bailey below. He'd already tried jumping. What he needed to do was go somewhere that would slow the dreadman down. Expose him so the archers might be able to aim.

The moonlight shone on a work platform with repairs materials on it. Men had been assigned to repair the mortar there, removing any plants that had been growing and applying a coat of limewash to make the surface smooth. The platform hung against the outer wall of the tower in front of him, suspended on ropes that ran from a two-armed crane erected at the top.

The platform was a precarious distance away, but Talen didn't see that he had any other choice. Hoardings were being erected over the battlement. He could leap from the hoarding to the platform.

Talen dashed forward, jumped to the top of an uncovered merlon and then up to the plank roof of the hoarding. He ran across the roof to its very edge and leapt for the hanging platform. He sailed out over the wall. The drop to the outer bailey yawned below him. Then he slammed into the platform. The platform swung out with the force of his momentum, moving the crane arms above, and swinging him farther around the tower. The wild swing sent the bucket flying off the platform, and Talen would have followed, but he caught one of the ropes, pulled himself up, and turned.

Behind him, the dreadman raced across the wall walk. Talen had hoped to see a number of candidates chasing him, but there were none. Farther down the battlement was another attacker, keeping a number of candidates busy. A third cluster of candidates fought yet another intruder down in the inner bailey.

"Here!" Talen shouted into the wind, hoping to draw someone's attention.

The dreadman leapt to the hoarding.

Talen had seen this dreadman jump, and this platform wasn't nearly far enough away. There was another platform a little farther around the tower. It was smaller, big enough for only one man to sit upon, and hung a little higher. Talen took a step and leapt for it. But the platform he leapt from was not a sturdy launch. It swung back, stealing part of the power of his jump.

Talen careened through the air toward the other platform. He slammed into it with his side, almost fell the neck-breaking forty feet to the ground, but caught one of the platform's guide ropes. Then instead of climbing up, he used what momentum he had left to run a bit around the tower face, swinging the crane that suspended this platform farther around the tower.

Behind him, the larger platform swung back toward the dreadman. Below, the dreadman leapt from the roof of the hoarding. His jump was astonishing. He sailed up to the first platform and landed on it squarely.

And Talen realized that if the dreadman had caught him in his barracks, he would have had no problem dispatching Talen's fistmates and subduing Talen. He would have done it in the blink of an eye with hardly a sound.

Talen climbed up to stand on the small seat of his platform and immediately saw he wasn't far enough away to escape.

"Holy One," said the dreadman. "One way or the other, we'll have you. It is best come now."

In answer, Talen yanked his main support rope, trying to swing the wooden crane still father away, but the crane arm had moved as far as it was going to go.

The dreadman did not jump for Talen. Instead he stood at one end of his platform and, like a child standing on a tree swing, pushed. He swung forward, swung back, then gave it another push with more power, and this time when he swung forward, the crane swung around and moved the dreadman closer.

Talen looked up. He could climb his ropes. But the dreadman had ropes to climb as well, and that blackheart would reach the top well before Talen did.

Shouts rose from the fortress bailey. Lightning flashed again, illuminating the storm that was almost upon them. Thunder boomed.

"Here!" Talen shouted into the wind. "On the tower!" But the other candidates were too busy. Or they didn't hear him. Or worse, now that he had swung his platform around, they didn't even see him. The first scattered drops of rain kissed Talen's face. Clouds began to scuttle across the face of the moon.

The dreadman pushed his platform again. This was it, Talen thought: the crane holding the dreadman's platform would swing father around, and then it would be but a hop for that dreadman from his platform to Talen's.

There was only one way out. Talen looked down and prepared to drop to the ground that lay much too far below. But the dreadman's platform suddenly lurched and swung back.

There were voices above. Then someone up there grabbed onto one of the ropes, leapt over the battlement, and dropped from the top of the tower above, using the rope to guide his fall.

He was a big man who dropped quickly and landed on the platform with a heavy thud. The platform shuddered. Part of the rope fastened to one corner loosened, and the platform sagged sideways a bit.

Talen recognized the man's big silhouette. He'd recognize it anywhere.

"He's quick!" Talen yelled to warn his brother.

The dreadman struck at Ke, but Ke countered the attack and slammed his fist into the dreadman's face. The dreadman staggered back a step, then drew a knife that flashed in the pale moonlight. He thrust, but Ke grabbed the wrist of his knife hand. The two men held onto a rope with one hand and struggled for the knife with the other.

Men shouted from above. Talen looked up and saw archers leaning out over the edge. But there was no way they could get a good target with Ke and the dreadman struggling in their current grip.

The platform under Ke and the dreadman sagged further, and then the ropes supporting one end gave out altogether. A brush and other repair materials that had been with the bucket all fell, bouncing once off the sloping side of the tower. Moments later, both the dreadman and Ke followed. The two men plummeted, striking the tower wall where it widened. The collision knocked them apart, and they disappeared into the night shadows below.

The wind gusted, howling about the edges of the battlements. If Ke had broken a leg or his back in the fall, he'd be no match for the dreadman.

"Give me slack!" Talen yelled up to the men above. "Drop me down!"

Moments later his platform began to drop, but not quickly enough. When Talen thought he was about twenty feet from the ground, he jumped. It was a foolish thing to do because the exact location of the ground was hidden in the deep moon shadow, and, sure enough, Talen landed just slightly after he expected to and was leaning too far forward. Instead of rolling, he smacked into the ground. It was like being hit with a board. He lay there for a moment, stunned.

A number of yards to his left, in the deep shadows of the wall, there was a grunt, a snarl, the sounds of a struggle.

Back up on the tower the guards yelled for a mark.

"Hold your shots!" Talen shouted.

On the far side of the moonlit outer bailey, a group of soldiers ran to help, but they were headed the wrong way. Talen pushed himself up, and felt around for a rock. But it was all hard dirt and goat-chewed grass. In the darkness a few paces away, Ke and the dreadman wrestled upon the ground. The dreadman broke free and tried to scramble away. Ke lunged after him and caught his foot.

Talen rushed forward and prepared to do damage with a flying kick, but the dreadmen yanked himself free of Ke's grasp. One moment he was there, and the next he was racing away, sprinting for the outer wall.

"There!" someone shouted from the battlement.

Bows twanged. But it was dark, and gusting, and the dreadman was moving fast. The arrows were blown wide. Ke raced after the dreadman. Talen followed.

The bows above thrummed again, but the dreadman was speed itself, a shadow fleeing across the bailey in the dappled moonlight. Ke ran much faster than Talen, but even he could not match the speed of their attacker.

They weren't even halfway across the bailey when the dreadman reached the outer defenses. Lightning exploded in the sky. Deafening thundered blasted the bailey and the stone walls around them. When the flash passed, the dreadman had already gained the top of the outer wall. Lightning cracked again, and the dreadman leapt away in a great arc over the wall and disappeared. A moment later the belly of the sky split open, and the rain poured down.

Ke slowed, then stopped. "Where, by Regret, do they get such speed?"

"Goh," said Talen. "What was he?"

"He wasn't some backwater scum, I can tell you that." Ke held his hand up and looked at it. The two small fingers of his left hand were twisted at odd angles, obviously broken.

The rain fell in sheets, but within the fortress a cry rose above its sound.

At first Talen thought it was another alarm, but then realized it was a cheer.

"Find out what's going on," Ke said.

"What are you going to do?"

"I knocked our visitor's knife out of his hand. I'm going to find it to see if it has any stories to tell."

Talen left Ke and ran back to the fortress gate. He entered the inner bailey and found a group of candidates crowding around a body lying upon the ground. Commander Eresh stood among them. He was livid. "You fool!" he said to Flax.

"I just killed you a dreadman," Flax said.

"You just killed someone we might have gotten to talk."

"He wouldn't have talked."

"He would have talked to me!" Eresh roared. He turned to a group of candidates. "Drag his body into the hall so we can get a better look at him. And bring his head."

Four candidates picked up the body. Another grabbed the severed head that was still dripping gore.

Flax stood to one side, a number of the candidates slapping him on the shoulders in congratulations.

"What happened?" Talen asked.

"That big blond is a wonder," one of the candidates said. "He caught the whoreson."

"We were pressed," another man said. "Commander Eresh came. He drew first blood."

"Aye," the first candidate said. "But that Flax, he was lightning! The dreadman bloodied us and was about to kill another when Flax caught him in the back. Spitted him like a pig. The dreadman turned to strike, but Flax pulled his sword out and hacked his head off. One blow, like he was slicing butter, and so fast you could hardly know he'd actually made the stroke."

"Yes, and put him beyond our questions!" Eresh roared back.

The men silenced.

Commander Eresh stormed into the hall.

Flax glanced over at Talen and their eyes met. "So much for repairing relations, eh? And so much for curfew."

Talen nodded at the headless dreadmen. "It was curfew for him though."

Flax smiled wryly, the rain soaking his blond hair. "Yes, he took one too many risks."

They followed the candidates out of the rain and into the hall. When they entered, Eresh commanded a number of lamps be lit and brought over. The attacker was laid out on the cobbled floor, his head placed on the stones beside him. Blood from his wounds and severed neck ran onto the stones and mixed with the water dripping from the men and their clothes.

Eresh knelt next to the man and pulled up his sleeves. The tattoos there were the same odd markings Talen had seen on the man in his dream. Eresh searched pockets and pouches. He sliced open the tunic with his knife to bare the man's chest. Nothing. No necklace, purse, pendant. Only the weave of might around the man's arm and a weave of tattoos over his body.

"What is he?" a candidate asked.

"A slayer," Ke said from behind.

The men turned. Ke stood in the door holding up a dagger. He walked over and dropped the knife onto the table.

The knife had whorls etched into its curved blade.

Eresh raised his eyebrows and walked over to look down at the knife. "So it is," he said.

Talen marveled. Slayers were dreadmen of the highest level. They fought in battles as no others could.

"Well, men," said Eresh. "Tonight you have fought a dreadman I gauge to be of the fourth level at least. I hope it's to your taste because I can guarantee you more will follow."

Talen shook his head. A dreadman of the fourth! Few could survive such a multiplication of their Fire. However, he suspected the man chasing him had probably been the same. No wonder he was so quick, so strong. Then Talen thought of Ke, struggling with the dreadman, and holding his own. Ke had been stronger than that dreadman. He hadn't been faster in a dead run, but he'd clearly had more might.

Talen looked at his brother with new eyes. Ke had bested a man of the fourth!

"Let us pray you all survive your quickening," Eresh said. "Mokad has come. And for all our sakes they had better find an army here to meet them."

* * *

Berosus looked over at Talen. This should have been an easy snatch, but it was clear the boy hadn't drunk the drugged wine. Not enough of it, anyway. It annoyed Berosus that he'd lost Rosh. But there was no way he was going to let him fall into the hands of that Kish. At the same time, his death hadn't been for naught. Berosus had seen how Eresh and Argoth looked at him. He knew they wouldn't trust him until he'd proven his allegiance and worth.

Well, tonight's display should convince them. They might not completely trust the Hand, but he had shown he was no friend of their enemy. As for Rosh, when the loose souls were collected in this land, Berosus would cut him out of the pack and reward him.

Berosus reached down and sliced a lock of hair from Rosh's severed head with his knife. He kept remembrances of all his men. Then he took an ear in good sleth fashion. Finally, he slipped the weave from Rosh's arm. As Rosh's killer, it was his right to take the booty. He suspected Argoth would demand he turn it over, but he'd stand on principle, just as any man of the Hand would.

Berosus considered taking Talen now. But he needed to remain under cover until the plan was in place to capture them all.

One thing was clear: this rabble didn't know what Talen was. You didn't bunk such a one as he with common men. Of course, maybe they did know and wanted him to blend in. However, after tonight, they would know that wasn't going to be possible. They would have to try to hide him somewhere else.

And that too was a bonus. It would make taking him all the simpler, which meant, in the long view, tonight's raid had actually been a success.

18

Nilliam

ARGOTH STOOD UPON the tall wind tower in the northeast corner, looking out into the night. Shim stood next to him. The rain fell loudly upon the roof and blew in from the gaps between the roof and battlement, wetting the stone floor and Argoth's legs.

Down in the great hall, Matiga and Eresh were already putting another group of candidates to the test. It would take more than two days to finish them all. Argoth prayed the ancestors they wouldn't all break.

He looked out at the dark woods. There was no way they'd find any trace of the two slayers that escaped. Not with this rain. More than fifteen candidates had been wounded in tonight's attack. Eight were dead. Another, he suspected, would not live to see the morning.

"How are we going to fight them?" Shim asked over the din of the rain.

"We're not, remember? This is exactly why we're breaking up. They caught us unaware. And they did it with some help."

"What do you mean?"

"You and I both inspected the work done on the walls. There was no way anyone, even a dreadman as powerful as Ke, could scale them silently in the night." Argoth picked up the rope he'd found hanging over the wall. "Our ship," he said, "has rats."

Shim looked down at the rope.

"This is how they got in."

"Who was it?" Shim demanded.

"I don't know," said Argoth.

"They were targeting Talen," Shim said, "weren't they?"

"It appears so."

"What is that boy?"

"I don't know, but I don't think he's safe staying with the troops."

"Find a place then. We're breaking up anyway. And put all the hammer-men we know we can trust on alert. Tell them to keep an eye out for any-thing suspicious. In the meantime, we'll figure a way to flush the rats out."

Argoth nodded.

"I'll tell you one thing," said Shim. "I'd rather face Slayers than another one of those grass and earth things you battled down in the caves."

"Creators spare us," said Argoth. "But I don't think we'll have to worry. I did get some insight as a thrall to Mokad. When I told the Skir Master Rubaloth about the creature Hunger, he was surprised. It was clear Mokad didn't have that lore. If they did, I believe they would have already sent it against us."

"Thank the Six," said Shim. "We have our hands full with normal flesh and blood. And I have one particular flesh and blood woman that needs to be alerted. I want you to get a carriage and bring my wife in. I don't think it's safe for her to be visiting relatives any longer."

"No, but will *you* be safe if you bring her in?" Argoth asked.

Shim smiled ruefully. "I'll be a sight better with her than you are with your Serah."

Serah, Argoth's wife, was not happy with the lies he'd told her and the secret life he'd kept from her for all these years. But she could deal with lies and secrets. The problem was Nettle, his son. Saying that he was not doing well was an understatement. Half his mind was gone. And she blamed him, as was right, for his condition.

"I'll send a carriage for her tonight," said Argoth. "In fact, I think that will be the perfect ruse to smuggle Talen out."

"Good," said Shim. "And now I'm going down to submit myself to the Creek Widow. I'm not waiting another minute to be forced."

* * *

Argoth knew Talen couldn't just ride out in full view in daylight. He'd have to be smuggled out under the cover of darkness. For that, he'd need a car-riage or wagon. But all the wagons in the fortress were full.

Shim was a practical commander and there was no room here for any-thing but what his army would use. But the village that stood close by would make up the lack. The tavern owner there hired out his carriage and wagon.

Argoth found Oaks and ordered him and his fist of men to join him. By the time they saddled their mounts, the storm had broken up. They rode to the village, the cold wind cutting through their clothes, the mud sucking at the horses' hooves.

He found the village homes dark and quiet, but Argoth built his Fire nevertheless. There were two taverns for the soldiers. Argoth rode to the first and dismounted, but instead of calling to the house, he softly rapped on the shutters to the tavern owner's bedroom around back. He rapped again.

"Who's there?"

"Argoth."

"Aye," the innkeeper said. "A moment." A minute later the tavern owner opened the back door and held his lamp aloft.

"Captain Argoth," the man said too loudly.

Argoth motioned for him to speak quietly. "I need to be discrete. We don't need a driver. Just the carriage and horse."

"Goh, it's a freezer tonight," he said. "Can it wait until morning?"

"Quietly, man," Argoth said. "It can't wait. We're fetching Lord Shim's wife."

The man's eyes widened in surprise. "Why didn't you say so right off? G'alls, we'll have everything hitched and ready in a moment. Do you want to come in?"

"No," said Argoth. "We can hitch the carriage. I just didn't want you thinking Fir-Noy thieves were taking it."

"I won't hear of it," the man whispered. Then he shouted into the house for his two sons to get up.

Argoth sighed. This tavern owner did not know the meaning of quiet.

By the time Oaks and a few of his men pushed the carriage out of the barn, the tavern owners' two sons were dressed and hitching the team to the carriage. "I'll have my Courage drive; he's a good lad."

"We've got a driver," said Argoth, pushing a piece of silver into the man's hand. It was more than what it should cost to rent a carriage and team and driver. "What I need is for you to prepare a breakfast. There will be at least ten people to feed when she arrives."

The tavern owner rubbed the silver between his fingers. "Aye, we can do that."

"We're keeping this just between us," Argoth said.

"Right," the man said and touched the side of his nose with his finger. "I'm the very picture of a mouse."

"Indeed," said Argoth. By this time the team was hitched and one of the men sat up top as driver. The others mounted, and then the carriage and escort moved down the lane at the side of the tavern and out into the dark street. Argoth lingered behind and bid the tavern owner and his sons good night and saw them to their door. Then he turned back to his horse which was tied up by the barn.

He had just taken the reins and was going to mount when a man spoke from the deep shadows. "I heard the fighting at the fortress tonight."

Argoth dropped the reigns, drew his sword, and spun. He flared his Fire.

The man stood under the eaves of the thick thatch roof. "I mean no harm. In fact, I bring good news."

His accent was odd. There wasn't much light, but the storm had passed by and allowed the slim moon to shine through. "Step out so I can see you," said Argoth, pointing the tip of the sword at the man.

The man walked out of the shadows. He was a tall man. His beard was cut short and tidy. His clothes were fringed with tassels and decorations. Argoth did not need to see his tattoos to know where he came from.

"And what would I have to talk about with a man of Nilliam?" Argoth asked.

"An offer."

"From whom?"

"From the Glory herself," the man said.

The hackles stood up on Argoth's neck. He glanced about him, looking for others, but couldn't see anybody else. Argoth's Fire flowed through him. He raised his sword.

"I come alone," the man said. "Why would I want to threaten a potential ally?"

"Mokad has no love for Nilliam," said Argoth.

"Ah, but you're not of Mokad, are you? No, you are of the Grove, if I'm not mistaken. And such a Grove that it was able to slay a Skir Master that all the lords of Nilliam could not."

"You do not know of what you speak," said Argoth.

The wind whistled about the barn eaves.

"But I do. Let us not prevaricate. I am come to offer you, Argoth, root of the Order of Hismayas, the opportunity to rule in power."

The man was guessing. He had to be. How could he know Argoth was a root of the Grove? "Lord Shim rules here."

"Lord Shim is a distraction. Mokad seeks the fledgling Glory prepared to rule you. But why should you give him to Mokad, who offers you nothing? Deliver him to us. Deliver your kingdom to us, and you shall be made a ruler over it. You shall become one of those consecrated for greater things."

Argoth did not know what powers this man had. But he knew he must be careful. "Do they teach the consecrated of Nilliam who really controls the Glories of the earth? Do they teach you that your masters are slaves to Devourers?

"It is the order of things. I have accepted it. As should you, because when you rebel against creation, you only follow Regret."

"Is that the excrement parading about Nilliam as reason?" asked Argoth. He was waiting for the man to attack, but the man held his arms out.

"You don't know what's coming for you," the man said.

"I think we have a good idea," Argoth said. He didn't drop his guard, but did lower his sword.

Somewhere in the village a door or shutter came loose and began to bang in the wind.

"No, you don't. But I shall endeavor to explain. When Glories fight Glories on behalf of their Sublime—'Devourers' is such a vulgar word— they do so with restraint. Our masters have accords with one another, even if they bend at times. But, you see, you fight for no Glory. You are literally a wolf among the sheep. And so the forces which have been gathered against you are not coming to subdue or conquer, but to exterminate."

"That's obvious. Do you think the Grove is made up of babes?"

"When a wolf comes to a vale, all members of the vale turn out to hunt it, even if some are enemies. If Mokad will not remove you, then all the oth- er Glorydoms will be bound to do so. If you're lucky, you may win a battle or two against Mokad. But you will not beat the combined might the Sub- limes will bring to bear. I give you a way out. Join with Nilliam. When you do, Mokad will have no claim. You'll be ours then, and their coalition will unravel. Toth and Urz will both stand with Nilliam. Mokad will be forced to retreat. Our Glory is gentle and fair. You will prosper and grow fat."

"You sicken me," said Argoth.

"I have walked this land. There are sicknesses Divines can heal. Furthermore, the borders your last master established are gone. Haven't you noticed?"

Argoth didn't know what he was referring to.

"No," said the man. "I see you haven't. There are many creatures that would prey upon us—Fire, soul, and flesh. But our sublime masters keep them out. Their servants work on our behalf to keep us safe."

Argoth thought of the creature in the river, of the village and the infestation of frights, of the wurms that had broken through the gap.

"You have no wisterwives. You have nothing to protect you now. The world outside will soon discover your lack of defense. And then you will beg for us to help."

"Listen to me," said Argoth. "We defeated one of your Sublimes down in her cave. We destroyed her monster. We do not fear you or any other goblin you might conjure." He stepped closer and raised his sword again, holding the point only a few inches from the man's chest. But the man seemed not to care.

"It can be a difficult thing for us to contemplate man's position in the world. But perhaps the choice will be clearer if I bring it closer to home. Join us and you will not only spare many in this land, but you will be able to repair the damage you did to your own son."

Nettle? How did he know about that?

"I don't ask you to make a decision now," said the man. "Just think on it. In the end you will see it's wisdom's path."

The man took a step back.

Argoth did not follow.

The man took another step back. A moment later a huge gust of wind banged into the buildings behind Argoth. The wind howled down between the barn and the house and slammed into Argoth, knocking him a step forward. Wet leaves and debris pelted him, forcing him to squint.

And then he felt the wind go through him. Felt a chill along his bones. A chill he'd felt once before out on the Skir Master's ship. Argoth gasped for breath.

And then the wind moved off. Argoth tensed for an attack, but the lord of Nilliam was gone.

19

Nettle

ALL THE WAY BACK to the fortress the wind blew. The ragged clouds rushed across the night sky, obscuring the moon and then letting it shine again. And Argoth pondered what had just happened next to the tavern owner's barn.

All that rubbish about the order of the creation! The Creators had endowed men with brains and the will to use them. Men were not grass to be sown and harvested as others saw fit. That lord, with all his smiles and confidence, was a coward who had traded his freedom for a snug spot in a sheep's fold.

The perils he talked about—they were nothing more than the burden of freedom. And if the Devourers could contend with these dangers, then so could humans.

Argoth crossed over the bridge spanning the creek in front of the fortress, his horse's hooves sounding on the timbers. How did Nilliam know who he was? How did they know about Talen?

Mokad would have known about Argoth's role in the Grove because Argoth had been, if only briefly, a thrall to one of its Divines. As a thrall, Mokad had been able to force him to reveal many secrets. But the Skir Master that had held his bond had been destroyed, and the bond of the thrall had gone with it. Moreover, that bond had been destroyed *before* they'd fought the Devourer in the caves, so how could anyone but those who had been in the cave know about Talen's part in that final battle?

Perhaps this was evidence that the thrall had not been completely broken when the Skir Master died. When Argoth's thrall had been quickened, a door opened in his mind that connected him to the Skir Master. Then another door had opened connecting the Skir Master to the Glory of Mokad. And then yet a third door had opened connecting the Glory to a Sublime—no, he wouldn't use that word—to a Devourer whose beauty still smote his heart.

Perhaps the link to the Skir Master had died, and the bulk of the power of the thrall had died with him. But was it possible the link with the Glory and Devourer still remained?

He had felt a ghost of that connection in the hours and days after he'd been freed. It had faded. He hadn't felt any of it these last weeks. Surely, their connection to him was now gone. Still he wondered: was he a source of information for the enemy? Were they spying upon Shim's fledgling army through him?

He cursed. The things the Grove did not know!

Then another idea occurred to him. If Nilliam had made contact with him, had they attempted to make contact with any of the other leaders? In fact, any of the candidates would be good targets. If he were in Nilliam's shoes, he wouldn't target just one person.

Argoth rode through the field and now approached the gate in the outer wall. He called up to the men there who opened for him.

It made sense that if the Devourers had their own society, they would communicate with each other. And why not? They probably also had their hierarchies and territories and disputes, their alliances and antagonists. In fact, wasn't this ploy by Nilliam evidence of such an antagonism between two masters?

Argoth thought it was. Which meant there was a whole world of power and politics that none but the Divines even knew existed. He corrected himself—none but the Divines and now the Order of Hismayas. No wonder the glorydoms were coming to exterminate them.

And with that thought of extermination, Argoth understood something of the history of Hismayas that he hadn't before. Hismayas had once been a Divine. But he'd rebelled and taught the people of his vale the secrets of the lore. And for that crime all the Divines who could be called from all the surrounding glorydoms, both friend and foe, came to the vale of Hismayas. They and their armies camped about it. And when all had gathered, they entered his vale and slaughtered all his people. Hismayas they took and tortured upon a stone for a full year. Then they sacrificed his soul.

Now Argoth knew why the Divines had reacted the way they had to Hismayas. He and his people threatened the whole community of Devourers. If people really knew and believed the truth, mankind would rise up in rebellion. These accords the lord of Nilliam spoke of probably defined how they would face a common threat.

Luckily, Hismayas had sent a seed into the wilderness to preserve the secrets long before the Divines and their armies were mustered. A seed that had, over the ages, grown into the Groves. The problem was that this was a very old war they were waging. So old that the Groves had forgotten who the real enemy was.

As Argoth rode up to the inner gate, he thought of the Book and Crown of Hismayas that Harnock kept in his fastness beyond the borders of the New Lands. None had been able to open that book and live. Many had tried. All had failed to be found worthy. But now, more than ever, they needed the power that would come with the secrets kept there. If they were going to face the glorydoms of the earth, they would not be able to stand with an army of a few hundred dreadmen. Maybe River was right. As soon as the current crisis was over, he would send her to Harnock once more.

Argoth thought about these things as he dismounted and gave his horse to the stable hand. He thought about them as he walked back to his quarters where his wife and children slept. He lit a lamp and went to the room where Nettle, his son, usually lay.

Argoth found the bed empty. He held the lamp higher and saw Nettle huddled in a corner asleep, lying with his bare legs on the cold floor. A blanket lay on the floor next to him. Argoth set the lamp on a table and went to his son. He felt Nettle's legs and hands; they were ice cold.

Nettle had a slight beard. Not the scratchy whiskers of a man, but of youth. Nevertheless, he was a man. He'd received his man's tattoo and had almost immediately made a man's choice, choosing to sacrifice his Fire so Argoth could fight the Skir Master. He'd chosen knowing that Argoth would have to take that Fire, and by so doing would also take part of his soul. He'd chosen, knowing he'd never be the same again.

Except as every day passed and Argoth saw more and more clearly what he'd done to his son, that reasoning became more and more brittle. Even if Nettle were technically a man, youth was impetuous and rash. Youth didn't understand the consequences even when they were explained to them. Had Nettle really chosen when his mind was still full of a boy's idea of valor?

Argoth worked his hands under Nettle's knees and carried him back to his bed. Then he lay down next to him and pulled the blanket up to warm the boy with his own body heat. Nettle stirred but did not waken. He was almost as tall as Argoth. In stature he was a man, but it was only in stature. When Argoth had taken the Fire, it had taken parts of Nettle's mind. He was not an imbecile, but he certainly wasn't full-witted either. This had also affected his coordination, for where he'd once been able to run like a horse, Nettle now moved with a gangly lope.

My son, Argoth thought, smoothing back Nettle's hair. *My bright boy.* The regret at what he'd done to Nettle clenched his heart.

He found no use in trying to suppress the fact that Nilliam's offer tempted him. Trying to ignore such things only seemed to make them worse. You had to deal with such thoughts head on, acknowledge them and pin them down. He'd kept the filtering rods through which he'd drawn Nettle's Fire, rods used specifically to catch soul. He'd kept them hoping beyond hope that lore existed which would allow him to restore the parts of his son he'd torn away.

He wanted to believe that the lord of Nilliam was speaking the truth. But he also knew a cunning adversary would use just such a hope to turn someone traitor. It was probably a well-spun, half-truth that would only disappoint.

But what if it wasn't?

He wouldn't make matters worse by sullying Nettle's gift with perfidy.

But what if it was true? Perhaps such lore was in the Book of Hismayas.

To have his son back! To ride with him as they once had, galloping down the road to Stag Home in a pell-mell race, the dust rising from the hooves of their horses. Or listen to him tease his sisters. Or labor in the fields and talk about the men and whether the blight would take their new variety of grape.

Those and many other bright memories burned in his mind, beckoning. Argoth allowed himself to revel in those dreams as he lay next to his son, trying to warm his limbs. But he knew he could not stay. When Nettle's hands no longer felt like ice, he rose and tucked the blankets securely about his son. Then he picked up the lamp that had burned low and quietly moved past his sleeping family and out the door.

* * *

Argoth found Shim, not in his chambers, but in the armory. His shirt was off, and he was sweating, practicing with his sword in the light of one single candle flame. Upon his upper right arm was a new weave. Shim was all muscle, hard and knotty and scarred. He danced past Argoth in his bare feet, the sword slicing the air, glinting in the small candlelight.

"So you survived the forcing," Argoth said.

"That woman Matiga is a torturer. I think she actually enjoyed watching me writhe."

"How do you feel now?"

"Jittery," Shim said and thrust.

"But you feel strong."

"I feel like I'm riding a horse that's much too big for me and galloping far too fast."

Argoth nodded. "Your body, marvelous thing it is, will grow accustomed to its new powers."

Shim leapt, but he leapt too far and had to correct himself at the last moment to avoid crashing into a table he'd moved aside. "You realize how dangerous this clumsiness will be until it passes?"

Argoth nodded. "And I'm afraid that's not all that has increased our peril."

Shim paused. "What? Mokaddian dreadmen aren't enough?"

Argoth told Shim then of his meeting with the lord of Nilliam. He told him of the offer for power and the enemy's accords. He told him everything except for what had been said about Nettle. He didn't know why he kept that part back, but he told himself it wasn't a necessary part of the discussion.

When he finished, Shim said, "The fact that they are making offers suggests to me they are not strong enough to simply come in here and take what they want. They may even fear us."

Argoth nodded. "Two Divines have died on these shores."

Shim scratched the beard growing under his jaw. "And all this attention on Talen. He's a good soldier, but fearsome would not be the first word to come to mind when describing him."

"The hatchlings of a Mungonese crocodile are not particularly fearsome. And yet they grow up to be horrors."

"True," said Shim.

"I still say we proceed as planned. We send Talen to a safe place. Then we break up and increase our reconnaissance. I fear there are more enemy troops here than we realize."

"You need to watch yourself as well, since I'm merely a—what was the exact word the lord of Nilliam used?"

"A distraction."

"Yes, a distraction. You thinking of taking my place?"

"And have to answer to all the wives of the Clans? Never."

Shim grinned. "Very wise."

* * *

A few hours later in the darkness of the early morning, Berosus worked with the newly forced candidates on the training field, trying to help settle them into their new powers, for none of them could sleep. The last of the storm clouds had blown away, and the moon shone down on the training bailey bright and clear.

Argoth's methods had proved to be effective. Of the candidates they'd forced so far, they'd only broken a handful. Berosus was impressed; these sleth had come up with a number of surprising innovations.

Next to him, two of the candidates practiced swordplay with wooden wasters. They looked like children, swinging with all their might. "A light touch," he said to them. "Your range of speed and power has just been extended. Stop going right up to the top. Ease into it."

The candidates modified their strokes, but not enough. He moved to another pair, and then another, always keeping close to the road from the inner fortress to the outer gate. A carriage wheeled past. But there was nothing of interest in it. A few minutes later a wagon loaded with two large barrels rolled by. He almost passed over the wagon, but caught a glimpse of the horse's shoe in the moonlight. The shoe was not open, but completely round. And with large caulkins to boot. You didn't put that kind of shoe on a draught horse. That was a shoe used for horse sport. And for firesteeds. He looked at the horse again. It was River's horse!

He felt for the small escrum in his pocket that held a bit of the soul of the captain of his dreadmen, allowing him to communicate with him over distances. *Follow the wagon*, he said to the man's mind.

The line of communication was not as clear as with a full thrall's bond, but the reply was clear enough. *It will be done, Bright One.*

The wagon disappeared through the gate. Berosus smiled. Soon Talen would be in hand. Once he was secured, there was only one piece left—he needed to know the identity of the real power behind Argoth and the others, the one who had actually defeated the Sublime Mother in the stone-wight warren. He'd visited the warren when he'd first arrived, but this Grove had emptied it. There was very little there that would give him any clue as to what had happened.

So what he needed was someone to tell him the truth. Of all those who had been present, it was clear who the weakest link was—Legs is where he'd begin his investigation.

He turned back to the candidates. One almost tumbled into him. Berosus helped the man up. "Think of it like a voice," he said. "Start off with a whisper. Move up the scale of volume slowly until you get control."

20

Suckle

SUGAR WOKE TO something pulling on her toe. She kicked at it, but found it too large to be a ferret.

"Good morning," Legs said and pulled her toe again.

She opened her eyes. The cellar door hadn't been shut all the way, and a sliver of early morning light shone through the cracks.

"The others have gone to eat," Legs said.

"Why didn't you wake me?"

"Last night the Creek Widow said you needed rest. Who am I to gainsay her?"

She turned and sat up. She had been tired to begin with, and the chaos with the Mokaddian dreadmen had only kept her up longer. She couldn't quite believe Mokaddian dreadmen were already here. The upcoming battles had seemed so far away. "I'm famished," she said. It felt like she'd been fasting for two days. Then she noticed in the wan light that Legs was wearing the necklace.

"What are you doing with that?" she asked.

"Nothing."

Her alarm rose. "What did you do?"

"I don't know how to use it," he said.

"That isn't an answer."

He was silent, which meant he *had* tried to do something.

"We're playing with lions," she said. "If we're not careful, one of us is going to end up being eaten."

"I didn't quicken it."

"Legs," she said.

"Would you deny me sight?" Legs asked. "I want to see. And not just the enemy. I want to see you, sister, even if it is only with the eyes of my soul. I want to see Mother and Da."

"Give it to me," she said.

Legs removed the weave and handed it to her. "Don't deny me this," he said.

"It's not about denying. The vitalities are not to be toyed with. The last thing I need is to lose you. Whatever Urban teaches me, I'll teach you. But you need to be patient."

"Patience is overrated," he said and put a few mint leaves in his mouth to chew.

"So says Legs the Wise. Come on."

Sugar dressed, and they exited the cellar. The morning air was clean from last night's rain. Much of the ground was cobbled, but where it wasn't, the earth was still dark with moisture. All about the bailey, soldiers were moving things, loading up wagons. Two fists of candidates worked with Ke and Eresh. Then she saw what they were doing and corrected herself—they weren't candidates any longer. These fists had been forced some time during the night. They were dreadmen, albeit of the first level, but dreadmen all the same.

Part of a dreadman's training included running various courses designed to increase strength, speed, and endurance. The saying was "multiply a runt and you just get a bigger runt." So you wanted to do everything you could to increase your normal base strength. The courses also taught you how to move at those higher levels, for, as she had learned, it was one thing to run through a forest. It was quite another to try to run through that same forest at double the speed.

Ke had a fist of dreadmen working on the platforms. One of the new dreadmen jumped from a standstill straight to the six-foot platform. That was like jumping over a man standing straight up. And he didn't squeak by—he had room to spare. He sprang off the other side. Another followed him up. A third candidate didn't quite make it. He tried again and failed and moved down to the five-foot platform and succeeded.

Eresh worked with another group scaling a fortress wall with ropes. Each man climbing the wall wore a fall harness made of rope around his waist and legs. A man above on the parapet reeled that in as the man below climbed. The men were scampering up the walls like squirrels, and Sugar wondered if they needed fall harnesses. But then Eresh started shouting at one man above him. "Breath!" he yelled. "Watch your breath!"

The man didn't seem to hear. He was wavering, barely clinging on.

"Breathe, you idiot!"

The man collapsed and would have fallen to some damage if it weren't for his harness and the man above slowly letting him to the ground.

Eresh bent down next to him and put his ear to the man's mouth to see if he was breathing. A moment passed, then Eresh said, "He's alive. The fool."

Sugar made her way over to the great hall where she assumed her fist was since they'd been helping with the forcing the night before. A fist of candidates waited their turn by the entrance. Inside, Argoth and the Creek Widow were taking a breather by one of the massive hearths. On the far side of the hall, a dozen or so men lay unmoving on tables and cots. They were bundled up in quilts and blankets. And all about them godsweed braids burned, filling the hall with smoke to keep frights and other creatures away.

"Are these the last?" Sugar asked.

"Those are the ones that broke," one of the waiting candidates replied.

Sugar remembered the night Talen had almost died. His da had forced him on accident, and he'd bled out a horrendous amount of Fire. He would have bled it all out if River hadn't been there to stop it. Talen must be made of tough stuff, for he'd survived and was using the lore. She hoped these men here survived. Her heart went out to them. Yesterday, they'd been dreaming of what they could do as loremen. Today that was now gone. She knew she'd be devastated if she'd lost the chance to learn her mother's lore.

"There you are," a woman said.

Sugar turned to find the Mistress.

"You're with me today, slug-a-bed."

"Where's my fist?" asked Sugar.

"They're with me too. Come on. Have you taken your breakfast?"

They hadn't, so the Mistress led them over to the cook's for a generous helping of swamp and hard bread.

"Can you believe it?" the Mistress asked. "There were Mokaddian dreadmen on this very ground, swords clashing, men shouting, and I slept like a baby through the whole thing. Slept late, and I never sleep late."

"Maybe that will teach you not to dip into someone else's wine," said Sugar.

"Ach," said the Mistress, "that Creek Widow doesn't want you drinking spirits. Besides, the wine was fair payment."

"For what?"

"For having to be fistmaiden over you, the other fell-maidens, and Master Legs."

Sugar furrowed her brow. River was their fist leader.

"Temporarily, of course. River's gone. The Creek Widow is still working with the candidates. She didn't sleep a wink last night. Just worked right through. I tell you that woman is iron. If Shim weren't here, I think she'd be running this whole show. Anyway, with both of them gone, you are assigned to me. The rest of the fist is already out working."

"Where did River go?"

"That's the question on everybody's lips. It appears both she and Talen were sneaked out sometime last night. Disappeared like ghosts."

"Sneaked? Why would they need to be sneaked?"

"You tell me."

"I don't know."

"Don't you? Those dreadmen were after him. Not Shim or Argoth or that fine piece of beef that's his brother. That's the word. I tell you, there's something about that boy you're keeping mum."

They had been told not to reveal all the details of what happened in the Devourer's warren. It would not play well to spread it about that Talen was some tool of the same master that controlled the monster that had terrorized the land. She didn't like lying to the Mistress, but what else could she do? "I'm sure I don't know what it is," Sugar said.

The Mistress turned to Legs. "And what about you, Master Legs? What do you know?"

"Me?" Legs asked. "I'm blind. What would I know of such things?"

"Plenty," the Mistress said in a tone that clearly revealed she wasn't buying any of that. "There are many secrets not meant for the chief washerwoman's ears. I'll grant you that. But, sooner or later, I find them out anyway."

Sugar said, "Then you must tell me when you solve this mystery."

"Oh, I shall," she said.

Sugar changed the topic. "Did the Creek Widow convince that Kish to force the fell-maidens?"

"I heard tomorrow," the Mistress said. "But I wouldn't depend on it.

That Kish has Shim's ear. From what I hear he convinced our warlord that the women's fist should be the last to go. Mark me: with all that's going on, he'll push it out for weeks."

"I don't know that I like that man," said Sugar.

The Mistress shrugged. "If the old badger is as good as Argoth thinks he is, we don't have to like him. And after yesterday's demonstration, I'm inclined to think he might be. I can tell you I don't intend to fight him. I suggest you do the same and content yourself with slaying piles of laundry and an equal mound of ducks instead."

The Mistress told Sugar to fetch a bowl of swamp. When she and Legs finished, the Mistress led them to the outer bailey. A number of crows congregated on the wall.

"They've got the dreadman that Flax beheaded out there on a pole next to Pinter," said the Mistress. "He's holding his head in his own hands. Want to have a look?"

Sugar did. They walked out of the fortress to view the spectacle. The naked body was already beginning to stink, but she held her hand under her nose to mitigate the smell. Half a dozen crows flew about trying to get their chance at the flesh. Flies and wasps buzzed about too. She described the man to Legs, including the strange tattoos.

"No mistaking Lord Shim's defiance now," said the Mistress.

"He's clearly Mokad's," Sugar said of the dreadman. He'd also been very clearly a powerful man. Even in death his muscled limbs and torso looked fearsome. And Mokad would be sending hundreds more. They contemplated him a bit longer, then went back inside.

The Mistress assigned some of the women to gather firewood and others to pick more wild rosemary for the laundry. Sugar and Legs she assigned to the group scalding and plucking a large quantity of ducks that would be roasted for the candidates. The hunting boys had brought back more than a hundred of them. The pile was mostly green-heads with some smaller browns mixed in and a half a dozen geese. Big as it was, the candidates would eat through this pile in short order.

The pluckers kept a small cauldron of water hot, not boiling. Sugar sat and dunked her bird in the hot water, holding it by its head. When it was good and wet, she hauled it out and began with the big feathers of the wings and tail. Once those were out, she held the bird belly-up in her left hand, picking and rubbing out the feathers from breast to tail, careful not to break the skin since it was what would keep the meat moist while cooking. Once the belly was done, she did the same to the back and sides, going from neck to hind, in the direction the feathers grew.

After the fourth bird, her hands stunk of the duck's feather oil. After a dozen more, the muscles in her shoulders and back tightened up and began to ache. She plucked on, wet feathers clinging to her tunic and trousers and catching in her hair, but her mind was not on the ducks.

The whole time she tried to find and follow a thread of her mother's weave about her neck. Twice she thought she had found one, but both times it slipped from her. It was like trying to hold a pea on a knife.

Candidates rode past. Some called out greetings to the women. To others, the women made their own calls. At one point Commander Eresh rode out along the path to the bridge, a fist of men with him. When he was only a number of yards away, he turned to the Mistress. "Good morning, Mistress," he said. "I've talked to Shim. You'll be given a rank in short order. Captain, I would think."

The Mistress rose and bowed to him.

"You tell those women the army's built on the backs of the laundresses," he said. "Tell them they're saving lives! I'd trade a whole hammer for a good crew of washerwomen. Remember it!"

"Aye," the Mistress said and put her fist to her chest in salute.

He rode on.

"Captain is it?" one of the other women teased. She was plump and missing a tooth at the side of her grin. "And when did you have time to get into his bed?"

"This has nothing to do with his bed," said the Mistress.

"Is he mocking us?" Sugar asked.

"He's an odd one, to be sure," said the mistress. "But he's not joking. He made it a point to visit with me earlier. After looking me over quite openly, he proclaimed that if I were to marshal my troops correctly, I'd save more of Shim's army than he would."

"I don't think that one's rowing with all his oars," said the plump woman. "Did someone hit him in the head during last night's fighting?"

The Mistress continued. "He said disease and pestilence can do more damage to an army than most foes. He said a clean army is a healthy one.

'I'll train them to fight flesh and blood, my good woman, but it won't do a lick of good if you don't keep the vermin out.' Those were his very words. And he was particular in verifying how we go about our wash and the consequences if we failed to follow his odd demands."

"If you're a captain," the plump one asked, "what does that make me?"

"The captain's boot polisher," another of the women said.

Sugar laughed along with the other women. But she wondered about this Kish even more. She would not complain about fewer lice and fleas, but to say the army was built on laundry?

"So, my lovely warriors," said the Mistress, "back to work."

They turned back to the ducks and conversation. As they approached lunch time, the Mistress nudged Sugar. "You keep watching the road. Who are you pining after? Certainly not that foreigner."

Sugar realized she had indeed been continually glancing up the road. "I'm going to be working in his crew," she said. "Nothing more."

The plump woman said, "Oh, dearie, that lie is written plain on your face."

"It's not a lie," Sugar said innocently.

"How many hares are you trying to catch?" another woman asked and brushed a curly lock of hair out of her face with the back of her hand.

"None," Sugar protested.

"Sweet Pie," said the Mistress, "you can't hide it from the likes of us."

Sugar thought of Talen. He'd certainly become more attractive to her. And then the weaver from Koramtown, although now that Talen had pointed it out, he did have a nose that was fairly dainty. There might be others. But she couldn't tell these ladies. It would fly through the camp before dinner. "I'm training for battle," she said. "I don't have time to be worrying about men."

"So who are you looking for then?" asked the Mistress.

Sugar sighed, rolled her duck, looking for any pin feathers she might have missed. "I admit I was looking for Urban, but—"

"Aha!" said the Mistress.

"That Urban's a long side of beef," said the plump one longingly.

The Mistress waved her finger at Sugar. "A word of advice. Foreigners are tempting. And I'm as liberal as they come, but I suggest you stick to what you know. It's always best that way. A man who's got his feet planted here is likely to stay. Someone just in off the boat, well, who knows if the next day he'll step back on again and sail away, leaving you behind with another responsibility growing in your belly?"

Sugar was not going to get pregnant.

"You're one to talk," said one of the women.

"I am," declared the mistress. "I've learned by hard experience."

The curly-headed woman guffawed at that comment. Sugar expected some coarse joke to follow, but the mistress said, "Don't you go letting a set of good teeth and an interesting accent mislead you."

"You underestimate me," said Sugar. She picked up another duck and dipped it in the pot, holding its head out of the water. Legs sat beside her plucking with the rest of the women. He couldn't always catch all the pin feathers, but he did a good job on the ones that were easy to feel with your hand. "Legs," she said, "help me out here."

Legs shook a couple of feathers from his hand. "Well, if the truth be told, he did call her 'your loveliness'."

That brought a round of titters.

"But Sugar wouldn't have any of his nonsense," he continued. "I was there. I heard it all. Still, I don't want her to shun him just yet. I believe he has a song I want to learn. A singer's always got to be increasing his basket of songs."

"What song is that?" asked one of the women.

"A tale about soft women," said Legs.

The mistress looked at Legs. "And what would a little whip like you know about soft women?"

"Nothing," said Legs. "That's why I wanted to learn the song."

The mistress laughed. "And why haven't you sung for us? Is all your entertainment reserved for men?"

"There's a cost, you know," Legs said. "I don't come cheap. Not even to the Ladies of the Tub."

"Ladies are we?" one said. "Looks like we're moving upstairs, girls."

A number of the other women laughed.

The Mistress said, "What cost? It's not like we're rolling in coin."

"A kiss," Legs said matter-of-factly.

Sugar smiled to herself and shook her head. Such the performer, but she was glad he'd taken the focus off her.

"You're taking kisses from the men, are you?" asked the Mistress. "I didn't peg you as the type."

For a moment Legs was speechless. The women laughed. Then Legs recovered. "To be truthful, the men's breath stinks, and so I demand nothing but hard copper from them."

The mistress grinned. "What do you say, girls? Do you think we can muster up a little coin for our singer?"

Legs held his cheek up, waiting for payment. But the mistress and two others gave him solid kisses on the mouth instead. When they released him, Legs staggered back, blushing, and that only made the women laugh more.

Sugar decided that perhaps, in the Mistress, Legs had finally met his match. Still blushing, he straightened himself and declared, "For such lips I shall sing of epic love and glory!" He cleared his throat. The women waited. Then he proceeded to regale them in serious tones with a silly song about a group of goats who outsmarted a farmer's wife. The women laughed and plucked and laughed some more. When Legs finished, they applauded.

Thank the Six for Legs, she thought. Then she realized she held a thread to the weave of her mother's necklace. She'd found it sometime during the song but was too preoccupied with Legs's singing to notice. The shock of it made her lose the thread, but she soon found it again.

The weave had been impenetrable. But now that she'd found it, this part of the pattern was clear as day. It was like those moments when someone points to the grain in the side of a board and tells you there's a face in it. At first you see nothing. But once you find the face, you can see nothing else.

Legs and the women continued to banter, but she tuned out the conversation and followed the thread. It was long and complicated, but she eventually came to a terminus of sorts. Weaves, she had been taught by River, had mouths. Quickening the weave required you to feed it Fire. Was this a mouth?

She opened herself just a bit and felt the weave pull. She released her Fire, and the weave took it. At first, she only gave it small amounts, thinking the weave would quicken at any moment. But it was far more hungry than that. And so she fed it a steady stream until it almost felt as if it were suckling.

And then she stopped. What if she was doing this wrong? What if the Fire was not filling it, but simply spilling into the air? It would attract frights.

And even if it wasn't spilling, she couldn't really gauge how much Fire she was giving. She hadn't learned that skill yet. What if it sucked years from her? The thought scared her.

She sat there a moment more, then decided to press on. Urban had told her to do this, and was there really any other way to quicken it?

The mistress ordered the women to stand and stretch and share some watered ale before they finished the last of the ducks. Sugar rolled her duck over to start on that side, and the weave suddenly thrummed about her neck.

She jumped. Then she realized what she'd done, and a thrill ran through her. She'd done it!

She had scarcely begun to enjoy her success when an itch began to build along her limbs. It quickly grew into a heat that ran along her very bones. Then the heat turned into a sharp pain.

She gasped.

The Mistress looked at her.

Sugar's vision began to double. There was a rushing in her ears. Her panic rose. What had she been thinking, doing this alone?

This was wrong, terribly wrong!

The pain grew. Sugar dropped her duck, fumbled with the necklace's clasp, then tore it from her throat and flung it to the ground like it was a snake. A moment later the pain receded.

Sugar blinked. Her vision returned.

The mistress looked at the necklace lying on the ground. "The foreigner gave you that, didn't he?"

"It was my mother's."

The Mistress nodded and took a large drink from her cup. "Best pick it up, girl."

Sugar did and put it in a pocket. The Mistress offered her a cup of watered ale, a knowing look in her eyes. Sugar took it and drank.

After a few moments she calmed, and the realization of what she'd just done filled her. Despite the pain, she'd quickened a weave! At least, she thought she had. She'd done *something*. Which meant she was that much closer to her mother and the lore Mother had wanted Sugar to have. But the pain gave her pause. Maybe this pain is what Urban had felt. Maybe the weave had rejected her too.

She replaced her cup and started in on another duck, the necklace in her pocket. Just as she was finishing, one of the women said, "Don't look now, but here comes that glittering side of beef."

Sugar glanced up the road toward the fortress gate. Urban was indeed coming, driving a smaller wagon pulled by one horse. His own white horse followed behind on a tether.

The Mistress watched him for a bit, then cocked her head. "That one's definitely not for a new woman like yourself. Someone more mature, on the other hand, might reconsider a scruple or two."

"Two?" one of the women asked. "I thought you tossed all yours out with the bad fruit."

The Mistress gave her a look, then smoothed a stray lock out of her face and tucked it back with the rest of her hair she'd braided up off her neck.

Urban hailed Sugar.

She rose. "Take care of Legs," she said to the Mistress.

"Aye," said the mistress. "We'll keep our little singer as snug as a bean in a barrel. And you save some of that foreigner for those better able to handle such men."

"You can have all of him. I'm not planning on taking even a nibble."

"Bold words," the plump woman said.

The Mistress took on a more serious tone. "You be careful, girl."

Sugar patted the knife belted at her waist, the one her father had taught her to use. "I've got a friend to keep me company."

21

Withers

SUGAR WALKED TO the wagon. Urban was wearing brown trousers and a dark gray tunic with a black leather vest. The bruise about his eye had already begun to turn yellow, which meant he must have been multiplying his own healing.

"Today you meet my cook," he said.

The Mistress called after Sugar: "Keep that knife ready!"

Urban glanced down at her belt, and then he grinned and offered her his hand.

Sugar waved his hand off and climbed up onto the wagon seat on her own. He smelled of sweat and leather and the spiced oil in his hair. When she was settled, he flicked the reins. They rode out of the fortress, over the bridge, and along the road to the village. A young girl leading a red steer to the fortress moved off the road to let them pass.

When the girl was behind them, Urban said, "Have you been practicing?"

"I have," she said.

"Are you wearing a weave?"

"My governor."

"Give me your hand."

Sugar placed her hand in his and readied herself for an attack, but none came. He turned her hand over and examined it. "Not a lady's soft-gloved skin, is it?"

Sugar couldn't help her station. She was not so rich as to be able to afford servants and pleasant lotions. She did use a little fat now and again to keep her hands from chapping to the point where they cracked and bled, but she knew they were not beautiful.

"You can read a lot about a person from their hands," he said. "You've got a very old scar here. What is that from?"

"A knife."

"Cooking?"

"I was practicing with my father, trying to disarm him."

"Oh?" he asked and cocked an eyebrow.

"My Da liked to fight and wrestle. He was teaching me. Said no daughter of his was going to be a helpless thing."

"And are you helpless?"

"I can hold my own."

Urban nodded. "We'll see." Immediately, he attacked, trying to push through the doors of her soul.

She slammed herself closed, more in panic than anything else.

"Good," he said. "Open."

She relaxed and opened the doors of her soul again.

He struck again. Again, she shut him out. He tried three more times, but she blocked his every attempt. The panic was still there, but she also felt a bit of pride.

"You *did* practice," he said. "And what about your mother's weave?"

"I believe I found the mouth," she said.

"What do you mean?"

She prepared to explain, but he struck again, and this time caught her off guard. He pressed past her barrier toward the center of her being. It was suffocating, bewildering. She fought, trying to dislodge him, but she could not shake his presence. Her panic rose until she felt he truly did mean her harm. He held his presence one terrifying moment longer, then retreated.

She slammed her doors shut and wrenched away from him. Lords, she could take a punch, but this was something else—a feeling of total loss of control, as if she were slipping uncontrollably toward a precipice.

She looked at him and wondered if anyone knew what Urban's true intentions were.

"Keep working," he said. "There are things in the world of soul that would possess you. Where you're going, one slip might mean the difference between coming back to your body and never coming back at all."

She swallowed, but then she reminded herself that Mother had done this. If she had been brave and mastered it, then Sugar could as well.

They rode the wagon into the village. A number of the folk there waved in friendly greeting as they passed by. Sugar returned their greeting.

"You said you found the mouth?" he asked.

"Yes."

"I'm not surprised. Progress with the lore seems to come in spurts. You'll work for some time with no noticeable result, and then it's all epiphanies. Did you feel a heat, a tearing along the bones?"

She nodded.

"Disorientation?"

"Yes."

"Perfect," he said. "You're going to do it again."

"I almost passed out. Maybe the weave rejected me."

"No, if it had rejected you, you wouldn't have been able to suckle it. You almost walked with your soul."

"What about the pain?"

"The pain is but a moment, and then you are free."

It sounded ominous to her. "What if I can't get back into my body?"

"That's why I wanted you to practice opening and closing."

There had to be more to it than that. "But what happens if things go wrong?"

He held his hand up. "I'm going to defer to one wiser than I. You can ask him when we get to camp. In the meantime, how good are you at multiplying and diminishing?"

"I'm okay."

He shook his head. "Weaves of might can become a crutch. You want to get off of them as soon as possible."

"That's what River said. She sat with me a number of times, but with so many candidates our sessions were brief."

"Take off your governor and give me your hand again," he said.

Sugar was wary of another attack, but she took off her candidate's weave, and placed her hand in his.

Urban reached out to her soul, just a touch, and connected with her so she could sense him. She'd done this with River. This hand-to-hand practice allowed a more experienced lore user to guide a less experienced one until she could do it on her own.

He multiplied his Fire. She multiplied hers to match. He diminished. She did the same.

"I've heard about your father and mother," he said. "Tell me the full story of these last few months."

"I'm sure you've heard it from Argoth."

"Not your version. I want to hear what happened to you. I want it from the beginning."

They followed the road out of the village and into the surrounding fields. Sugar started with the birth of Cotton, her little brother, and Lanky the stork. As she talked, he continued to multiply and diminish. She followed and felt the joy of the Fire grow and decrease, felt the vigor in her limbs multiply and diminish. She told him about the mob, her flight. Urban listened and nodded, making small changes to his Fire. They entered the woods. At one point an enormous flock of birds wheeled over head, landed in a tree, and took flight again. She continued and told him most of the details of the fight in the cave. He listened and prodded her with questions.

When she finished, he said, "Captain Argoth knew my father decades ago. Argoth had a different name then. He was a different man. A frightening man. But my father brought him into the light, made him a tree in the Grove of Hismayas. He was a man of many secrets then. It appears some things haven't changed."

Sugar said nothing.

"Have you thought about what you and your brother will do should this dream of Shim's fall apart?"

"You're not committed to Shim's cause?"

"I'm committed to certain principles, and to my crew, of which you are now a part."

"Sounds a bit fair-weathered to me."

He smiled. "I stick with mine through thick and thin. On the other hand, I'm not a big fan of committing myself to another man's suicide."

"You think that's what this is?"

"Not at this moment. Right now it's a wondrous opportunity. But opportunities don't last forever. Conditions change. New facts come to light. I suggest you think about that. You have a brother to take care of."

"I'm committed to my friends," she said.

"And have you thought of how you might help save them if Shim fails?"

"I assume Argoth and the Creek Widow have such things planned."

"Have they shared them with you?"

"No," she said defensively.

"Then don't assume. I owe your mother. I aim to see you're taken care of. Shim's dream carries a great amount of risk. When was the last time someone tried to build an army of sleth and take on a glorydom? I'm not sure even Hismayas attempted this, and you know what happened to him. It never hurts to run scenarios of potential risks through your mind. So, have you made contingency plans?"

She ignored the question. He had just said he owed her mother. What did that mean?

He waited for an answer.

"Look, I'm not going to abandon my duty when things get rough."

"I'm not asking you to. I'm just suggesting you look down the path a bit. Just as your mother would have."

"You knew my mother?"

He smiled. "We're almost to the camp," he said. "We already passed through the first picket."

Sugar looked around. "I didn't see anyone."

"You're not meant to."

"What about my mother?"

"All in good time," he said.

Another fifty yards and they turned down a lane that was starting to grow weeds at the edges. Through the trees an old woodman's shack came into view. Half of it was covered in vines. Smoke trailed up out of a stone chimney.

"Not much to look at," she said. "And where are all your men?"

"A big show of force would only attract attention," said Urban. "But our sentries are posted."

As they came closer, she saw Soddam, the big man that had first scared her at Redthorn, sitting on a stump, skinning an apple with his big knife. When they entered the yard, Soddam plopped a slice of apple in his mouth and stood. "I don't think I've seen a more pretty ferret," he said. "Welcome."

The slit pupils of his orangish-brown eyes still unnerved her. "I'm not the ferret yet."

"You will be," he said. "Old Withers is waiting expectantly."

She caught a whiff of the appetizing odor of roasting meat.

Urban pulled the horse to a stop, then set the wagon brake. They clambered down, and then Urban led her over to the door of the shack and opened it. The delicious aroma of cooking washed over her—meat, sweet onions, and some type of bread.

Inside the shack stood a table, some bunks, a hearth with a small fire. A thin old man squatted next to the fire stirring a pot. Other pots sat next to him in the coals.

"Withers," said Urban. "This is Sugar, Purity's girl."

"Keep that door open," the man said without turning. "Any visitors need to find an easy way out." He lit a braid of godsweed in the coals. When it caught fire, he waved the braid back and forth, spreading the sweet smoke into the corners of the room and up into the rafters, working from the back of the shack to the door. When he finished, he whistled for Soddam, handed him the braid, and instructed him to smoke the area around the house. At last he turned to Sugar. His face was wrinkled and brown. His mouth was missing a number of teeth. "I've been waiting for you," he said kindly enough. Then he took a step back and looked her up and down. "Hum," he grunted and took her wrist. With his other hand he pinched the skin along her arm, gauging its thickness. When he'd gauged the back of her arm, he shook his head. "Not good." He pinched her waist in three spots. "Not good at all."

"She's ready to learn," said Urban.

Withers poked her in the ribs. "Starve her, I told the Captain, and then all we'll have is bones. If you're going to walk, you need some flesh to come back to. I'm not going to teach you anything until your belly's full. That's the first order of business. Everything's easier when you eat, especially walking." He motioned at the table. "Sit."

Sugar sat at the wooden table. Withers turned back to his pots. In moments he produced a bowl full of some kind of fowl, which he'd been cooking with vegetables and raisins. In another pot were biscuits covered with melted cheese. In yet another pot were apples cooked down to butter.

"Here," he said and scooped some of the meat and raisins onto a wooden plate. "We found this fat fellow this morning strolling about the yard." On another table lay some pheasant tail feathers. She assumed those had, as recently as this morning, belonged to the fat fellow she was about to eat.

"And you'll have some of this," he said and added some biscuits. He laid the plate in front of her with a spoon. "Go on," he said rubbing his knuckles.

Sugar picked up the spoon and took a bite of the pheasant. It was pure delight in her mouth.

"Ha," Withers said and pointed at her. "Like a starved dog. Try the bread now. Go on."

She took a bite of the biscuit. It was flaky and redolent with butter. "This is very good," she said.

"No speaking," he said. "Chew. That is all."

And so she ate and chewed, him watching her, and ate some more until she was almost stuffed. Then he brought out one more pot full of walnuts candied with butter and honey.

"I can't," she said.

He tipped his head and looked out from underneath his eyebrows as if he didn't believe a word of it.

"No, truly," she said.

"You'll take them with you for later," he said and put the pot back. He sat down next to her and began to examine the working of her joints, clucking like a hen, asking her about twinges. He made her open her mouth so he could inspect her teeth. He opened a shutter to get a bit better light and checked her eyes. He smelled her hair and felt the quality of her muscle. He poked and prodded until she felt like a goose on the table.

At last he finished. "So let us see the weave," he said.

She produced her mother's necklace. He held out the end of a wooden spoon, and she looped the necklace over it. Then he held it up to the light and began fingering the segments and making small sounds of approval. He fingered the horse and a moment later snatched his hand back.

He said, "The soul and flesh are bound together, but the proper weave can loosen that binding without breaking it altogether and killing the wearer." He held the necklace out to her, and she removed it from the spoon.

She said, "Urban says you were a Walker."

"Oh, my dear. My sweet biscuit. I walked glorious paths."

"He doesn't walk anymore," said Urban. "Not for a long time. The ability was seared out of him."

"Seared?"

Withers sucked in through the teeth he had. "They were all dying anyway. I just made sure it didn't go to waste. No harm done. And then I'd use it on my pigs. I raised the most succulent pigs in the territory. I put it to good use."

"Many years ago he cooked for a warlord," said Urban. "After the battles, he'd go out among the fallen."

"Only the enemy fallen," Withers corrected.

"He'd go out to those who were wounded and dying, and he'd steal their Fire."

"Like a fright," Withers said. "And that's where their Fire was going anyway. I said to myself, why give it to those ugly monsters? It was only practical not to waste it."

Sugar asked, "What does it mean to be seared?"

"It's a punishment in the Groves. Somewhat like forcing. It scars you, makes it almost impossible to use the lore, even when you heal again. All skill was burned out of Withers."

"The Grove seared him?" asked Sugar.

"They were going to do more, but now he cooks for us. They took his lore, but they couldn't take the knowledge that littered his mind."

"No," Withers said, "but sometimes I wish they would have. Sometimes it would be easier to bear. But we aren't here to talk about old Withers, are we? No, indeed. The Captain wants a ferret, and that's what he shall have." He looked at Sugar. "Can you quicken it?"

"I think so."

"Then let's not waste a moment," he said and rubbed his hands in excitement. "Put it on."

Sugar put the weave on.

"To be free," he said, a wild longing in his eyes.

She hesitated.

"Don't mind him," Urban said.

"Something happens," she said, "and I'm going to haunt you both."

"Ho," Withers laughed in delight. "I like this one, Captain. I do. Now find the mouth, Sweetness, and feed it."

Sugar knew that despite her reservations she really had no choice. She wanted to learn the lore, so she braced herself with a deep breath and felt for the thread. It was easy to find now that she'd already done it once.

"I'm going to feed it now," she said and gave it the smallest amount of Fire. Almost immediately she heard the thrumming. The heat ran along her bones, and she gritted her teeth.

"It hurts," Withers said. "It burns, but only a little, and then it will pass."

The heat built, a tearing along her bones, and then the room shifted, and she was seeing double. She blinked and blinked again.

"Your vision is blurring?"

"Yes," she said.

"That's because you're seeing with both the eyes of the flesh *and* the soul. You could step out of yourself if you wanted to. Close the eyes of your flesh."

She closed her eyes and the double vision vanished, leaving everything cast in yellow. Everything looked strange, the surfaces textured differently. Withers and Urban sat at the table. Their bodies were dark, but shone with a wavering aura. Outside the door, the sky was yellow with a lavender tinge at the horizon.

She looked at her hand and found she was looking at the hand of her soul, including, surprisingly, her tattoo. She'd thought that would have only been a part of the flesh, but it appeared more solid here. "What if something gets into my body while I'm out?"

"Is there anything here that looks like it might get in?"

She looked about. "No," she said.

"Then go, dear," said Withers.

"How?"

"Can you feel your soul?"

"I think so."

"Just take a step then."

Sugar stepped forward, felt the soul pull away, and exited her flesh. Some part of her remained back with her body, but the bulk was standing outside. A world of sound rushed in—pops and cracks and some odd singing in the distance. She took a step and then another, but didn't feel in control. She moved differently here, and suddenly she wondered if she might float away. She panicked and stepped back to her flesh, which accepted and cleaved to her again along the bones as if there were something sticky binding the two parts of herself together.

She immediately removed the weave. The odd vision left. The house returned to normal, but the heat still prickled along her bones.

Withers touched her arm gently. "Do you realize what you've just done?"

She did, and for the second time today, she was both amazed and terrified.

"That wasn't so bad, was it?" he asked.

"It's a bit disconcerting," she said.

"Like falling in love," he said wistfully.

"I don't know I'd compare it to that," she said.

"Oh, you will," he said. "You will. But you're going to have to do more than peep in and out. I want you to walk. Just walk and tell me what you see. Can you do that?"

"What about frights?" she asked.

Withers rubbed the knuckles of one hand. "What you need is a soul cleaver in your hand and a skir to do your bidding. That's how it's done in the world of light. But I don't suppose you're any sort of Skir Master."

"No, Zu," she said.

"No," he repeated. "So you'll have to do with a poker. Blackspine should be enough to give the howlers and ayten something to think about. Do you know how to handle a staff?"

"Yes," she said.

"Blackspine is nothing more than a long staff with a deadly point at one end. It's a good weapon. I've used it myself to chase off frights. And I'm not talking about the little ones. I'm talking about the disgusting ancient ones, all fat and knobby with multiple eyes. Monstrous sows that will suck you dry in a blink. But they don't like pokers; no they don't."

"I'm afraid I don't know what blackspine is."

"It grows in every land I've walked," said Withers, rubbing his wrist. "No reason why it shouldn't grow here. But you're going to have to walk to find it."

Sugar nodded.

"And here's another thing: I'm sure your soul's lovely in its nakedness, but you can't walk around like that in the world of soul, even if the Captain fancies it a fine idea. It's not practical or safe. No. A little bit of protection is what we're wanting. And a weapon. That's what we need, and old Withers can help you get both." He rubbed his knuckles again. "Let's walk for real this time, shall we?"

22

Soulwalk

SUGAR QUICKENED THE WEAVE for the third time today. She winced again at the pain along her bones, then stepped out of her flesh into the yellow world of souls.

"Captain," said Withers, "we're going to have to bring her body with us. I don't want her straying too far. Make it nice and secure on a horse."

Urban picked up her body of flesh and carried it out of the shack. Withers gestured for her to follow. "Outside, my dear."

His voice came from the wrong direction, and then she realized she was hearing him with the ears of her flesh that was now outside the house.

Withers picked up a small box that had been covered in copper and walked out of the shack. Sugar followed into the sunlight and dappled shade of the trees outside. Urban straddled her body upon a horse and secured it to the saddle. The horse's flesh was dark, but it too shone with an aura.

Above her, a flock of small blue creatures flew in a wavy line across the lavender-tinged sky. They looked and moved more like a school of sting rays.

"While you roam, you will talk to me with the mouth of your flesh," said Withers. "You will listen to me with the ears of flesh. When you ferret, this is how it's done. What do you see?"

She described the blue creatures.

"Did you try to speak?" he asked. "It's tricky in the beginning to control the flesh while most of you is standing outside of it."

Sugar focused and used the mouth of her flesh to repeat what she'd said. The ray-like creatures flying high above were mottled robin egg blue and white. Their heads trailed long black hairs. They were much larger than she first thought.

"That's much better," said Withers. "Every land on earth has some common animals, some wholly unique. It's the same in the world of souls. What you see are minor urgom. They like to feed at the mouths of rivers."

Sugar watched the minor urgom recede in the distance, then turned her attention to the area about the shack. The trees appeared odd here, as if they were made of felt. She took a step toward one and moved much farther than she would have suspected. She looked down at her legs and realized Withers was right—she was naked.

Her body was in the form of a human, but it shone with a faint luminescence. She raised her arms, looking at herself and saw some sort of membrane that extended a hand's span out from either side of her body. The membrane undulated, augmenting her movements. It was like she was some kind of eel from the sea. "Withers," she said. "My body . . ."

"Beautiful," he said, "isn't it?"

"I—" she said, gazing at her limbs. "I am not the creature I thought I was."

"None of us are. I think this is one of the truths the Divines destroyed when they rose to power."

Her hair moved to the side and in front of her as if the wind were blowing it. But there was no wind. Furthermore, she could feel things, sense something off in the woods with it. It was as if she'd grown a new sensory organ. "My hair," she said in wonder.

"Marvelously alive," he said. "The soul guides the growth of the flesh. But the flesh has limitations. Or perhaps it's more accurate to say it has its own needs. And so our bodies of flesh look like our bodies of soul, but they are not identical. There are some things our souls can do and feel that our flesh cannot, and vice versa. In this sphere of existence, the soul and flesh are not yet fully joined. One or the other dominates. But when we journey to the brightness that awaits, we are reborn. We become new creatures."

She could have never imagined this. She felt in a way like a hermit crab or oyster out of her shell. "I feel like a butterfly that has stepped out of its chrysalis before its time."

"Exactly," Withers said. "Which is why you need protection. The Creators endowed the flesh with wondrous properties. Chief among these is the ability to keep your soul safe. It's like a fortress. Safe, unless you let something inside. And there are many things that would want to get in there. Some to gorge, others to nest. So when you leave that fortress, you need something to protect you."

He set the small copper box he'd carried out onto the ground and opened the lid. "Put these on."

Sugar moved over to the box and looked in to see an odd set of clothes neatly folded. She pulled out a cap, shirt, and trousers. But they weren't solid. They looked like thick-whorled lace that would certainly not provide much protection in the world of flesh. "There's nothing in the box but moth-eaten clothes. If there are indeed moths on this side."

He laughed. "Sweet girl, those moth-eaten rags are worth more than the wealth of all the Shoka put together. You'll find them quite adequate against those that would want a nibble of you. Put them on. Put them on."

Sugar put the strange clothes on. The hat fit like a knitted cap with thin strips of the strange lace hanging down that tied to the shoulders of her shirt. The fabric was thin and exceedingly supple, clinging to her like a second skin. The shirt tied to the pants. When she'd fastened it all to her, she felt invigorated.

"Are you dressed?" he asked.

"I am." Then the clothes shifted slightly of their own accord. "This odd lace, it's moving."

He laughed again and rubbed his hands with excitement. "It's a very old and excellent servant, handed down from the ancestors. Woven and trained by their own hands."

"You've seen the ancestors?"

"In all my years, mine never made themselves known to me. I've seen the dead, but the ancestors, the bright ones, I only saw one once, very far off. It disappointed and troubled me. I walked far and wide and never found the Ways. But that's another matter. I have seen the recently dead, and I have seen the famished ones. You avoid them at all costs. But this wasn't given to me by some soul. I received it from my grandfather who received it from his until the names are forgotten. It's a skenning. It protects and conserves you even as it draws strength from your soul."

The clothing moved in small ways until it was snug against her. "Just when I think things can't get any stranger," she said. She held up her arm and saw that the gaps in the lace were now much smaller.

"It's not impervious," he said. "But it's strong against many things on that side. And when it's torn, it grows to renew itself."

"Like a skin of flesh."

"Precisely," he said. "Soul wants to be joined with another substance. This is one thing that can be worn outside the world of flesh. Now, let's walk. You still need blackspine."

Withers led Urban and her body upon the horse down a trail. She followed, but it felt so wrong to see her body riding away without her in it. She said, "How far away can a soul travel from its body?"

"You're not all outside yourself," he said. "If I were to take your body a distance down the road, you'd know exactly where it was, just as your body would know exactly where your soul stood. You can roam some distance, but the farther you go, the more your longing to be reunited grows until that longing consumes you, becomes almost a pain. I myself traveled three miles once; there are some who can go farther."

"What are the limits?"

"It all depends, but I've heard of some who walked great distances. But most must stay close."

"What about the weaves that employ bits of soul? Don't those travel?"

"Those bits are in a body of sorts, so different rules apply. But they still feel that discomfort of separation at great distances. There's a tale of a lord of Trolumbay who had part of his son's soul put into a soul stone. The soul stone was to be given to a warring neighbor as part of a treaty in an exchange for one of the enemy's own. But the ship wrecked out at sea and the soul stone was lost. The son went on with his life, but as the years past, he was often to be found standing in the surf, looking out to sea. His father tried to guard him to keep him safe. But early one foggy morning the son slipped away. The last anyone saw of him he was rowing out into the mists."

The tale gave her chills. "I supposed it will require some time to learn the hazards in this yellow world."

"Time and a good guide. There are very few Walkers who learn it on their own. Most of those who go it alone simply do not return. Now, tell me what you see."

Sugar did, and after each report Withers talked to her about the flora and fauna in the world of light. Numerous times he asked her to look up in the sky and tell him what she saw. If there was anything at all there, she described it to him, and he named it and detailed its behavior and habit and whether it posed a danger.

He told her about other things she had not seen yet: ayten, hoppen, shades, seven-arms, racers, wind mums, urgom. He'd ask her to watch the ground and give a report. She did. He asked her to listen, to jump, to feel the difference in motions. She realized he was savoring a place he loved through her. As they walked he told her stories of spying, of fighting ravening predators and chasing frights. He told her how water, air, and earth affected soul. He explained how stone was hard in both worlds and could damage her and protect her soul just at it could her body of flesh.

She found she could move more easily as a soul. As they walked she began to venture farther from her body of flesh. Up ahead a row of tall narrow poplars rose into the sky. She ran for them, leapt, and zoomed into branches and leaves which were all edged with fine pale hairs as thin as dandelion fluff. The tree was not solid, not nearly as solid as her body and the horse had been. It felt instead like sand or small gravel. She reported this.

"The structure of things is different in that world," Withers said. "Press into it."

She pressed her arm through a branch, feeling a heat as she did so, and retrieved it again. She was clinging to the tree about a dozen feet from the field below. Above her a group of small flying creatures startled from their hiding places and fluttered out of the tree. They looked like white butterflies. Some landed on her shoulders and body. One landed on the back of her naked hand. She looked down at it. It was a pretty wispy thing. She described it to Withers.

"Careful," he said.

Suddenly her hand stung. Two more stings lanced into her foot.

She cursed and swatted at them with her hand. The strange butterflies lifted off. Those she'd hit dropped away, spiraling to the ground.

Sugar jumped out of the tree. As soon as she hit the ground, she was running, expecting the biting butterflies to follow her like an angry nest of hornets. But when she glanced back, the butterflies were trailing down, falling upon those she'd injured or killed.

"Sugar?" Withers asked.

"I'm okay," she said.

"Good thing you had your skenning, eh?"

It was. What if the whole mob of them had been able to sting her? It would have been excruciating.

"Those pretties are called gossamers. You'll often find them about bodies of fallen souls. Sometimes the bodies of flesh that Walkers leave behind attract them as well."

"How many Walkers are there?"

"Very few sleth know the secrets. But there are Walkers employed by the Divines. Myself, I tried to avoid areas where Divines were working."

Sugar smelled sulfur and reported it.

"You're not smelling that in the world of souls," said Withers. "We're coming up on a sulfur spring. We asked around when we learned you'd agreed to be our ferret. If you're going to find blackspine, you'll find it here, next to hot springs."

They walked a little farther to a hillside where waters burbled out of the ground. The smell of rotting eggs was strong. True to its name, blackspine grew like the spines of monstrous urchins here. Withers directed her to wrench one of the spines out of the ground.

She grabbed one that looked solid and was the right diameter for her hands and twisted this way and that until it broke off at the root. The spine stood as tall as she. It was invisible in the world of the flesh, but in the world of the soul it had heft and strength. It was more like a javelin or short spear than a staff.

Withers produced a strap from a pouch and looped it around the head of her body and one shoulder. She opened the eyes of her flesh and saw the strap and pouch in that world as well. They were both made of well-worn leather. The strap was scraped, nocked, and stained. At various intervals along it were worked small bits of metal. But what appeared to be a plain strap in the world of flesh turned out to be a pack in the world of the soul with fasteners and ties. She wondered what lore allowed someone to weave in material from the world of souls.

"You have to carry your things around with you," Withers said. "This strap allows you to do that. Now you have a weapon and some armor. I think that's enough for the first day. Let's go back now."

She realized he was taking her in a large circle. They'd walked a few miles, but she'd been so absorbed, she hadn't realized they'd come so far. On this part of the walk, a number of black gnat-like things zipped past her and gave her a scare, but Withers said they were benign. As were a cluster of dull amber creatures moving about a jumble of stone at the bottom of a hill. There were about a dozen of them, no larger than a knuckle. When she approached, they fled into the gaps in the rocks.

She crossed a stream, and found soul sank like everything else, but if she moved quickly, she could run across the face of the water. Her abilities, the sights and sounds—it was wondrous. Of all of them, her hair was the most strange. She'd sensed things all along the way, but realized something was following them through the woods. She couldn't see it with the eyes of her soul. Nor could she hear it. But it was there. She reported this to Withers.

"I wouldn't worry about it. But if it starts to come close, retreat to your body to be safe."

They continued on and followed the road up a hill, Urban staying with her body. When she crested the top, a shimmering flickered behind a thin stand of trees below. She looked closer and saw that it was a soul, a person, walking through the trees. She immediately thought of the ancestors, of Mother and Da.

She described this to Withers. "I want to investigate."

"Is this wise?" Urban asked.

"She'll meet them sooner or later," said Withers. "Better to learn her lessons now. Besides, sometimes these souls have insight." He patted the hand of her flesh. "Go slowly. You don't know what such a soul's intentions might be. Always assess before you jump in."

Sugar's excitement rose. The soul might have seen her mother and father, might have news. It might lead her to them.

There was a small path next to the creek that ran at the bottom of the hollow. Withers and Urban descended with the horses and turned onto the trail, but Sugar didn't wait for her body of flesh. She ran ahead.

The thing following them had paced her, but it now stopped, then began to move away at speed. A moment later something grunted and growled in the distance. She reached out with her senses. There were other living things about, but none of them felt far enough away to be associated with the growl, so she decided to continue to move forward.She was now some distance ahead of Withers and Urban. With the bends in the trail she'd lost sight of them, but she could still hear them with her body. She continued for maybe a hundred yards along the trail, came to the edge of a clearing, and stopped.

A number of bodies lay about the grass. There were a few goats, but also the bodies of a man and a boy. The man was alive, but mortally wounded in his leg and belly. The boy was clearly dead, two arrows sticking from his chest.

The man stroked the hair of the boy's body of flesh and wept, oblivious to the half-dozen frights that had latched onto him, the body of his boy, and the goats. The frights were twisted like driftwood, knobby and misshapen, their many fingers split and spread like the pale roots of a plant, sinking into their victims. Each was as long as her arm. They grunted as they fed.

The soul of the boy yelled and charged the fright clinging to his father.

The fright turned menacingly, and the boy aborted his attack.

She described the scene to Withers. "Should I chase the frights off?"

"Patience. Do you hear a clicking?"

"No."

"That means the ayten haven't found them yet."

Ayten, Withers had said earlier, were orangish skir that fed on souls. "I did hear an awful growl earlier, but it was in the distance."

"I think it's time to come back," said Withers.

The soul of the boy charged again. This time he kicked at one fright and sent it scurrying away, but another fright turned on him, and he backed away. The man groaned and slumped to one side.

"Da," the boy said and dropped to his knees weeping.

A beat passed and something began to emerge from the man's mouth. Sugar watched in horror as his soul pulled itself out of his body.

"Da?" the boy asked.

The soul of the man pulled the last part of himself out and stood before his son.

At that moment, a howl rose at the far end of the field. The souls of the dead goats there panicked and ran. A dark beast shot out of the trees and chased them. It was followed by another. And then four more. The creatures were angular and long-limbed like nightmare versions of whippets or greyhounds. They had no tails. Instead, short spikes ran down their backs. One howled. It was the howl she'd heard before. And she realized she'd felt the presence a few minutes ago but hadn't been paying attention to them.

The frights looked up, then broke from the bodies and scurried away into the woods.

Two of the beasts stopped to tear into the goats, but the rest spied the boy and the soul of the man.

"Run!" the father yelled, then grabbed his son's hand and sprinted for the woods. But Sugar could see they weren't going to be fast enough. And where would they go anyway?

Sugar held the blackspine in her hand. She described the beasts to Withers. "What do I do?"

"Come back," said Withers.

"I can't just leave them."

"Come back!" Withers commanded.

The dark nightmare whippets sprang onto the boy, taking him down. He screamed in agony. Two others fell upon the father.

Sugar took a step forward blackspine in hand, hesitated, but it was clear she was too late. Then one of the dark creatures spotted her.

Fear shot through her.

"Sugar!" Withers said.

"I'm coming," she said and backed away.

The creature moved forward.

Sugar turned and fled, running faster than she ever could in the flesh. The dark creature howled and raced after her, angling through the trees.

Back upon the horse, her body tried to rise to its feet.

"Sugar!" Urban shouted. "Talk to us."

But she was too busy to talk. The spiked beast rushed through the woods. Sugar ran, leapt, raced back down the trail. She tried to release her body from the saddle, to run to her soul, but her fingers fumbled at the ties holding her in the saddle. She tried opening her eyes briefly. The double vision disoriented her, and she almost ran into a tree.

"Bring my body!" she said with the mouth of her flesh. "Down the path!"

She fled around a bend, and this time she did careen into the trunk of a tree and sank partway into the wood. The impact hurt and she realized, again, that soul was mortal. She wrenched herself out, scrabbled back up to right herself, but the miscalculation had cost her. There was no way she'd make it back to her body now. However, as she charged down the trail, Urban appeared around a corner ahead, leading the horse with her body. Withers hurried behind, trying to keep up.

"I'm here!" she said. "I'm here!" Four long strides and she reached the horse. Just as she did, the hideous whippet burst onto the trail behind her.

Her body strained against its bindings, and she leapt upon the horse and tried to enter her flesh, but couldn't.

Panic flooded her.

Then she realized she was wearing the skenning. She couldn't inhabit two bodies at the same time. And she didn't have time to take it off.

She spun around.

The whippet howled, raced toward her. It did not have a mouth like a dog, but more like a lamprey.

She faced it, held her blackspine in front of her. Just as the horrible thing leapt, she lunged. The blackspine sank deep into its body. The whippet writhed and cried out. Its brothers back with the souls of the man and boy answered.

Sugar pulled the blackspine out and stabbed the thing again and again. It fell to the earth and writhed.

She turned back to her body and shed the skenning. The other whippets raced through the trees toward her.

Withers had finally caught up, panting.

"Where do I put it?" she said with the mouth of her body.

"Put what?" Urban replied.

"The skenning?"

"Here," Withers said and opened the copper box. She stuffed it in. Then she jumped up behind where her body sat on the horse. The creatures galloped through the woods. She fastened one clasp of the strap she wore on her body around the blackspine, then tried to slip into her body as she'd done before, but she could not.

Then she remembered she'd closed her doors. She opened them and stepped into her body. Outside her body, the approaching whippets howled. She slammed her doors shut, then remembered Urban saying weaves make an opening. It was how they worked. Which meant that even though she was shut, it could be a weakness. The howls rose to a pitch, and she untied the necklace and tore it from her.

Immediately, the awful vision and noise vanished. Moments later a chill slid past her. And another, then they were gone, and there was nothing but the blue-hued world of the flesh, Urban standing next to her, the creek burbling to the side.

"Merciful lords," she said.

"What happened?" Urban asked.

"Howlers," said Withers.

"We need to get out of here," she said.

"You're safe now," Withers said. "There is no need to panic. You are safe in the fortress of your flesh."

"What happened?" Urban asked again.

"It was horrible," she said. "Horrible."

"They took the man and boy, didn't they?" Withers asked.

"They ripped them apart."

Withers rubbed his knuckles slowly. "It is a beautiful world. A perilous world. I think your first lesson is now complete. You did well, ferret. Very well."

She thought about the man and boy. "Nobody came for them," she said. There were no ancestors guarding them. None to bring them to safety. She thought about her own mother and father. Had anyone come for them?

"You need to be smoked," said Withers. "Then we'll talk."

"And I'll send someone back to investigate the deaths," said Urban. "It was probably a Fir-Noy raid."

They traveled the rest of the way back to the shack in silence. Along the way she realized being apart from herself had strained her and that merging back into her flesh brought a relaxing comfort.

When they got back to the shack, they found Soddam still sitting on his stump. She dismounted and followed Withers and Urban into the shack. She said, "I knew the stories about the perilous journey in the world of souls. But they were all stories."

"Not the same as witnessing it firsthand," said Withers, "is it?" He retrieved a godsweed braid and laid it on the embers in the hearth.

"Do you think those horrid creatures followed us?"

"They might have," he said. He retrieved the braid and began to wave it about. "Sometimes walking attracts attention. It's always wise to burn a little godsweed afterwards."

"I should have helped that man and boy," she said.

"You weren't ready," he said. "You would have fallen."

"I should have tried."

"Not everyone can be saved," he said. "A Walker has to reconcile himself to that fact."

She knew his words made logical sense, but that didn't mean they felt right. The images of the man and boy being torn by those howlers filled her mind. "Dear Creators, where were the ancestors?"

Withers said nothing.

Urban said, "With more skill, you will be able to do more in the world of souls. Maybe next time you can help. But first you have to learn. I told you I don't compel any of my men. I think you now know the nature of your work. And its risks. Are you still in?"

Everyone in Shim's army took risks. Her fellow candidates needed a spy. If she could increase their odds of victory, she'd be a coward not to do this thing. "Of course I'm in," Sugar said.

Urban smiled. "Purity's daughter indeed."

"There you go again," Sugar said.

"She was part of my father's Grove. She did not bind herself to weak thinking."

Sugar smiled. No, Mother never did.

"She came here as one of those traveling to the city of Hope."

"Yes," Sugar said, "Matiga told me. When it was time to move on, she realized the promise of a distant city didn't quite compare with the here and now of a certain smith she'd come to know."

He nodded. "Exactly. She had her own mind. And a good thing too."

Sugar knew the story of the trail. The One Root, the leader of all the Groves of Hismayas had led a company into the wilderness here to establish a city where they could practice their arts freely and yet be hidden from the eyes of the world. For a number of years, members of various Groves had secretly traveled to the New Lands. They'd sought out Hogan the Koramite who gave them the directions that would take them to a lake somewhere in the Wilds beyond the borders of the land to wait. Every few weeks or months, someone from the city would come and lead them into the wilderness, never to be heard or seen again. But that had all stopped. No guides had come to the lake in many years. The trail was dead. There was much speculation on what had happened and whether the city had failed or was growing, preparing to reveal itself to the world in power.

"Why do you say it was a good thing she didn't go?" asked Sugar.

"There are some people who serve the lore. And there are others who let the lore serve them. Your mother didn't let the Order rule her. She married and found joy in a family."

"She came to a bad end," said Sugar. "I don't know if I'd call that good."

"Are you telling me that one awful day wiped out everything that had gone before? Your mother lived and loved while she had the chance.

She was a great woman. At least, she was when I knew her."

"She was splendid," Sugar agreed.

"And you'll do her proud," said Urban.

Withers reached out and stroked the end of Sugar's hair. "How are you feeling, Walker?"

Now that he'd asked, she realized she had a bit of a headache. "A few aches here and there," she said.

Withers nodded. "Perfectly natural. To be expected. They will go away, but there are some that won't. If you are ever walking and start feeling real pain, like the very flames of a fire are licking your bones, you run back to your body. You don't hesitate. Or you may find you can't get back at all. Do you hear me?"

"I hear," Sugar said.

"Walking is not for everybody. For some it means death. Remember that."

"I will."

"Good," he said. "Your job now is to practice with the spine. Don't get cocky after bullying a few frights about. A spine's good, the skenning helpful, but when you hear the howls or the wicked singing of the ayten, you run back to your body. You run back to the defense of the flesh until you know how to handle such things."

"I will," she said.

He rubbed his wrist and said, "You come back to old Withers. There's no need to fear—I'll fatten you up, then teach you how to weave a soul cleaver. Great Lords, then you will be a terror in your own right. In the meantime, you need to eat." He pushed a number of dried biscuits into her pockets. Then he fetched the candied nuts.

She took his food, then climbed back onto the wagon seat next to Urban. They left Withers and the shack. Soddam waved good-bye. She thought she saw another one of Urban's crew as they rode back to the fortress, but she couldn't be sure.

When they had ridden a good distance from the shack, Urban said, "So, what do you think about Withers?"

He'd been so kind and patient, like a grandfather, and yet he'd done abominable things. "I don't know."

"He was a villain once. But he didn't need killing, did he?"

She thought on that, then said, "I truly hope not."

23

Rabbit

BEROSUS NOTICED the man tailing him before he had walked a hundred yards from the fortress. It was one of Eresh's men.

Shim and Argoth had wanted to give Berosus leadership of a terror, but he didn't want to be under their eye, so he'd argued that Eresh would only balk and that it would be far better to use him as a spy. As a member of the Hand, not only did he know how Mokad worked, but he also knew the names of various Divines and lesser lords and could recognize them on sight. Furthermore, unlike anyone from the Clans here, his tattoos wouldn't give him away. His honors had nothing to do with the New Lands, which meant he could pose as a Mokaddian scout and get in close to the enemy.

His argument had convinced Argoth and Shim, and they'd agreed. However, it still didn't mean they fully trusted him. Argoth, for example, was still wary. Berosus could see it in his eyes. And Eresh, of course, didn't trust him at all. Still, his role as spy meant he could come and go as he needed, at least for now.

Berosus walked past the fields between the fortress and the village that served it. Shortly after entering the village, he made a number of turns through the houses, outbuildings, and back yards. The man tailing him followed at a discrete distance, and then was replaced by another who was eating what looked like a fine bun of some sort.

Very good, Berosus thought. He was impressed yet again with these sleth. In fact, if he hadn't been looking, he would have never noticed the second man, or the man on the porch of the tavern, or the woman out with her cows. There was a whole network of eyes and ears here.

Shim and Argoth had probably alerted them to note the movements of certain people and watch for anything suspicious. The attack on Talen proved they had a breach in their security, and so all eyes and ears would have been ordered to step up their vigilance. Any sleth who had come to join Shim would certainly be on the watch list. It would be the prudent thing to do. There was never any telling what a sleth might be hiding.

So the tail following Berosus wasn't the result of Eresh acting on his own. It was surely Argoth's idea as well. But they wouldn't find out any of his secrets today.

He entered the woods outside the village. The original tail followed, albeit with a different hat and shirt, which anyone with normal senses would have missed.

But Berosus wasn't your normal dreadman. He wasn't your normal Divine. He built his Fire and increased his pace. He increased it again. A few strides later, yet again. The woods on either side of him flew past, his lungs taking in far more breath than a normal human's could. By the time Berosus came to the river, he was two miles ahead of his tail.

Berosus entered the river and swam downstream a few hundred yards. Then he exited through some willows on the far side and disappeared into the woods beyond. The tail would spend an hour here, going up and down the banks. By the time he found a trail, if he found one at all, Berosus would be beyond catching.

* * *

A few hours later Berosus waited by a small secluded waterfall in the woods savoring a small basket of blueberries as his captain reported that the army would arrive on the morrow. There would be more than a hundred ships, almost fifty thousand normal troops, a few thousand dreadmen, plus dog-men, plus his Skir Masters.

A whole army was descending upon this land, and Argoth was back at the fortress trying to force the last of his candidates. It made Berosus smile.

The captain finished his report, and they discussed other plans and tasks, which the captain would need to fulfill. Then they waited for Nashrud. His dog appeared first. It wasn't a big mastiff, but a smaller hound, black and brown with a salting of white hairs. It had one brown eye and one that was pale blue, both of which looked at you with far too much intelligence. The dog padded down to the waterfall, sniffed about, then sat on its haunches and looked squarely at Berosus. Normal dogs avoided prolonged eye-contact. This one did not, but that was to be expected with Nashrud. He was more Divine than dreadman, and his powers focused along one track.

Moments later Nashrud appeared, coming through the trees.

When he was close, Berosus held out the small basket of blueberries. "They're quite good." Nashrud took two and ate them without question as Berosus knew he would, but he did not show any delight. Nashrud was a hard man. An excellent servant. He enjoyed his animals and red meat and the thrill of the hunt, but he didn't betray much emotion.

"We have the rabbit's location," said Nashrud. His scar stood out in the muted light of the woods. It ran from the top of his forehead, cleaved his eyebrow, and continued down his cheek to the corner of his mouth.

Berosus said, "You've confirmed this with human eyes?"

"The Holy One and his sister are hiding at a farm close to the mountains. All we await is your command."

The water burbled across the rocks. The autumn leaves had begun to fall, and the whole woods smelled of leaf mold. It was delicious.

"Secure him," said Berosus.

"And what of the sister?"

"If she dies, it won't be a troubling loss. The fledgling Glory is the main thing."

Nashrud inclined his head. "The rabbit will be in your hands by breakfast tomorrow."

* * *

Miles away, in the barn of the Koramite farmer Len and his wife Tinker, Talen sat down upon a milking stool. On the dark wooden platter between River and him lay a duck, two squares of soft pumpkin, and a number of small apples, all of which had been roasted to perfection.

Talen said, "The whole time in that barrel I was thinking we'd be laying up in some nasty cave or wet, mosquito-infested knoll in the swamps. I thought we'd be eating snakes and squirrels. But I believe we're going to eat better here than in Len's barn we did back at the fortress."

River said, "A cave or knoll would have meant Uncle would have had to supply sentries, and that would have attracted attention."

"True," Talen said and carved off a piece of the duck's breast with his knife. Len had many children and grandchildren. Two more bodies wouldn't attract attention. And with so many, he'd been able to position a number of these to watch the ways to the farm. Talen bit into the piece of meat. It was moist and seasoned. "He used salt," he said with delight.

"Len and Uncle go way back," said River. "You be sure to show your gratitude." Then she picked up a square of pumpkin and ate some of the flesh with her knife.

Talen's craving, to his incredible relief, had diminished over the last few hours. He didn't know why, and he didn't care.

He said, "This is a good hiding place, but there's going to come a time when we have to face the servants of the Devourers."

"Even when you're as strong as Da or Ke, there will be times when running is the best option."

"The day's coming when I will hunt *them*."

River smiled. "When you can beat your sister, then you can talk about hunting. In fact, I think this barn will make a fine spot for some hard lore work."

"You underestimate me," said Talen.

"Finish your duck, and we'll see who's the one doing the underestimating."

* * *

High above Len's farm two hooded crows circled and watched the landscape below them. There was the bright river, the dead badger they so very much wanted to descend and eat, and the barn that hid the two humans.

24

Alert

ARGOTH WAS EXHAUSTED. He and Matiga had spent the whole night forcing candidates. One had died. More than twenty others lay broken. But two hundred and twelve had been raised. It was an awesome thing to contemplate, even if he feared their numbers weren't going to be enough.

He stood in the smoky great hall checking the pulse of a man who'd just broken. He was a strong fellow from Bain, the brother of one of Mokad's official Shoka dreadmen.

"Such a waste," Matiga said, bringing a thick woolen quilt over.

He didn't want to think about that. The fall of each one of these men hurt him. "We'll hope for the best," said Argoth. "I'm sure he'll recover."

"I'm not," she said and unfurled the quilt over him. Argoth helped her wrap the man up. They checked the others who had broken, making sure their hearts were still beating and their Fire hadn't broken forth again.

Matiga fetched another bit of godsweed and put it in the fire. "We should take a break," she said. "Get some sun. We've still got a stretch to go."

"Aye," he said, but it took him a moment to muster the strength to leave the hall. Outside in the bailey, some troops had already begun to move out. Eresh and Ke were somewhere else practicing with the new dreadmen. Argoth made his way over to his family's quarters. He entered to find Serah packing up a bundle of clothes.

Nettle squatted over by the wall, tracking a spider as it ran across the floor. Just as it was about to slip under a bed, he crushed the spider with one finger, then brought up the gooey remains to examine them. He paused a moment, then flicked his tongue out to taste it.

"Nettle," Serah said, reprimanding him.

Argoth's heart sank. Nettle was getting worse.

Serah folded a tunic and looked at Argoth. She didn't say a word, but he knew what that look meant. She still didn't forgive him for what he'd done to their son.

"We're more than halfway through the candidates," he said.

She didn't reply, just picked up a pair of woolen socks and rolled them together.

A commotion arose outside. A moment later a man rushed to the open door. It was one of those he'd sent to watch the ways leading to Talen's and River's hideout.

"Captain," the soldier said. "We spotted a hammer of mounted men moving along the road you told us to watch, proceeding toward West Hill by way of Smoky Ridge."

"Why did you not engage them?"

"We did. They were dreadmen, and there weren't enough of us."

Argoth cursed. Mokad *was* here. And it was more than a few spies. He wondered how many dreadmen had already arrived and why Shim's ears had not even heard a rumor. Worse still, West Hill was where Len's farm lay. There was nothing of value to Mokad out there, not unless you knew about Talen. But how could Mokad have found out Talen's true location? Nobody but he, Ke, Shim, and Matiga knew where he'd hidden the boy. The driver who'd taken the wagon out hadn't even driven to Len's place. Argoth had sent him elsewhere so River and Talen could slip through the woods on foot and attract no attention at all. Even Eresh was in the dark.

"Thank you," Argoth said to the man. "Find Oaks. I want a hundred of the new dreadmen mounted up immediately." Mokad was taking a roundabout way to Len's farm. If he took the direct route, he just might beat them there.

The man nodded and raced back out into the bailey.

Serah looked at Argoth, then back down to her folding.

Argoth followed the soldier out. Less than ten minutes later he and a terror of Shim's new dreadmen were mounted on horses and thundering through the outer gate.

25

Scruff

TALEN DIDN'T HAVE time to step back and avoid the blow that surely would have broken his jaw. Instead, he leaned away and turned his face, River's fist just barely brushing past his cheek. Her swing had exposed her, but before he could strike, she moved, elbowed his forehead, and the next thing Talen knew, he was thudding to the barn's dirt floor, a small puff of dust and hay flecks rising about him.

River put her fists on her hips and shook her head. "Your footwork is sloppy. You've got to remember to keep a stance that will let you move. Stand up like a wall and someone's going to knock you down."

Talen felt his forehead where she'd struck him, then climbed to his feet. They'd been practicing combat sequences the whole morning and were now using them in an open fight. All their work had raised a cloud of dust in the barn. "I'm choking," he said. "We need to open a window."

"Cleaner air isn't going to get you to stand right."

He was sweating and itchy from the flakes of hay and dust that stuck to him. He knew they shouldn't risk open windows, but the farm was secure. Len and his wife Tinker were as loyal to Uncle Argoth as any of his soldiers. In fact, three of their older sons had fought under Argoth's personal command. But it went beyond that. They had a true friendship with him. So much that the farmer had posted three of his younger sons and daughters to watch the roads. "I'm opening a window," Talen said.

River rushed him, as he knew she would. He dodged left, spun, and delivered a perfect kick to her side. Except by the time his foot arrived, she wasn't there, and his perfect kick mortally wounded nothing but a few dust motes.

She snatched Talen's leg in a two-arm hold, and before he could cry out in dismay, she twisted and he was off his feet and thudding to the ground yet again. Another puff of dust and hay flecks curled up around him.

She pointed at him. "How many times have I killed you today?"

Talen groaned. "I think you just broke my back." He rolled over and got up, gingerly feeling just above his tail bone. "It's not quite a fair fight."

"No," she said. "Fights never are. Do you think Mokad's dreadmen are going to tie a hand behind their backs to give you a sporting chance?"

Talen was irritated now. River had forced him to a higher level, and he was still dealing with the vestiges of clumsiness that came with his newfound power. But even if he'd mastered this new level, River was still stronger than he was, faster, more experienced. "The only way to even the odds is to run away from you and come back with help," he said.

"That's one way," she said. "But what if that option isn't available?"

He sprang to the top of the horse stall wall about five feet off the ground.

"What are you doing up there?"

"Despite your powers, you're not as nimble up here as I."

River picked up a block of wood from a small stack leaning against the wall and hucked it at him. He tried to move, but it struck him in the side. River was a thrower and always had been. Deadly with shoes, cooking spoons, and pots.

"Don't restrict your movement," she said. "Restrict mine. Find an equalizer, something to let you strike from a distance or block my blows."

His eyes stung; his head was buzzing. She was going to send him to the world of souls before any of Mokad's dreadmen had the chance. And as if to prove him right, she picked up another block of wood and threw it at his head. He ducked, and it banged into the wall.

He spotted a hay fork, jumped down, and ran to it. He brought it around like a staff. River came at him with a stick of firewood in her hand.

He was tired and angry. She was supposed to train him, not beat him to a pulp. If she wanted him to equalize this fight, he'd equalize it.

"Careful," River replied. "You're losing your calm. You need to be angry, but not enough that you can't think. It's a fine balance." She was going to throw that stick and immediately follow it with an attack. But he wasn't going to let her get that far. Talen charged her with the business end of the fork. He didn't hold back.

River moved to the side. He shifted his weight and swung the other end of the hay fork at her head. She blocked the blow with her stick. He parried, but as he did so, she grabbed the shaft of the hay fork, wrenched, and the hay fork leapt from his hands.

Impossible.

She shook her head. She was going to teach him a lesson. He could see it in her face. She swung the handle end of the hayfork around to clout him.

But Talen had had enough. His anger rose, and suddenly he was in two places. The part of him that was in front of her ducked, barely avoiding a blow to the head. The other part reached around and struck her from behind.

Her eyes went wide and she faltered. That gave Talen an opening, and he took it, striking her solidly in the gut.

She gasped and winced. He struck again. "Ha!" he said.

River clutched her stomach and stepped back. "What did you just do?" she asked.

"Taught you some respect," he said. Although he still didn't feel quite himself and the double vision was confusing him. He closed his eyes.

"I felt you clawing at me."

It was like the dream he'd had the night before where he'd seen the slayer upon the wall. "I don't know," he said, blinking. The room whirled, and then his vision resolved.

"Yes, you do," she said, "and you're going to tell me even if I have to beat it out of you."

"I think that's exactly what you just—"

River held her hand up for silence. Outside someone whistled loudly.

That was the signal warning of danger coming down the road. Talen raised his eyebrows. They ran to the window and cracked the shutter. A dark column of smoke rose in the distance.

Farmer Len had placed his children to watch both of the approaches to the farm. When a pair spotted someone on the road, one of them was to ride back to the farm on a pony. If the other that stayed behind perceived danger, he or she was to ignite a heap of straw that would burn with a thick black smoke, and then flee.

"Saddle Scruff," River said and ran for the barn door.

His given name was Blue Boot, an obvious reference to the coloring of his legs, which was the coloring of the wild horses on the Kish plains. But Scruff wasn't one of those wild horses; he was a mix of who knew what. His body was a sandy brown that gave way to a neck and head of mottled gray.

His coat was a bit too long in places. His build was odd, looking to be a poor mix of charger and runner. However, the important thing was not his lack of beauty, his ancestry, or name, but his surprising acceleration and sure foot. River had been training with him to become a firesteed. But not like the mounts some dreadmen rode that wore weaves full of horse Fire. Scruff received Fire directly from River's touch, often to his neck or withers. This meant she had some control over his multiplication. The weave was only there to help guide her.

Fire, Talen had learned, could be given without harm from any living thing to another. But it was not so when taken. Filtering rods could catch much of the soul of the specific creature, but there were essential parts of a species that no rod could touch. And so humans couldn't breed animals for their Fire because humans couldn't consume animal Fire without consuming those essential parts and becoming twisted by them.

Scruff had taken to the training. He liked to run and jump. But horses, just like men, had to learn to wear their power, and that took a lot of time. Scruff was not a full firesteed yet. If River pushed him too hard, his body would be overmatched. He'd suffer the clumsiness Talen did. But even worse, it would become easier to run the animal to death. One had to be careful and give the animal plenty of time to recover from a firerun.

Scruff stood in the corral outside the barn, snuffling the last bits of hay from his feeding. Talen grabbed the bridle, opened the door to the corral, and whistled. River did not believe in using food to entice a horse to you because what happened if you needed to catch the horse while out riding and didn't have some treat? She felt it was a bad lesson to teach them. So Talen hadn't used food to catch Scruff, but that hadn't prevented him from using food to curry some friendship. He had an old carrot in his pocket; he held it up and whistled again. Scruff eyed the carrot, then began to mosey over. Talen didn't want to spook him, so he didn't run to the animal, but did quicken his gait. When he reached the horse, he slipped the bit into Scruff's mouth and the bridle onto his head. Then he fed the horse the carrot.

Two hooded crows swooped low over the corral, cawed, and took positions on top of the fence. Behind them the thin pillar of black smoke rose in the distance above the trees.

Talen tied Scruff to a post and fetched the blanket and his special saddle. The saddle used by firesteeds was slightly different from a normal saddle because both the front and back were built higher to help keep the rider upon the animal. Talen put the big saddle on the horse and straightened it. He attached the saddle bags and tightened the belly strap.

River came running to the corral with Farmer Len, carrying a water bladder. "Quickly," Len said. "Out the back!"

Because firesteeds accelerated and stopped so quickly, they required both chest and rump straps as well. Talen tightened the chest straps while River secured the rump.

Len packed the water and some food in the saddle bags, and they mounted. Then Len opened the gate to the corral. "Go!" he said and waved them out.

Scruff wanted to run. If they'd been training, they would have made sure to trot him for a distance first, but this wasn't training. River gave him his head, and Scruff shot forth with such a surge that if Talen hadn't been clinging to River, he would have tumbled right off the rump.

A group of hens scratched the dirt in the road. Scruff raced toward them; the hens looked up in alarm, then scattered with squawks and a flutter of wings.

Talen scooted closer to River and took a better grip on the saddle. Just before they turned a bend in the narrow road, he looked back. Len was closing the gate and was motioning to his wife and girl to walk slowly and act calm.

Talen hadn't really known Len, Tinker, or any of their children. Yet they'd been willing to put themselves in terrible danger for his sake. His heart swelled with gratitude. He hoped this was all a false alarm and that whoever was coming just passed through.

The road bent left into the trees and then down into a small wash and out of view of the farm. Water ran in a small stream at the bottom. Scruff raced down the bank, splashed through the water, surged up the other side onto a good path with not too much incline, allowing him to stretch his gait into a full gallop.

Talen leaned forward. "Have you multiplied him?"

"Not yet," River shot back.

She obviously wanted to give him time to warm his body. They galloped for a short distance along the trail through the wood, Scruff kicking up the fallen autumn leaves that littered the ground. Behind them, the trail was mostly long and straight. Anyone coming up from the wash would see them, and Talen expected someone to appear at any moment.

His tension built until River rode Scruff around a bend along the base of a hill, and Talen sighed in relief. They galloped down a short stretch, and then River cursed and brought Scruff up short. It took Scruff a number of steps to stop, and Talen had to brace himself from falling forward and off the horse.

"What is it?" he asked. The road continued in a line for about fifty more yards and then opened onto a wide meadowland where some of the Shoka lords ran cattle and goats. The trees had dropped a good portion of their leaves and the meadow was visible through the gray trunks.

"There's someone up ahead."

Talen looked, but couldn't see anything. Scruff snorted. His ears pricked forward.

"I saw the hind end of a horse," River said.

"You sure it wasn't some stray cow?"

"With a saddle on it?"

River backed Scruff up. Up ahead, those who were waiting must have known their game was up, for there was a sudden commotion, and three men and their horses rose from the ground. A fourth charged out, already on his mount.

The men did not wear any clan colors, only dark clothing. The same clothing he'd seen the night of the attack. "Lovely," Talen said.

River turned Scruff and gave him her heels. Again, he shot forth with his marvelous acceleration. They galloped back down the short stretch to the bend around the hill only to find three more riders down at the far end of the long trail from Len's, pushing their horses hard.

That made at least seven of them. There was no way he and River would ever equalize those odds.

River slowed Scruff from a gallop into a trot. "Watch the branches," she said and turned Scruff off the road into the trees. There would be no galloping here.

A small branch whacked Talen in the face. He ducked the next one. River bent as low as she could over Scruff's neck. Talen bent low with her.

"We should go back to the fortress," he said.

"No," said River. "They'll be expecting that. And there's only one way back, which means they'll probably have men waiting on that road."

"We can go along the coast, cut through the woods."

"And remove Scruff's speed? They'll catch us for sure. No. I'm taking you where I should have to begin with."

"Where's that?"

"Shush," said River and led Scruff deeper into the woods. They skirted a tangle of brambles, pushed through a wet area, Scruff's hooves sinking deep, then quietly rode through a scattering of large stones. Talen could hear their pursuit shouting through the trees. They were fast.

He realized the children watching this approach should have lit their warning beacon, but there wasn't any smoke. He hoped they hadn't been caught. But how had the dreadmen even known to come here? How had they known to set a trap? Nobody had visited this farmer. In fact, Len had hung yellow scarves on the road to warn travelers that people were sick with fever and they should stay away.

He and River rode into a clearing made by a fallen elm and turned toward the meadow again. Above him two hooded crows cawed. There had been two hooded crows back at the farm. Crows and ravens knew to follow armies because they'd eventually get a feast. But there was no army here.

"Can you enthrall birds?" he asked.

"Anything with soul can be enthralled," she said.

Talen looked back up at the birds. "There are two crows keeping pace with us. I think they're the same ones that were at the farm."

River glanced up. "And they call us sleth," she said in disgust. "First chance you get, you shoot them."

Talen strung his bow, but there were too many branches between him and the birds for the bow to do much good. They traveled on, Talen watching the tree line. Scruff passed a lone white birch, its leaves a column of blazing yellow. Not much later the edge of the wood appeared through the trees ahead, the sun shining down on the meadow grass beyond. Once they reached that open ground, they could give Scruff his lead, let him run with Fire, and leave these whoresons to chew on his sod.

Something moved off to Talen's left. He turned. Through the trees a dark-clad rider angled his bay horse on an intercept course.

"On our left!" Talen said. He ducked to miss another branch.

River saw the threat and turned Scruff away from it and urged him faster. Scruff's pace quickened, but it wasn't the full gallop of a firesteed. It couldn't be.

Then the dreadman leapt from his mount and begin to run on foot, easily outpacing his horse.

"He's coming!" Talen said.

River kicked Scruff who broke into a canter. The tree line was so close, the meadow shining in the sun, but the man was faster. He charged from the side.

Talen nocked an arrow, but River suddenly rose from the saddle. She swung her leg over and jumped to the ground. She took two strides, keeping pace with the horse. "Ride!" she shouted at Talen. Then she drew her two knives and turned to face the dreadman.

Talen bumped along behind the saddle. He wasn't going to ride. Hadn't she been the one to say the first thing you did in any fight was try to out-number the enemy? He hopped forward into the saddle, shoved his feet into the stirrups, and grabbed the reins. Then he pulled Scruff into a halt and turned him around. Talen scanned the woods. He didn't see any other slay-ers, but that could change in a moment.

The dark-clad slayer charged River. She stepped aside, slashed at him. He parried her blow, forced her back.

"Gee!" Talen yelled and put his heels into Scruff's flanks. Scruff had been trained as a warhorse. That word and heel pressure together were the command to charge. Scruff shot forth. If nothing else, Talen would ride that dreadman down.

Talen still held his bow. There were too many branches in the way, but he needed to distract the slayer. He dropped the reins, gripped with his thighs, aimed, and released. The arrow missed, flying just past the man, but the slayer glanced in Talen's direction. It was enough: River lunged and thrust her knife into the dreadman's thigh.

He grimaced.

River pulled back, but she wasn't quite fast enough, and the dreadman sliced down, cutting her forearm.

Talen and Scruff thundered down upon them. Talen picked up the reins. "Faw!" he shouted, and Scruff surged forward.

The dreadman rolled to the right.

River stepped to the left, but as Talen and Scruff charged past, she leapt, grabbing the saddle with her good hand, and swung a leg up and over. A moment later she sat behind the saddle. "I told you to ride!" she shouted.

"What do you think I'm doing?" he shouted back.

Behind them the slayer tried to hobble after them, but the thigh wound had done its job.

Talen turned Scruff, dug in his heels, and headed at a different angle for the wide meadow. Scruff surged forward, and they raced toward the tree line and the sunlit grass. Talen wondered why River had gone for the dreadman's thigh, but now he saw the foresight of that move. That dreadman would have expected a mortal blow to the chest and might have slipped her attack. As it was, River hadn't killed him, but she'd certainly taken him out of the fight.

A rock glanced off a tree just to Talen's left. Talen looked back to see the injured dreadman pick up another rock. Maybe he wasn't out of the fight just yet. Talen urged Scruff faster.

"Riders!" River yelled.

Out in the meadow two dreadman raced along the tree line to intercept them.

Talen kicked Scruff again. He leapt over a small pine and thundered toward the tree line and the meadow beyond, but there was no way he and River would beat the dreadmen at this pace.

"You've got to multiply him!" Talen shouted.

"Give me the reins!" she said.

He held them up to her, bent low and to the side, then slid out of the saddle and stirrups. River used a bounce from Scruff's gate, leapfrogged over Talen, and landed in the saddle. She slid her feet into the stirrups. "Hold on!" she said.

Talen gripped Scruff with his thighs.

The riders drew their swords.

River leaned forward. Talen pressed himself into her back, bracing for what was to come.

"Grab the front of the saddle!" she said.

Talen reached around her waist with both arms and grasped the saddle barley a second before Scruff shot forth.

River gave him her heels, and he accelerated even faster. This was only the third time Talen had ridden Scruff. His power was frightening, and Talen clutched the front of the saddle for all he was worth.

The dreadmen's horses were stretched out at a full gallop, but Scruff's stride was so quick, so long, that he covered the remaining few yards to the tree line in a blink. Scruff charged through the brush, another branch whipped Talen's hat right off his head. Then they burst from the wood into the sunlit meadow only a pace in front of the dreadmen.

The lead dreadman raised his sword and slashed at Scruff's rump as he passed. Talen cringed, expecting Scruff to falter or stumble, but Scruff was running so fast the dreadman's sword connected with nothing but air.

Scruff, impossibly, surged forward even faster. Talen leaned into River and gripped the front of the saddle tighter. He squeezed Scruff's flanks with his thighs. Truly, they were flying. They were the wind itself. If he was careless for one moment, he would tumble off and break upon the ground.

He glanced back. Scruff's hind hooves threw clumps of turf in huge arcs twenty feet high. Back by the trees, the dreadmen turned their horses to give chase.

River aimed Scruff for the road.

The dreadmen who had been chasing Talen and River through the woods broke from the trees into the meadow. He expected them to multiply their mounts, but as he watched, the distance between Scruff and their lead horses lengthened.

Talen didn't know how far Scruff could run at this pace. River had said firesteeds could easily be run to death, which was why River hadn't multiplied him until it had been absolutely necessary. Furthermore, firesteeds, like any horse, were not immune to stumbling, slipping, or stepping into the hole of a groundhog and breaking a leg. Talen didn't want to think about Scruff taking a tumble at this speed.

Scruff hurdled something and Talen found himself nearly flying over River's head. He clutched at the saddle, then slammed back down behind her and righted himself, trying with all his might to stick to Scruff like a tick on a dog.

The trees lining the meadow flew past. River shouted, "Hold tight!"

Scruff slowed, and Talen strained not to lose his seat. Then they turned on the road and Scruff shot forward again. The road was hard, perfect for speed. Scruff surged forward. In half a dozen strides they were flying over it, literally. His gallop was a thrump, thrump, thrump, the trees along the road speeding by impossibly fast. They raced through brightly colored leaves fluttering in the breeze. The thrill of the ride rose in him, and Talen couldn't contain himself. He whooped for joy, turned to watch their pursuers fall behind, and whooped again.

Above the tops of the trees a crow cawed, but Talen didn't dare let go to use his bow.

They kept the same blinding pace for two, maybe three miles. And it *was* blinding. The rushing of the wind from their speed made Talen weep and squint. Firesteed riders sometimes wore goggles. He'd thought it silly. Now he knew it wasn't silly at all.

River sucked at the slash the dreadman had given her and spat. When she'd done it a third time, he shouted into the wind, asking her what she was doing.

"I can't feel my toes!" she called back.

"What?"

"Poison," she said, her lips smudged with her own blood. "The dreadman's blade was poisoned."

26

Beyond Land's Edge

TALEN GLANCED BACK. The dreadmen were nowhere to be seen. "We need to get you to Matiga and Argoth," he said. "We need to take the coast road back to Rogum's Defense."

River slowed Scruff into a trot. But this wasn't the trot of a regular horse because the length of each of Scruff's strides was much longer. A normal trotting horse might average eight to twelve miles an hour. They had to be going at least half that again or more. The gait, however, was not the glide of Scruff's gallop, and Talen had to work not to be bounced to pieces.

"You didn't answer me," said Talen.

"We're a half day's ride from Rogum's Defense. More importantly, this is twice someone there ratted you out. I'm not taking you to the fortress."

"Then where?"

"We're going into the Wilds."

"The Wilds?" Why in the world was she taking him there?

Then it came to him.

"It's not going to do us much good to escape dreadmen only to die at the hands of some crazed, abominable half-beast."

"Harnock's not a beast."

"He tries to kill all males that come into his territory."

"Harnock was bred for killing, but he knows healing. He learned arcane parts of the lore trying to reverse what Lumen had done to him. It's where you should have gone to begin with. Besides, I might not make it if we try for Rogum's Defense."

Lords, the tales he'd heard of Harnock from Ke!

"Are you sure?"

"Talen," she said.

He sighed. If River needed Harnock's lore, then she needed his lore.

"He's close?" Talen asked.

She sucked at her wound again. "Closer than our other options."

Talen took in a big bracing breath. "Forget Rogum's Defense, then."

"I knew you'd see sense."

"If he kills me, don't you let him eat me."

"He's not going to eat you."

"My bones go back next to Da's."

"He's not going to eat you," River said again.

* * *

After another few miles, they came to a small stream. Talen's pants were soaked with Scruff's sweat and smelling like twenty horses.

"I think we all need a drink," River said.

"How long can he keep this pace?"

"I don't know. We're going to have to get off and walk a bit alongside," she said.

"We were flying," Talen said. "Lords, almighty." He slid off, happy to give his sore legs a rest, but even happier to break contact, for his cravings were back. "I'm going to train a firesteed when we get back. I don't care if I never use him in war. The thrill alone is worth the years of Fire that it will cost."

River dismounted. "Maybe, but you've got to be careful, Talen. It doesn't seem like much. But a few years here, a few years there, and suddenly your life is spent."

Talen bent to the stream and drank straight from the flow. When he finished, he said, "I say use the years up when you're young and lively and can enjoy them. Who's going to miss a few extra years hobbling around as an old man?"

River checked Scruff's legs for injuries. "It's not the hobbling that you'll miss," she said. "It's your children and grandchildren. Who knows? Maybe you'll be like Mother and find you need that Fire to be a blessing to someone you love who's in need."

"And yet none of that prevented you from getting yourself a Fire-gobbling mount," Talen said.

She ignored him and bent over and pinched the tendons above one of Scruff's hind legs. Scruff raised his hoof to be inspected.

"You don't have an answer to that, do you?" he said. "So much for prudence. I'm training me a firesteed."

"Yours will probably be an ass," she said.

He saw himself charging into battle on the small animal, zipping about the other steeds' legs. "I'd be murder on the belly straps."

She laughed, but it was weak.

"How bad is the poison?"

"I'm fighting it," she said.

Talen opened one of the saddlebags and retrieved a number of large pellets made of oats, honey, and salt. Just as with humans, horses that were multiplied needed rich feed. He held the pellets out to Scruff while she checked the rest of the hooves. When she lifted the right front hoof, she sighed in frustration. "He's knocked the front caulkin completely off."

The force and speed of a firesteeds' stride created such a stress that normal horseshoes couldn't handle it. Firesteeds required a special shoe of thick steel or iron that made a complete oval instead of opening at the rear. It also required three small knobs called caulkins, one front and two in the back, to provide more traction. "Can he still be ridden?"

"It's not as bad as knocking a caulkin off one of the hind shoes," she said. "But it's going to need to be fixed. I don't want the uneven traction to make him lame or cause him to slip. We certainly won't be able to—" She groaned and fell to her knee.

Talen rushed to her. "River?"

"It was just a bit of dizziness."

"Don't you go dying on me."

"We need to get to Harnock."

"You're going to get up on Scruff," he said. "I can run alongside."

"Let's let him walk for a bit," she said. "He needs a breather."

"He's just fine." Talen picked her up and helped her back onto Scruff.

When she was in the saddle, she said, "We need to go west. Harnock's home is in the mountains."

The wind hissed through the trees, sending a gust of leaves fluttering across the road and into the stream. The storm clouds were blowing in from the sea.

"I never got the full story on Harnock," he said.

"He was a Koramite captain," River replied. "After the war with Koram, Mokad sent Lumen to take charge of the New Lands. Harnock refused to bow. He and a group of outlaws fought against Mokad. They lost. Lumen captured them, sacrificed their families. Then he took Harnock and the other rebels into his dungeon. All thought he'd executed them, but he kept them alive and experimented on them. The Divines have always tried to create a new type of warrior by blending soul."

Talen shook his head. He picked up Scruff's reins. The horse resisted Talen, wanting more water. Talen let him drink more, then gently pulled on the reins. A few slurps later Scruff complied and started to walk.

"How far is it?" Talen asked.

"Seven or eight miles past the border."

Talen nodded. It was a relief to be off the horse, away from both of them and his maddening longing. "I don't ever want you to teach me how to take Fire," he said.

She didn't respond.

"I don't know if I can be trusted," he said.

"Your longing will pass," she said.

"That's what you keep saying, but it's only intensified. Before, it came and went. Now, it's always gnawing at me."

"Always?"

The wind in the trees masked the sound around them. He glanced back to make sure their pursuers weren't catching up.

"More or less," he said. "And it's worse when I touch something living." He paused, then said, "River, I don't want to be someone's tool."

"You are what you choose to be," said River. "Just because you feel an urge doesn't mean you must act upon it. We are, all of us, full of urges."

"This isn't an urge," he said. "And I'm not like other men."

"How do you know what other men feel? For some, the desire for drink or sinnis rides them like a beast. And yet they choose to resist. Some men have a disposition for a neighbor's wife or daughter. Some are full of anger. But they refuse it. Are you telling me you think you're a special exception?"

"No," Talen said, "which is precisely why I don't want to tempt myself. If you teach me how to take Fire, I might lose control."

"There's your fallacy," she said. "You already know how to take Fire."

"No, I don't."

"You tried to take my Fire when we were fighting in the stable. I don't know how you did it, but that's what it was."

"I wasn't trying to take your Fire," he said, but, actually, he didn't know what he'd been trying to do; it had all happened so fast.

"Let me tell you how it's done."

"No!" he said. "I just said I didn't want to hear it."

"You also just said there's no use running from the truth."

He didn't want to know this. Once you knew a skill, it was only a matter of time before you used it. If it was a mystery, if the possibility was hidden, then it couldn't be used.

She said, "You need to know how others will try to take from you so you can defend against such attacks. Mokad's chasing us. You need to be ready should we fail to escape."

"I'll kill myself before I fall into their hands," he said. "I'm not going to be enthralled. I've felt that power in the cave, and it's irresistible. You heard what Uncle Argoth said about the thrall the Skir Master put upon him. You know what the Bone Faces do to those they enslave and how they use one finger to twist a man's heart. So don't tell me all urges can be resisted. It's simply not true."

River said, "Are you enthralled right now? Look, if you put a drop of honey on your tongue, it's almost impossible not to swallow. You can feed a desire until it's so large you don't want to control it anymore. You need to know when you're trying to take someone's Fire, so you can stop yourself from putting that honey on your tongue."

"I don't want to know," he said stubbornly.

The wind gusted in the trees.

"I believe it's a good thing we're going to Harnock," she said. "I think he has a few things to teach you."

"If he doesn't kill me first," said Talen.

"You're so scrawny, I don't know if he'll think it's worth the effort."

High above them the two hooded crows dived and circled in the winds. "Those birds are starting to irritate me," he said, but they were too high up in the winds for any accurate bowshot.

River shaded her eyes and watched the birds. "There's a Vargon farmer who taught a raven to eat food from his finger tips. Then he taught it to talk. It followed him around everywhere. He soon died, and the people said he befriended it because the raven could see in both the world of the flesh and the world of the soul and saw his death coming. And he wanted a guide."

"What kind of morbid talk is that? You're not dying."

"I'm not talking about dying," she said. "I'm just saying that if I were to enthrall an animal, I think it would be handy to have one that could see in both worlds."

"Well, let's hope they get close enough for us to make a crow pie. And we'll see if they taste as good in this world as they do in the next."

They walked Scruff for another quarter mile, and then River said, "I think we can pick up the pace again. We can both ride. When we go down any large hills, we can get off and spare him the extra load. We'll make good time that way."

"You stay on the horse," he said. He was multiplied and could run, and before she could protest, he set off at a jog, Scruff trotting behind. The wind picked up, knocking small branches out of the trees. A few miles later, they moved into the foothills. An hour after that, they reached the borders of the land where the slope of a mountain rose before them.

The actual border of the New Lands was marked by a line of obelisks spaced a mile or two apart. The obelisks ran the length of the mountains. Each had a base made of mortared stones and a column made of wood. They were built tall enough to rise above the trees.

"I think I've realized something," Talen said.

"What is that?" River said weakly.

He fed Scruff one of his large honey pellets. All his life he'd heard that one must never go beyond the giant obelisks because that was woodikin territory. The Wilds lay behind the western mountains. As the name suggested, they were not tamed lands. They were full of wurms and other dangers. There were men who hunted in those parts and sometimes brought back wonders. But none of them ventured far. Those that did eventually failed to return. "I just realized, the border and these tales—they're there to keep the herd from straying. Maybe the Wilds are exactly where we should be heading."

"I hadn't thought about it that way," said River.

"All this time we've been penning ourselves in."

A beat passed.

He said, "It seems odd to me that Harnock can live there for all these years and not be discovered. Doesn't he need to trade every once in a while?"

"The laws keep most folks inside the bounds of the land," she said. "And when he needs something, he has contacts."

Talen knew she meant the members of the Order. "But he's not wanted contact for some time. That's what Uncle Argoth said. Maybe he's found other sources of supply."

"He's one man," said River. "He doesn't need much. He keeps to himself. And this vale is not exactly easy to reach."

"I think we should trot again," said Talen. "I don't know how far behind the slayers are, but I don't want to lose our advantage."

Talen fed Scruff another pellet. "Where do we go?"

"Do you see those broken cliffs?" she asked, pointing at a protrusion of rock columns and chutes at the top of the slope. "There's a chute on the right that will take us up to the top. When we get over to the other side, we'll follow a ridge for a few miles. It will end in a vale with a lazy river. From there we pick our way carefully over hill and through hollow. Harnock's vale is a number of miles farther in. When we get to the ridge that looks down upon his vale, we need to stand in a certain place and call out for him."

"And none of that takes us through woodikin territory?" The last thing he wanted was a poison dart in his neck, or worse: a nest of their wasps filling him with venom.

"If we keep to the ridge, we'll be okay. I've traveled it before."

"I hope you're right. At least the dreadmen won't feed us to the wurms."

"The woodikin wouldn't feed you to the wurms. They would eat you themselves to demonstrate their power."

"Well, that makes me feel much better," he said.

"I'd rather be devoured by a troop of little hairy men who can't touch the soul than what was down in the stone-wight caves."

"Aye," Talen said. "That's the truth."

Above them one of the hooded crows streaked across the sky above the trees. It fought against the wind to circle back.

To the east thick and dark clouds had formed. It was going to rain hard. It would probably freeze him and River, but a good strong rain would drive those blasted crows to ground, which meant if they could just keep themselves ahead of the dreadmen, they might lose them in the storm.

He hadn't seen any sign of the dreadmen, although he didn't doubt they were close. "How are you feeling?" he asked River.

"Not well," she said.

He looked up at her on the horse. Her face was pale and moist with sweat.

"Listen to me carefully," she said. "When we get to Harnock's vale, he must know you're one of the Order."

"Won't he recognize you?"

"That's not enough. Besides, I don't know what state I'll be in when we get there. So make sure you're magnified. Don't use the weave because if he's in one of his moods, you need to be ready to flee with all your powers. You'll make the sign of the Order when he approaches. And you'll ask him to respect the blood of Hogan that runs through your veins."

She sagged in the saddle.

"River?"

"Get moving," she said. "I don't want to be caught on the face of this mountain when the rain comes."

Talen stroked Scruff's broad jaw as he finished chewing the pellet. "Come on, boy," he said. "We've got to get her up and over." Then he tugged on the reins and set off at a faster pace, Scruff breaking into a canter behind.

* * *

By the time they'd climbed most of the way to the cliffs, Talen's legs were burning, and both his and Scruff's lungs were working like bellows. He took a break and looked back at where they'd come. The cursed crows had followed them up the hill and perched in a stand of tall pines some distance away. Talen tied Scruff to a branch and scrambled up a large protrusion of rock, hoping to get a better view of their back trail. The wind buffeted him, swayed the boughs of the trees around him.

Below the land stretched for miles. Only the approaching dark storm clouds prevented him from seeing all the way to the sea. At the foot of the mountain, their pursuers stopped where he and River had left the road. One of them looked up the mountain and pointed up the slope. It seemed he was pointing right at Talen. Then the group of slayers left the road, urging their horses into a canter.

Talen cursed and scrambled back down to Scruff, praying to the Six that the storm would overtake them.

27

Pursuit

ARGOTH GALLOPED AROUND A BEND in the wagon trail that led to the house of Len and Tinker. His mount was slick with sweat, soaping around the saddle and straps. Next to him rode Oaks, captain of a hammer of dreadmen. Behind them thundered a full terror—ninety-seven men, all of them new dreadmen.

At any moment the farm would come into view, but Argoth already knew he was too late, for a huge pillar of blackened smoke rose above the trees where the farm should be. It would take a burning house to make that much smoke.

He'd racked his brains trying to figure out how the traitor had found out about the hiding place. He'd been very careful to make sure people saw River and Talen in the fortress after the attack, very carefully slipping them into the barrels behind doors without notice. With all the preparations going on, the comings and goings that night, those two barrels would not have stood out. It was impossible, yet there was the smoke piling up in the sky.

A gust of wind hissed down the hill on Argoth's left, blowing through the tree tops and shaking loose great sheets of fluttering orange and yellow leaves. Argoth and his terror of men galloped through them.

The road dipped and bent around the hill. When he rounded the last corner, he saw Len's burning house. The flames, bright and roaring like rushing waters, leapt above the tops of the trees and poured smoke into the sky. The fire had engulfed the roof of the house, but the other buildings had not yet been touched, which meant the fires had only just been lit. Maybe he wasn't too late.

Argoth raised his arm, signaling his men to ready themselves for attack. Argoth's own Fire was raging inside him. He was multiplied to his limit. His whole body was a spring, compressed, yearning to be released.

Oaks motioned for the line of horsemen to fan out, and the riders spilled out into the field on their right. A third of his dreadmen carried crossbows. The other two-thirds had recurved horse bows. All they needed to do was pin the dreadmen in place. Some of them might still be suffering from the clumsiness of the forced progression, but, if the report was right, he still had better than a three-to-one superiority in numbers.

In the corral on the far side of the barn, a girl fled from three men, but one of them cut her off. Back in the yard, two men prepared to fire the barn. Len, Tinker, and a number of their children crouched, bound to the door-posts, which meant these maggots were planning on burning them alive. Two more men stood back from the fire, watching, waiting for the fire to work its way down the roof and consume Len and his family.

But these men weren't dreadmen. They were dressed as common Fir-Noy soldiers.

One of those preparing to burn the barn must have heard the thudding of the hooves for he turned and saw the attack. He yelled something to the others, dropped his burning brand, and dashed for a line of horses tied to a fence post. The other man tossed his burning brand through the barn's open doors and followed. The three in the corral either didn't hear or were too focused on their victim. One of them grabbed her by the hair and threw her to the ground.

Argoth counted seven horses tied to the fence. The message he'd received said there were thirty men moving toward Len's farm. It was clear these were the ones left behind to clean up after the initial raid.

"I want them alive," Argoth shouted. "I want answers!"

The men shouted the command down the line.

The horsemen thundered over the field. Two Fir-Noy mounted and galloped down the road that led south. Those in the corral finally saw their predicament. Two sprinted for their horses. The other ran for the woods. But Argoth's men galloped into the yard of the farm and cut off all escape.

Argoth and Oaks dismounted while their horses were still moving and ran to Len and his family. The fire roared overhead. The children were huddled as low as their bonds would allow, Tinker trying to covering them from the heat. Len was tied up straight, and couldn't crouch. He coughed and wheezed in the smoke.

Argoth ran to him, cut the bonds at his wrists and legs, and carried him a number of yards away from the blistering heat of the house. Oaks freed Tinker, then set to work on the children.

Len continued to cough and hack, gasping for breath. His eyes were blood-shot. His hair singed. Argoth laid him on the ground.

A man brought a bucket of water from the well. Argoth ripped off a piece of his tunic, dipped it in the water, then daubed Len's face, trying to cool him. Even though he was a number of yards away, the heat from the burning house was so hot Argoth could feel it through his padded tunic and armor. A few minutes more and the heat and smoke would have killed Len before any flames could have reached him.

Len had been a tenant on this part of Argoth's land for many years. He'd managed it well and with good humor. So well that Argoth had come to admire him. "My friend," he said. "I'm so sorry."

Len gasped for breath.

Tinker coughed behind him. "Do not be sorry for the wicked deeds of other men," she said. "They're only a few minutes ahead. You can catch them."

"Did they get Talen and River?"

"No," she said hoarsely, "they escaped on that ungainly steed."

"How many were there?"

"We saw nine, all dressed in dark colors with foreign honors," she said. "Your job's with them. Me and mine will take care of these rot."

Tinker—practical and level-headed in every crisis. "When this is all done, I'm going to make you a captain," he said. "Then our enemies will indeed shake in their boots."

"Go," she said.

Argoth looked down at Len. "I'll be back, old friend."

Len wheezed horribly and nodded. Argoth stood. His men had tied up the Fir-Noy. Despite Tinker's capability, he couldn't leave her here alone. Who knew if there were other Fir-Noy coming? He commanded a fist to stay behind.

Argoth walked over to the captives, who, to his surprise, weren't all Fir-Noy. Three were Shoka. "Who's the leader here?"

None of the men answered or looked him in the eye.

"Fools," Argoth bellowed. "Your only hope in this life and the next is in Shim." He turned to one of the Shoka. "What did these Fir-Noy idiots promise you? Eh? Lands, cattle? And for what? You think they want to rid the land of a dangerous rebellion? Let me tell you something. I fought one of the gods of Mokad down in the caves. I saw what rules over the Divines. I saw what took Lumen and fashioned him into a beast of grass and stone. That monster was a Divine's beast. Not one of sleth making. The master of Mokad does not want land or cattle. It wants your very souls. That's what guides Mokad. That's what you're trading your good names for."

The house fire raged behind him, sparks and embers flying into the sky. The intense heat of the blaze still licked his skin even at this distance.

Argoth needed to give the captives a reason to talk. He lowered his voice. "I can understand you don't know what you're dealing with. And you were just obeying orders. A man can't be faulted for that. But you can't cite ignorance any longer. You'll see proofs back at Rogum's Defense. Then it will be your time to choose. I hope you choose life."

By this time many of the horses had been watered and the fire in the barn put out. Some horses had been given a handful of oats from Len's barn. Argoth walked over to the scummy watering trough, pushed a horse aside, and knelt, using both hands to scoop up a number of handfuls of water for himself. He wanted to gallop after the dreadmen, but he knew the animals needed a short break. He wiped his mouth with the back of his hand, stood, and took his horse by the reins. "Get yourselves watered, men. We're going to run."

A minute later, he and the terror of dreadmen started out. They had formed two lines, each man holding the reins of his horse. The columns ran down to the creek bed, across, and up the other side.

The tracks made by the caulkins on River's firesteed lay easily enough to see in the dirt as did the hoofprints of those that pursued them. They followed the tracks for a mile to where the turf had been churned at the wood's edge. The sign on the forest floor was clear, so Argoth followed the tracks into the woods. The trail bent around toward a meadow. At the edge of the tree line he found Talen's hat, and then he saw the tracks of the firesteed. The animal had shot forth here. At this point, River and Talen had still been free.

Oaks brought a handful of leaves to Argoth. They were splattered with blood. Blood that wasn't fully dried yet.

They were close. Very close. "Mount up!" he commanded his men.

Argoth followed the tracks of the firesteed down the wash and up again.

He followed them through the woods, out into a meadow, and onto a road. Then he lost them, and his heart fell, but one of his men called to him from farther down the road. The tracks of the firesteed were so far apart, they'd thrown him off.He rode his horse farther down the trail and found another set. The horse must have been running full out while multiplied. The speed must have been astounding.

He and his men followed the trail in a fast trot. They wound their way through the woods and then toward the borders of the land. At no time did he see any sign that would suggest Talen and River had been taken. Then they came to a part where the road dipped down a gully and up again. The wind gusted through the trees.

On the far side of the gully the tracks turned off the narrow road and ran through a meadow with a trail of grass bent by the hooves of a number of horses. The trail ran straight past an obelisk marking the edges of the land to a mountain that marked the beginning of the Wilds.

Argoth looked up the slope. He knew exactly what lay back there and what it meant—River was going into the Wilds, leading dreadmen to Harnock's door. Not a good idea.

There was movement up the slope close to the cliffs. Two crows circled. Below them a number of men and horses flashed through a break in the trees.

That had to be Talen's pursuit. A determined anger rose in his breast. The Wilds were tricky, but he knew the ground behind that mountain. They did not. He could probably have them cornered before nightfall.

Moreover, he didn't want them anywhere near Harnock. Harnock had been twisted by Lumen. But the Divines weren't fools. Harnock might be fashioned to kill, but he was also fashioned to be controlled by a master. As mighty as Harnock was, if a Divine got his hands on him, Harnock would be turned against them.

Argoth was just about to order his men after them when shouts rose from farther down the road.

A group of about two or three dozen women and children hurried toward him and his men. They must have been hiding in the shadows of the trees. Some seemed to be injured. Two children were up on a white horse.

"Zu!" an old woman wearing a Shoka shawl cried. "Woolsom is attacked!"

Argoth looked back up the mountain to the men making their way to the cliffs, but urged his mount forward. His men followed.

Woolsom was one of five villages clustered along one part of the Short Falls River. Argoth recognized the woman. Her name was Larkspur. Many years ago when she and her husband were newly married, they had gone out to fell trees to build their first small house. In a terrible accident, a massive pine had fallen on her husband, skewering his leg and pinning it to the ground. He would have bled out and died, but she cut the leg off and saved his life. She'd built that first house on her own, put him in it, and brought him back to health. When he was better, he fashioned his own long peg leg, often festooning it with bright ribbons, and the two of them eventually raised five stout children just outside Woolsom.

Argoth rode up to the group and reined his horse to a halt. The faces of the women and children were full of horror and grief.

"They've slaughtered Woolsom," Larkspur said.

"Who?" demanded Argoth.

"I don't know. They wore a black and red sash at their waists. Their heads and faces were all shaved and painted."

A short thin woman behind Larkspur spoke. "There was a blackness, Zu. We were up on the hillside above the village gathering late season berries and acorns. We saw ships' masts on the river. Then the blackness descended upon Woolsom."

Woolsom, Larkin, Fishing and the other villages lay a number of miles from here, but not too far. Argoth turned to one of his men and pointed to a tall tree that stood on the top of a rise just a few yards away. "Get up there," he said. "Tell me if you see smoke from the warning beacons."

The man stowed his crossbow, then removed his helmet and padded tunic. Moments later he'd kicked off his boots and was climbing.

Up on the slope the dreadmen continued to move higher through the trees. Argoth turned back to the thin woman. "What about the blackness? Where did it come from?"

"I don't know."

"How many were there?"

"I didn't see them," said Larkspur. "Not with these old eyes. My daughter did. She went running to the village to gather her sick husband. But she never came back. And there's this—the mists groaned."

"What do you mean?"

"A great sighing. Like some great beast in the midst of it."

"It's the curse," another woman said.

Larkspur nodded. "We've offended the Six."

Argoth thought back to the words of the lord of Nilliam, about how the Devourers protected their herds from predators. "The only curse at work here is the one laid by our enemies," he said.

"Zu!" The dreadman in the tree called down. He stood braced at the very top. "Smoke's rising a number of miles northwest in the direction of Woolsom."

"What of the beacons?" The clans had located watch towers on the tops of a number of high hills. They used beacon fires to signal danger and to call for aid.

"I see no beacons."

Argoth turned back to the group of women and children. "How many ships' masts did you see?"

"I counted ten," a boy said.

Ten could mean two to three ships. Depending on the size of the ships that might have been enough to land a few hundred men. Maybe more. But why would anyone land there? Woolsom and the surrounding villages weren't strategic; they didn't possess any great treasure. Just as with Redthorn, it made no sense.

However, they were closer to Rogum's Defense. Maybe this was a landing for a surprise attack.

What Argoth did know is that he had a third of Shim's dreadmen with him. Others would be out on patrol, which meant Rogum's Defense might itself be threatened.

"You can't fight the mists, Zu," a grandfather said. "We sent men to investigate, but the blackness took them, struck them to the ground."

Argoth didn't dare split his men. It would be pure folly to send forty new dreadmen against a hammer of Mokad's most powerful. He'd need his whole force to overwhelm those dreadmen, which meant he either chased after them and attempted to rescue River and Talen, or he went to Woolsom.

If the enemy captured Talen, they'd enthrall him. In time, they'd turn him into a weapon, a Glory. At least, that was the plan of the Devourer that had planted him. Who knew what Mokad might do with him? But the Wilds were treacherous, and so Harnock would have the advantage there. River was fearsome in her own right. But against a full hammer of mature dreadmen?

Argoth cursed. By all that was holy! They were his sister's children! But the greater danger lay in Woolsom. He made his decision and turned to the travelers. "Did you send word to Rogum's Defense?"

"Yes," said the old woman, "but who knows if they made it through?"

If Mokad was landing, he had to be there. He couldn't leave Shim with only part of an army.

Argoth took one last look at the mountain and the crows. He prayed the Six that River and Talen would be able to get to Harnock's. Then he faced his men. "We ride to Woolsom!"

28

Woolsom

ARGOTH RODE INTO Woolsom too late. Dead animals lay about the houses. The bodies of the inhabitants were scattered about as well, but the bulk of them, both old and young, lay in piles next to the village workshop.

Argoth dismounted. The wind whistled about the workshop and houses. Great numbers of flies flitted about the bodies, filling the air with a loud buzzing. It was grim work searching through the bodies, especially when moving the little ones. He moved one small girl with a sprig of lavender woven into her hair. The sight of it struck him. That was something Grace would wear. In fact, not two weeks ago she'd tried to weave such a sprig into his own hair. Argoth laid the girl gently down and moved to another. With each body his dismay and anger built.

None had survived. All had an odd blackening about their necks and chests. The eyes of a few of the corpses had begun to cloud over, but the stiffness of death had only begun to set in. Furthermore, there were no frights. He suspected the last of these good folks had died less than an hour ago, which meant that whoever had done this was not far ahead.

Oaks was out by the road. "They're headed for Fishing," he called. "The tracks are clear as day."

Fishing was a small community scarcely more than a mile away. It was named, not for its fishermen, but because of its role in a practical joke played by locals on unsuspecting travelers. If he hurried, he just might be able to catch the murderers before they repeated there what they'd done here and at Redthorn.

Argoth ordered his men up. He sent a handful of riders to scout ahead and on both flanks. He also ordered a hammer to form up a rearguard. The remaining seventy-five dreadmen followed him and Oaks. The scouts raced ahead. The rest of the men came behind at a trot.

The road cut through fields with their short stone fences, then into the woods at the base of a row of hills. Fishing lay on the other side of the hill ahead. Argoth and the column of riders trotted into the wood. They rounded a bend and saw one of his scouts up ahead, a man lying on the ground next to him.

Argoth rode forward and looked down upon the man.

"We got him before he could blow a warning," the scout said.

The man's face and head were shaved and painted in yellow, white, and black. Sticking out of his side was the last few inches of a twelve inch crossbow dart. He wore a tunic of otter skins over his mail that was gathered with a red and black sash at his waist. About his neck hung a cord of shark's teeth. He was still breathing, glaring.

"He's Bone Face," the scout said and held out the man's sword hilt-first to Argoth.

Argoth took it. Letters in Bone Face script had been carved upon the leather wrapping. Argoth turned to the dying man. "Your chief?" he asked in Bone Face.

The man grinned through his pain and made a wretched face. He said something unintelligible in his awful tongue, something about the wind.

Argoth turned back to his scout. "Were there others?"

The man shook his head. "Just this one, Captain."

An army would have fists and hammers of men positioned as scouts and outriders, not a lone scout, which meant this Bone Face group was small.

Up the hill someone made the warning call of the black crane, signaling they'd found the enemy.

Argoth turned to Oaks. "We're going in quietly. Tell the men to dismount when they get to the top."

Oaks passed the order back, and the column moved forward. Argoth scanned both sides of the woods as they rode to the top of the hill and couldn't help wonder: in all the years the Bone Faces had been coming, they always came to steal goods, livestock, and people, not kill them. Why start killing defenseless villagers now? And what was this blackness?

They reached the top of the hill without incident, quietly dismounted, and tied up the horses. The men removed their bows and other weapons from the saddles. Argoth himself had brought a crossbow and sword. He slung his quiver of bolts across his back and drank the last of his water. When the men were ready, he broke them into three hammers, and then they slipped into the cover of the trees and carefully made their way down the other side of the hill.

As he descended, he got his first glimpse of the blackness through the branches of the trees. It was common enough on some mornings to see small patches of fog lingering in the folds of hills and valleys along the coast. But it wasn't morning and this mist wasn't white—it was dark brown, almost black, as if a smoke lay over the village. The mists stretched a few hundred yards across, concealing many but not all of the buildings. The thick heart of the mist flashed, but the colors were all wrong—instead of the red and orange of fire, they were pale lavender and yellow.

Argoth got a better look when he and the three hammers reached the bottom of the hill and crept to the edge of the tree line.

Fishing was a village that lay in the crook where two lines of low hills met. A Y-shaped crossroads sat in the middle of the village. That's where most of the houses and workshops clustered. But all that was shrouded in the smoky mist. Only a few of the outlying homes were visible. One such home stood along the road up ahead in the thinning edges of the strange darkness.

Three horses lay on their sides in a corral next to the home. In front of the house in the road lay the bodies of a woman and a dog. The mists here were unusual, but they did not move as the Redthorn children had reported.

Argoth scanned the area and heard men's voices down the lane, from within the village. He took a footlong crossbow bolt from his quiver and placed it in the crossbow. It was true he could put more shafts into the air with a horse bow, but numbers weren't the only thing he was looking for. A crossbow had a higher speed at close range. Besides, if there were Bone Face dreadmen here, and Argoth encountered them up close, he'd only have time for one shot anyway.

He was about to give the order to move out of the trees, when a man's scream rose from deep inside the mists. Moments later a great sigh followed it, as if the mists themselves had taken a breath.

The hairs on the back of Argoth's neck stood straight on end. The men looked at each other in alarm. Argoth turned to Oaks, but he was as baffled and alarmed as the rest of them.

Argoth had never read about or seen anything like this in his life. But he reminded himself that those who held the lore were nothing more than men. Men who fed their own kind to their masters. And he suddenly wondered if they had stumbled upon a feeding, if what created this blackness was one of the Devourers.

He motioned the hammers forward, and the men emerged from the tree line and crossed the open space before them, entering the thinnest parts of the mist. The hammer on is left ran forward and took cover behind a fence. The one on his right found cover behind the corral. Argoth ran up to the house, his hammer behind him. The door and windows stood open. A fire burned low at the hearth, but other than that the house was dark and empty.

Ahead, the towering mists flickered, and another great sigh rose from the heart of the village.

The sound unnerved him. What sort of rough beast would make such a noise?

More houses and buildings lay ahead. Argoth thought he heard the sound of men talking in the Bone Face tongue, but couldn't see anyone, so he motioned the hammers forward again.

They stole silently across the gardens to the next set of buildings. The homes here were just as the first one had been—dark and empty, thin trails of smoke rising from the chimneys. The hammers moved forward again, hopping fences and passing bird pens.

The mists were thicker here, turning the sun into a smoky, blood-red circle in the sky and partially obscuring the other hammers.

There was another flicker and the mists sighed again, much closer this time. A jolt of fear shot through him. This was surely the breath of something large.

He motioned his hammer out from behind the house, but as they fanned out, something in the corner of his eye caught his attention. He dropped behind a two-wheeled handcart and motioned for the others behind him to get down.

A small lane ran past a home up ahead and joined up with the road that ran to the heart of the village. Through the mists, two Bone Face warriors forced a short line of women and children down the lane at sword point. The Bone Faces wore the same black and red sash as the man they'd found in the wood. Their faces were painted the same white, black, and yellow. Argoth had not seen this combination of colors on Bone Faces and wondered what it signified.

He gave the signal for his men to hold their bows as the Bone Faces and their captives disappeared into the mists down the lane. Argoth waited a moment more, then motioned the hammers forward.

The men in the hammer on his left moved like ghosts in the mist and disappeared behind a barn. The men in the hammer on his right took up a position alongside a house, the top of which disappeared into the dark, thickening fog. Argoth and his men crossed the road and moved up behind a low wall.

They were close to the Y-shaped crossroad at the heart of the village. He could see movement ahead, but the mists were thick, cutting visibility. It would be foolish to charge in without knowing what they faced. Somebody needed to find out what lay before them, and of all the men here, he was the one best suited to recognize this lore for what is was. So he signaled for the hammers to stay put. Then he quietly lifted himself over the fence and made his way forward through the unnatural murkiness.

The voices of men rose from the mist ahead. A horse nickered. Argoth crept forward to the side of the house that faced the crossroad.Across the road three horses with Bone Face saddles stood tethered to a hitching post in front of another house.

Whatever force the Bone Faces had landed, it was becoming apparent the full army was not in Fishing. This was some small advanced unit.

At the edge of the village the murk was thin, but here it was thick. The mists suddenly glowed and flickered, flashed with the witching yellow and lavender light, and then they exhaled loudly all about him.

Argoth swallowed and crept forward until he saw the crossroad before him.

Long tatters moved in a slow wide circle around the crossroad. Suddenly a thick smoky apparition broke away from the circle. It floated along the roof top of the house across the road and curled down its chimney. Another tatter about six feet long moved along the ground and curled around one of the horse's hind legs. The horse whinnied in alarm and pulled at its tether, the whites of its eyes showing in fear.

A wave of alarm washed up his back and prickled the hairs on his neck. What were those *things*? A foreboding rose in him—this wasn't going to end well. But they couldn't fight an enemy they didn't know, so he readied his crossbow and crept farther down the side of the house.

A woman pleaded. "Please," she said. "Please." A man laughed. But there seemed to be other voices all about him murmuring.

A tatter of mist floated around the corner of the house and came toward him. Argoth pressed himself back against the wall and froze. The tatter approached, but it slid past and continued on.

Argoth exhaled a huge breath. What in the name of Regret had he and his men walked into? His whole body shouted for him to flee, to turn around now, but he forced himself forward. When he reached the edge of the house, he crouched low and looked out at the mist-shrouded crossroad.

A tall wiry man stood in the center. His head was shaven. His chest was bare and painted, not the normal black and white of the Bone Faces, but red and yellow. About his neck hung a necklace of teeth and another of feathers tied to fingers. He held a rough black stone in his hand.

The Bone Faces didn't order their Divines like the Western Glorydoms. Instead, they had wizards that they called Kragows, which was their term for chief men. This was one of them. There were about a hammer's worth of warriors with him, some of them dragging bodies away, some of them guarding villagers. Two of the warriors held a woman before the Kragow.

The Kragow muttered something, and it seemed as if the very air about him began to melt, to ripple like old glass. The rippling extended up a number of yards above him and flickered at its edges.

The Kragow spoke again, and the flickering turned violent. A moment later there was a flash of lavender and pale yellow light as a huge rent tore through the rippling. Black mist poured out. As the rippling tore open, it breathed, as if some great beast had opened its maw. But it wasn't any beast for Argoth could see some different place on the other side of the gash.

Great lords, had that Kragow ripped the very fabric of the world?

Then the Kragow reached, impossibly, into the woman. She groaned, and he pulled forth something as long as his arm that bucked and shone with a pure light.

Argoth watched in horror as the woman cried out and slumped in the arms of her captors.

The Kragow held the shining high. It thrashed, trying to escape, but it could not break free of the Kragow's grip. It was not clear through the rippling what he did, but the shining thing slowly stilled and stopped resisting. Moments later it began to dull and turn gray. The Kragow shouted and the rippling about the

Kragow slowed. The gash between worlds closed up with another sigh. With it went the lavender and pale yellow light. Then the rippling was gone.

The Kragow released the grayness, which rose up and joined the other mass of tatters circling in the mist, circling this Wizard like dogs on a chain. The graynesses seethed, and he realized they were the source of the murmuring.

And then it came to him—wraiths.

That's what they had to be, but wraiths were things of the world of the dead, not this one. Yet what else could these be?

The woman groaned in pain. A part of her had been ripped out, but not all. Nevertheless, the wounds to the bonds between Fire, flesh, and soul would be fatal. She would die, just as those at Redthorn and Woolsom had. Just as those piled about this crossroad were dying.

Argoth found his breath. He tried to estimate the number of wraiths that roiled in the mist. Were there a hundred, two? Just about the number of those who lived in Woolsom, Fishing, and Larkin.

Argoth slowly drew back around behind the corner of the house, his heart pounding. He had no idea what this Bone Face abomination was doing, but he did know he and his men had to kill him. They had to kill him now.

He turned to his men and signaled the numbers of the enemy, their armament, and placement and waited while his men passed the signal to the other two hammers. He raised his crossbow, checking to make sure the bolt was properly placed. He'd have one good shot, and it needed to sink deep into that wizard's wicked heart.

Oaks signaled back that the message had been received. Argoth prepared to give the order to charge.

Then a small group of Bone Face warriors with more prisoners marched around a corner and saw his hammers. One of them shouted a warning. Two others drew their bows.

"Charge!" Argoth bellowed and stepped around the corner of the workshop.

The Kragow turned to look at him. Argoth leveled the crossbow, blew out a breath, squared the man in its sights, and pulled the trigger. The crossbow thocked, the bolt shot out and sped like lightning across the crossroad at the Kragow.

The Kragow twisted, snake-quick, and the bolt flew into the inside of his forearm and out the other side, blood shooting out in an arc.

Argoth tossed the crossbow to the side, drew his axe, and charged with a bellow. He was multiplied, his Fire raging.

The Kragow raised his good hand, holding his ragged stone aloft.

Argoth's men charged past the house. The Bone Face warriors picked up their weapons, but Argoth's men released a volley of arrows, which streaked across the short distance and pin-cushioned five or six of them.

The Kragow did not flee or draw a weapon, merely looked at Argoth with disgust, the blood running down his one arm and mixing with the yellow paint. The Kragow shouted a command.

Argoth raced across the road, raised his axe for a killing blow, but one of the wraiths shot down and struck at his face. Argoth reeled back. Another wrapped about his arm.

The faint murmuring he'd heard before turned into a wailing of anguish. The first wraith tried to push into his mouth and down his throat. Then the one around his arm bit in, trying to enter his flesh.

He slammed shut his doors, but the dark creature that writhed at his wrist, pushed its way partially through. It clawed and bit its way in further. It was crazed, maddened. Argoth recoiled then realized it was the tattoo—somehow it was giving the thing ingress.

He yelled in anger and focused. The thing was full of menace, but Argoth pushed it out and closed the doors at his wrists. Immediately, the wailing receded.

All around him the wraiths fell upon his men who cried out in terror and dismay. One dreadman slumped to his knees, tearing at his chest. Another stumbled backward.

Many of the Bone Faces had been killed or injured, but the dozen or so that remained raised their weapons. One shot a dreadmen from a pace away with an arrow into his throat. Another charged a dreadman and thrust him through with a spear. One man with a long knife charged Oaks, who was down on one knee, struggling with a wraith wrapped about his arm.

Argoth yelled and hurled his axe. It flew with massive velocity and sank deep into the side of the man rushing Oaks. Argoth turned back to the Kragow who was holding his wounded arm.

But another gray tatter attacked Argoth, and he was forced to stop and fight to keep it from entering him and taking possession. A few more wraiths and Argoth would be immobilized.

The Kragow backed away and shouted out another command. More of the wraiths broke away from the mist.

Argoth glanced about him. All but four of the men in his hammer were clutching at their throats or arms, staggering and fighting the things. The second hammer was reeling in the same way.

It was their weaves, he realized. The weaves opened a door! And even though his dreadmen had practiced closing the paths to the soul, the weaves would prevent a complete closure.

"Take off your weaves!" Argoth roared. "Remove them!"

Some of the dreadmen complied. Others seemed to take no notice, lost in the fight to retain possession of their own bodies.

Argoth ran over to one of them and ripped off his weave. He tore off the weave of another. But the Bone Face warriors were wading in with their weapons. One hacked into one of his men's neck, then stabbed another in the back.

Two more wraiths fell upon Argoth. Their cries reverberated in his mind, and he staggered and yelled in frustration, struggling to keep them out.

And he realized this fight was lost. They needed to flee.

"Fall back!" Argoth shouted. "Fall back!" He picked up the bow of a fallen dreadmen, nocked an arrow, and shot at the closest Bone Face. Nocked and shot another.

Many of the dreadmen began to fall back, a number of them dragging fallen comrades with them. Most of the third hammer were moving. They'd had been farther back when the attack began and had been able to remove their weaves.

"Give us cover!" he shouted to them.

A volley of arrows sped past him at the Bone Faces. A few struck targets. The rest sent the Bone Faces diving for cover, and that gave Argoth and his men a chance to escape. "Run!" he shouted. "Run!"

The third hammer continued to fire at the Bone Faces, and then the wraiths found them, and they too fled back past the dark silent houses, past the dead animals, down the main road and away from the horrors of that crossroad.

The wraiths attacked Argoth and his fleeing men the whole way. More of his men fell, tangled in the horrible coils, before the remnants of the hammers reached the edge of the village and staggered out of the thinning mists into the sunlight.

They fled another fifty yards, but the wraiths did not follow them into the full sunlight.

"Look," Oaks said.

The wraiths roiled at the edges of the mist, some darting out, then immediately racing back in.

"It contains them," Oaks said.

"I don't want to test that theory," Argoth said. "And I don't want to wait for that Kragow to realize he made a mistake. He should have sent his men to chase us."

Argoth looked at the number of men that had made it out, and his heart sank. Not even half were with him.

Shouts rose above them at the top of the hill followed by the sound of many horses. An army of horses. Probably the rest of these Bone Face whoresons. He ordered the men to flee to the woods, but a horn sounded the Shoka call to battle.

That was not an army of Bone Faces.

Argoth rushed to the hill road and looked up its length. At the top he saw two columns of riders wearing the blue and white of freedom. Shim led them on his stallion, which meant the messengers the villagers sent must have made it to Rogum's Defense.

Shim kicked his horse into a gallop, and he and the column behind him descended the hill, bringing the horses for Argoth and his men with them. Argoth did not wait for them, but raced up to meet them.

"What is that?" asked Shim.

"Bone Faces," Argoth said. "The mists are full of wraiths fashioned by a wicked lore."

Shim furrowed his brows. "How many are they?"

"It's not men you need to worry about."

"Lord," one of Shim's riders said and pointed toward the village.

On the far side of the village, the Kragow and the dozen or so of his remaining men sped away from the village on their horses. They raced their mounts up a small hill and paused. The Kragow turned his horse around, raised a lance with three human heads tied to it with cords, and drove it into the ground. It was a Bone Face gesture of warning, a boast of what they would do.

"I don't see any wraiths about that maggot," said Shim.

"If we take him, it has to be from a distance," Argoth said. He took his horse from one of the riders and mounted it.

Shim ordered two hammers to wait and watch the mists, and then he dug his heels into the flanks of his mount. "Do not close with him," Argoth shouted and put his heels into his own horse. The riders galloped across the field outside the village, then raced up the hill and swarmed past the lance with its Bone Face script and gory heads.

In front of Argoth and the other riders the fields and meadows stretched out toward the sea. Off to the right the Short Falls River ran through them. The Bone Faces had split up. The Kragow's men followed the road back to the bay. However, the Kragow himself had broken off from the main group and galloped across a rolling meadow toward the river.

Shim and his dreadmen charged down the hill. They followed the road for about a quarter mile, then fifty chased the Bone Face warriors. The rest followed Shim off the road after the Kragow.

The Kragow reached the rivers' edge and slid off his horse, disappearing down the river's bank. A few minutes later, Shim and his men approached the spot where the Kragow had been. The Kragow's horse stood munching grass. It looked up at the riders as they approached.

Shim motioned for his riders to fan out so more could shoot their arrows at once. He rode forward with his own short recurved horse bow in hand. They closed the distance until they were only a few dozen yards from the Kragow's mount.

"Show yourself like a man!" Shim shouted.

The grass waved in the wind. The river flowed past. There was no response.

They continued forward. The Kragow's horse, seeing the line of men closing on it, trotted a few paces away, its reins trailing along the ground.

Argoth waited for the Kragow to rise and summon his wraiths out of the air, but nothing happened. Shim urged his horse forward to the bank of the river. The land here was flat, the banks of the river short and gentle.

"Look at that," said Shim, pointing at the bank of the river.

From the river's edge up to where Argoth sat on his horse, the wild grass was pressed down and wet. Argoth walked his horse over to the water's edge. A fifteen foot wide swath of the river bank and bottom had been churned.

Shim pointed at a huge swale of mud that had been thrown up. "No ships' hull would make that."

"No," said Argoth. "There's no keel or hull mark. No footprints. And why is the grass wet a dozen yards up the bank?"

"Something came out of the river," said Oaks.

As soon as Oaks said it, Argoth knew it was true. The Short Falls River was maybe thirty yards wide at this location, but it was deep and slow.

Argoth said, "I think we should back away from the water, Lord."

"I was just going to suggest a swim, Captain."

"Lord," said Argoth in warning.

Shim said, "If there's something in the river, let it show itself. We have three hundred arrows waiting." But nothing showed itself. A few minutes later, Shim ordered a hammer of men to cross. They did so without incident. He sent more to follow, ordering men to scout up and down both banks of the river.

After an hour of thorough searching, they returned, having found nothing. The Kragow had not been hiding in the grass or willows, hadn't left a wet spot in the grass or footprints in the mud as he climbed out of the water. The man had simply disappeared.

Those who had chased the Bone Face warriors did not bring back anyone Shim could question either. The warriors had raced to the coast and rowed out to a raiding ship waiting off shore.

Shim said, "They might have rowed another smaller ship up the river."

"You saw as far down the river as I," said Argoth. "There was no ship. And the scouts would have caught up to any small boat in these slow waters."

"Then where did he go?"

Argoth had no good answer.

* * *

After the failed search for the Kragow, Argoth and Shim returned to Fishing. The mists had dissipated. The wraiths, as far as Argoth could see, were gone, leaving behind the bodies of the villagers and his men. Sixty-three villagers and forty-seven of his new dreadmen.

They were good men. He knew each one of them well. With each body they found, the images of the men's loved ones rose in his mind. A whole multitude of wives and children, mothers and fathers and brothers and sisters and grandparents to whom he'd have to tell the awful news. It grieved him to the core. They had been *good* men who had been wasted because of his ignorance.

For each fallen soldier, Argoth and the others built a litter that could be dragged behind a horse. Then they placed the bodies of the dreadmen upon them. For the people of Fishing they dug graves. They did the same for those in Woolsom and Larkin. With every spadeful Argoth's grief hardened until it was cold as stone.

By the time they'd finished all the graves, the sun had dropped into the western sky. Argoth rode next to Shim. Behind them came the riders dragging the litters which carried the bodies of the brave Shoka sons, fathers, and brothers.

As they rode, Argoth thought through the implications of this new threat. The dark and smoky mists at Fishing had not quite covered the whole village, but what if the Kragow could extend those mists to cover a wider area? He'd be able to destroy a huge army with only a handful of men. Of course, anyone who saw the mists could flee. But what if the Kragows attacked at night when the black mists couldn't be seen and avoided? That thought chilled him.

"I think the Bone Faces might pose a greater threat than Mokad," Argoth said to Shim.

"Are you sure they're not allied with them?"

"No. But I do know our weaves will be useless against them in an attack. Our men need to grow in their ability to withstand those that would ride their souls. Although that probably won't be enough. I myself almost succumbed, and I've had years to grow into my strength."

Shim nodded. "There is one good thing in this bitter brew. Can you imagine what would have happened if we'd met this for the first time in a major battle?"

It was clear that if that Kragow had been with a few more men, they would have slaughtered Argoth and all those that had been with him. In fact, the only reason any had survived was because the third hammer had been standing farther back when the wraiths attacked.

Shim said, "It was not all a waste. We now know what those mists are. Maybe our Kish friend has a way to fight it."

"Yes," Argoth said. "The weapon for fighting this is called retreat."

29

The Practical Thing

ARGOTH, SHIM, AND THEIR ARMY of dreadmen rode toward the village that served Rogum's Defense. Out to sea a storm was brewing, dark clouds heaving toward the coast. Inland, the low sun shone slantwise upon the walls and roofs of the houses and across the fields, illuminating all with orange and yellow. A lone rider sat upon his mount at the crest of a low hill a few hundred yards off the road.

Argoth recognized the rider, even without seeing the tasseled fringe of his clothing, and pulled out of the moving column of Shim's men to face the man.

All the way back from Fishing Argoth had thought about the Bone Face Kragow and the wraiths. All the way back he'd seen clearly that the chances of Shim's army succeeding grew less and less.

The lord of Nilliam turned his horse and disappeared down the other side of the hill. Argoth loped his horse up to the crest of the hill. Below him, the lord of Nilliam waited at the wood's edge. When Argoth spotted him, he turned into the woods and disappeared in the trees.

Argoth knew there could be men waiting there in ambush. But if this lord had wanted to abduct him, he could have done it the first time. So Argoth urged his horse forward. He rode down the hill and entered the wood where the lord had.

He found the lord, with his tassels, tidy hair, and easy smile, sitting atop his horse a discrete distance from the wood's edge. "My friend," the lord said. "I came to see if you'd considered our offer. Your time is growing short."

"You're not merely a lord of Nilliam, are you?" asked Argoth.

"I am a lord, a messenger, a ditch digger—I am whatever I'm needed to be."

"Was the skir that spirited you away yours or another's?"

"The Divines of Nilliam sometimes share resources."

Argoth considered the man. "Show me your honors."

The man smiled and raised the sleeve of his left arm. His honors were elaborate and ran all the way to the elbow. What clearly stood out were the loops and whorls marking him as one of those consecrated as Divine.

The Divine of Nilliam pulled his sleeve back down and said, "You can see I am not making idle promises."

"What is your name?"

"When the Mother raised me, she named me Loyal."

Loyal of Nilliam. Argoth had heard that name, although he did not know much about the man.

"So what is your decision?" Loyal of Nilliam asked.

"How can I trust you when everything the Devourers speak is lies?"

"I am not lying when I tell you that you will be destroyed. You've done well to raise your terrors of dreadmen. But as impressive as your little army is, it will be no match for the combined might of the Western Glorydoms."

Argoth noticed he did not include the Bone Faces. "Combined might? Who, Nilliam and Mokad?"

"And Cath and Urz and Toth and Mungo."

"So this is what you came to do? Try to frighten me into compliance?"

"I came to demonstrate our good will," said Loyal. "I came because I'm a father, and I would want to help my own son were I in your situation." He withdrew a leather pouch and tossed it to Argoth.

Argoth caught the pouch.

"Open it," Loyal said.

Argoth loosened the draw string and pulled out a pendant the size of his thumb. It was black and silver and shaped in the form of bird that looked to be a nightingale. Argoth turned it over in his hand. It was alive, a weave.

"Let your son wear it on a string around his neck."

"What is its purpose?"

"It will slow your son's deterioration. The longer you wait, the harder it is to join soul to soul. Wait too long, and it will be impossible."

Argoth slipped the weave back into its pouch and tossed it back at Loyal. "Do you take me for a fool?" Argoth had no idea what this weave did, but he was sure it wasn't something to protect his son.

"Whatever you are, you are not a fool," said Loyal. "We would not choose a fool to elevate to our ranks. The weave is a gift. You're running out of time to save your son. It will help."

"You do not offer salvation," said Argoth.

"You still do not understand," Loyal said and shook his head. "When Mokad finishes, there will be nothing left. But it doesn't have to be. Not all masters are the same. Our master is fair. Only a portion of our people are harvested. Many of us go into the world of souls not only unmolested, but with escort. You can be one of those."

"I have a better proposal," said Argoth. "Why don't you join us? Why don't you throw off your shackles? Become a free man."

"Now who is taking whom for the fool? Men have never been free."

"In the beginning men submitted to none but the Creators. Then entered envying and strife and covetous desires. And that is how men fell."

"Come," said Loyal, "let us be men of truth. It's a good story. A noble dream. But that's all it is. That's all it will ever be."

"The Devourers are not invincible."

"Zu," Loyal said. "You face an army of three thousand dreadmen. You face multiple Divines, including a number of Skir Masters."

"We'll take our chances."

"I appreciate the fact that you must be strong in the face of your enemy. But there are no chances to be taken, except the one I'm giving you."

"No, that's not true. The Bone Faces have made us an offer."

Loyal of Nilliam cocked his head in surprise. "The Bone Faces? You truly think those backward savages can stand against the Western Glorydoms?"

Argoth shrugged.

"The Bone Faces are gnats, nothing more. They will be crushed and you along with them."

He was either bluffing or knew something about the mists that Argoth didn't. Or maybe he didn't know about the mists at all. One thing was clear: the Bone Faces were not allied with Mokad, and that was good news. Argoth decided to play this hand a bit farther. "They offer us defense," he lied.

"And you think they won't sacrifice you up to their gods? Right now you are outside the protection of a Sublime. You are alone. But if you become the property of a Sublime, then all sorts of agreements come into play. And because you are no longer a common threat but a responsibility of Nilliam instead, Mokad's coalition will dissolve."

"Responsibility? I find that an odd word. What you mean is we will become the property, the meat of the Devourer that holds your Glory's chain. I don't see any difference between you and the Bone Faces."

"You have not heard me. The Sublimes are not all the same. Our master is not void of all feeling for her subjects. She is beautiful, strong, and kind."

"Do you hear your own words?" asked Argoth. "You feed your people to these creatures. You do not preserve life. You destroy it."

"I am serving those I love. I am serving my wife and children. I am preserving my seed. That's where a man's duty lies. That's where your duty lies. You have a son. You have daughters. Your job is to preserve them. And not just here, in the world of flesh, but also in the world of souls. Once you've done that, you extend your protection to as many others as you can. You don't begin by betraying your own seed. And if that doesn't move you, then think on this: I will help more souls find that glorious brightness, my friend, than any man in any Hismayan Grove ever has or ever will."

They'd been smart to send this Loyal. He was persuasive, even though Argoth knew he lied.

"I'm giving you a chance to make a difference in this world," said Loyal. "I'm giving you an opportunity to seize real power. Save your daughters. Save your wife, your son. Save as many as you can. And do not delude yourself—if your son dies now, his soul torn, he will only become prey to the hungers that roam that other world."

Loyal's offer was tempting. Argoth had to face that fact. Furthermore, it seemed the more Argoth learned, the more he saw he didn't know. A small doubt crept into his mind. How did he know the Devourers were not the intended masters of the earth? Argoth had never seen an ancestor, never talked to one who had returned from the brightness. No Creator had spoken to him. So how did he know that humans received any salvation? He'd read scrolls and codices written by men, been taught stories handed down from other men. But who was to say the things he'd learned were only part-truths or maybe outright falsehoods? What if it was Loyal of Nilliam, and not Argoth, who was the one that possessed the fuller measure of the truth?

Loyal watched him, not with the look of a predator, but a caring friend. Oh, but he was good.

Argoth said, "I need more assurance than your promises."

Loyal nodded. "Of course, you do. So let me give you this. Mokad will be landing her many ships tomorrow at Blue Towers. The Mokaddian Kains that supply the Fire for the weaves of this army will arrive together."

"Where's the Skir Master?"

"We don't know, but we can give you the Kains."

Knowing the location of the Skir Master would be better. But you took the opportunities you were given, not the ones you wished for. Besides, if they could take out Mokad's Kains, it would be a tremendous blow. It was true many Divines knew the lore of drawing and storing Fire, but the Kains knew secrets the others did not. A handful could keep an army's weaves black with Fire. Furthermore, it was they who conducted the Fire sacrifices. Without the Kains, those caught in raids wouldn't be sacrificed. The weaves for 3,000 dreadmen required prodigious amounts of fire. Remove the Kains and the weaves would soon run dry.

Loyal said, "They come in the death ship with the red eye upon its sails."

If this information was correct, Loyal was giving them an opportunity to hobble Mokad's army. Argoth looked at his opponent, his gentle smile and honest face. A man who looked like he had nothing to hide. "Why would you give us this information?"

"How many times must I say it? Our Sublime is not like the others."

"More likely you simply see a way to gain the upper hand over Mokad without spilling your own blood."

Loyal held out the pouch with the nightingale weave in it. "Test us," he said. "Test *me*."

Argoth looked at the pouch. That weave might be anything, but, then again, wouldn't they want to deliver something that would actually work and build his trust? Besides, he could examine its operation well beforehand. He wasn't going to join them, so what harm could there be in accepting a gift?

He reached up and closed his fist around the pouch. It would do no harm to lead Loyal and his Glory on. In fact, it might do great good. "I will indeed test this," he said.

Loyal of Nilliam nodded. "You're doing the right thing." He said this without revealing any sort of deception or gloating, just honest sympathy. "It is a hard decision you have to make. I know. It was offered to me once as well. But do not delay. You do not have the time. Raise a red pennant on your north tower when you are ready to talk. I will be waiting for you on the same hill you found me today."

Argoth put the pouch into his pocket. "Who else in Shim's army have you made this offer to?"

"I told you: we are careful about who we raise to our ranks. This offer has been made to none other."

That was a lie. It had to be. Moreover, why would Nilliam be the only one playing this game? Could Urz, for instance, be making their own offers? Maybe they were behind the traitor in Shim's midst. What about Mungo and Cath? Both of them were neck-deep in their own games; why wouldn't they be trying to steal the New Lands from Mokad just as Nilliam was? Surely someone had made a similar offer to Shim or Eresh.

"Who is the traitor in our midst?" Argoth asked.

"Mokad does not share such secrets with us."

Argoth told himself Loyal of Nilliam was wrong about the nature of Divines. He told himself he'd just given Shim's army an advantage, perhaps an opportunity, by discovering the Bone Faces were not part of Mokad's coalition. Furthermore, Argoth might be able to play this Loyal for even more information or feed him lies.

But underneath all that he wondered: there was so much he didn't know. Over his many years, he had learned, as painful as it might be, it never did any good to fight against the truth. Was it possible the teachings of Hisma-yas were dreams? Was Loyal of Nilliam actually bringing light?

Loyal smiled.

Argoth did not return the gesture. He simply turned his horse around and rode it out of the woods. Above him the storm clouds darkened the sky.

* * *

A thunderstorm broke upon the troops as they rode into Rogum's Defense. Argoth settled his horse in the stables, then walked across the bailey to Shim's quarters. He climbed the stairs, his clothes dripping rain, and reported everything that had occurred with Loyal to Shim. Everything except the last bit about the red pennant.

"We have to act on this knowledge," Shim said.

"It could be a trap."

"It could be their undoing. Their dreadmen don't know any lore. They rely on the Kains to fill their weaves. What happens when their weaves begin to run dry while ours wean themselves off weaves and begin to learn how to wield Fire on their own? Every day our forces will grow stronger while theirs diminish. We need to plan."

"We need to send word to the families of the men that have fallen. We need to send word about the mists to all our outposts."

Shim nodded. "It's going to be a long, rough evening."

Argoth sent riders with messages, then helped Shim oversee the preparation of the dead bodies in the great hall. As they worked, the rain lashed the fortress walls and the cobbles of the inner bailey. Lightning cracked and boomed. At one point Serah, his wife, and the girls entered the hall to silently view each of the bodies. They somberly added coins and gifts to the small piles forming next to each of the men. On their way out, Grace ran over to Argoth and put a small straw girl she'd made in his pocket. She was always giving him things to remember her by.

When the bodies had all been prepared, Shim said to Argoth, "Get something to eat. Then meet me in my quarters."

Argoth wasn't hungry, but he knew he should eat. So he got a bowl of cold swamp from the cooks and took it to his quarters.

Grace and his other daughters sat around their mother stitching various bits of clothing. They'd shuttered the window against the storm and worked by candlelight. Nettle sat to one side on the floor with a piece of chalk and a slate, painstakingly drawing something Argoth could not recognize. A few moments later a tremor began to shake Nettle's head and arm.

"Serah?" he asked.

"It comes and goes," she said. "It will pass. Matiga is reading her codices to see if there might be an herb to stop it."

He knelt by Nettle and put his arm around him. Nettle trembled in his embrace. A few minutes later the trembling stopped. Argoth rocked with him. He thought back over the last weeks. Nettle *was* getting worse, just as that Divine of Nilliam said.

In the beginning, there had been flashes of the old Nettle. He would say something or do something, and Argoth would think that maybe he'd come back despite the soul he'd lost. But those flashes were coming less and less. Sometimes it seemed Nettle hardly even knew who Argoth was.

He looked at his family. He knew what would happen to them if Shim lost. A man had to take care of his family. They were his first duty. He had to take care of them in this life and the next.

Serah poked her bronze needle through a quilted tunic that soldiers wore under their armor and tugged a sturdy piece of thread through. She was pregnant, only a month away from delivering.

He said, "Will you talk to me?"

She glanced at him, then went back to her work in the candlelight. He took that as a yes. "Let's say you had a choice. Perhaps you were in a capsized boat in a heaving sea. Or you were on the beach and saw a sleeper wave coming toward you. And you knew you could save our children, get them to safety, but not the children of your sisters. You know that if you try to save them all, you will all perish together. What would you do?"

"I have not forgiven you," she said.

"I'm not talking about Nettle," he said. "I'm asking you a question. How do you prioritize? I want to know."

"Why do you even have to ask?" She tied a knot and then bit the thread off.

"What would you do?"

She sat up straight and felt her pregnant belly. Their child must have kicked. "You know what I would do," she said and turned back to her work.

And he did. She would save her children. Then she would go back and perish trying to save the rest. Which was how it should be.

"I think I know how to heal Nettle," he said. The moment he uttered the words, he regretted having said them. He didn't know that Nilliam could restore his son. It was probably a lie. But what if it wasn't? What if it could save Nettle from going into that world unprotected?

Serah stopped, bronze needle in one hand, thread in the other.

"Forget I said that."

"Do you wish to torture me with false hopes?"

He wondered how much he should tell her. He had kept her in the dark for so many years. He'd thought keeping her in the dark would keep her close. In the end, it only led him to lose both her and Nettle. But he couldn't tell her he was thinking of Nilliam's offer. "It might be nothing. Just an old scrap of something I remember. I shouldn't have mentioned it."

Serah looked up at him. The anger and hurt were plain on her face. She knew he was lying. "You'll never give it up," she said referring to his secrets and lies, "will you?"

How could he bring her into his confidence on this matter? How could he not keep some secrets from her? If he told her what he was thinking, she would tell Matiga who would tell Shim and Eresh. They would watch him. And then this opportunity, if it was one, would be forever beyond his reach. Besides, he hadn't committed to anything. He didn't know yet if Loyal even spoke the truth.

He felt the pouch in his pocket with its bird weave. "We have information that might turn the upcoming battle before it even starts. I'll know better tomorrow if it will work," he said. "That may give me more time to focus on our son." Then he finished his food and went out into the rain and across the bailey to Shim's quarters.

30

Mission

SUGAR WAS RIDING back from her meeting with Withers. It was raining and, despite Urban's riding cloak, she was soaked. Up ahead, yet another messenger galloped toward them from the direction of Rogum's Defense. She and Urban moved their mounts off the muddy road for the third time.

The messenger rode up on the shoulder where the grass would provide more traction instead of down in the mud of the road, but the horse's hooves still threw up soggy clumps of earth. Sugar recognized this Shimsman as he approached. She waved a small hello as he went by. He gave her a nod as he flew past, his face grim with determined purpose.

"Something's up," said Urban.

Sugar agreed, and they urged their horses into a trot. Not much later they arrived at the fortress. Despite the rain, it was buzzing with activity.

Sugar had been excited to return. She'd walked for hours today. She'd beheld wonders, and couldn't wait to tell Legs all about it, but then she saw the faces of the soldiers and knew something terrible had happened.

They received the news from the grooms at the stables. She and Urban hurried to the great hall and saw the dead men lying there. She had not known any of them well, but their deaths still struck her. She had nothing to give, but Urban opened his purse and placed a coin next to each of them. Off to the side, one of the men who'd been at Woolsom was telling the tale of the battle. She and Urban moved into the crowd of people about him. She listened with horror as he told of the Bone Face Kragow and the wraiths.

As the story progressed, Urban's expression became more and more concerned. When the soldier finished telling the tale, Urban turned to her. "I need to talk to Argoth."

She nodded, and they left the hall, him to speak with Argoth and her with Legs. Sugar found Legs sitting on a barrel under the eaves of the kitchen with group of men eating swamp. Flax sat next to him. He stood when Sugar arrived, smoothed both sides of his long blond moustache. "Just the person I've been waiting for. I was under strict command from the chief lady of the tub not to leave the boy's sight." He paused.

When she didn't respond, he repeated, "not to leave the boy's *sight* . . ."

"Ah," she said and faked a laugh.

Some of the other men shook their heads at the joke.

Flax stood. "I dared not risk the wrath of that formidable woman. But now that you're here, I deliver him to you and take my leave." He turned to the other men. "Take heart, boys. The Bone Faces will pay."

"Thank you," Legs said to Flax.

Flax reached out and gave Legs's hand a friendly squeeze. "You remember what I told you."

"I will."

Flax gave a sympathetic look to Sugar, then walked out toward the stables.

"He's grand," said Legs.

"He's a foreigner," one of the men said as if that trumped everything else.

"Foreigner or not," another said, "he's the one I want next to me when the fighting gets thick."

Sugar put her hand on Legs's shoulder.

"So?" he said to her.

She didn't feel comfortable sharing everything that had happened today with these men. "Come with me," she said. She took his hand, and he hopped off the barrel. Then she led him away. When they were in the privacy of their own cellar, she said, "Brother, you cannot imagine. You won't believe the things I saw." Two of the ferrets were awake in their cage, playing, wrestling with each other.

"Start from the beginning," he said.

She did and told him everything from the moment she found the thread while working with the washerwomen to the goatherd and howlers. When she finished, she remembered the honeyed nuts. She withdrew the cloth from her pocket. "Here," she said. "I saved these for you."

She pressed them into his hands, but his face was cast down. "What's wrong?"

"Do you think they made it?"

He was talking about Mother and Da. She put an arm around him. "If Mother can't make it, nobody can. Remember, she went to find Da. I'm sure they're safe as stone."

But in her heart she wondered. Furthermore, after the tale of Woolsom, she realized how important Urban's suggestion had been. She and Legs did need a plan should things fall apart, one for this world and the next. War was upon them, and soldiers died all the time. What if she and Legs were killed, and the ancestors didn't come? What if the same happened to her friends here?

She thought about the skenning and blackspine and realized she might be the only thing standing between those she loved and the perils of the yellow world.

A few minutes later Urban darkened the doorway. "It's begun," he said. "The ferret is being sent to war."

"Where?" she asked.

He looked at Legs, glanced behind him to make sure nobody was there. "Blue Towers."

31

The Wilds

TALEN KEPT an eye out. They were in the Wilds proper now, and who knew what foul thing might attack them here? He held Scruff's reins, leading him along the rocky crown of a ridge. River sat up in the saddle, every minute growing worse, looking like she was going fall off with the slightest nudge. In front of him, the maze of wooded hollows and hills that made up the Wilds stretched for as far as he could see. And Talen was about to see much less, for the thick clouds of the approaching storm were not far behind, blotting out the sky and moving fast in his direction.

The wind picked up, gusting into the trees with a heavy hand. Talen loped as fast as the terrain would allow, weaving his way along the rocky crown of the ridge in his bare feet, taking them both deeper into this forsaken wilderness.

He'd taken his weave off a few miles back. He needed all the might he could muster, not only to move faster, but also to defend himself and River should some abominable thing come at them through the trees. His Fire burned inside him, filling him with vigor.

The crows flew above, fighting to keep pace in the increasing winds. Behind him thunder boomed. A smattering of hail fell from the sky, bouncing on the ground. The brief hail stopped. Then a gust of wind brought another squall, the pellets stinging his face and arms. Then the winds picked up even more and the hail was replaced by a sweep of rain, a huge curtain of it hissing as the drops struck rock and tree.

The wind buffeted the two crows. They cawed, tried to stay aloft, but then dived out of sight.

Now was his chance. He dropped off the ridge, down the slope River had told him to take and into the trees. He made sure to wrap the reins tightly around his hand. Scruff was a calm horse, but the lightning could spook the best animals, and he didn't want to throw River.

The leading edge of the rain crossed over and engulfed them in a gray torrent of water that soaked his hair and clothes. Then the thick rain and clouds folded them in, cutting visibility.

A few minutes later he struck out along a saddle and then climbed back up to the crest of another hill at a lower elevation. They were going to come to a vale with a lazy river. They would cross that, climb the slope on the far side, then drop down into a hollow, which would lead them along for a few miles. There was a cutoff, and a jutting rock that looked like a rabbit's head, which was the marking that would tell him Harnock's vale was close.

Talen led Scruff along the hill, trying to keep to the thinner parts of the wood because River seemed barely able to avoid the branches. After about fifteen minutes they came to the far side of the hill. Talen looked down the slope and saw a gentle valley below with the serpentine coils of a slow river.

"Is this it?" he asked.

She didn't reply.

"River," he said. Her cloak's hood hung down over her face. He went to her and grabbed her hand. "Sister, is this where we go down?" He pushed the cowl of her hood back so she could see. Her eyes were rolling in her head.

Good lords, not here. Not now. He patted her hand and called her name again.

She slurred something.

"What?" he asked.

"Down," she moaned. At least, that's what he thought she said. Then she slumped to one side and almost fell off the horse.

Talen grabbed her and righted her in the saddle, and then he retrieved some rope from the saddle bags and lashed her feet in the stirrups and legs to the saddle flaps. With her securely tied in, he set off, descending the slope slantwise, hurrying through the trees and scrub.

Toward the bottom he jammed his toes on a fallen branch and stumbled. He cursed and proceeded on. When he broke from the trees onto the valley floor, he stopped.

Wurms were said to make their burrows in the valley bottoms. He scanned the tall meadow grass, then quickly realized there would be no burrows here—the whole valley bottom was a boggy marsh. He moved forward. As he proceeded, he sank to his thighs in the brackish water, the mud sucking at his legs. The good thing was that the rain kept the mosquitoes grounded. He was bound to pick up a few leeches before he made it to the other side, but that was far better than falling into the hands of what chased him.

The river in the middle of the valley was not fast, and he and Scruff were able to easily swim to the other side and climb up into slightly less boggy ground. When he reached the base of the far slope, he looked back across the valley. The slope he'd come down was shrouded in mist and rain. He thought he saw something brown flash through the trees, but when he looked closer, nothing was there. The hackles rose on his neck. The last thing he wanted to meet was woodikin. He waited, but whatever it was didn't reveal itself again. It was probably just some animal—a deer or badger seeking cover.

He checked River's lashings to make sure they were not too loose or tight, then climbed the hill on this side, crested, and dropped down into the hollow on the other side. When they reached the bottom, River pointed the direction they should go.

Talen didn't think she had much time left, and he began to run along an animal trail under the drenched canopy of trees. The storm rumbled overhead, darkening the sky. The rain was falling hard, erasing any tracks they left. He thanked the Six for the cover, even if it was cold.

They followed the folds of the hills and hollows, twisting and turning, and he soon realized why people entered this place and never found their way out again. He counted the cutoffs and then couldn't remember if he'd counted five or six. Or was he at seven? Had he missed the cutoff entirely? Then he saw a break in the trees up one rocky slope and the large formation that looked like a rabbit's head.

This was it. "We're almost there," He said. "Hold on." He turned up the hollow. A creek ran noisily down the middle. Talen hurried along a thin trail that ran alongside it.

The rain lessened and then stopped, even though water still dropped from the leaves. He led Scruff along a trail at the bottom of a hollow that ended in a bowl. Harnock's vale was just on the other side of one of the slopes, but without the sun, he couldn't tell his directions. But even if he could, he'd forgotten which way River had said to go.

"River," he said. He turned and found her leaning back, her arms limp at her side. Her hood had fallen back, exposing her face to the sky. She sat like someone petitioning the clouds, her face upturned, her open mouth collecting the rain.

"River!" he repeated and grabbed her hand.

She did not respond.

Scruff blew out in weariness and shifted his weight. River sagged to one side and would have fallen if not for his lashings.

"Lords, no," he said, and righted her. He patted her hand, slapped her face. No response. He felt for a pulse in her hand and found only the faintest beat.

Which direction had she told him to go? Had she said left? He couldn't see any sign of a trail that might tell him which slope to choose. He dithered for a moment, then decided it didn't matter which slope he chose. If necessary, he would try them all.

The low cloud ceiling was beginning to rise, and he knew he had to find Harnock before those crows began to fly. He followed an animal path up a slope, scrabbled over the ridge at the top, and found a narrow hollow below, but River had said Harnock lived in a wide vale.

He didn't panic. Instead, he stayed on top of the ridge and circled around, trying to keep the low branches from whipping River. When he'd gone a good way around, the trees parted and revealed a wide meadow in the vale below.

This had to be Harnock's. He knew there was a place where he was supposed to stand and call out his desire to visit, but had no idea where that was and knew River couldn't wait. So he skirted a cliff and descended the slope, calling Harnock's name as he went. When he got to the bottom, he began to alternate the calls with loud whistles.

He broke from the trees into the meadow he'd seen from above. A well worn path cut through the waist-high grass and his spirits soared. This had to be the right vale, which meant Harnock's house would be somewhere up ahead.

"Harnock!" he called and entered the path. The grass here was lush, perfect for grazing livestock. Harnock's home was probably down the vale a bit, maybe behind the trees a few hundred yards ahead.

Still holding the reins, Talen picked up his speed. Scruff broke into a fast trot behind him. River didn't sit the bouncing well, but his lashes held her on.

He followed the smooth trail for a hundred yards, running with the speed of his Fire. Then the trail took a tight turn, and Talen stumbled into a burrow six feet across. Scruff stumbled in after him and knocked him flat on his face partway down the gaping hole.

Scruff nickered and climbed out, River sagging to one side in the saddle. Talen raised up on his hands and knees and wiped mud from his face.

The burrow's run was well-worn and smooth, angling gently downward into blackness. Whatever lived here was large. Fear washed over him. An odd odor rose from the depths. It was sharp, almost like vinegar, almost—

Wurm scent! He'd stumbled into a wurm hole.

He scrambled out of the hole in a panic. Two paths led away from this burrow. Another smaller burrow sank into the ground only a half dozen yards away. Beyond it was another, and another.

Wurms lived in colonies. He hadn't run out into a grazing meadow, but a wurm field. Furthermore, he wasn't at its edge. He was inside the outer ring.

A deer or wild goat would see the grass of this meadow and be unable to resist coming down to take a bite. And when enough had come, the wurms would rise and devour them. It was said that wurms waited underground, listening. And all this time he'd been whistling and hollering with Scruff clomping behind. His mouth went dry.

He had to get out. There was no way to muffle the thuds of Scruff's hooves. They were going to have to run for it. He turned to flee back the way he'd come, but a dark figure on horseback emerged at the edge of the woods there. A black and brown dog was with him. It padded forward to sniff about the edge of the tall grass. A hooded crow flew low over the field and cawed. Then it turned and swooped over to light on the man's shoulder.

The man wore high leather riding boots, a dark padded tunic, and a sword. His hair was cropped short. His face had a long scar running down one side. Moments later riders filtered out of the trees behind him.

Talen looked at the Mokaddian dreadmen. How had they found him? The rain had been so intense it would have quickly covered any tracks they would have made. Then he looked at that dog. His mind shot back to the shape he'd seen on the slope behind him after he'd crossed the marsh and lazy river. It had been the dog flashing through the trees, not some woodikin or badger.

"Holy One," the lead dreadman called across the meadow. "It's useless to run."

Maybe, but if these greasy whoresons wanted him, they would have to catch him. He grabbed the saddle and swung up behind River. It was awkward, holding the reins from behind.

"Holy One, come out of there."

"Better the wurms than you!" Talen called back and dug his heels into Scruff's flanks. The stallion surged forward, springing past the large wurm burrow and deeper into the field.

From his height atop Scruff, the crisscrossed wurm trails were now easy to see. What a fool he'd been. He urged Scruff faster.

Behind him the lead dreadman kicked his horse and galloped forward. The crow sprang to the air. The dog barked and shot out ahead. Some of the dreadmen skirted the meadow on the near side. The rest followed their leader into the tall grass.

The wurms would be listening below. And what they'd hear was one lone horse running out front and a number behind. Talen hoped they were greedy.

Scruff leapt over a wurm burrow and just about unseated Talen, but he righted himself and tightened his grip with his thighs. They galloped for a number of yards, but a thick clump of burrows lay up ahead. So Talen pulled the reins and turned Scruff off the path into the grass. He pointed Scruff for the far side of the meadow.

River, unable to support herself, bounced to the side. Talen tried to hold onto her and the reins and keep himself from falling off, but it was a mad juggle, and he had to slow to right her. He glanced back. The lead dreadmen was closing the distance, his face hard as stone.

Suddenly a low sound began to rise about the meadow. Low like the wind, moaning through the trees, except there were no trees out here. He turned his head; the sound was coming from in front of him. He changed course. A few moments later the sound rose in front of him again.

His first impulse was to turn yet again, but perhaps that's exactly what the wurms wanted. It was said that wurms liked to confuse and surround their prey. Maybe this was how they tricked their prey into running around in circles. He held his course, urged Scruff on, straight toward the sound.

Off to Talen's right, something large moved through the tall grass. Ahead lay a cluster of three wurm holes. The grass around them had been beaten low. If he could get past them, he'd have a clear shot to the edge of the meadow.

The odd moaning of the wind about the field grew. "Come on," Talen said and urged Scruff faster. But then Scruff's ears pricked forward and to the side, and he balked. Came to a complete halt.

A moment later a wurm shot out of a hole in front of them and rose twelve feet into the air, the rest of its long length disappearing down its hole. The wurm was as thick as Talen's leg with wrinkled gray skin. The head was shaggy, not with hair, but odd growths of skin. Its eyes were small and ugly like a salamander's.

Scruff whinnied in fright, jerked to the side, throwing Talen. He landed with a thud in the grass just a few feet in front of the wurm. Talen scrambled to his feet, the sharp tang of the creature filling his nostrils.

The wurm pulled back to strike, opened its mouth full of short sharp teeth.

Scruff ran wildly toward the edge of the field, River jerking on his back. Talen, filled with Fire, shot out after them.

But the wurm was surprisingly fast. It struck, slamming him with the side of its head, and knocked him down. Talen rolled away, sprang to his feet, shot forward. The wurm slammed him again, this time with much more force, disorienting him. Talen sprawled to the ground, stunned.

The wurm pulled back, opened its mouth.

At that moment the dreadman with the scar rode up at a full gallop and hurled himself from the saddle, sword flashing. He struck the wurm and sliced deep.

The wurm pulled back in pain and rent the air with an ear-splitting bellow.

The dreadman landed in the tall grass, rolled, and charged back, sword ready. This time when he swung, he almost cleaved the wurm in two. Blood pumped out in a huge arc, bone popped, and then the severed portion toppled heavily to the tall grass.

All about the field a clamor arose as if they'd awakened all of Regret's foul minions. Wurms of various sizes rose out of a multitude of holes.

One struck a dreadmen, pulling him from his saddle. Another one attacked the scarred dreadman's horse, biting into its throat. Someone shot an arrow into the wurm's body. It trumpeted in pain and turned to face the threat.

Talen sprinted after Scruff and River only to find another beast rising in front of him. Then another dreadman rode up behind Talen, grabbed him by the back of his tunic, and lifted him up, laying him across the withers in front of the saddle. They raced past the wurm for the slope ahead.

Behind them the field of tall grass writhed. Dreadmen fought and ducked. A monstrous wurm as big around as a cow slammed its head into the rump of a horse and sent both horse and rider sprawling.

The scarred dreadman and the others that had not been trapped by the wurms galloped for the edge of the field. A horse tried to dart through a gap between two creatures, but the wurm closest to it struck, biting deep into the horse's leg. Another dreadman on foot turned to defend himself, but a smaller creature struck at him, bit into his arm, and yanked him to the ground.

Talen and the dreadman thundered past the edge of the field and began to climb up the slope above the vale. Below them the black and brown dog broke from the grass and ran up the hill, followed by the scarred leader running with multiplied speed. In the field, the wurms converged on the horses and men they'd caught and injured.

Talen's heart was pounding. He was *not* going to be captured by these men. And where was River? He looked about and didn't see her. Lords, was she still back on that field?

He pushed off the horse, stumbled and crashed into the ground, but then he was up and began to sprint away. But the dreadman who had lifted him onto the horse flew from the saddle and bore him to the ground.

Talen drew his knife, but the dreadman knocked it away. Talen swung his elbow back into the man's jaw, tried to twist free, but the dreadman was too fast. He wrapped around Talen like a snake and held him fast.

Moments later the scarred dreadman caught up. He slid something cool around Talen's neck. When he snapped the clasp shut, something slipped inside—his grip on his Fire weakened. And then it was like trying to hold a fish with frozen hands, and it was gone.

Talen bucked and fought, but the vigor in his limbs leaked away.

The scarred dreadman bound Talen's hands, then rolled him over. "Now, Holy One," he said, "we will take you to your master."

He reached out to pull Talen up, and Talen got a good look at the honors on the man's hands. He wasn't merely a dreadman.

"Filth!" Talen spat.

"Holy One—"

"I'm not your holy anything," Talen said. "I do not betray my own kind and serve them up on platters."

"Sooner or later, we are all meat," the scarred Divine said. "It is the order of creation."

Another one of the men rode up leading Scruff along by his reins. River was still lashed to the saddle.

Below them the wurms in the field moaned and sighed like the wind. A smaller one broke from the grass and began to slither up the slope.

"We're not out of this yet," the Divine said. "Move."

* * *

About a mile from the wurm field they stopped in a piney wood. Talen had been put up on a horse with one of the dreadmen riders. The scarred Divine, his horse dead on the field, had been running. He now walked over to Scruff and began to cut River free.

"We need to get her some help," Talen said.

"We do not have time to bear the dead," said the Divine. "She will not last the hour. Your sister's soul will be free. You should rejoice in her good fortune." He removed the lashing from her legs and stirrups and slid her from the horse. Then he laid her upon the thick carpet of pine needles that covered the ground.

River's skin was pale. Her hair was wet and tangled. She lay unmoving. Just hours before she had been springing about Len's barn, giving him instructorly wallops. This didn't seem real. "You keep calling me holy, then do as I say. Help her."

"My skills do not lie in that path," he said and began to lower the stirrups to accommodate his greater height.

This wasn't happening. River couldn't die. She couldn't!

"You may bid her farewell," said the Divine. "Then we must go."

The dreadman holding Talen helped him slide off the horse, then led him over to her. Talen knelt beside her, stroking her face with his bound hands. "River," he said, but she did not respond.

He smoothed her wet hair back with his bound hands. Why hadn't he insisted on taking her the other way? They should have gone to the coast.

The Divine finished adjusting Scruff's stirrups and mounted. "It is time."

Talen ignored the Divine and bent over to kiss her brow. Then the dreadman he'd been riding with hauled him up by the arm.

"Leave me alone!" Talen growled and snatched his arm back.

But the dreadman did not listen. He grabbed Talen by the arm again and half dragged him back to the horse.

River lay motionless. He'd missed Harnock's vale. He'd failed, and she was going to die. Despair and anger roiled in him. He hated them. He hated them all.

The dreadman bent over and cupped his hands to give Talen a leg up.

"Deliver me to your dark master," Talen said, "and one day it will be me coming for you and your children."

"Holy One," the scarred dreadman said. "Put your foot into his hand, or we'll just throw you across."

These men were blind, but he could see there was no use fighting. Talen did as he was told and was soon sitting astride the horse. The dreadman got up behind him, and then they all rode forward through the trees. The dog padded along by Scruff's side. The crows cawed above the pines.

As they rode away, Talen turned to get one last glimpse of River. She lay like a pale flower in the shadows of the forest floor. The sight of her stabbed him through the heart. He'd broken when Da died. He was breaking now.

They rode around some high scrub, and River disappeared completely from his view. He thought he might catch one last glimpse, but she was gone, lost in the shadows of the wood.

Talen turned around, grief mixing with his rage. He'd had no mother. She'd died when he was but a boy. So River had taken her place. River had been his mainstay; she'd been everything. She'd laughed with him, chased him, thrown innumerable spoons at his head. She tried to teach him how to talk to girls. She'd always been there for him. An image rose in his mind of the time she'd shown him the trick of how to fillet fish down by the river, the sun glistening off the water. Why that should rise now, he had no idea, but it filled him with a terrible loss. Some awful denizen of the Wilds would find her body. As for her soul, would Da come? Was he even around?

Talen's grief crested, and in that pain he saw what he had to do. He was not going to allow himself to be delivered to Mokad's master. When the time came, he'd simply remove himself from their clutches permanently. He would not turn River's and Da's sacrifices into things of naught. Until that moment came, there had to be some way to fight these men. If he could get free, if River just hung on, he might be able to deliver her yet. And with that thought his anger rose.

The king's collar prevented him from multiplying his might. And even if he could, he was outnumbered. There was no way he could take this fist of powerful dreadmen in a physical struggle. No way he could outrun them. Lords, there was no way he could even beat his own sister—

He pulled his thoughts up short. That was not true. His mind raced back to what had happened earlier today in the barn. He'd been able to strike River without touching her. That thought banged around in his mind and came back with renewed force. He'd been able to strike her *without touching her*. No, that wasn't right. A part of him *had* touched her.

The Devourers wanted him, which meant he obviously must have some ability or power. He'd been bred to be a tool. Whatever had happened in the barn was surely part of that. And if he could figure out what he'd done to River, maybe he could attack these men.

All this time Talen had been resisting his sense of the Fire and souls around him. Maybe it was time to quit fighting that desire and open his eyes instead. Maybe it was time for the tool to rise up against the master.

Talen reached out with his senses and tried to remember what he'd done back in the barn. Tried to do it again. But it was like groping in the dark.

32

Dreadman's Camp

JUST BEFORE THE last bit of daylight totally failed, the Divine ordered his men to make camp in the lee of a ledge close to the top of a ridge still in the Wilds. Since the time he'd left River until now, Talen had struggled to repeat what he'd done in the barn and failed.

The dreadman Talen rode with helped him off the horse and led him under the cover of the tall ledge. This site was a good one and would provide a shield not only against the wind, but also give them a defensive position against creatures of the Wilds.

The dreadmen tied up their horses to the trunks of some trees thick with yellow autumn leaves and made a fire. The scarred Divine asked him to strip so they could dry his clothes. Talen complied. There was nothing to be gained by sitting around wet and cold.

"What is your name?" Talen asked.

"Nashrud, Holy One."

Talen had not heard of any Nashrud, but he supposed the identity of a hunter was best kept secret.

The Divine searched Talen's clothes before hanging them by the fire. He found Talen's governor and weave of might. He looked over their design and pronounced them fair. Then he put them in his pouch. He took Talen's knife and laid it to the side. When he was satisfied there was nothing else in the clothing, he set them to dry and rummaged through Scruff's saddlebags.

"It's a fine steed," he said, "even if it is rather ugly."

"Ugly and far too good for the likes of you," Talen said. The scarred Divine said nothing.

While the clothing dried, the men ate. Talen did not refuse the dreadman biscuits and water they offered him. Nashrud settled himself across the fire from

Talen with his own biscuit. He was a fearsome man clearly weathered by much experience. The scar that ran down one side of his face wasn't his only one.

"So you're a Divine," Talen said.

"Holy One, I am not one of the lofty ones that rule," he said. "The title of 'Divine' has not been bestowed upon me."

Talen pointed at his honors. "And yet you wear the markings."

"I am a hunter. A servant. Nothing more."

A hunter of criminals and sleth. Talen motioned at the crows. "A hunter that enthralls beasts."

The man shrugged as if that were a small matter. "Tomorrow I will put a thrall of the Mother upon you as well. But we will have to first go back to that wurm field and retrieve the weave from my fallen horse."

Talen remembered vividly Uncle Argoth's description of what the thrall had done to his desires. Talen couldn't allow that to happen to himself.

The scarred Divine took a drink from his water skin.

"You are no better than any sleth," Talen said.

"I never claimed to be," Nashrud replied.

There were eleven men with Nashrud, all of them dreadmen. Three of them took up the first watch in a wide perimeter. Talen finished his meal as the last light of day faded. Above them the clouds blocked out the stars and moon, leaving them in total blackness except for what was made by the small fire. Out in the woods, the wind picked up and whistled over the ledge and through the trees.

Nashrud checked the lashings about Talen's ankles and wrists, then lay down. Talen did not sleep. He lay there struggling to figure out what he'd done before, searching his new senses. He could smell the Fire of the men around him. If he concentrated, he could just catch a whiff of the life in the horses. He tried and tried again to split himself. The camp fire died down to glowing embers. The night wore on. The dreadmen changed watch, and those that had stood guard settled into their sleep.

Talen began to despair. He turned his mind to his other option. There was a forty- or fifty-foot cliff they'd passed coming here. If they took the same trail back tomorrow, he might cast himself off it. He began to plan how to push himself off the horse quickly enough to put himself beyond the dreadman's reach. He retraced the trail in his mind and identified the best spot. It would be close, but he figured he could reach the cliff.

His eyes drooped. He relaxed. A moment later part of him slipped, and suddenly the camp and ledge were visible in the muted yellow light of his dream. Except he knew now that this wasn't a dream. He looked about, saw the horses, the dreadmen sleeping in their bedrolls about the embers of the campfire, the dog lying next to Nashrud. He saw himself staring up into the black night.

How he could be in two places at the same time was frightening to contemplate. But he pushed the fear down. He could see, and his captors could not. Talen brought his other self down to look at the ropes about his hands. There was no way he was going to wriggle out of those lashings. He'd already tried. He'd also tried gnawing on them, but the sun would be up before he'd chewed hiw way out. So he carefully sat up and moved to the embers of the fire. The dreadmen about him slept on, a couple of them snoring lightly.

He picked up a twig and used it to pull a big ember away from the others. None of the men stirred, so he crouched low and pressed a part of the rope that bound his hands to the ember and carefully blew on it. The ember glowed; the hemp rope blackened. The heat burned against the skin of his hand. He carefully blew again and pressed the cord against the ember. He blew again, and the cord began to smolder. He kept blowing and pressing, gritting his teeth against the pain, then bringing the sides of his hands up to lick them. A thin trail of smoke rose up from the rope. He continued, his hand scorching, until the cord was burned most of the way through. Then he snatched his hand away to lick the burned part, trying to cool it.

He picked at the mostly burned rope with his teeth, and in moments it broke. Using his teeth he loosened the rest of the lashings and soon his hands were free. He reached forward to undo the knots at his feet.

The dreadman that had been sleeping next to him rolled over. "What are you doing?"

Talen struck him with the part of himself that was outside his body. He didn't know exactly what he did; it was more a reflex.

The man flinched back. Talen grabbed the knife from the dreadman's sheath.

The dreadman lunged forward, but Talen struck him again with his other self. Then he sawed through the lashings with the sharp knife and kicked his feet free.

Nashrud sat up. His dog rose to its feet and barked. Talen struck at Nashrud with his other self, then scrambled back, out of the dim glow of the fire's embers. He stumbled over a bush, then brought his other self back to see where he was going.

"Stop!" Nashrud commanded. He rose and ran a few steps into the dark, but it was clear Nashrud could not see in the pitch blackness. "Frost," he said. "Get him." And the dog raced out into the darkness after Talen.

Talen took a number of strides, then struck out with his other self, biting at the weave of the dog's body. The dog ignored it and raced forward. Talen picked up a big stone and flung it. It glanced off the dog's head. The animal yelped in pain and veered to the side. Then it shook itself and continued forward.

Talen struck at it again with his other self, but this time instead of pulling back, he felt for the dog's weave, examined it. He could smell the dog's Fire and soul, and then he found what he thought was a gap, a weakness. He pressed in and the dog yelped and bit at its side as if some tick was there. Talen pressed again, and the dog whirled, trying to dislodge him.

Behind the dog, Nashrud felt his way forward holding up a burning branch to see with. "You're a danger to yourself, Holy One."

Talen backed out of the light.

"There!" a man shouted.

Talen turned and ran.

"Holy One!" Nashrud yelled.

Talen raced down the hill, but running using the vision of his other self proved tricky, like trying to use your left hand to do only what the right has been trained to do, and he slammed his shoulder into a tree, knocking himself to the ground. He shot to his feet and continued forward, clutching at the pain in his arm.

Back at the camp, dreadmen were shouting, pulling out torches. Talen continued to run, but taking more care this time. He ran down the slope, then back along the trail the way they'd come. When he was a good distance away, he stopped to send his one part back. Nashrud and his men were far behind, a few of the men holding torches, the rest ready with their weapons, but they were following the dog, which would sniff its way right to him. Talen struck at Frost the dog until he scurried back with a series of yelps. Then Talen chased him all the way back to the campground.

Then he raced back to his body that was standing in the dark along the trail. River was still out there. He couldn't multiply because of his collar, but if he was lucky, he'd find her before the other things that lived in these cursed woods did. But he knew he didn't have much time.

* * *

Talen followed the trail, working on getting the hang of seeing with his other self. Every now and again, he'd send his self back. Every time, that rotted dog was following the trail again. He chased the dog back another two times. The third time he chased it off a small ledge into a ravine. Then he focused on getting to River. He couldn't tell how long it was taking, but he knew it had been too long. He knew that with every minute his chances of saving River grew less and less. He had started to get the hang of moving with his odd vision, even if it still felt wrong, so he increased his speed and raced along the carpet of pine needles.

He ran up and down the rolls of the hills, the wind gusting through the trees, and entered the piney wood they'd left River in. He raced along the path and finally turned the corner where he'd last seen her, and then thought maybe he'd made another mistake. He ran a bit farther, then stopped. This was the place, but where was she?

His fear rose, and he scanned the ground with his other self for signs of what happened. In the yellow light, he saw the scuffs and hoof prints from when Nashrud and his men had been here earlier.

Maybe she'd awakened. But then he came upon markings that looked liked she'd been dragged from the path.

His heart fell. *No*, please *no*.

He sent his other self forward to follow the tracks and saw her legs a few dozen yards away. Something hairy hunkered over her body. Something else lay dead next to the side. Talen's panic rose.

He still had the knife he'd stolen from the dreadman. He was unmultiplied, but sometimes a bluff was all you needed. He pulled his other self back so he could see where he walked, and then he raised his knife and ran forward, yelling with all the battle anger he could muster. He crashed through the brush and spied the beast ahead.

The creature turned. Talen yelled again and charged. If he was going to die, it was going to be right here. He sent his other self forward and struck at the thing.

The creature did not flinch. It snarled and with blinding speed rose from River's body and met Talen's charge. It batted away Talen's upraised arm, sending the knife flying into the trees. Then the hairy thing took him by the throat.

The creature was as tall as a man and stood upright. Its breath stank of rotten meat. It bent its head in close and sniffed about Talen's chest and face. "Mokaddian filth," it snarled.

Talen blinked. The creature had spoken Mokaddian with a Koramite accent. This wasn't a woodikin. It was far too big for that.

"Harnock?" Talen asked.

It squeezed Talen's throat with iron fingers. One jerk, and it would snap Talen's neck like a twig.

"I'm Hogan's son," Talen croaked. "I'm part of the Grove."

"Lies," Harnock said. "You reek of the Divines. But your masters won't have me." The creature increased the pressure of its grip.

Talen began to feel dizzy. "No," he said. But the woods about him began to slide. Then his vision grew dim, and he fell into a tumbling blackness.

33

Nightingale

IT WAS DARK, and Argoth was in his chamber sitting on a bench against the wall, holding Nettle who'd been shaking. Serah lay sleeping on the bed with the girls.

Argoth and Shim had received Urban's report earlier, and Blue Towers was indeed preparing itself. The town merchants were stocking up. The dock masters were clearing all the boats and ships from their moorings to make room for others. Up in the fortress, the Fir-Noy commanders were making room in their barracks and in the fields around the fortress for what appeared to be a large host of men. An enormous quantity of grain and other food was being brought in on wagons. All the mills along the river were grinding at full capacity. And probably the most telling of all, Fir-Noy soldiers had been positioned up and down the river and on the docks.

The plan Shim had come up with was risky. In an hour or so, he and the others would move out and try to get in position at Blue Towers. Ke would lead a small force that included Urban's crew. Argoth would lead another, Shim the third. Tomorrow they'd know if Loyal was speaking the truth. If he was, they'd engage in a bold attack against the Kains that, if successful, would shake Mokad's army. A bold attack with a high likelihood of failure.

On a table next to Argoth lay the nightingale weave Loyal of Nilliam had given him. It was a weave similar to other healing weaves he'd seen. He'd quickened it and used it on himself to see if it was a trap, but had not detected anything ill. He believed Loyal had been telling the truth about its operation.

Argoth's leg was going to sleep on the bench, so he shifted Nettle in his lap and rocked slightly back and forth and felt Nettle begin to shake again. His tremors had been coming with greater frequency and intensity. This one built much quicker than the last one. He pulled Nettle close, except this time the shaking didn't pass. It continued and grew.

"I'm here, son," Argoth whispered. "I'm here."

Nettle twisted and accidentally struck Argoth in the face.

Argoth grabbed the arm. "You're going to be okay," he said.

But the tremors grew, and Nettle scrunched up his face and began to grunt in pain.

"It's okay," Argoth murmured and rocked on.

But the spasms built, and then Nettle tensed up and contorted as stiff as a board. He stopped breathing. Argoth waited, waited. Nettle gasped for a small bit of air, couldn't get it. His eyes were wide with fear.

Argoth hesitated for a moment, then retrieved the nightingale weave. He quickened it, then pressed it into Nettle's clenched fist.

Nettle remained frozen for a few moments more, then suddenly drew in a great gasp of air. He continued panting, gaining his breath.

Serah rolled over in the bed. "What's wrong?" She whispered in alarm.

"Nothing," Argoth said. Nettle's breathing slowed back to normal. He relaxed, clutching the nightingale at his chest.

"There we go," Argoth said and smoothed his hair back. In the spasms and twitching Nettle had worked loose of his blanket. Argoth gathered it up and wrapped it around his son.

The tremors had been coming every thousand counts or so. Argoth sat and waited for the next one, not quite believing the weave had worked. But the next one didn't come. He waited, counting another thousand, and then another, until Nettle fell into a relaxed sleep.

Argoth continued to hold Nettle, thinking on Loyal's words. Sometime later a soft knock came for him to prepare for the mission at Blue Towers. Nettle was still sleeping peacefully, the weave secure in his fist.

Argoth took the weave and strung it around Nettle's neck. Then he tucked him into his narrow bed. He looked down at his boy. Tomorrow would tell him much about Loyal and Nilliam and the course of this war.

34

Beetle

BEROSUS WATCHED SHIM'S new dreadmen soldiers don their armor in the light of the lamps and moon. They moved as quietly as they could, but it was hard to mask the chinking of armor and whispers of two hundred men. Nor could they keep the horses quiet as they led them out of the stalls and saddled them. In the smithy two men sat at grindstones sharpening up an axe and a long knife.

He'd asked a number of the soldiers what their destination and mission was, but none of them knew it. Shim and Argoth were obviously keeping that to themselves until the last moment, probably when they were a number of miles from here, when they were sure it couldn't be given away. It was a very wise policy.

But that didn't mean Berosus couldn't add two and two together: this mission probably involved the landing of his army on the morrow—it was simply too great a coincidence.

Eresh quietly moved through the men, inspecting their buckles and deportment, giving them a good word. He crossed over to some men hauling a casket out of the cellar where the seafire was kept and spotted Berosus. He faced him and put his hands on his hips. "You can go," he said.

"I'm waiting to report to Argoth," Berosus replied.

"You can wait until tomorrow. This is my fortress. I want you out of it now."

Technically it wasn't anything of the sort. "It's obvious you're gearing up for something. Let me help."

"Sure," Eresh said. "I dropped my lamp down the privy hole. Be a dear and fetch it for me."

Berosus smiled. "I'm on that," he said. "I'll have it back to you in a jiffy."

Eresh said nothing, just stood there with his hands on his hips and glared at Berosus with his one good eye.

Berosus moved off. Argoth and Ke and Sugar had left a number of hours ago with another group. It was significant that the whole command except for Eresh had gone. It was significant they'd taken Sugar. Legs had revealed to him that they were training her to be a Walker. They were up to something big, and he needed to know what it was.

He walked over to the cellar where Legs slept, except Legs wasn't behind the doors sleeping. He was outside sitting on a barrel, wrapped up in a blanket against the cold. It was the boy's habit to wait for his sister when he was worried.

Berosus approached him. When he was still a number of feet away, Legs said, "So it sounds like you and Commander Eresh have begun courting again."

It was uncanny how the boy knew he was there, and without any multiplication. He must have the ears of an owl. "All his coy protestations only serve to reinforce my determination to win his deepest affections."

Legs laughed. "Sounds like you're stuck here just like me."

Berosus drew up next to Legs and reached in his pocket for some dried pork to share with him. "I was out scouting. I think they assumed I wouldn't be back in time."

"Their loss, my gain," said Legs. "Maybe you can tell me the rest of that business you had with the Urzarians."

"This looks big," Berosus said. "They're going to need every sword they can get. Did Sugar tell you where they were going?"

"No," Legs said, but Berosus had lived and worked with fabulous liars for decades: he could spot the boy's lie a mile away.

"I saw a number of things tonight that they should know about. Things that might affect a raid being conducted deep inside Fir-Noy territory. Especially around the port at Blue Towers," he guessed. "Your sister is going to run into unexpected trouble there."

Legs shifted on his seat and took just a little too long to reply. "I don't know anything about a port."

Another lie. However, he didn't have time to play cat and mouse with Legs. He tapped a piece of dried pork against Legs's hand. "Want a bite?"

Legs accepted the jerked meat and bit into it, working a piece free.

Berosus leaned casually up against the wall next to Legs. "I don't feel like stories tonight. However, you said before that you hoped to learn more about the lore of Kains."

Legs's face lit up in the moonlight. "River says I have a knack."

"Then I suppose with us two being left behind to guard the goats and chickens, now might be the perfect time to learn a bit about how weaves are made. Some basics, nothing dangerous." In another pocket he kept a pouch that contained a minor thrall. It was the work of the Mungonese house of Kains. It wasn't a massively powerful weave, but a small thing in the form of a beetle, a bauble really. He'd found the simple things were often the most effective. There was no sense raising an alarm with a frontal attack when the barest whisper of persuasion would do. He pulled the weave out and placed it in Legs's hand. "This is a practice piece."

Legs took it and explored it with his fingers. It moved, and he made a small exclamation of delight. "Is this alive?"

"It is," Berosus said. The thrall righted itself, then crept across Legs's palm to one of his fingers. It latched on like a ring.

"Oh," Legs said in delight. "What does it do?"

"Open yourself and see."

Legs hesitated. "We're not supposed to accept weaves from anyone but Argoth himself."

"It's harmless. And it's not like I'm some candidate playing with things above my understanding. But if you don't want to go forward, I understand. Rules are important to keep you safe."

Legs gave it a bit more thought, then shrugged. "I'm okay," he said. Moments later Berosus felt the faintest link to the boy's mind. Just enough for him to oh-so-carefully nudge the boy in the right direction.

And, indeed, not an hour later he was on the road to Blue Towers having deftly persuaded Legs to offer up everything he knew. He didn't have all the details because Legs hadn't known them, but he knew enough. Shim's plan was bold. It might even work. He shook his head and smiled. By Regret's stones, he liked Shim's style.

He tried one last time to feel after the Glory of Mokad through his own thrall to send a warning which could then be relayed to the Skir Master, but the distance was too great. Berosus would simply have to take the message in person. He felt after the captain of his dreadmen through his escrum and told him to leave enough of the men to watch the fortress and follow with the rest.

The night breeze gusted through the trees. Everything smelled fresh from the recent rain. It was quite lovely. He began to jog, then increased his speed and increased it again. The road flew under him in the moonlight. It was still dark, but the first light of morning was not far away. If he ran hard, he just might make it in time and effect his own surprise.

He increased his speed again, until anyone who saw him would have thought him nothing more than a flicker of a night shadow.

35

Kains

SUGAR HID WITH Soddam in a two-story house that fronted the main road running up from the docks through the Fir-Noy town of Blue Towers. The road led to the fortress on the hill from which the town got its name. Blue Towers had once been an outpost, but the town had grown up and was now one of the Fir-Noy's biggest with more than fifteen thousand inhabitants. Today it was getting a lot bigger as Mokad's army, and the many people and animals needed to feed, maintain, and supply it, debarked at the docks and made their way up the road.

The house where Sugar hid, which had been scouted by one of Shim's many eyes and ears, belonged to the old widow of a cobbler who had died the previous year. The widow herself had been gone for two weeks now, visiting relatives out across the bay in Fog Town, and had closed the house up nice and tight.

The dark workshop on the first floor still held the implements of the cobbler's trade. There were shelves for leather, drawers for stitching and nails, and lines of hooks on a wall upon which hung the cobbler's assortment of awls, leather cutters, hammers, and various wooden shoe trees. Over in one corner stood a low cobbler's stool along with a number of lasts of different sizes the cobbler would have used to form the shoes and boots into the right shape and hammer and stitch them together. There was a pair of gorgeous knee-high boots set out as if the cobbler had just stepped away from his shop, indicating that the widow or her sons must be continuing with the business. Sugar and the others had entered via the back and wedged the front door with shims and barricaded it with a work table.

On the second floor were the living quarters—four rooms with beds and desks. Three of Urban's men were stationed in a bedroom with a window that looked down over the main road. With them stood a deep barrel of seafire, a force-pump, a firelance, which was a three-foot brass tube with a flared nozzle and burning igniter at the tip, and lengths of leather hose to hook the firelance to the pump and the pump to the barrel. There were also thick leather gloves, an apron, and a face mask for the one who would hold the lance. Right now Sugar and the others were all watching the crowds below through the shutter the men had cracked open.

The docks lay just down the road and over the bluff. From her position, Sugar could hear the raucous cry of flocks of gulls and see the forest of ship's masts at the docks as well as many others offshore waiting their turn to unload their people and cargo. The breeze was blowing in from the bay, filling the air with the scent of the sea.

People lined the street from the docks all the way to the fortress, watching the army march up to the fortress and the western fields where a good number of them would set up camp. They cheered as each group passed, even those driving wagons and carts laden with cargo. When a unit of soldiers marched by, they threw a few late-season flowers and autumn leaves. Sometimes they ran out with a basket of apples or meat pies to give to the men they obviously saw as their deliverers from Shim. Children with baskets of food for sale moved through the crowd.

It was a festive atmosphere, but the whole sight struck terror in her heart—she'd never seen an army this big in her life. Already some six thousand troops had marched up the road, and the ships had only just begun to unload. And here she was in the middle of it, a Koramite, on the verge of attacking the army's core.

Furthermore, Mokad had kitemen in the sky, riding the winds, keeping an eye on things below. She and the others were going to be hard pressed to make a clean escape with them above.

Half a dozen more of Urban's men were on the street below, some of them standing in the crowd, some of them, including Urban himself, keeping a low profile in an alley up the road. Ke and his fist manned an alley at the other end of this section of street.

A number of wagons laden with grain and other stores rolled up the cobbled street, pulled by teams of horses.

"The ship's coming in," Soddam said. "Time to ferret."

Sugar nodded. They'd been waiting for one of Mokad's big death ships with the red eye of Mokad upon its sails. Her job was to verify that there were no skir protecting the Kains when the moment to strike came—it simply would not do to have seafire thrown back in their faces.

Soddam took a coal from the hearth where they'd made a small fire and lit a candle with it.

One of the three men in the house with them grinned. "Good luck, Oh Great Master of Balls."

Despite his protests, Soddam had been assigned to the roof, not to shoot arrows, but to rain down two-dozen hollow pottery balls the size of a man's head. Argoth called them fireshot because each five to six pound ball held a half gallon of seafire.

"Large flaming balls," the second corrected.

Soddam narrowed his eyes. "You'll think flaming balls when I put one through this window."

All three men broke up laughing.

Soddam picked up his candle and the staff sling. "Come on," he said to Sugar. "Can't reason with those who are full of envy."

That only made them laugh harder.

She followed Soddam up the ladder into the attic. It was hot and the candle threw odd shadows. The windows at either end were shuttered up tight. Soddam led her to the one in the front and leaned the staff sling against the wall.

The staff sling was bigger than normal. Regular staves for slings were four feet long. This one was five. Someone had painted "Havoc" on it in white letters. The end of the large strap that made the sling hung about seven inches from the head of the staff. The other end of the strap looped around the curved iron horn that extended from the head of the staff.

To use the staff, a slinger would cast from back to front in an arc over his head, whipping the attached sling. As the staff came forward in front of the slinger, the looped end of the sling would slide off the iron horn, and the missile would fly. You could cast stones much harder and farther with a staff sling than you could with one you whirled about your head. It was the only way to hurl the big clay balls.

Soddam shook his head at the staff, "Those fireshot belong in a ballista."

"I think you're big enough you could be a ballista."

He smiled. "Have you ever thrown six-pounders?"

"No," she said.

"Neither have I. This is going to be interesting." He cracked the shutter, peered across the street to make sure nobody was looking. "You're a brave one," he said, "just like your beautiful mother."

Sugar waited, hoping he'd go on about Mother, but he opened the shutter instead. "Time to ferret. You remember what you're looking for?"

"Yes," she said and sat down against the wall. She put on her mother's necklace, took a breath, then closed her eyes and quickened the weave. In moments she felt the tearing along her bones, and swore it was worse now than it had been last night when she'd scouted their way in. The wave of pain crested and receded, and she stepped out of her body into the yellow world. The attic and Soddam were recognizable, although the colors and textures were different. She looked about for danger, saw and felt none, then retrieved the skenning and put it on. Last of all she picked up her blackspine.

"I'm ready," she said with the mouth of her flesh.

Soddam moved aside, and she crawled out of the window onto the shingle roof with her soul. Withers had said some souls could speak to the living, voices and whispers on the wind, but he didn't know how it was accomplished. So she was forced to communicate with her body. "I'm out," she said. Up the roof a bit were the crates filled with fireshot that Soddam and another of the men had positioned before the sun had risen.

Above her the sky was yellow and lavender. At her feet the shingles gave a little like hard wet sand. She could still hear the muffled sounds of the street with her body in the attic, but she now also heard the sounds of this world. A trumpeting carried from out in the bay where three skir flew above the ships.

The creatures looked like giant manta rays. Except they were immense—hundreds of yards across, dwarfing the ships below them. They trailed long black whips from their chins, although she could only surmise it was their chins for she saw no mouth or eyes. Their coloring was mottled fading to a lighter blue on their huge wings. "Lords," she said and described them to Soddam.

"They are urgom," he said, "the largest skir men can control. It usually requires three masters to enthrall them. There are skir even larger, huge beasts that live in the vents of volcanoes or the depths of the sea. But they are too powerful for even a hammer of Skir Masters. Those that try to harness them eventually break."

She was happy they were out over the bay. Such mountainous creatures could probably inhale her and not even know it.

"Can you see the ship?" Soddam asked.

"I can," she replied. It was already in its mooring. Far above her Mokad's kitemen looked like shadows; she hoped they couldn't see her. She scanned the rest of the skies. In the distance past the urgom, a small flock of orange skir flew. Withers had told her to watch out for those. There was nothing else in the skies surrounding the town and fortress, just a small group of amber creatures milling about the chimney stones. Nevertheless, Sugar felt exposed.

The roofs were of different heights, but they butted up against each other. She moved down a few houses to a roof that was a few feet lower than the others and crouched in a space between a chimney and a house wall.

Below her the procession moved along the street. She heard the sounds with the ears of her body and saw with the eyes of her soul. It was a little disorienting, but she was getting used to it. All last night she'd scouted the way for Argoth and the others in the pitch black, helping them navigate the boats and avoid detection while stealing through the woods, into the town, and setting up in the widow's house.

She spied a young boy hurrying along one of the back alleys with a basket of meat pies. "I think I see the messenger," she said.

"How many pies?"

The boy turned down the nearest alley out of her sight. Sugar moved over the peak of the roof, spotted him, and looked down in the basket. "Three pies. There are some small cheese rounds and golden apples as well."

Argoth and his fist were stationed down at the docks with seafire. Their job was to mark how many Kains debarked, wait for the attack to begin, then cause a massive distraction. If the Kains rode in carriages, Argoth was to specify which carriages they rode in. The boy knew nothing of this. He was simply someone Argoth paid to deliver food to a certain man standing in front of Marsh the Cobbler's house. They'd already worked out what the food items would mean. The meat pies represented carriages. The other items represented the number of Kains. All that was left was to know in which carriages the Kains rode.

She watched the boy weave his way past people in the alley, then turn into the crowd on the main road and make his way to one of Urban's men. The boy delivered the goods. They exchanged words, then Urban's man gave the boy a green scarf to take back to Argoth as a sign of thanks. Once the boy returned with the scarf, Argoth would know his message had been delivered and pay the boy.

Urban's man on the street unobtrusively signaled up to the house by running his fingers through his hair and scratching the back of his neck. Three carriages, five Kains, two in the second carriage, three in the last.

Sugar couldn't believe they were about to do this.

"Any skir, darling?" Soddam asked.

Sugar searched the sky. The urgom were still out over the ships. She looked down the road. Most of the last supply wagons had passed. "All's clear as far as I can see," she said.

A roar of cheering rose down by the docks.

"I suspect that clamor means the Kains are on the move," Soddam said.

She listened as they waited and could mark the approach as the cheering moved closer. A drum beat a marching cadence to the sound of the soldier's boots striking the cobbled stones. A low chorus of voices mixed in with the cheering. The chorus built as the men singing the slow haunting march song approached the top of the hill. The column was five men wide. The soldiers wore the blue and orange of the Fir-Noy as well as helms with pheasant feathers arrayed on one side. An escort of Fir-Noy armsmen—their best troops.

The crowd went wild, clapping and whistling. The soldiers were led by their standard bearer and captain on his stallion. Five wide and twenty men long—a full terror, followed by about a dozen more mounted Fir-Noy officers.

Their march song was punctuated by shouts. The crowd continued to hoot and holler as the unit passed, but then some beast barked down the road. The sound was so low and full of menace that it silenced the crowd. Moments later three giant men walked up the road amidst a pack of monstrous dogs.

"Regret's eyes," Soddam cursed.

Sugar had never seen a dogman of Toth before. They were indeed men, but they were so distant a race that the offspring born to human-dogmen crosses were often as sterile as mules. According to the dogmen, men had been giants in the beginning, but only the dogmen had kept their original size. All others had diminished with inferior breeding.

The lead dogman here must have stood seven to eight feet tall. He was broad, at least four feet at the shoulder. His chest was deep. He would have fangs. Not huge canines, but they would be much more pronounced than those of a Mokaddian.

Their faces were angular. Long black hair ran down their backs. But their size, Lords!

She said with the mouth of her flesh. "And I thought you were big, Soddam."

They carried poleaxes. The weapon weren't huge, but these dogmen obviously knew they were going to be fighting humans, probably dread-men. Those poleaxes would be light as a stick in their hands, and more than enough to pierce armor and sever limbs.

"They make the armsmen look puny," she said. "I think I'd rather face a hammer of dreadmen."

"They *are* dreadmen," he said.

Sugar gulped imagining such multiplied might. "I suppose we should look on the positive side. Their size will make them fine targets."

"You haven't seen them move, Love."

The stories of the fierce dogmen of Toth were bad enough, but they did not run alone. Like humans, they bred their hounds for different purposes. Some were sentries, others trackers. Some carried messages or pulled carts to fetch the wounded or carry loads. Maulers were what they brought to war. And that's what the dozen or so huge dogs on the street were. They were the size of bears. And they were wearing body armor with spiked collars.

"Those dogs aren't leashed," she said.

"Why would you leash your comrade?" Soddam asked. "Some say the bonds between the dogmen and their beasts are slethwork; others say its long years of training and the fact that the man and dog are raised together."

She didn't care what method they used—they were horrible. Standing on all four, these dogs could look a shorter man in the face. Their heads were huge. Their great mouths hung open, pink tongues lolling. Mouths that could easily accommodate a man's head.

"Gah," Soddam said.

The crowds shrank back up against the fronts of the houses. Somewhere along the street a small girl began to cry.

"Can you smell 'em?" Soddam asked.

She sniffed. "No," she said, and wondered if Soddam's eyes weren't the only thing that was different about him.

"When a pack is given by the lords of Toth to other Glories or Divines, they are required to wash themselves daily. These brutes obviously didn't get the message."

She looked at the chain armor over the dog's bodies, the plates covering the tops of their muzzles and heads. She tried to imagine how you'd battle such a creature. You'd have to strike its belly, but how could you get close enough?

"Seafire will stop them," she said, trying to reassure herself.

"We'll find out soon enough," Soddam said. "There's the first carriage."

It came into view down the street, followed by the other two. They were closed carriages, each painted white with gold trim and drawn by four horses. On the doors were the blue and orange standards of the Fir-Noy. Two lines of Mokaddian dreadmen walked on both sides.

Unlike the armsmen whose armor was a bit of a mix, the armor of the Mokaddian dreadmen was all of a piece. They had the same helms, same boots, same shields. The brass outer parts of their armor shone brightly in the sun. Their garments were red. Except for their greaves, their forearms were bare, showing their honors. They were, all of them, massive men. And unlike the Fir-Noy armsmen, not one of them smiled. Their standard bearer held a pole with three cross pieces to which skulls had been affixed.

The prickle of fear rose in her. These men were death itself.

As the carriages approached, Urban's and Ke's men readied themselves below. At the signal, those stationed in the two alleys would each push a wagon out into the road, blocking the carriages from going forward or back. Then the pyrotechnics would begin. She and Soddam had the fireshot, as did Argoth down at the docks. But it was the three men below who would immolate the Kains.

"Are we clear?" he asked.

Sugar scanned the skies about her. She looked over the rooftops and down the alleys. One of the massive blue urgom was flying slowly toward the docks, but it was still a ways out. There was nothing in the vicinity of the carriages. "We're clear," she said.

"Then get yourself back. You and I have got a job to do. It's time to rid ourselves of some excrement."

She hurried back over the shingles, past the crates of fireshot, to the little attic window and slipped back inside. A number of small pale creatures that looked like tiny beetles marched along the crack of the attic wall to her body. A handful milled about her neck. Horrified, she shooed them away, then took off her skenning. She stowed it and the blackspine and entered her body.

A great relief washed through her upon entering her flesh, and she opened her eyes. It wasn't right splitting her soul, and her body knew it. Soddam was lighting a firebrand with the candle. When it was burning, he handed it to her.

She took it.

"Remember what we practiced," he said. "And keep yourself low. Are you multiplied?"

"Not yet."

"Get it going. You don't know what's going to happen."

Sugar nodded, took off her governor, and began to nudge her Fire. Then she crawled out the window again, this time in the flesh. Below her the first carriage was approaching the spot on the street in front of the window. As soon as the other two were in front of the window below, they'd spring their trap. But as she was moving out of the way to allow Soddam through, she heard the sound of galloping hooves on the cobbles up the street. A rider pulled up to the captain of the Fir-Noy armsmen, shouting and gesticulating wildly. He pointed at the cobbler's house. The captain turned, looked up the front of the house and then saw her there holding the firebrand on the roof. His face filled with thunder, and he shouted at his men to turn.

"I think we've just been found out," Sugar said.

"Go!" Soddam said.

The first carriage below stopped, preventing the other two from moving into place. Up the road, the Fir-Noy captain shouted at his bowmen. The dreadmen below looked about, not knowing where the threat was coming from. The last driver, seeing the commotion ahead, began to back his carriage up.

She and the others needed to act now or this chance would slip away. Soddam must have realized this as well. Having the best vantage point and being the one to receive Sugar's report on skir, he was the one assigned to give the signal. He whistled three times loudly.

A clamor arose in the alley a few yards up the street, smoke rose, then Urban and three other men pushed a burning wagon doused in seafire out in to the street into the gap between the dogmen and the first carriage. The fire leapt a dozen feet in the air. The horses of the first carriage pulled back in fright. Down behind the last carriage, Ke's group pushed their burning wagon out. Then the men in the cobbler's second story room below lit the firelance.

There was a great whoosh, and then a gout of liquid fire shot out of the window. Dark brown smoke billowed up from the arc of flame. The seafire splashed onto the Mokaddian dreadmen below and the first coach. Then the man working the lance turned the arc of fire on the second coach, dousing it and the horses.

The horses screamed in terror and bolted forward, knocking a few dread-men down, but the first carriage was in the way. The men with the firelance tracked the carriage with their arc of flame, splashing dreadmen and throw-ing fire over the street.

A Kain inside the carriage kicked the door open, his arm on fire. There was a thwunk, and the crossbow bolt of one of Urban's men down on the street took him in the chest. Three men tried to bail out of the other carriage door, but the lancers hit them with the fire. They burned like wood, scream-ing, and stumbling to the ground.

The lancers turned the seafire toward the last carriage. The stream of fire shot out about fifty feet, but it wasn't far enough to reach. The man working the lance shouted to the two other men to pump harder. The spray surged a dozen feet more and splashed up the exposed side of the carriage onto the roof, but it wasn't going to be enough. A number of the dreadmen guarding that carriage raised their shields around the door on the far side, making a protective shield. The Kains in that carriage were going to exit on the other side. They were going to get away.

"Sugar!" Soddam yelled.

She realized she'd been frozen with the spectacle. She turned and scam-pered up the roof to where he stood next to the three crates they'd positioned up there earlier. The tops of the crates were off, and Soddam stood with the staff sling loaded with one six-pound cabbage-sized ball of fireshot.

The clay balls had a small hole through which they'd been filled with seafire. A cord soaked in a sulfur mixture had been slipped into the hole and fixed into position with wax. She put the flaming end of her brand to one cord. Immediately, the cord flamed and spat.

"Get another one ready," he said and stepped out into position.

Sugar grabbed another ball.

Below them the panicked horses of the first carriage charged through a gap between the burning wagon blocking the road and the buildings on the far side. The flaming carriage rammed into the wagon, then careened past, through the pack of dogmen and maulers. At the other end, the Kains of the last carriage exited onto the street.

Soddam adjusted his grip on the staff sling, waited the last second for the fire to burn down the cord and into the ball. As the ball began to spew smoke out its hole, he took aim at the knot of dreadmen protecting the Kains, and hurled the ball with a deep grunt. The sling moaned as it whipped up and over his head. The ball flew with a whir, smoke pouring out its hole. It sailed twenty feet over the heads of the dreadmen and crashed into the front of a building down the street. The ball shattered, splashing the wall with flame.

"Load!" Soddam said. He reattached the free end of the sling to the staff's horn and held it out to her. Sugar placed the ball into the sling and put the firebrand to its fuse. Except this time she lit it at the base, not the end of the cord.

Smoke began to spew out of the ball almost immediately. Soddam took aim and, with a mighty heave, whipped the staff forward and pointed the end low. The ball flew with a flatter trajectory this time. It sped down from the roof and slammed into the shield of one of the dreadmen, knocking the shield aside and splattering liquid fire on a number of men. That part of the circle around the Kains collapsed with men batting at the fire on their arms and faces.

"I've got you now," Soddam said, "you stinking excremencies. Load!"

Sugar went to load, but out of the corner of her eye she saw a dreadman down on the street with a bow pointed up at them. "Dive!" she shouted and shoved Soddam aside. They landed heavily on the shingles. The arrow whistled past, a foot away, exactly where Soddam had been standing.

"Lamborn!" Soddam thundered at the man holding the firelance below. "Mind the street in front of your rotted eyes!"

Below them the spray of seafire swept back across the road at the dreadman with the bow. He and two others scattered. The whole scene down on the street was chaos and smoke. Men scorched and writhing, the second carriage on its side aflame, two of its horses dead, the others trying to escape their harness. And everywhere the flames—burning on the cobbles and men and in great lines on the houses on the other side.

Down the street the dreadmen were forming up around the Kains again. "Quickly," Soddam said.

She scrambled up and retrieved another fireshot. By that time Soddam was in position. She loaded the ball, lit it.

Soddam hurled it at the Kains. It sped down, trailing dark brown smoke, and broke in front of the dreadmen clustered about them, splashing their legs.

Soddam reattached the free end of the sling and held it out to her. She loaded, but Soddam cursed. "The other way, Lass!"

Down the street, two of the giant dogmen climbed the face of a house. There were only a handful of rooftops between those houses and Sugar's current position.

"Quickly," he said.

She lit the ball. Soddam moved higher to get a better angle. Smoke began shooting out of the ball's hole, making a whistling sound. He waited a moment, then two. Then the dogman's arm appeared over the edge of the roof followed by his head.

Soddam hurled the ball. The dogman turned to look just as the ball struck the shingles in front of him. The seafire splashed onto his face and torso. He roared in pain and fell back.

At the other end of the street, the dreadmen had formed back up around the Kains and were moving them quickly toward an alley. Below her, something crashed. The next moment a small group of dreadmen rushed into the house.

"We've got company!" Lamborn yelled up to them from the window below.

"Load," Soddam said.

Up the street, the second dogman reached the roofs.

Sugar placed the ball in his sling and lit it. She nudged her Fire further. Then she heard the continuous sound of a thousand doors slamming and banging. The sound grew as it approached from the docks. She and Soddam looked up.

A great churning wall of sea water and dust engulfed the houses down the street. It stretched out a hundred yards on either side. The squall was moving toward them at great speed, its winds whipping up debris, knocking people to their knees, ripping shingles from the roofs.

"Sweet Creators," Soddam said in awe. He tore his gaze from the squall and turned to hurl the fireshot, but the Kains were already disappearing down an alley. The violent squall raced up the road. It was clear the winds would carry away anyone foolish enough to be standing on a roof.

"To the attic!" Soddam cried.

They scrambled down the roof back to the window. Sugar dove through the window first, Soddam coming in after her. The sound of men in battle rose from below. Outside the banging grew louder. The whine of the wind grew to a fever pitch. The shutters against the side of the house slammed, then tore away completely. Shingles above their heads ripped loose.

"Down," Soddam roared over the wind, "and out the back!"

She and Soddam raced to the hole and ladder to the floor below, but the ladder had been knocked aside. Below them men grunted, weapons clashed. The wind doubled in force. It screamed across the window and through the holes in the roof. Then the water hit, pounding the house like a cataract.

Soddam drew his axe, dropped through the hole, and landed on his feet. He charged forward out of sight. Sugar was multiplied. She nudged her Fire further, decided the long knife her father made her would be better in these close quarters and drew it instead of her axe. She dropped through the hole down to the hallway below.

The stairway from the workshop was next to her, running up to the landing at the end of the hall that led directly to the room where the fire-lancers had stationed themselves. On the landing, one of Urban's men lay on his back with javelin sticking out his chest. Another, a younger man named Vance, swung a crossbow, fighting off a dreadman coming up the stairs and losing ground. Behind them in the room, Lamborn was still in his leather mask and apron, picking himself up off of the flooded floor. Outside the window, the squall raged, sending in sheets of rain. Inside, spills of seafire guttered on the wet floor and walls. One spot burned on Lamborn's leather mask.

The wind blew like a storm gale through the hall, howling off the corners and banister. The dreadman caught Vance's crossbow with one hand and tore it from his grip. Vance slammed the dreadman's face with the palm of his hand, but the dreadman shoved his knife into Vance's gut and drove it deep.

Soddam roared, raced to the landing, and charged the dreadman. The dreadman turned to face him, but Soddam, snake quick, drove the spiked end of his axe through the man's helm and deep into his head. The dreadman slumped back, his eyes full of shock.

Below, two dreadman leaped over a fallen comrade and rushed up the stairs. Soddam grabbed Vance's crossbow and hurled it into the first man, knocking him to his knees. "The seafire!" Soddam roared.

Sugar saw exactly what was wanted. She sprinted down the hallway past Soddam and into the room. Lamborn was trying to lift the barrel of seafire, but his forearm was bleeding. An arrow must have sailed clean through it. "Help me!" he said.

Sugar bent low and together, with their multiplied strength, picked up the barrel. As they lifted, she lost her grip on her knife and it clattered to the floor. Lamborn took the barrel from her, balancing it from the bottom with his bad forearm. "Coming through!" he yelled and charged forward. Soddam stepped out of the way. Lamborn sped past him and hurled the barrel. The barrel slammed into a dreadman, knocking him back and spilling its stinking dark contents all over the stairs and the dreadmen below.

Lamborn turned around. "A flame!" he said. Then a crossbow bolt flew up from below and took him in the back.

Sugar frantically looked around. There were spots of flame everywhere, but nothing to ignite the stairs with. Then she saw a burning blanket. She ripped it off the bed and ran back to the landing.

"Move!" she yelled.

Below her on the stair, a dreadman soaked with seafire looked up at her. He snarled, the thick liquid clinging to his face, and charged. Sugar threw the burning blanket at him. He batted it away, and the blanket fell to the stairs behind him into the seafire spill.

A beat passed. Then a blue flame raced over the stairs and up the dreadman's body. The next moment it all ignited.

The dreadman roared and charged up the stairs, his seafire-soaked clothing aflame. Sugar reached for her long knife and realized it was back in the room. She set herself, planning to turn away from his charge and throw him past her, knowing she probably didn't have enough room, but as he reached the top, Soddam charged into him, thrusting him through the side with the javelin that had killed the first of the firelancers, and pinned the dreadman to the wall.

Pain and hate twisted the dreadman's face. He tried to pull himself off the javelin, but the wind-whipped flames spread and grew and he burst into a pillar of fire. He thrashed and screamed, and succeeded in pulling himself free from the javelin, only to fall to the floor in a burning, sizzling heap.

Down on the stairs the seafire flames raged, sending up billows of choking smoke.

"Out the back window," Soddam yelled over the wind and turned to Lamborn who was on his hands and knees. Sugar raced into the room and snatched up her long knife, then raced past Soddam who was lifting Lamborn up onto his shoulders.

They fled down the hall and flung open the door to the largest of the two backrooms. Outside the pitch of the wind lessened, then began to fall off. She threw open the shutters and looked down at the street below. Sodden debris lay everywhere.

"I'll hand him down," Soddam said.

Sugar stepped up to the ledge and hopped out the window. Multiplied as she was, it was no great distance, but she didn't want to break anything, so she rolled as she'd been taught by Ke and Argoth. By the time she came up, Soddam was already letting Lamborn down.

Sugar grabbed his legs and took him from Soddam as best she could. As she stumbled back, trying to bring him down easy, two large drops splattered on her face and mouth. She licked her lips and realized it was Lamborn's blood.

Soddam leapt out the window to the street, then turned and took Lamborn from her. Above them the back end of the squall passed over the houses. The rain diminished.

"What about Urban and the others?" she asked.

"Who knows where they are?" Soddam said. "Can't worry about them now."

A shimmering thing the size of a man's hand fell from the sky next to her and bounced off the cobbles. It was followed by another, then another. They were yellow barred surfperch. Sugar looked up and saw hundreds of the small bodies flashing in the sun, speeding down toward them.

"Into the doorway!" Soddam said. He grabbed her wrist and pulled her with him across the alley. The striped fish rained down, striking her painfully on the head and back, bouncing off the stones about them. Mixed in were a few crabs and seabirds. Then she and Soddam were in the doorway pressing themselves back under the lintel. The rain of fish continued, Lamborn taking a couple of blows, and then as quickly as it had come, the rain of fish fell away. The sun shone down on an alley glistening with fish and crab and seaweed. The few fish that hadn't died on impact flipped about. A number of crabs flailed their spider legs and tried to right themselves.

"Come on," Soddam said. "Now's our chance."

They raced out of the doorway, trying to pick their way through the fish and crabs, slipping on those they trod upon. She wished she wasn't so fond of bare feet and had brought some boots.

She led, and Soddam followed, for it was she who had led Urban and the others into city. She, out of all of them, knew best the way out.

Behind them, around a corner, someone shouted something in a language she'd never heard before. It was followed by the awful bark of a number of maulers.

"Lords," Soddam said.

"This way!" Sugar said and turned down another lane. The barking grew, and she decided at that moment she really didn't like dogs.

36

Ke

BEROSUS ROSE FROM the cranny on the roof where he'd taken shelter from the squall and surveyed the scene below. Out in the street, the charred carriages, men, and horses lay in a jumbled mess. Here and there, a few small slicks of seafire still burned in the drenched street.

The three remaining Kains were well away from the attack site. He'd almost been too late. The blackened bodies of two of his Kains and their servants slumped in the middle carriage. The Mother would not be pleased. He shook his head. These sleth had now killed five Divines. It was unheard of. Which was why he needed to know what was really going on—now, before he launched his full attack.

One street over, the dogmen and maulers howled and barked, chasing those that had been in the house. Shouts rose a few streets away in the other direction. He ran along the rooftops toward the second commotion, leaping narrow alleys and streets. In a few short minutes he leapt to a row of roofs and looked down.

Below him Ke and a number of Shim's men ran down the street. They were moving fast. The hammer of Mokaddian dreadmen chasing them hadn't yet turned the corner. Under normal circumstances, with their knowledge of the area, Ke and Shim's men would probably escape. But not today.

He saw where Ke was heading, then leapt across the alley, over their heads, to the next row of houses. He climbed over to the other side, ran down the roofs almost to the end, then dropped to street just before Ke and the others turned the corner.

Ke startled in surprise.

"Goh!" said Berosus. "I found you!"

Ke slowed to a stop. "What are you doing here?" The men behind him were panting.

"I was watching the parade, buttering up a fine Fir-Noy lass who had access to people we need. And suddenly Regret's torture pits open up with fire and smoke. I saw you. What just happened?"

"There's no time," said Ke. "We need to get out of here."

"Well, you're not going to get far the way you're running," said Berosus. "Mokad's whole army is set up in that direction. And running will attract the attention of the kitemen anyway. Follow me; I know a way out."

Ke glanced up at the skies, then back at Berosus. "We need to get to Loon Point. That's the arranged meet."

"I don't know any Loon's Point. You might get there, you might not. But at least you'll get out alive. Now, come." He hurried away at a brisk walk. Ke and the others followed.

"There's a hammer of dreadmen on our heels," Ke said urgently.

Berosus held up his hand to say he had it all covered and led them off the road into a thin alley no wider than a man that connected to a lane that ran behind two rows of houses. They walked a bit, exited the lane down another thin alley. The shouts of the dreadmen passed by behind them. Berosus led Ke and his men across another street and slipped down a lane between two houses that led to a barn. "We'll smuggle you out in a wagon," he said. He motioned at their clothes. "A wagon will be far safer than a Koramite and eight Shoka running around in broad daylight with blood and soot drawing everyone's eyes."

He opened the barn door and motioned them in. Ke slipped in first followed by the others. Some of them were wounded—a little blood around the knuckles or caking an ear, but nothing that would worry a man hardened to battle. These were all powerful soldiers. Glorious works of flesh. And by Regret's rotted stones, they'd just helped murder three Kains! They would have matured into fine dreadmen, maybe become something more.

He stepped in behind them and shut the door. Light streamed in through an open shutter illuminating dust motes. Berosus slid the bar in the barn door home.

"There's no wagon," Ke said.

"No," Berosus replied. He drew his knife and slit the throats of three of the men. The others turned. They were fast and strong, but he was as far above them as a man is a babe. His Fire filled him, turning his sinews and muscles into iron, giving him unnatural reflexes.

He killed the next one by slamming his head into the edge of a workbench.

A fifth lunged forward. Berosus struck him a glancing blow, whipping his face to the side and breaking his neck.

The other two Shimsmen hesitated. Ke reached for his knife and found it missing.

"Looking for this?" Berosus asked. Then he threw it, burying it deep into one man's throat. The man tried to breathe, his face full of shock and dismay, and fell back.

The last Shimsman drew his sword. He thrust at Berosus, blinding quick, but Berosus was quicker. He sidestepped it, grabbed the man by the head, brought up a knee, and smashed the man's face into it. The man fell to the floor, his sword clattering on the stones. Berosus brought his foot down and staved in three ribs with his heel. He turned to Ke.

"So Eresh was right," Ke said with disgust. He wore an axe, but did not draw it. A wise decision in these close quarters.

"Eresh is a fool." Berosus said, then stepped over a dead man and skirted around a work table.

"Who paid you off?" Ke asked, finding his own good ground.

Berosus laughed. "Paid? There is no treasure that can compare to the Mother's sublime approbation."

Ke narrowed his eyes. "You're not of the Hand."

"Oh, I am. I am the soul of the Hand."

Disgust filled Ke's face. "So the Hand is run by a lapdog, a thrall."

"I am whatever the Mother wants me to be."

Ke attacked, rushing him. Berosus tried to sidestep the charge, but Ke caught him by the jaw and hurled him back. Berosus banged into the wall, surprised. Ke followed with blow that would have crushed his throat, but Berosus caught it. He grabbed Ke by the arm and tried to twist his wrist, but found it much harder than he expected. Then Ke spun himself free of Berosus's grip and stepped back to a workbench.

"You are quite the specimen," Berosus said. He was going to need more power for this one and increased his Fire. "Back in Mokad you'd make a great breeding stud, I think."

Ke snatched a hammer off the workbench.

Berosus stepped toward him. "I need to know what's going on," he said. "Who really defeated the Sublime down in her cave?"

"Truth defeated that creature," Ke said. He swung with the hammer.

Berosus was forced to take a step back to avoid the blow and almost stepped on a dead man. "You will tell me. Everyone talks, eventually."

"You will have nothing from me. Tell that vile thing you call your master we are coming." Ke pulled back the hammer for another blow, and Berosus lunged.

But Ke blocked him.

Incredible. Berosus struck again, and, again, Ke blocked it.

"Lords, you are wonderful. An excellent mix of Koramite and Mokaddian blood. You *are* going to Mokad. The Mother is going to want to cross-breed you with some fine ladies. I think you'll like that."

Ke growled and hurled the hammer.

Berosus flinched to the side and the hammer kissed his cheek with cold iron as it sailed past his face and banged loudly into the wall behind him.

Ke picked up an iron pry bar and lunged at Berosus's throat. But Berosus's full vigor was now upon him. He swatted Ke's hand aside, slammed his fist into Ke's gut. Ke struggled for breath. It was a momentary pause, but enough for Berosus to move behind him and put him in a head lock.

Ke thrashed—his power spectacular—and the two of them fell to the floor, crashing into one of the dead men at their feet. They rolled over the man, into his blood, banged into a table. Berosus held on, squeezing the blood flow to Ke's brain with an arm hold of iron. Moments later Ke's thrashing lessened. The he mustered his strength, heaved both himself and Berosus up. Berosus hung on. Ke pulled at his arm. Struck at him, but Berosus squeezed tighter. Ke went down to a knee, fought, but Berosus was not going to be dislodged. After some ineffectual flailing, Ke slumped in Berosus's arms.

Berosus held on for another second, then quickly drew a king's collar out of his purse and clasped it around Ke's neck.

By the Mother's eyes, that had been lovely. He took a satisfied breath of relief. How long had it been since he'd been in a true fight? He'd almost forgotten the thrill.

He cradled the boy in his arms and felt for a pulse. Blood beat steady and strong in Ke's thick neck. He was a veritable bull. The Mother was going to be pleased indeed, but first Berosus needed to extract this Grove's secrets. The weave he'd used on Legs wasn't going to work here; this was going to require a true seeking.

He found some cord and bound Ke's wrists and ankles. Then he opened the barn door and dragged Ke away from the dead men and out into the sun.

37

Black Harvest

SUGAR AND SODDAM ran down the lane between the houses and workshops of cobblers and tailors, Lamborn still on Soddam's shoulder. The barking of maulers followed a few turns behind.

Sugar barreled with multiplied speed past a man pushing a cart of beets, almost bowled over a group of dumbfounded children. Above them, people, who were leaning out of windows to watch the receding skir squall, pointed and exclaimed as they ran past. Soddam knocked over a man with sausage links for sale, careened off a boy holding two dead pheasants. On his shoulder, Lamborn groaned.

Then the maulers entered the lane a number of houses back. A man shouted in panic. A mother screamed for her children to get off the road.

The maulers snarled, vicious and low, and the people on the lane began to shout and scream.

Fear surged through Sugar.

"We've got to lose them," Soddam said.

Sugar's mind raced. She didn't know if they could outrun the beasts, even multiplied. There was no canal nearby where the water would sink the beasts in their armor. If she and Soddam took to the roofs, the maulers would just pace them. Furthermore, the kitemen would easily direct the Skir Master to them. *Where could they go? Where!*

She remembered a row of sail and net makers' workshops in this area, and an idea began to form. "This way!" she called and raced down the lane, the people scattering before her. She turned the corner into a blind end. This was it. There were only five buildings here. The end was dominated by a sail maker's workshop.

The double doors at the front and back of the workshop stood so she could see through the workshop to a ship builder's scaffolding down by the water. A lone woman knelt in the workshop, stitching a sail with a whale-bone needle. Two kittens played with the thread at her feet.

Sugar raced toward the workshop. "Out, Good-Wife!" she cried. "Out!"

The woman looked up, alarm on her face.

"Out!" Sugar yelled.

The woman stood, backed away, then fled when Sugar and Soddam raced through the front doors.

The shape of a large sail had been chalked on the tight wooden floor of the workshop. Wide strips of linen sail cloth were laid out to fit. The woman had been stitching together two wide strips of linen about twenty feet long.

Sugar looked about and saw what she wanted. "Take Lamborn out the back way," she said. "Bar those doors."

"What are you doing?" Soddam asked.

"Just go!" she said. "When the dogs come in, you come around and bar those front doors."

"You're not staying in here with those animals."

"I'm not planning to. Get!"

Just at that moment the maulers barreled around the corner.

"Go!" she said.

Soddam ran out the back the way the woman had gone. He shut and barred the doors behind him.

Sugar backed up, looked at the maulers and felt her heart just might fail her. They were monsters. They spotted her and charged full speed toward the workshop, baring their teeth. One bite, and they'd rip her in half.

The workshop was a large space, big enough for a sail maker to chalk out sails for medium-sized boats. Big enough to give her the room she needed. When the maulers were only a few yards away, and she was sure they were coming in, she ran to the ladder leading up to the loft. She was halfway up when the dogs entered the workshop.

They leapt for her, crashing into the ladder. She jumped, grabbed onto the banister, and swung herself onto the loft. Below, the dogs and ladder crashed to the ground.

The maulers rose and snarled at her with such volume it felt as if the bark had bite. One of the monsters jumped and almost reached the loft. She raced for the small window in the roof. At the front of the workshop,

Soddam swung the double doors behind the maulers shut. Sugar shouted, hoping to keep their attention away from the doors, then opened the shutter and slipped out onto the roof.

She dropped to the ground, ran around the corner, and found Lamborn on the ground, Soddam straining with all his might to hold the doors shut against the maulers. "The bar!" he said.

She grabbed it, slammed into the door with her shoulder to knock it back just a bit, then slammed the bar down in its braces. The maulers barked. One of the animals charged into the doors. The doors shuddered, but the stout bar held. The maulers' barks became more violent and angry. They were so loud it felt as if the sound itself would tear the doors to pieces.

"Holy Creators," Soddam said and stepped back. "You're as mad as your mother."

"I'll take that as a compliment," she said.

"Let's get out of here," Soddam said.

They turned and found the maulers' dogman standing in the lane, watching them. A grin spread across his face. He held a big poleax in a two-handed grip. He threw his head back and howled. A moment later howls from his brethren a number of streets away answered him back.

Soddam drew his axe. It looked like a toy in comparison to the dogman's weapon. "Fight or run?" Soddam said to Sugar.

If they were quick, they might be able to make it around the house and down to the dock.

"Run," Sugar said.

"I think you're right," Soddam said. "Go!"

Sugar ran, but realized a few strides later that Soddam hadn't followed. Instead, he charged the dogman. Sugar knew Soddam was mature in the lore, and he was big, but the dogman was bigger. Soddam flew at the dogman, a blur of fury, and struck with his axe.

The dogman countered and stepped back, clearly surprised.

Soddam twisted and struck again.

The dogman blocked his attack.

Soddam slashed him with a knife. The dogman snarled and took the initiative. He swung the bladed end of the poleax at Soddam and knocked his axe back. Then he swung the butt of the staff around, landing a glancing blow that knocked Soddam to the ground.

Sugar rushed forward with her knife, but the dogman swatted her away, and she crashed painfully into the cobbles. The dogman turned back to Soddam who was getting up.

The dogman licked his lips. "Sliced thin, your heart will be succulent," he said with an odd accent. He swung, blinding fast. Soddam ducked under the blow and charged into the dogman, lifting him off his feet for a stride, but the dogman twisted and hurled Soddam to the ground.

Sugar rushed the dogman again. He straight-armed her, took her by the throat, and threw her on top of Soddam. He raised his poleax high for a blow that would skewer them both, and then a sword protruded from his chest. His eyes went wide.

The sword tip disappeared. The dogman turned.

Argoth stepped back, his face grim.

The dogman swung his poleax, weakened.

Argoth stepped to the side and, with one blow, hacked the dogman's head off. It landed heavily and rolled a bit. A moment later the body toppled to the ground.

Relief washed over Sugar. She rolled off Soddam and got to her feet.

"Where are the others?" Argoth asked.

"Scattered from here to breakfast," Soddam said, hauling himself up and feeling his battered head.

Argoth's small fist of men were all with him, watching the street. "We need to get to the cover of the trees," Argoth said.

"Follow me," Sugar said.

Soddam fetched Lamborn, and they all ran past the sail maker's workshop. Behind them maulers barked and scattered dogmen howled. Battle horns sounded up by the fortress and down at the docks.

"Look up," Soddam said.

Sugar looked. Two kitemen soared like vultures above, tracking their progress.

Kitemen rode the winds, but were also said to be kept aloft many times by smaller skir. They were sometimes used as messengers. More often they were used as scouts, giving Mokad's Divines eyes in the sky so they could see exactly what the enemy was doing over a huge area. She didn't know how they communicated with the ground, but had heard they had special methods using hand mirrors, pennants, and specific aerial maneuvers. These flew in a harness attached to huge triangular linen sails. The sails were painted with the eye of Mokad.

They would have been a wonder to behold if they weren't directing the whole Mokaddian army to Sugar's exact position.

Sugar led Argoth and the others through the streets to one of the town's lesser-used gates. The guards saw her and moved to bar the way, but then they saw the rest of the crew round the corner, and the guards scattered. A few moments later, Sugar and the others were through the gate and running along the outlying streets. And then they left the streets behind and ran across a field to the shelter of the woods.

Mokad would send out mounted men. In no time, this whole area would be crawling with troops. But Sugar had lived among the Fir-Noy her whole life. She'd been to Blue Towers many times for her father's smithing work, and she knew about Sharp's Cave.

They entered the woods and ran another quarter of a mile. One of the kitemen dropped lower to see better through the canopy of trees. He skimmed low enough she could hear the flapping of his sail and see his face. But even though it was autumn and a number of the trees had lost their top leaves, there was still enough cover that they were able to give him the slip when they entered the cave.

The cave itself was a rather simple affair. There were some dangerous holes and a few blind ends, and parents forbid their children from exploring it, but the youth explored it all the same. It ran for half a mile, branching about two-thirds the way in. Argoth had seafire soaked torches, but they didn't need them, for they'd stumbled upon a boy and two girls who were obviously not there to listen to the bats. The men tied them up and gagged them. Then they stole their lamps and continued their journey over the wet rocks deeper into the cave.

As they went, Sugar prayed the ancestors that Urban and Ke and the others had escaped.

* * *

Berosus felt after the captain of his dreadmen, then waited patiently for Ke to rouse. His hammer of dreadmen guard soon arrived and formed a perimeter around the barn and drive. Not long after, Ke opened his eyes. He was none too happy. Shouts rose in the distance about them in the town. The chase for the attackers was still in progress.

"You and I are going to chat," said Berosus. "I'll give you credit. This was a breathtaking strike. And you yourself are a surprise. An equal to any of my dreadmen in might. In fact, I'm sure you surpass a good many of them."

"Shim will hound the Divines that hold your chain," said Ke. "When they're dead, you'll be free. And I'll try my best at that time to forgive you and not run you through with a sword."

"Divines?" Berosus asked. He smiled. "My dear boy, I don't think you understand who I am."

Uncertainty shown in Ke's eyes. "Your honors tell me nothing."

"Of course, not," said Berosus. "It would not do to walk into a nest of sleth and proclaim that the chief Guardian of Mokad was among them."

Ke expression changed from alarm to fear.

"Yes, now I think you finally see your situation."

Ke renewed his struggle against his bonds.

"I need some information," said Berosus. "And you're going to provide it. Do not chastise yourself when you give in. Resistance is not something you or anyone else is capable of." He pulled back the sleeve of his right arm. In the palm of his right hand the symbol of the eye of Mokad glowed red. He placed his hand upon Ke's forehead. The boy's resistance was strong, but this was not a power to be withstood. He tore open the boy's doors and pushed into his mind.

"Tell me what happened in the battle in the Mother's cave. Tell me who the real power of the Grove is."

Anguish wracked Ke's face, and he resisted, but even this bull could not hold out for long. Not with the hooks of the Sublime already deep within him. Berosus asked questions about the history of the Grove here; he asked about the current war plans. And Ke answered. When he'd retrieved all the information he wanted, he sat back on his heels satisfied but somewhat disappointed.

These sleth had not killed Lumen or Rubaloth. Nor had they really killed the Sublime Mother who had been behind everything. They'd had a stroke of luck, that was all. That Mother's own thrall had failed, and her creation had turned on her. The dark killing mists at Redthorn and Fishing were also not of their making. All of which meant that there was nothing in this Grove to fear.

He had been looking forward to a true struggle, but that was not to be.

Which meant there was no need to wait. Tomorrow he would destroy Shim and his army. He motioned to the captain of his dreadmen.

The man approached. "Holy One," he said.

"Take the gloryhorn to the harvesters. Tell them to begin today."

He wouldn't have the fight he'd been hoping for, but the weather was still holding—it was still going to be a magnificent harvest.

* * *

Sugar's body lay hidden next to Soddam who crouched behind an outcropping of rocks on a hill with a good view of Blue Towers. They had traveled through the cave without incident and joined up with Shim's escort. Urban and the survivors in his group had also joined them. Only Ke's group was missing.

"What do you see?" Argoth asked.

Sugar had soulwalked to an open bluff that looked across the river. She had a clear view of the surrounding area. "I don't see Ke's fist anywhere."

"Come on, boy," Argoth said. "Show yourself."

But they'd already waited as long as they could; Mokad's forces were starting patrols on this side of the river. Down below, two packs of dogmen debarked from a boat.

"We need to move," Urban said.

Argoth sighed heavily. "Come back, Sugar."

But one of the immense blue urgom was flying up the river toward her. She dove under the cover of some rocks. The mountain-sized creature blocked out the sun, filled the sky. Other smaller things flew about it, but even these were large. She quailed at the creature's sheer size, and made herself as small as possible. The air filled with the clicks and tones it made.

The front edge of the wind passed over her position throwing debris in her face and hair. Moments later the massive skir followed, and for four long breaths all she could see was its belly and the creatures that accompanied it. Then it passed by, heading up the river. The tail end of its wind tossed the tops of the trees, and then was gone.

Lords, how were they ever going to fight that? And the Mokaddians had two more like it still out over the bay.

She prepared to move back up the slope to her body when a man walked out into a field across the river close to the fortress. He held a horn in his hand. Sugar should have ignored him, but there was something about him, about that horn. The man brought the horn to his lips and blew.

The note sailed out clean and clear, and the part of the tattoo that was in the wrist of her soul moved. The skenning tightened around her arms. She startled and looked down at her wrist and the tattoo there. The man blew the horn again. Again her tattoo moved. This time joy filled her. It was like when she heard the horns announcing feast day. Or the fiddles striking up before a dance. She wanted to run to the sound. But the skenning moved again, covering the tattoo, and the desire subsided. The horn sounded again, but this time it was only a sound in the distance. She shook her head, and not for the first time wondered what they were doing sending her, a girl with no experience, out as a spy. She knew nothing and wished Withers was back with her body, giving her instruction.

A flock of orange skir that undulated flat and thin like huge leeches flew out over the field where the man stood. The blue urgom dove at them and chased them away. And then, from the trees at the edge of the wood, a man appeared.

No, not a man—the soul of a man. He walked out onto the field. Others appeared in the trees. On the rooftops of the houses on the streets below, another handful of souls appeared. The man in the field blew the horn again. The souls on the field began to run to him. Those on the rooftops leaped toward him from house to house. They were like children running to a juggler.

The orange skir evaded the blue urgom and dived toward those souls out on the field. But a number of men in spiked armor rushed out from the fortress. She recognized them from the description Withers had given her. They were Walkers, those that soulwalked for the Divines.

The Walkers rushed out onto the field brandishing their weapons at the orange skir. One of the creatures dove at a soul, but a Walker fought it off. Then the big blue urgom was there, and from a clump of hair a long whip struck out at one of the orange skir and knocked it to the ground. The blue urgom struck another orange skir.

More souls filtered out of the trees and from the streets, running to the Walkers. All her life Sugar had been told that the ancestors came for the souls of their fallen dead to protect them and escort them to safety. She did not see any ancestors.

Howlers bayed in the distance. The blue behemoth chased orange skir. One darted down and caught a soul and carried it away. The rest of the souls began to panic and ran to the field with the hornsman and the Walkers. A few souls held back by a house, but a Walker approached them with his spear and moved them along like a cowherd prods reluctant cows to join back with the herd.

More of the flock of orange skir tried to dart down and take a soul, but then the whole flock startled and fled, scattering like pigeons before a hawk. A moment later Sugar felt something behind her. She turned and scanned the field, the cliff's edge, and the sea beyond. Suddenly, a large skir rose up over the precipice. It was followed by three others. They were not the beautiful blue of the urgom or the frightful sickly orange of the long flat skir. These were golden with bellies of hair that was long and dark.

They cruised over the field and hovered above the souls being herded into one big group. The souls of the fallen stood looking into the sky. The Walkers backed away.

The first golden skir snaked down a whip-like arm, snatching a soul and nestling it in the hairs of its belly. It whipped down another arm and took another soul. And then another arm and another until it seemed it was grabbing the souls with a dozen arms, nestling them in the long hairs of its belly.

The souls of the fallen did not run, did not move. The horn sounded yet again, and the other golden skir joined the first, their whip-arms plucking up the dead like a farmer picked pods of peas. They worked methodically. Two of the souls yelled in alarm and tried to flee, but it was too late. One skir snaked out a whip-like arm and wrapped it around the man's leg before he could get away and lifted him aloft. Moments later another skir grabbed the second man's soul by the waist.

Sugar was petrified. This couldn't be right. Surely, this isn't how it would end. All the stories of the life after death talked about the ancestors coming to gather their seed, protecting them. Her mind raced to make sense of what she was seeing.

Why weren't the souls running? Her only guess was the horn. Somehow it had pacified them. Or maybe the Walkers had said something to them.

The skir picked up the last few souls and buried them in their grasping hairs. The souls hung from the bellies of the skir, wrapped in the long dark brown hairs, row upon terrible row like insects in a spider's web. The sight revolted her. Then the skir rose and flew away toward the sea. A lone soul of a woman stood upon a rooftop watching the spectacle in shock. As one of the skir flew over, it snatched her up, trailing her along behind in its whip-like arm.

The skir flew out past the fortress, down to the shore, and out to a large Mokaddian death ship. One descended to the deck while the rest hovered above. Sugar couldn't see clearly at such a distance, but she saw enough.

The Walkers hadn't been sent by the ancestors. They were servants of Mokad. Servants of a Devourer. This wasn't a reunion—it was a harvest! The souls of the dead were being taken to the ships, to be killed or transported to some terrible slaughter pen that was kept somewhere else. All those people going, not to the loving arms of their beloved dead, but to their end. To nothingness. To the bellies of their masters.

She thought about her mother and Da, their deaths. Had they been snatched up like this?

"Holy Six," she prayed, unable to finish the thought.

"Sugar," Argoth said. "We need to go."

Across the river, the horn sounded again. She felt it tug at her wrist again. Felt something stir inside her. The skenning was protecting her, but she could still feel the horn calling.

A pack of howlers bayed close by, startling her. Sugar raced back to her body. She removed the skenning as fast as she could and slipped back into the comfort and security of her flesh. The horn pealed in the distance, calling to her, beckoning her, enticing her, compelling her to come. But she closed herself up tight in her flesh and shut out the sound.

38

Urban's Warning

SUGAR AND THE OTHERS retreated in haste from the precipice that looked over the river and followed a wooded road to the south. Shim's escort of two hammers rode horses. Some of Argoth's men rode doubled-up with them, but Sugar and Urban's crew ran, leading the wounded Lamborn along on a mule. All of them watched the sky for Mokad's kitemen.

She could not get the horror of the souls coming to that field out of her mind. She could not unhear their cries. She could not unsee them wrapped in the living hairs on the bellies of the creatures that collected them.

A few miles later, Shim halted the group to let a handful of his men scout the road ahead. While they were waiting, Argoth asked her to report.

She told them what she'd seen in exact detail. "I think the horn calls to them," she said. She held up her wrist and pointed at the tattoo. "There's something here. I felt it leap to the call of that horn. Had I not been wearing the skenning, I believe I too would have gone to the field."

The men about her looked at their own wrists.

Shim spat. "Skir masters. Their kitemen and winds—it's all show. Their real pupose is to help with the slaughter."

Argoth said, "We saw the Skir Master out on his ship with his priests and skirmen."

"You know him by sight?"

"Aye," Argoth said and motioned at his men. "We all marked him."

"We're not done," Shim said. He turned to his men. "I want you to think about what you accomplished today. You killed two Divines, at the very least. We will kill more. A couple more Kains, a Skir Master. Five or six men. That's all that stands between us and victory."

Urban and Soddam glanced at each other, and Sugar thought they did not share Shim's assessment.

Shim continued. "I don't know where the ancestors were today, but it's clear it's time for the living to help the dead."

Sugar thought about her parents. If Mokad wasn't stopped, she was sure that evil horn would be taken to every hollow and plain in the New Lands, and if Mother and Da had not already made their journey, what protections would they have? They'd be as helpless against the call as those souls today, leaping across the rooftops to their doom.

One of the soldiers sent to watch their rear came running up the road and reported that a kiteman was winging their way.

"He'll have a harder time finding us if we split up," Urban said.

Shim agreed, and they broke up into their respective hammers and moved out. Sugar went with Urban. He'd lost five of his crew on the streets, and it looked like Lamborn would be next. The shaft had gone right into his gut, and gut wounds did not heal well. Lamborn told them to leave him, but Urban wouldn't hear of it and ordered him to stay on his mule.

They burned their Fire and jogged, Sugar keeping them headed in the right direction. One man stayed some distance ahead to scout their way. Another lagged behind to watch their backs. Sugar had been multiplied for many hours now, and a burning thirst was upon her, and she wasn't the only one. When they came to a brooklet, all of them rushed to the clear water. Some of the men fell to their knees and scooped up the water with their hands. She knelt at the bank next to Soddam on a carpet of bright autumn leaves that were soft with moisture and slurped straight from the cold, delicious flow.

When she'd had her fill, she sat back on her haunches and wiped her mouth.

A few moments later Soddam sat back and smiled at her. "You did well today."

She shrugged. The loss of men and the horrors she'd seen didn't make her feel like celebrating.

"How's your Fire?"

"Steady," she said. "It flared once, just after we exited the cave, but I brought it in control."

He nodded. "I'm still thinking about you and those maulers in that workshop. That was steel, girl. Hard steel."

"Only because I knew a fearsome sleth had my back. How is the hand?"

He held it up. The bandages were bloody, but it looked like the bleeding had stopped and dried. "I've had worse," he said.

She thought about him on the roof, the seafire and the men screaming in pain below as they burned. The sights and smells of burning flesh and the stink of seafire pressed in on her mind and sickened her.

"You look troubled," he said.

"I'm just thinking about those men we burned today. I know it was us or them, and the Divines have to go, but I just can't shake the faces. I can't shake the feeling I've done some horrible thing. Some of them were probably good men. Had children or lovers they were faithful to. And that one in the hallway . . ."

"It was gruesome," Soddam agreed. "That's for sure. But is it worse than what the Divines did to the souls out on that field? Those Kains were ugly as sin and deserved to die. So does that Skir Master."

"Even when they're enthralled?"

"Especially when they're enthralled. Being a thrall does not excuse their actions. Think about what they're doing. The only way to stop them is to kill them."

"I suppose you're right," she said, "although it doesn't feel any better."

He reached out and smoothed her hair, looping it behind her ear, and looked at her with his slit-iris eyes. "I have a daughter like you: all heart." He was about to say more, but a look of pain flickered across his face, and he drew his hand away and looked to the side.

"You knew my mother from before," Sugar said.

"Aye," he said tossing a yellow leaf onto the water. "She was a fiery thing."

"Was she in this crew?"

He laughed wryly. "Now, that would have been the sight. Her submitting to the likes of Urban. No, but she did help train him. She was a grand woman, open-hearted, destined for great things. I'm very sorry to hear how she died."

Sugar wanted to hear more about what Soddam knew of her, but Urban approached. "It's time to move," he said and held some dreadman biscuits out to them.

Soddam took a few biscuits and rose. "I'll take point," he said.

Urban nodded.

Soddam turned Sugar. "We'll talk later," he said, then headed down the road.

Sugar accepted a biscuit and dipped it in the water to soften it a bit. "I wonder how much of our futures we've consumed with our Fire. It's a strange thing knowing you're hastening your end."

Urban shrugged. "I tend to think it's what you spend your days upon that matters. Not necessarily how many of them you have left. Those that forget that are the ones that go awry."

Sugar pulled her biscuit out of the water. Dreadman biscuits were made with honey and fine milled flour and salt. Sometimes the bakers would mix in seeds. She bit down on this one and began to munch.

She said, "Soddam seemed quite distressed a moment ago."

"About what?"

"His daughter."

Urban nodded. "The sight of you probably causes him pain."

"But why should that distress him? Has he been away from them long?"

"They're dead. His wife, daughters, all of them butchered."

"Oh," Sugar groaned in sympathy.

"It would be nice if the world were neat and tidy," he said. "Clean sheets, clean beds, pretty flowers. But it's not."

"He talked as if his daughter was still alive."

"Let me ask you something. There are some who join the Grove and lose their way. They make a mistake. What happens to them?"

"I don't know."

"Yes, you do. Your mother was one such."

"I don't know what you're talking about." She swallowed and took another bite of her biscuit.

"The Order has its discipline."

"Well, there are rules."

"Do you agree with them?"

"The lore is not something to be trifled with. I suppose it's necessary."

"Is it? Were they right to mark your mother for death?"

"She wasn't marked," said Sugar.

"Have you asked Argoth and Matiga? Did you think it was chance your mother was so sick after your encounter with the Devourer and the others were not? I would wager they decided on poison."

"It's not like that," she said. "She'd been pierced through by arrows, and who knows what the Devourer did to her."

He shrugged. "Maybe you're right."

"There's a difference," Sugar said, "between someone who makes a mistake and turns away from it and one who turns toward the sin with appetite."

"How right you are," he said. "But the Order doesn't see it that way. It culls any member who has sinned against the light. It's to preserve the rest of them, they say."

Sugar didn't know how to respond to that. This was the first Sugar had ever heard of this.

"Soddam made a mistake long ago," Urban continued. "He lost his daughters and his wife for it. He suffered for his crime, but the Grove sent me to hunt him down. They always sent me. I found him living on roots and insects, haunting his wife's grave. He looked like an animal, but he was a man, with a man's heart, who made one mistake. It was very clear to see."

"So they listened to you and spared him?"

Urban shook his head. "If only it were that easy. I decided not to carry out the orders they'd given me. They didn't know about it, or they would have sent another. But it wasn't the first time I'd chosen not to carry out their orders. And by the time they found out, it was too late."

"You think the Order is wrong."

"I think the Order has strayed a bit. Not all who sin deserve to die."

"But surely some do. It sounds like you just have a different measuring stick to determine who that is. And what says yours is the right measure?"

"That's the question," he said. "That's the very heart of the matter."

She suddenly wondered how many sleth he'd saved. "How big is your crew?" she asked.

"As big as it needs to be," he said.

She thought about Withers and Soddam and the fact that Argoth had asked them to make their quarters outside the fortress. "You seek them out, don't you? You seek out the fallen."

"We rescue those we can."

She thought about that and wondered what had started him on this path, wondered if he himself had fallen and some Grove had put a bounty on his head. Then her mind turned back to what he had said. Had Matiga and Argoth really ordered her mother's death?

"Soddam said my mother trained you."

"She was part of my father's Grove." He smiled, reminiscing. "I think we were all in love with her. And not just because of her looks. When everyone else in our Grove had determined to kill my brother, your mother spoke out against it. She went tooth and nail against my father."

"Your brother?"

"My father killed him. Oh, he wept a river, but he killed him all the same. I vowed on that day never to bind myself in a similar manner."

Sugar was speechless. She couldn't imagine what that would have been like. She could no more kill Legs, or imagine Mother doing it, than she could fly to the moon.

"Soddam was once like your mother," said Urban, "all fire and life. I hope one day he becomes that man again."

Sugar's mind whirled. Had Zu Argoth poisoned her mother? Is that why she had died when everyone else had survived?

They left the stream and followed the path Soddam had taken. As they ran, Sugar thought about Urban's words. About a mile later they came to a hill that gave a wide view of the bay.

Up ahead, Soddam had stopped to wait for them.

"I thought you were on point," Urban said.

"I sent Sniff ahead." Then he pointed out at the water. Ships stretched out for miles. Dozens upon dozens of fighting and cargo ships, all making their way to the Blue Towers harbor. Sugar had never seen so many ships.

"How many do you calculate?" Urban asked.

"I'm thinking an army of forty to sixty thousand."

Urban looked out at the ships, shook his head, and blew out a sigh.

"They already had a few thousand dreadmen coming to dock when we were there," Soddam said.

"And a full ship of priests, skirmen, and lesser Divines with the Skir Master," said Urban. "And Kains, and eyes in the skies, and who knows what else."

"And look there," Soddam said and pointed, "out past the big ship with the striped sail. Those are from Toth, which means there are more of those blighted dogmen out there."

Urban turned to Sugar. "What do you think about Shim's odds?"

Shim's army had about six thousand men in it. A few terrors of dreadmen. "We're outnumbered almost ten to one."

"More than that with the Skir Master and his crew," said Urban. "It's going to be a slaughter."

"But commander Eresh's strategy," Sugar said. "That's exactly why we're breaking up, to avoid a slaughter. We'll hide. We'll strike as we can."

Urban said, "They're going to raze every Shoka village. How long before Lord Shim's own people give him up?"

"All we have to do is take out the Divines."

Urban smiled. "Just like that, eh? With sixty thousand troops surrounding them, and every last one of them alert to our intentions now."

It had to be possible. There had to be some way to sneak a hammer or two of dreadmen in.

Urban shook his head. "I truly wanted this to work."

"We can still do it," Sugar said.

"So says the great warlord Sugar." Urban's eyes took on a gentle look. "It's important we face the facts. Not what we hope and wish might occur. Impossible odds are for fools; and you don't want to be gambling with the lives of thousands. I've seen my fair share of battles," Urban said. "This one is not going to end well."

"Lord Shim—"

"Lord Shim is noble. He's brave. But this is now nothing more than a glorious dream. The opportunity to build an army here has passed."

"What are you suggesting?" she asked.

"Do you remember our discussion of an exit?"

"You're just going to leave?"

"I'm surviving. It's what I do."

"You're abandoning us."

"I will not waste my men," said Urban. "They have put their lives in my hands. Think about what's going to happen when Mokad sends its thousands into Shoka territory to rape and pillage. Think about that horn and what's going to happen to you and Legs and everyone else they slaughter. And I haven't even started with the Bone Faces."

"I can't leave my friends."

"No true friend would ask you to throw your life away."

"So I just leave them?"

"Warn them."

"What? Now you want me to start a revolt against Shim and Argoth?"

"No. Respect their agency. Let them make their own choice, but do not bind yourself to a lost cause. There's more than just one Order. The Groves of Hismayas have done good things. But the Groves were made to support the people, not the other way around. Live and fight another day."

Sugar couldn't believe he was just turning his back on them. They needed every dreadman they could get.

"Shim took a high-risk gamble," Urban said. "If we could have killed all the Kains, that would have shaken them. It would have put their dreadmen at risk. If we could have taken the Skir Master, they would have had to resort to traditional tactics. And we might have been able to harry them through the winter. But there's nothing to stop them now. You think you can beat a hammer of dreadmen on your own? Because if we're to win, that's what every one of us will have to do. They'll have Walkers watching the night, kitemen watching the skies by day. And there are already traitors among us."

She turned to Soddam. "You agree with him?"

Soddam rubbed his beard. "I think we have twenty-four hours. And then Mokad will unleash its fury. Shim's little army will be brained like so many rabbits. There won't be one of us left to piss against the wall. Shim's dream is now over."

"You can't just slink away," Sugar said.

"I don't plan on slinking," said Urban. "I plan to talk to Argoth and Shim. But I already know what they're going to say."

39

Ferret's Choice

SUGAR AND URBAN left the crew at the edge of the woods and jogged down the road that led across the field to Rogum's Defense. They entered through the gates and were met by the smell of roasting meat and found the cooks feeding the last of the troops that had returned with Shim and Argoth at the great hall.

"Get yourself some food," Urban said. "I'm going to talk to Argoth."

Sugar was all too happy to get herself a bowl of swamp. She'd been multiplied for some time and was famished. She made her way over to the great hall, got a bowl, and let the cooks fill it. The thick stew was warm and savory and had large bits of fatty goat meat in it this time. She ate two bowls and a thick heel of bread, then made herself stop even though her hunger had not yet abated because she needed to look for Legs.

She found him up on the edge of the north parapet petting a big calico, one of the fortress's cats. He sat on an embrasure between two merlons, his legs dangling over the edge of the wall. There were still a number of people in the fortress below, but not near as many as there had been earlier.

"I thought you'd be by the gate waiting," she said.

He looked up in her direction and smiled. "There was a lot of coming and going with the troops moving out, and I was only getting in the way."

The calico cat nudged his hand with its head for another scratch. Legs scratched its head and said, "I heard the mission failed."

"Not completely," she said. "We killed a couple of Kains."

"You should have taken Flax with you," he said. "I don't think Shim was smart to leave the only Divine killer behind."

"Argoth hunted Divines once in his past."

"If you'd taken Flax, you would have probably killed them all."

"I see you've become one of his admirers."

Legs shrugged. "You don't need to be an admirer to see it was stupid to leave him."

Sugar looked down the outside of the wall. It was a steep drop. "And I don't know that this is a good place to sit. One bump and you're over the edge. Come off of there."

Legs helped the cat off his lap, then slid off the embrasure to the wall walk. "I'm weary of being left behind," he said. "I want to fight. You and I could be our own fist."

"We've only the one weave."

"Flax says he might know how to make another."

Flax again. "That's a big promise, but I don't see him much."

"You're not supposed to see him. He's a spy. But he was here to kill that dreadman assassin, wasn't he? It's not easy to kill a slayer."

"I suppose not," she said. She looked at Legs and knew just what he was thinking. With a weave that would allow him to soulwalk, he could become a warrior. The Blind Warrior. That's what they'd call him. And he could grow up to kill himself a slayer. Of course, it would take a number of years for him to train to become the fearsome thing he hoped to be. Right now he was just a boy. And if Urban was right, that's all he would ever be. Yet another reason for her not to remain in a Grove that was going to be destroyed.

An insect moved on Legs's hand. She looked closer and saw it was not an insect, but a ring that was black as flint. It shifted on his finger again. "What is that on your finger?" she asked a bit alarmed.

Legs stroked the ring. "Flax is teaching me the Kains' lore."

"When did this start?" she asked in surprise.

"Yesterday."

"Nobody talked to me about it."

Legs shrugged.

A faint alarm rose in Sugar's mind. "Does the Creek Widow know?"

Legs didn't reply.

"Legs, we aren't supposed to accept weaves from anyone without her approval," she said.

"The Creek Widow and Argoth are too busy to help me. But Flax isn't. Besides, I was going to talk to her."

"Sure you were," she said, not believing a word of it. She could see this was going to be a problem. Legs had seen an opportunity, and he wasn't going to let it slip away. It didn't matter who he learned the lore from. Of course she couldn't blame him. Wouldn't she do the same? "I think I'm going to have a talk with Flax when he comes back. Take it off."

"You're going to push me aside like everyone else? You run off, risking your life, and leave me behind. Why can't I learn just a little bit?"

"You know I'm not pushing you aside."

"Let me keep it. I've been studying it, following the pattern. I'll be careful."

She knew it would be hard to always stay behind, fretting and worrying. Da had made sure she could fight. To be something that acts for herself, and not just something to be acted upon. He'd probably want Legs to do the same. "I don't know," she said.

"There's something about it," he said. "Something odd."

"I should say."

"No, not the fact that it moves. There's something else. I can't quite describe it. But I feel it's important. Please. I'll make sure Flax goes and talks to the Creek Widow. We'd do it now, but they're both out."

"Let me look at it," she said.

Legs hesitated, then he wrested it from his finger and gave it to her. She held it up to get a better view. Its legs suddenly moved, and then it flipped over and latched onto her finger. She gave a startled yelp.

Legs laughed.

"Do you have to quicken it?" she asked.

"It's already quickened," he said. "It doesn't do anything. It's just a piece to learn on."

She waited expecting it to reach out to her in some way, but nothing happened. "Did Flax make this himself?"

"I think so," Legs said.

"It's a powerful lore to animate such a thing. From what the Creek Widow said about that monster the Devourer controlled, it's very rare."

"Which just goes to show they shouldn't have left Flax behind."

The ring clung to her finger with its legs, but it released when she gave it a good tug. "You promise to talk to the Creek Widow?"

"Promise," Legs said. "I'm just practicing feeling its weave. Flax says that's one of the first lessons."

She looked more closely at the beetle: it was a wondrous thing, and she felt a little stab of jealousy—she wanted to learn this lore as well. And what harm could this do? Flax was obviously a master. "I think it's nice that Flax has taken an interest in you," she said, "but we still need to be safe."

"Flax is safe."

"I don't want you wearing it until you talk to her. Promise."

His shoulders slumped. "Fine," he said.

Satisfied, she handed it back. Legs took it and put it in his pouch.

Down below, Urban exited Shim's quarters. He walked over to the cellar where she and the washerwomen slept. The Mistress was there with a few of the women. He spoke to them, and then the Mistress pointed up at the wall where she and Legs were. He turned to look, and the Mistress pinched his bottom. Urban jumped and backed away to the merriment of the other washerwomen.

"I'll be right back," Sugar said. "Don't go anywhere."

She ran along the parapet, then down to the bailey and caught Urban as he was coming over to the stairs.

"A man is not safe with the company you keep," he said.

"And yet you keep returning to them," she said. "You talked to Argoth?"

His face went hard. "Yes," he said.

Behind them, a number of soldiers were filling a wagon with bedrolls and packs. "Let's talk where it's less busy," he said and led her out of the inner bailey to the empty goat pens.

"I explained my issues," he said.

She waited.

"And they didn't want to hear them. Shim says there's a woman who can get them into the fortress."

"Do you believe him?"

"He's grasping at straws. Even if he could get in, I want you to think about what happened on the street today."

"I don't fear a little danger."

"I'm not talking about danger. A man ran out onto the road and alerted the captain of that Fir-Noy terror. He pointed right at us. How could anyone have known we were there or what we were doing? We were all just part of the crowd trying to get a view."

"What are you saying?"

"Somebody betrayed us."

"Who?"

He shrugged.

"Not the Creek Widow. Or Argoth or Eresh or Shim."

"I don't know who it is, and we don't have time to find out. More importantly, the facts are laid out in front of anyone with eyes to see. This army is going to be decimated and their souls carried off to Mokad's Devourer."

"You don't know that."

"I've learned by hard experience not to ignore my instincts. There are many who depend on me."

"We just need to remove a few of their men."

"That's what everyone keeps saying. Just a few guarded by thousands of dreadmen. Not to mention their Walkers that can see at night. Or the dogmen that surely will be on patrol. Sugar, even if Shim and Argoth do take this Skir Master, they still have an overwhelming army to contend with. There will still be Divines among them. I will not waste my men. Three died this morning. It was a risk we knowingly took. But facing Mokad's army at this time in this place serves no purpose."

If Urban, who was brave and skilled, saw no hope, then how many lesser men would be seeing the same? For the first time since the caves, she began question Shim's odds. But running just didn't feel right.

"Your hesitation does you credit, and I wouldn't expect less. But consider what's to be gained and lost. I'm a fair master. You'll have equal rights with all the others."

He reached out and lifted her chin with two fingers so he could look her in the face. "Purity's daughter, carry on your mother's legacy. Don't waste her gifts."

She looked into his glittering, but weary eyes. He'd never given her any reason to doubt his intentions or abilities. And it was true that he cared for his men and put them first. If she went with him, she could travel away from all these dangers and worries. She and Legs would finally be safe with people who accepted her as she was. And yet, it still felt like betrayal.

"Tomorrow the armies of Mokad will spread out," he said. "Their ships will move away from Blue Towers and lock up the ports. My ship is faster than most, but I can't outrun a chaser racing with a skir wind. Tonight is our window to escape. I'm all for fighting and risking my life in a good cause, but I'm not going to participate in a mass suicide. Meet me at Potter's Crossing. Bring Legs."

She couldn't believe he was saying this.

He raised her hand to his lips and kissed it. "I'll wait until sunset."

She didn't know how to respond.

He released her hand, smiled, then put on his hat. "Think about Legs," he said. Then he turned and walked away, leaving her standing by the pens, the remnants of his kiss still tingling the back of her hand.

She watched him stride out the gate, and then she looked about her, at the men still on the wall, and the fortress where she'd spent the last months learning the lore. She thought about Legs. When all was said and done, her first duty was to protect him. And if Shim fell, that task would be impossible.

She walked back through the inner gates and into the inner bailey, lost in thought. All about her, the remaining soldiers and support folk were preparing to leave, but she didn't really notice them. Nor did she notice the Mistress and two of the other washerwomen until they were almost upon her.

"There she is, ladies," the Mistress said. She and the others were carrying baskets of rosemary for the laundry.

Sugar looked up. The Mistress smiled. "And are his lips honeyed? His bum certainly is."

"What?"

"Honey, indeed," the rotund one said. "Look at her. His presence has put her in a daze."

The Mistress tsked. "I can't blame you; he tempts the best of us."

Sugar shook her head. "I'm not in a daze." She turned to the Mistress. "I need to talk to you."

"Oh," the rotund one clucked, "it *is* serious."

Sugar gave her a look.

"I suppose we can't talk here," the Mistress said.

Sugar shrugged.

The Mistress read her look. "I suppose not," she said and stacked her basket in a wagon. She took Sugar's arm, then led her away from the others.

"I warned you," The Mistress said, patting her hand. "Foreigners are tempting. You haven't been rash, have you?"

"No," said Sugar. "Nothing like that. He's been nothing but considerate." And kind, and helpful, and about as decent as any man she'd ever known.

"Well then?"

"Did you hear about Mokad's army?"

"Honey Cake, nobody's talked about anything else since Shim and Argoth rode through the gates."

"There are some that say it's hopeless to fight them."

The Mistress looked down at her, gave her hand a squeeze. "It was bad this morning, wasn't it?"

"It was close. The men were burning. We fought a dogman who struck with the force of a sledgehammer."

"A dogman of Toth?" The Mistress said and raised her eyebrows. "Lords, girl, but you've got guts. Probably more than I do. You're going to have to tell us this tale. I insist on it. And I think the ladies and I deserve the first audience."

"You'll have the details in full."

The Mistress nodded, then took on a reserved air. "Were the dogmen at all"—she paused—"fetching?"

"Lords," Sugar said, "you've got to be joking."

"Maybe a little."

"Only a little?"

"A woman can be curious," the Mistress said.

"Of course," Sugar said. She shook her head to herself. Where in the world would she find another like the Mistress? And how could she leave her? Or the others? How could she not fight to give them a chance?

She'd run away once before, when the odds were against her mother and Da, and she regretted it every minute.

Sugar said, "So if you thought this fight was hopeless, what would you do?"

The Mistress narrowed her eyes.

"We're outnumbered ten to one," Sugar said.

"Aye," said the Mistress, "that's what I heard."

"That doesn't bother you?"

"I've faced ten to one odds before."

"You have?" Sugar asked.

"You're not the only lass who's had to pick up a sword. Or know that men are coming for you with murderous intent. I know what's going through your head. Don't let it take you. Don't give into the battle dread. Everyone's feeling it. But you hold on; it will pass."

Battle dread—those were the words Da had used with Mother on that awful morning. But he'd misdiagnosed Mother's intent just as the Mistress misdiagnosed hers.

The Mistress said, "This was your first encounter. It's always the worst. Listen to me. When those Mokaddian whoresons come, I will be standing up on that wall, my staff sling in hand, throwing murder down upon them. And if not that wall, it will be another."

"And their skir?"

"Let them come. That's Lord Shim's and Commander Eresh's province. My job is to wield my pile of stones. Your job is to do whatever you do with that foreign crew. And"—she took a confidential tone—"wield your slethery."

"Right," Sugar said. Her fearful slethery, which consisted of nothing more than being able to run fast. And use her mother's necklace. But neither would defeat Mokad's army. She looked at the people milling about the bailey. Chances were they would all die.

"Look there," said the Mistress. "Here comes our charge."

Legs was exiting the stairway to the parapet.

She called out to him. Legs turned toward the sound and made his way to them, feeling his way with a stick, his other hand out in front.

"He's got all the ladies eating out of his hand," the Mistress said.

"Is that our lovely Mistress of the tub?" Legs asked and walked over to them.

"Charmer," the Mistress said and pinched him on the cheek. "Too bad he's not a few years older."

Legs blushed, and the Mistress laughed.

Sugar smiled, but inside she was roiling. Inside she was imagining the Mistress being battered by a troop of Mokaddian soldiers. The Mistress had not seen the power of the skir nor the dogmen nor the endless ships. Confidence only took you so far.

"Thanks for your wise words," Sugar said.

"You're a good lass," the Mistress said. "You'll do what's right."

At that moment, Argoth exited Shim's quarters. He began to walk toward hers, then spotted her and turned to talk to her.

"It seems you're very popular today," said the Mistress. "But you remember your promise—we have dibs on first audience."

"Of course," Sugar said.

The Mistress nodded, then walked away to join the washerwomen as they continued to load a wagon.

When Argoth was close, he called out to Legs. "How's our singer?" he asked.

"In want of sweetcakes," Legs replied. "And pillows. And a few silks. I'm terribly underpaid."

Argoth laughed. "Yes, Lord. I shall work on the pillows. In the meantime, may I speak to your sister?"

"I just got her back."

"I will return her as soon as I can. She needs to do some studying."

"Another mission or patrol?" Legs asked.

"Perhaps," he said.

Legs squeezed Sugar's hand tighter, reminding her about his desire to be useful and fight.

"Let me go with Argoth for now," she said. "I'll meet you a bit later."

He let her go, the frustration of being left behind yet again clear on his face.

She walked with Argoth back to Shim's chambers. They passed by the clerk and climbed the stairs to the waiting room above. The doors to Shim's audience chamber were closed. Argoth stopped, and motioned for her to sit down with him on a bench. Across the room, a small window let in the light and sound from the bailey.

He pitched his voice so low she had to lean forward to hear. "You're going back to Blue Towers. You're going in."

"But—"

"Not through a gate or over the wall. And not alone. The Fir-Noy have many enemies. And that is to our advantage. Especially when one of them knows a secret way, not only into the fortress, but into Lord Hash's very chambers. A woman came to us with information. She was one of Lord Hash's servants who cleaned his chambers and filled some of his other needs. But Hash is heartless, and so are his men. She was treated worse than a dog. I won't go into her tale, but the short of the matter is that she knows the way in. It's how she escaped."

"So why do you need me?"

"She's not coming with us. Furthermore, this has to be done in complete darkness. We need your eyes. We need you to guide us through the pitch black passages, scout ahead, peer through doors."

"You yourself are going on this mission?"

Argoth nodded. "A handful of men stand in our way of victory. Eliminate them, and humanity rises to stand upon its feet. Today we finished off some of the Kains. Tonight we'll take the Skir Master."

"How do you know this woman isn't a plant sent to lead you into a Fir-Noy trap?"

"We don't know that for certain, but she came to us two weeks ago, before Mokad stationed itself in Blue Towers. And we've confirmed her story. The Fir-Noy killed her family. They have no leverage with her."

Sugar said, "Urban thinks this is suicide."

"Urban thinks a lot of things," Argoth said.

"Be honest with me, Zu," Sugar said. "Do you think this is possible? The Skir Master will have guards, Walkers. Those dogmen and their maulers will be on patrol."

"If we were just a fist of dreadmen, I'd say we had no chance. But we have you, my dear. You're our secret weapon. You're the key."

"I see," said Sugar. She saw it all very clearly. They were desperate, grasping at straws. If she left, they would surely fail. If she stayed, they might fail anyway. But she might be able to help give them a chance, even if it was a small one.

A beat passed.

"Did you poison my mother?"

"What?"

"Did the Grove order her death?"

Argoth shook his head. "Urban's been talking to you, hasn't he?"

"I deserve to know the truth.

Argoth blew out a breath. "Indeed, you do. Here are the simple facts. We went to her, down in the cleansing room at Whitecliff. We wanted to save her, but there was no way to accomplish that. In the end, she herself asked for the poison to protect all of us so that we could protect you and Legs."

That sounded exactly like Mother. She shook her head and thought about Urban, his pleasant smile, his eyes, the beauty he held on the inside. She thought of Soddam and Withers. Of freedom. Of being among those that treated her as a person of worth. Urban was probably right—going into the heart of the enemy camp was suicide.

"I'm asking you to take a great risk," Argoth said. "I know you're new to your powers, but you've proven yourself. I would not ask unless we had extreme need."

She could leave her friends to die, or she could help. When put that way, the decision was clear. "Zu," she said. "I've been trained as a ferret. I say send this ferret in that Shim may go hunting."

Argoth smiled. He looked about the room. "Purity," he said to the air, "I hope you're listening. This is the quality of yours and Sparrow's blood." He turned back to Sugar. "You do your ancestors proud."

Sugar nodded, but knew the dead were not watching over their living kindred. Mother was not here to approve or disapprove of her decision, which Sugar was already starting to regret.

"You're going to need to memorize the layout of the passageways," he said. "Are you ready?"

Sugar nodded, even though she didn't want to, and Argoth rose and opened the doors.

Inside, Shim, Matiga, and Eresh stood around a candlelit table, and she realized the time of preparation was over. The war had begun. Humankind's moment was upon them.

She wondered about Talen, River, and Ke. One of them should be here, not her. But she was what Argoth had. And she would not quail. Not while her mother's blood flowed in her veins.

Sugar thought about Urban again. She thought about his ship. She thought about Legs.

Then she followed Argoth in.

The End

Dear Reader

I HOPE YOU enjoyed this volume of the Dark God series (I can tell you I loved writing it). If you did, please consider leaving a review at your favorite bookseller's website. Even if it's only a line or two, a hearty huzzah not only helps your fellow readers, it also helps me continue to bring you more books.

Reviews help us independent authors a great deal.

As for the foundations your review helps me support, they are looking for vegan orcs this time, since the first batch tried to eat the hobbits.

Terms & People

Political Hierarchy

While there are many variations, the basic power hierarchy in the realms of the Western Glorydoms flows from the Glory down:

Glory
|
Lesser Divines
|
Territory Lords and Warlords
|
District Lords and Village Bailiffs

There are still some small areas of the known world ruled by barbarian kings or chieftains, but almost all these pay tribute to one Glory or another in the form of treasure, slaves, or Fire. The major western glorydoms include Kish, Koram, Mokad, Mungo, Nilliam, and Urz.

The Six Orders of the Divine

Fire Wizards
Kains
Skir Masters
Guardians
Green Ones
Glories

Infamous Divines include: The Goat King, The Witch of Cath, and Hismayas, the ancient lord of the sleth.

Major Mokaddian Clans with holdings in the New Lands

Birak
Burund
Fir-Noy
Harkon
Jarund

Mithrosh
Seema
Shoka
Vargon

Koramites

Hogan
River
Ke
Talen
Sparrow & Purity
Sugar
Legs
Harnock

Mokaddians

Argoth & Serah
Nettle
The Creek Widow (Matiga)
Lumen (The missing Divine of the New Lands)
Rubaloth (Skir Master of Mokad)
Rose (Sister to Argoth, wife of Hogan the Koramite)
Shim (Warlord of the Shoka clan)

Armsman

Every clan has various martial orders within it. The ranks of the vast majority of these orders are filled with those who are not full-time soldiers, but farmers, laborers, and craftsmen. However, there are orders in some clans of elite and sometimes professional soldiers. These are the orders of the armsmen.

Bone Faces

Barbarian raiders from the South who have begun striking Mokaddian holdings by sea.

Dreadmen and Fell-maidens

Those without lore who are endowed by Divines with weaves of might. When such weaves are worn, they multiply the wearer's natural mental and physical abilities. However, the weaves carry a cost: worn too frequently, the body wastes, consuming itself to fuel the magic.

Escrum

A weave that binds the wearer to a master, allowing communication over long distances.

Frights

Not completely of the world of flesh, frights feed on Fire. They most often prey on the sick and dying, attaching themselves like great leeches.

Godsweed

An herb with properties said to repel some creatures such as frights and the souls of the dead. The smoke from one thin braid can rid a house of an infestation for many weeks. But its effect does not discriminate between frights, ancestors, or even the servants of the Creators. Hence the saying: take care to appease those you've chased with smoke.

King's Collar

A weave wrought by a special order of Divines called Kains. Such collars not only prevent a person from working magic, but also weaken the wearer, making those captured easier to handle.

Kragow

A weilder of the strange lore of the Bone Faces.

Military Units

A fist is made up of 8-12 soldiers. A hammer contains 2-4 fists. A terror contains 4-6 hammers. The leaders of these units are called fistmen, hammermen, and terrormen. A cohort contains 4-6 terrors.

Skir

Orders of beings that inhabit the heavens as well as the deep places of the earth and sea. While invisible to the naked eye, many do exert power in the visible world and can be harnessed by those knowing the secrets. But not all are useful to man. Many orders of smaller Skir are deemed insignificant, while other powers are so dreadful none dare summon them.

Stone-wights

A vanished race whose ruins are found in the New Lands. Some claim plague or war took them. Others find evidence they were destroyed by the Six themselves.

The Six

Seven creators fashioned the earth and all life therein. However, upon seeing the flaws in what he and the other six Creators had wrought, the seventh, called Regret, wanted to destroy the work and begin again. The remaining Six, whose names are sacred, refused, but they were not able to overcome Regret. And so it is that the powers of both creation and dissolution still struggle on the earth.

Sleth

Another term for "soul-eaters." In Urzarian tongue it literally means "The East Wind," which dries and kills life. Applied to those who, in rebellion of the Glories, use an unsanctioned form of the lore of the Divines. They are beings and orders of beings supposedly twisted by their polluted draws. Said to have gotten their lore from Regret, one of the seven Creators who, having once seen the creation, realized its flaws and wanted to destroy it.

The Three Vitalities

All life is made up of one or more of the three vital powers. There are many names for these life forces. The most common terms in the western glory-doms are Fire (sometimes called Spirit), Body, and Soul. There are rumors, among those who know the lore, of lost vitalities: powers that have passed out of human ken.

Weaves

Objects of power. Some can only be quickened and handled by lore masters. Others, wild weaves, are independent of a master and can be used by those who do not possess any lore. Weaves may be made of almost any material; however, gold is used most often for the wild weaves given to dreadmen.

Woodikin

Creatures that live in great families beyond the gap in the wilds of the New Lands. About half the size of a man, they are ferocious and spilled much blood in the battles fought with the early settlers. Although rare, single woodikin are sometimes seen in human lands.

Acknowledgements

Curse took a very long and crooked path toward publication, which makes the help and encouragement that so many offered along the way even more special.

My first thanks goes to the many readers who let me know of their eagerness to read this book. There are too many names to mention here (those of you who emailed and posted know who you are), but all of your support was much appreciated.

Smart beta readers are precious, and these folks provided loads of good reader insight: **Caitlin Blasdell, Darren Eggett, David Hartwell, David Walton, Garrett Winn, Hannah Bowman, Kassandra Brown, Larry Correia, Mette Harrison, Stacy Hague-Hill, Stephen and Liesl Nelson**, and **Steve Diamond**. A huge thanks goes to **Alex and Amy Lamborn** who were extra helpful with each iteration of the story.

A number of folks also provided excellent reader responses to a beginning I wanted to test. These helpful souls include **Adam Teachout, Alexis Cooper, Cameron Wilson, David West, Eric Allen, Hyrum Grissom, Justin Fisher, Krista Hoeppner Leahy, Laurel Amberdine, Lindsey Tolis, Mark Holt, Martin Cahill, Melanie Goldmund, Merrill Nielson, Nick Dianatkhah, Ray Solomon**, and **Wes Amodt**.

As for the art, **Victor Minguez** provided an awesome illustration. **Dixon Leavitt** stepped in at a critical juncture and made that illustration possible. And **Devon Dorrity** did a wonderful job on the cover.

Above all, my thanks goes to my wife **Nellie** who played the roles of reader, editor, listening ear (when this project ran into heavy weather multiple times), and business manager.

By John D. Brown

Thrillers
Bad Penny
Awful Intent

Epic Fantasies
Servant: The Dark God Book One
Curse: The Dark God Book Two
Raveler: The Dark God Book Three
Glory: The Dark God Book Four (in planning!)

Shorter Works
Bright Waters
From the Clay of His Heart
Loose in the Wires
The Scent of Desire

Don't Miss Out!

Join the many readers who have asked to be notified
when the next book is released by singing up at **johndbrown.com**.

About the Author

JOHN D. BROWN lives with his wife and four daughters in the hinterlands of Utah where one encounters much fresh air, many good-hearted ranchers, and the occasional wolf.

Feel free to drop by his website **johndbrown.com** to post comments or just say hello. He always enjoys hearing from his readers.